W9-ACG-260

Four Weddings
and a
Sixpence

Also by Julia Quinn

BECAUSE OF MISS BRIDGERTON
THE SECRETS OF SIR RICHARD KENWORTHY
THE SUM OF ALL KISSES

Also by Elizabeth Boyle

THE KNAVE OF HEARTS
MAD ABOUT THE MAJOR
THE VISCOUNT WHO LIVED DOWN THE LANE

Also by Laura Lee Guhrke

THE TRUTH ABOUT LOVE AND DUKES
NO MISTRESS OF MINE
CATCH A FALLING HEIRESS

Also by Stefanie Sloane

THE WICKED WIDOW MEETS HER MATCH
THE SCOUNDREL TAKES A BRIDE
THE SAINT WHO STOLE MY HEART

JULIA
QUINN

ELIZABETH
BOYLE

LAURA LEE
GUHRKE

STEFANIE
SLOANE

AN ANTHOLOGY

Four Weddings
and a
Sixpence

AVONBOOKS

An Imprint of HarperCollinsPublishers

This is a collection of fiction. Names, characters, places, and incidents are products of the authors' imagination or are used fictitiously and are not to be construed as real. Any resemblance to actual events, locales, organizations, or persons, living or dead, is entirely coincidental.

"Something Old" copyright © 2017 by Julie Cotler Pottinger.
"Something New" copyright © 2017 by Stefanie Sloane.
"Something Borrowed" copyright © 2017 by Elizabeth Boyle.
"Something Blue" copyright © 2017 Laura Lee Guhrke.
". . . and a Sixpence in Her Shoe" copyright © 2017 by Julie Cotler Pottinger.

All rights reserved. Printed in the United States of America. No part of this book may be used or reproduced in any manner whatsoever without written permission except in the case of brief quotations embodied in critical articles and reviews. For information, address HarperCollins Publishers, 195 Broadway, New York, NY 10007.

First Avon Books mass market printing: January 2017
First Avon Books hardcover printing: December 2016

ISBN 978-0-06-266011-4

Avon Trademark Reg. U.S. Pat. Off. and in Other Countries, Marca Registrada, Hecho en U.S.A.
Avon, Avon Books, and the Avon logo are trademarks of HarperCollins Publishers.
HarperCollins® is a registered trademark of HarperCollins Publishers.

17 18 19 20 21   LCS   10 9 8 7 6 5 4 3 2 1

Contents

Four Weddings
and a
Sixpence

Something Old

JULIA QUINN

Prologue

Kidmore End
nr. Reading
April 1818

*M*adame Rochambeaux's Gentle School for Girls was, as the name might suggest, not rigorous. Pupils received two hours of lessons per day, followed by dance, music, or drawing, depending on the day of the week. The girls did not receive instruction in the classical languages, as their brothers routinely did at Eton and Harrow, but they were required to know the names of the major Greek and Latin writers so that, as Madame Rochambeaux frequently pointed out, they should not look silly at a dinner party if the topic arose.

That was the crux of the curriculum, really. *Things that will make you not look silly at a dinner party.* Miss Beatrice Heywood, who had been boarding at Madame Rochambeaux's since the age of eight, had once suggested it as the school's motto.

This was not met with glad reception.

Bea had never much minded the lack of Latin and Greek, but she really wished that Madame Rochambeaux would see fit to hire a tutor for the sciences, stargazing in particular. When she was home, or rather her aunts' home—she didn't have one herself—she loved to lie on her back in the garden at night and stare at the skies. All of her pin money had gone toward the purchase of a book of astronomy, and she was trying to teach herself, but she was certain she'd have a much easier time of it with someone who actually knew what they were doing.

Not to mention a telescope.

Miss Cordelia Padley had been at Madame Rochambeaux's almost as long as Bea, having arrived at the age of nine. She was not an orphan, although with her father halfway across the world in India, she might well have been. Unlike Bea, Cordelia was a great heiress and arrived at school in possession of twelve day dresses and four pairs of shoes, which was precisely four times as many dresses as Bea, and twice the shoes. Luckily for them both (since they were to share a room for a full nine years) Cordelia's heart was as kind as her wallet was fat.

Two years later another bed was fitted into the dormer room, and much to the surprise of everyone, the Lady Elinor Daventry moved in. Madame Rochambeaux's was a respectable school, reasonably well regarded, but it had never boasted an actual *lady* among its ranks before. Lady Elinor was the only daughter of an earl, and no one—not even Ellie—understood why she'd been sent to Madame Rochambeaux's school when all of her Daventry cousins had been educated in Berkshire, at the exclusive Badminton School for Proper Ladies. Prior to her days at Madame Rochambeaux's, Ellie had had the services of a governess—an elegant and enigmatic French émigré, with blood rumored to be as blue as that of the Daventrys. (No one knew for sure, and Mademoiselle de la Clair did nothing to diffuse the air of mystery that wafted about her like a fine perfume.)

If the fair mademoiselle was not precisely up to snuff as a teacher of English history and literature, she more than made up for it with her delicious Parisian accent, and by the time she was six, Ellie spoke like a native. Which was why it surprised no one that, when she learned that Madame Rochambeaux had been born in

Limoges, she eagerly greeted her new headmistress with a lilting torrent of French.

Madame Rochambeaux replied in the same language, but only just.

Perplexed, Ellie tried again. Perhaps the older woman was hard of hearing; she did look rather ancient. At least forty.

But Madame Rochambeaux just grunted out her answer—a rather badly pronounced *je ne sais quoi*—and then announced she was needed elsewhere.

Limoges was never mentioned again.

"What on earth have we been learning?" Cordelia wondered, back in their room after Ellie's first day of lessons.

"I don't know," Bea muttered, "but I don't think it's been French."

"Combien de temps avez-vous étudié le français?" Ellie asked.

"I know what that means," Bea announced, pleased and relieved that she understood a question as simple as *How long have you studied French?* Unfortunately her reply—*"Depuis que je suis un éléphant"* was not quite the answer she'd been going for.

Eventually the group of friends managed to piece together the secrets of Madame Rochambeaux's past. Sadly, there was nothing scandalous to be found, just a letter from her sister advising that she take on a French name to sound more genteel.

Miss Anne Brabourne, who had arrived two years after Ellie, was the one to discover the truth.

"I don't see why she changed her name," Anne said as they sat on their beds after supper. "Who wants to sound French these days?"

"Everyone," Cordelia said, laughing. "The war's been over for ages."

The moment the words were out of her mouth, she bit her lip and gave Ellie a quick glance, as did the others, while Ellie pretended a sudden great interest in the buckle on her shoe. None of the girls fully understood the rumors that swirled around Ellie's family, just that they involved her father and some things he may have done during the war.

"Sorry, Ellie," Cordelia said after a moment.

Her friend looked up and managed a smile. "It's all right, Cordelia. I can't expect the world to stop talking about the war just because of malicious and untrue gossip."

"Still," Bea said, wisely veering the topic away from Ellie's father, "the fact remains that Madame Rochambeaux is, in actual fact, Miss Puddleford of East Grinstead, Sussex."

They all paused to absorb this. Or rather, reabsorb. They'd found the letter two days earlier. It was a testament to the monotony of boarding school life that they were still talking about it.

"That fact may remain," Anne put in, "but what are we going to do with that fact?"

"I like Madame Rochambeaux," Cordelia said.

"So do I," Ellie said. "Her French is dreadful, but other than that, she's been quite lovely."

Anne shrugged. "I suppose if my name were Puddleford, I should want to be a Rochambeaux, too."

They all looked at Bea, who nodded. "She's been very kind to me over the years," she said.

"How odd that we've expended so much energy in search of the truth, and now we're just going to leave it be," Ellie said.

"The pursuit of knowledge, and all that," Anne quipped. She flopped back on her bed. "Ow."

"What?"

"Something poked me."

Bea leaned over. "It's probably the sharp end of a feather."

Anne grumbled under her breath as she used her bottom to re-fluff the mattress.

"You look ridiculous," Ellie said.

"It feels like a bloody quill. I'm trying to get it back into the mattress."

"Oh, for heaven's sake," Bea said. "Let me help you."

Together they removed the sheets from the mattress and felt along until they found the offending feather.

"Can you grasp it?" Anne asked. "I just trimmed my nails, and I can't pinch anything."

"I can try." Bea frowned in concentration. The shaft was just barely poking through the mattress fabric. "I think it might be easier to push it back in."

"So that it might rise up again and stab her in the night," Ellie chortled.

Anne shot her a mildly disgruntled look, turning back when Bea murmured, "That's odd."

"What?"

"There's something in your mattress. I think it's a"—she palpated the object through the fabric—"a coin."

"A coin?" That was enough to get all the girls off their beds.

"In Anne's mattress?" Cordelia said. "How odd."

"Heaven only knows how old this mattress is," Anne said. "It could be a Spanish doubloon."

Ellie arched her neck for a better look, not that there was anything to see. "That could keep you in tea for the rest of your life."

"How are we going to get it out?" Cordelia asked.

Anne frowned. "I think we'll have to cut it."

Cordelia looked at her in shock. "Cut the mattress?"

"There's no other way. It shouldn't be difficult to sew it back up when we're done."

Indeed it wouldn't. All four girls were handy with a needle. That, at least, had been on Madame Rochambeaux's curriculum.

And so an expeditionary party was dispatched to the kitchen for a knife, and ten minutes later, Anne was holding in her hand not a Spanish doubloon but a rather ordinary sixpence. "It will keep me in tea for a week, at least," she said.

"More than that, I should think," Bea said, taking the coin from her. "It looks very old." She brought it near her lantern and squinted her eyes. "That's Queen Anne on it. This is more than a hundred years old."

"I hope that doesn't mean my mattress is more than a hundred years old," Anne said with a queasy frown.

"Oh, here's the date," Bea continued. "Seventeen-eleven. Do you suppose it's worth more than a sixpence? Perhaps to someone who collects coins?"

"I doubt it," Cordelia said, coming over to look at it. "But Anne can save it for her wedding."

Anne looked up. "What?"

"Surely you know the rhyme. Something old, something new, something borrowed, something blue—"

"—and a sixpence in her shoe," Ellie and Bea chimed in, joining Cordelia in the recitation.

"You wear the sixpence in your shoe during the ceremony," Ellie said. "It's supposed to bless the marriage with wealth."

"My mother did it," Cordelia murmured.

The group paused to take stock of that. Cordelia's parents had not been wealthy at the time of their marriage; it had been an unexpected inheritance three years later that had provided the family with their riches.

"I wonder what would happen if you put the sixpence in your shoe before you got married," Cordelia said.

"You'd get a blister," Bea said smartly.

Cordelia rolled her eyes in return. "Maybe it would help you *find* your husband."

"A lucky engagement sixpence?" Ellie asked with a smile.

"If that's the case," Anne announced, scooping the coin back from Bea, "then I'm holding on to it. You all know I need to marry before I turn twenty-five."

"Oh, for heaven's sake," Cordelia said. "You've *ages*. You're barely fourteen."

"It's highly unlikely you would still be unmarried by the time you turn twenty-five," Ellie said reasonably. "If your uncle had decreed eighteen, or even twenty-one, that would be a different story."

"Yes, but he must approve the match. And he's so dreadfully dull. I cannot even imagine what sort of man he'll force upon me."

"Surely he wouldn't force you . . ." Bea murmured.

"I won't be tied up and trussed at the altar, if that's what you mean," Anne said. "But it will feel like it."

"One of us should take it first," Cordelia protested. "We're older."

It was true; Anne was the baby of the bunch, nearly a year younger than Ellie and two years behind her other roommates. As such she'd had to learn to speak up for herself, and she did not pause before looking Cordelia straight in the eye and saying, "Finders keepers, I'm afraid. I need it more."

"All right," Cordelia capitulated, because she knew it was true. "But if it works, you must promise to give it to one of us after you're married."

"We'll use it in turns," Ellie added.

"You're all mad," Bea said.

"You'll think differently when we're all married and you're still living with your aunts," Ellie warned.

"Fine. If you all marry before me, I will put that silly coin in my shoe and leave it there until I find my true love."

"Deal?" Cordelia asked with a grin.

Ellie placed her hand atop Cordelia's. "Deal."

Anne shrugged and joined in. "Deal."

They all looked at Bea.

"Oh, very well," she said. "I suppose I must, since I'm the one who suggested it." She put her hand atop Anne's, and then for good measure, slid her other hand below Cordelia's.

"Deal."

Something New

STEFANIE SLOANE

Chapter 1

Grosvenor Square, London
Almost ten years later . . .

*M*iss Anne Brabourne's dedicated quest to find the ideal
husband was proving difficult. Standing at the edge of
the Marchioness of Lipscombe's ballroom, she took a small sip of
ratafia and watched the dancers before her, the ladies' gowns brilliant swirls of color in contrast to the men's somber evening attire
as the couples executed a waltz. Nearly five years after her debut,
Anne wondered if "difficult" was indeed the right word. She feared
"impossible" would soon apply to her situation.

She deposited her cup on the tray of a passing footman and
moved toward the far end of the room where her chaperone, Lady
Marguerite Stanley, held court. Smiling at acquaintances as she
passed, Anne directed her steps toward her chaperone, slowing as
she drew near. Marguerite was engaged in lively conversation with
a handful of her dearest friends. Reassured the older woman was
well occupied, Anne swept her gaze over the crowd.

Along the far wall, pocket doors were pushed wide to extend
the space and invite guests to circulate. With swift movements,
Anne exited the ballroom for the much less crowded hallway

beyond the doors and moved purposefully toward the residence's more private rooms.

The sounds of laughter, conversation, and strains of music grew less intrusive, fading to a murmur as she moved deeper into the house.

A door stood partially ajar, the warm light within beckoning her, and she paused to peer inside. Searching for occupants, Anne eyed the library and found the chairs arrayed before the imposing desk at one end empty. Directly across from her, a fire burned in the hearth beneath a graceful Adams mantel. Braces of candles glowed atop tables to her left and right but she saw no one. Satisfied she was alone, Anne stepped inside, closing the door behind her.

Blessed silence engulfed her. She exhaled with relief, the tension in her neck easing as she relaxed.

"Woof."

Startled, Anne's gaze searched the room for the source of the sound. A large dog was stretched out on the wide hearth rug, nearly blending into the rich, dark hues of his makeshift bed. Ears up, eyes alert, he watched her with tail-wagging interest but no alarm.

"Hello there," Anne said in welcome to the large mastiff. "You surprised me."

The big dog's tail moved faster, thumping against the thick rug in welcome.

Anne laughed softly and crossed the room. Ignoring the leather armchair, she sank down on its matching footstool.

"I'm pleased to meet you, too," she said softly.

She unbuttoned and stripped off one long glove before holding out her hand.

The mastiff sniffed her fingers, his breath warm against her palm. When he gave her a brief, approving sweep of his tongue, she chuckled again, charmed by his welcome.

"Are you all alone?"

He butted his head against her hand and she obliged his silent request. Smoothing her fingers over his head, she scratched him gently behind his ears.

"I will see to your ears as long as you promise to not scold me for taking a respite from my mission. Agreed?"

The dog woofed again, tilting his head to the side in a questioning manner.

"Ah yes, I forgot. You are not familiar with said mission." She bent closer and rubbed his silky hair. "In short, I must find a husband. And not just any husband," Anne added, smiling as the dog sighed with pleasure. "He must leave me be to do as I please—an impossible attribute in a man, if the last five years have taught me anything. Oh, and I must find him before I turn twenty-one—which is in less than six weeks."

Anne absentmindedly folded her hands in her lap and the dog huffed, nosing at her entwined fingers. "You might wonder why I bother at all," she continued, the oddness of discussing her private affairs with a mastiff beginning to wane. "Well, I've no choice. My well-meaning but misguided uncle insists I marry by my twenty-first birthday or I shall be packed off to the country, never to be heard from again."

The dog shifted and dropped his large head in her lap, eyeing her judgingly.

"You're right, I am being overly dramatic," Anne admitted. "Thank you. I needed reminding."

A log broke in the fireplace, the crack and flare of light startling her. The dog, however, paid the sound no heed and nudged her once again.

"You're quite single-minded, aren't you?" She resumed the slow stroke of her fingers, and the massive animal huffed with contentment. "But easily pleased. If only my uncle would accept a dog as a suitable companion for his only heir. You would be the perfect suitor."

A muffled laugh broke the quiet.

Anne glanced quickly at the entry. The heavy oak paneled door remained closed, just as she'd left it.

Under her hand, the dog didn't stir or show any signs of concern. Nonetheless, she gazed once more down the length of the room.

She caught a shift of movement at the edge of one of the wingback chairs that faced away from her. As she watched with dismay, a man rose and turned to stroll toward her.

Tall and lean, he moved with easy, prowling strides. Light from the candles and fire burnished coal black hair above a handsome face graced with strong cheekbones and a determined jawline. Ice blue eyes, set in a frame of thick black lashes, gleamed with amusement as he watched her.

Anne swallowed hard as he approached. She supposed some women would find him an excellent example of the male form. She swallowed a second time. Who was she attempting to fool? She found him the most excellent example of the male form she'd ever clapped eyes on, and he'd only been in her line of sight for mere seconds.

Anne abruptly realized she was staring. She also realized that she knew the man's name.

RHYS ALEXANDER HAMILTON, Duke of Dorset, studied the young woman as she quickly stood. She was unusually pretty, with gold curls caught up in a topknot, moss green eyes, and a lush mouth. The pale pink gown draping her body was backlit by the fire and semitranslucent, revealing a curvaceous, compact form. A delicate gold chain encircled her throat, the lower links concealed beneath the neckline of her gown. Rhys wondered what hung from the end of the chain—and instantly envied its position.

He knew the exact moment she recognized him because her eyes widened fractionally. Much to his surprise, she immediately frowned, her mouth firming.

A beautiful mouth, to be sure. But still, one currently conveying displeasure.

He was a duke. Young ladies didn't frown at the sight of him. They gushed. They simpered. They often tittered nervously and gave him coy glances while fluttering their eyelashes—all behavior he'd come to find annoying of late. Until now.

Intrigued, he halted several steps from her and bowed.

"My apologies for intruding on your solitude," he said smoothly.

"It would seem it is I who have intruded on your peace, Your Grace," she replied. "Had I known you were here, I would not have entered."

"Ah, but then I would have missed hearing your charming conversation with Jack," he replied, unable to restrain a grin. "And your look of—what, exactly? Disappointment? Displeasure?"

"None of the above—not exactly, that is." A blush colored her cheeks, her fingers toying with the delicate links of the chain at her throat.

"I apologize for not revealing myself sooner," Rhys offered, regret that he'd embarrassed her assailing him. "I should not have listened without your knowledge."

She waved dismissively. "I should have known better than to entrust such secrets to a mastiff." The heat faded from her face, the delicate skin once again clear and pale. "Everyone knows it's a hound you need for personal matters."

Rhys smiled, warmed by the unexpected humor—and something else. Something entirely authentic. He stared at her for a moment too long, realizing belatedly it was his turn to reply. "Let us start again, then—properly, this time. We have not been introduced," he said with feigned dismay. "I am—"

"I know who you are, Your Grace," she interrupted, holding up a hand to stop him from reciting his pedigree.

"Ah, then you have the better of me," he replied, finding his easy cadence once again. "For I have not had the pleasure of your acquaintance, Lady . . . ?"

"Not Lady," she corrected him. "Miss. Miss Anne Brabourne."

"A pleasure, Miss Brabourne." He bowed.

She sketched a curtsy and inclined her head with a graceful gesture that was perfectly polite. At the same time, she managed to imbue the acknowledgment with all the imperiousness of a queen greeting a subject.

Delighted by the act despite his earlier irritation, he smiled. "I hesitate to point out, Miss Brabourne, but you risk what I am certain must be a pristine reputation by sharing this admittedly large but very private space with me. I cannot be trusted to behave."

She eyed him dubiously. "Hardly, Your Grace."

His eyebrows lifted in surprise. She was something, all right. Something that fired Rhys's blood in a way he'd not felt for some time. Did she really believe herself able to resist his advances? Was he losing his touch? All but three minutes in her presence and his body begged for the opportunity to find out. "And why not, pray tell?"

"Because you are . . . well, you." She waved her hand dismissively. "And I am me."

"Would you care to explain that rather cryptic comment?"

"You"—she gestured, a pointed wave of her hand at him—"are Rhys Alexander Hamilton, a duke, and a gentleman notorious for avoiding matchmaking mamas and their hopeful daughters. It's universally accepted that you have no wish to marry any time soon. I, on the other hand, am engaged in the expected occupation of a lady and industriously searching for a husband. That alone makes me a female you would wish to avoid at all costs."

She paused, eyeing Rhys as though she worried he could not keep up. "I am also the niece and sole heir to Lord William Armbruster— General Armbruster. While you are rumored to be a rake of the first order, you are not known to be heartless. You could have no logical reason to practice your wiles on me. You'll keep to your widows and unhappily married women. To dally with an unwed young woman would lead to a scandal and disgrace for your family and ducal name."

"You seem to know much of me," Rhys replied, taking a step toward her. She was honest—brutally so. Scandalously so, even. And she was right. He valued his time and independence far too much to take on a wife. Oh, he would acquiesce at some point, of course. There was no other choice for a man in his position. But he'd be damned if he didn't live life to the fullest before being taken down by matrimony—at a ripe old age, if he could manage.

Rhys resisted the urge to close the distance completely and trace the length of her necklace to where it ended. "And I know so little of you."

"My uncle is determined I shall marry a man who is a pillar of society. A man with an impeccable reputation," she explained almost apologetically. "It is my business to know of you and your ilk, as well as the respectable eligible bachelors. How else am I to arrive at a suitable match? I have a list and you most certainly are not on it."

"Your enthusiasm for the undertaking threatens to overwhelm me," he commented dryly, trying desperately not to feel slighted by her statement. It was true enough, after all. He cared deeply for his family and would no more harm their good name than he would Miss Brabourne's. Still, did she have to make him sound so harmless?

Her eyes twinkled with restrained amusement. "I should certainly reprimand you for that comment, Your Grace, but alas, you are correct. I do not wish to marry a pillar of society or any other eligible man. I do not wish to marry at all."

"I'm unsure if I should be relieved or aggrieved that I and all of mankind have been so summarily dismissed," he commented, taking one more step toward her, purposefully cocking one eyebrow in the very manner that had been known to make multiple women swoon—at once.

She laughed, a low, melodic sound that sang to his very senses.

He took one last step and stood directly in front of her, realizing she'd grown more beautiful as he'd advanced.

A low, guttural growl emanated from behind Miss Brabourne, and Rhys looked past her to the hearth where Jack reclined, eyeing him with wise, dark eyes.

Rhys blinked hard. This was not how encounters proceeded between the Duke of Dorset and women. Somehow, the roles had been reversed. Clearly, he'd gone too long without a widow or unhappily married woman in his bed.

Coming to his senses, Rhys realized he should insist Miss Brabourne leave immediately, despite her claim of safety.

He looked again at Jack. He really ought to send her away at once. Rhys hadn't been so entertained by a female in months, if not years. And the truth of it was, he wasn't ready to let her go. He'd have to eventually, but not just yet.

Jack rumbled again, a second throaty growl of warning.

Rhys mentally pleaded with the mastiff, promising to behave—and willing himself to keep his word.

At that moment, the library doors opened, the creaking of the oak allowing just enough time for Miss Brabourne to gain a safe distance from Rhys.

"Anne, whatever are you doing here?" Lady Marguerite Stanley asked as she joined them. "And with Rhys? I wasn't aware the two of you were acquainted."

Rhys eyed his aunt's best friend. "Miss Brabourne did not know of my presence in the room, Lady Marguerite. She was just leaving."

"That's not entirely true," Miss Brabourne began as Marguerite frowned at Rhys.

"Your Grace, I assume your discretion is guaranteed?" Marguerite demanded, interrupting Miss Brabourne.

Rhys bowed to the two women. "You have my word. Go, return to the ball. I will wait here until a suitable amount of time has passed."

"Are either of you remotely interested in what I have to say?" Miss Brabourne asked, accepting Marguerite's arm.

"No, my dear, now come or your uncle will have my head," the older woman answered, tugging Miss Brabourne about and urging her toward the door.

But Anne stopped abruptly and turned back, offering him a charming smile. "You're far less frightening than everyone makes you out to be, Your Grace," she began, adding, "but I will keep your secret."

Rhys returned her warm smile, only this time without the cocking of his eyebrow. Or the lopsided smirk that showed his dimple so well. Not even the raking of his hand through his hair. No, Rhys simply smiled for the pure joy of it—for the pure joy of her.

He watched as the two women left the room. He waited a quarter of an hour, then returned to the ballroom, only to find the evening entertainment had lost its enticement. He searched out his aunt, promised to see her soon, and instead of joining friends at his club, went home. Settling in the library with a glass of brandy before bed, he realized he'd enjoyed his aunt's annual gala much more than usual.

And he wondered if Miss Brabourne always accompanied Lady Marguerite on her visits with his aunt.

Chapter 2

$\mathcal{A}$nne smothered a yawn as the door closed behind her maid. The gold chain with the simple locket attached lay next to her brush and comb atop her dressing table. She gathered the necklace up in her palm and opened the locket, pausing to contemplate the silver sixpence inside.

"You haven't brought me a husband yet," she murmured, smoothing her thumb over the cool metal of the coin. "Lucky charm, indeed. I don't know why Cordelia, Bea, and Ellie thought you were anything more than an old coin."

Anne smiled at the thought of her three dearest friends as she closed the locket and laid it atop the dresser. They'd been young girls together at boarding school when the sixpence had been discovered, hidden within a mattress. She couldn't remember who, precisely, had decided it was a lucky coin that would bring them all true love, and it didn't really matter. In truth, they were more sisters than mere friends, and Anne would willingly do whatever was needed to make them happy. Even if it meant pretending to believe in the power of a random coin. Yawning once again, she climbed into the turned-down bed and snuggled into her pillow.

She was far too practical to truly believe the sixpence would bring her a husband and true love. Not that she wanted true love, she thought with a sleepy snort. Observing her parents' passionate, emotionally explosive marriage for the first twelve years of her life had taught Anne that love brought intermittent and all too few bouts of pure joy along with misery and pain.

No, she reflected, she did not want a love match. But she did want, or rather required, a husband. And the undiscovered gentleman was proving extremely difficult to find.

"I'll write to Cordelia, Bea, and Ellie in the morning and solicit their advice," she decided out loud. Surely, one of the three would offer some bit of wisdom that would lead Anne to the right man.

The instant mental image of firelight highlighting Rhys Hamilton's face as he laughed made her shiver.

"He is not a possible suitor," she muttered. "I need a biddable husband. Easily controlled and one that will satisfy Uncle's requests. The duke is none of those things."

Anne closed her tired eyes. On their way home in the carriage that night, Marguerite had asked how long she'd been alone with the duke in the library. Of course she'd assured her chaperone it had been a short time at best, but she'd bit her tongue to keep from adding, *Not nearly long enough.*

She'd been sure the duke was about to kiss her when Marguerite had walked in. She could still feel the heat from his body on her skin. The smell of him continued to tease her nostrils still, long after they'd departed the ball. And his lips. The man's lips were made for kissing. She'd all but willed the duke to take her in his arms. Some sort of subtle yet feverish madness had taken her over, and it continued still. Perhaps she'd been wrong about him? Had he meant to add unwed young women to his list of accomplishments?

Anne drew the covers up to her chin and squeezed her eyes tightly. The Duke of Dorset would not make for suitable dreams. She needed to think on something else. A pastoral scene perhaps?

"No, he would not make for suitable dreams," she agreed with herself aloud. "But delicious dreams?" Anne groaned at the very suggestion and pictured cows. Lots and lots of slow, simple cows.

ANNE'S USUAL SOCIAL schedule kept her busy over the next two days—so busy, in fact, she convinced herself she'd forgotten the interlude with the duke in the library.

On the third morning, she followed Marguerite into Lady Sylvia Lipscombe's drawing room. A wash of genuine pleasure swept over her when she realized the duke stood near his aunt Sylvia, sipping tea, but Anne only smiled politely, the sense that she had something to hide nibbling at the back of her mind.

The two older women, bosom friends since the cradle, greeted each other warmly. Rhys bent to kiss Marguerite's cheek.

"It's a lovely surprise to see you here, Rhys," she commented with a genuine smile.

Marguerite lifted an eyebrow and glanced at Sylvia.

Anne saw the significant look but didn't have time to wonder what it meant before Sylvia abruptly turned to Rhys and began to talk.

"I assume you know Miss Brabourne?" She didn't allow Rhys to reply, only nod, before she continued. "Excellent. Now, if you'll be so good as to take Anne for a walk in my garden, I have a matter of some urgency to discuss with Marguerite, in private. I believe the roses are quite lovely at the moment."

She made a shooing motion, her lace handkerchief fluttering.

Anne's eyes widened at the abrupt command but Rhys smiled wryly as he bowed. "Miss Brabourne, I believe we have our orders. Shall we?" He gestured to the French doors leading out onto a terrace overlooking the garden.

She nodded and moved past him. He leaned close to open the door and his arm brushed hers. She shifted quickly, startled by the shiver of awareness at the brief touch.

"Watch your step," he murmured, taking her arm as they left the terrace for the garden path.

Anne glanced up at him through the screen of her lashes. He walked beside her, hands clasped behind his back, his gaze on the flowers lining the path.

It seemed rather unfair that he appeared completely unaffected by her presence while she . . . Anne wondered where the thought was going and decided not to follow.

"Not very subtle," Anne commented astutely, aiming the subject of the conversation purposefully away from herself and the duke.

A smile curved his mouth. "No, but that's hardly unusual for those two. Machinations will wait for no man—or woman, as the case may be. From what I am told, Lady Marguerite can quite often be found here with my aunt in the mornings."

Anne met his gaze and laughed, pausing on the path. "Did you purposely visit your aunt today to see Marguerite?"

"No. I came hoping to see you." He glanced at the windows overlooking the garden. "Perhaps we should find the rose my aunt suggested?"

He gestured to a curve in the walkway. "I believe the rosebush lies just beyond the bend." He bent toward her and whispered. "Where we shall thankfully be out of sight of my aunt Sylvia's keen eyes."

Anne breathed in the irresistible scent of the duke, the sensation of tiny butterflies winging their way about her stomach. "Should I fear being unobserved, sir?"

"My dear Miss Brabourne," he said dolefully, shaking his head. "I thought we addressed this subject at my aunt's ball. You are in dire need of a husband, while I"—he pressed his palm to his chest—"am assiduously avoiding all things matrimonial. You are as safe as the crown jewels, my dear Anne."

She was flirting and enjoying the act far, far too much.

He is unsuitable. And even if he was not, the duke wants nothing to do with marriage, Anne mentally repeated twice, then once more for good measure.

Pastoral cows were clearly in order. Anne attempted to focus her mind.

They wandered down the path, the strengthening breeze teasing a tendril from her pinned hair.

The duke touched her arm, turning her to face him. "You've come undone," he teased, reaching out to tuck the loose curl behind her ear, his fingers brushing her cheek and lingering.

Cows. Was that a soft, mournful moo she heard?

"Tell me why you won't marry for love."

The duke's wholly unexpected question did everything the imagined cows could not. Anne stepped back, searching the man's face. "But why?" she asked, vulnerability settling upon her skin.

The duke pointed to a rosebush a little farther up the path and urged Anne on. "All will be revealed. But first, tell me."

"Well, I suppose you've a right to the whole story," Anne reasoned, eyeing him questioningly before turning her gaze back to the path. "You've heard half—and only half a story is never enough."

Chapter 3

"My parents were a love match," Anne began, her gaze fixed straight ahead. "One of Shakespearean proportions. My mother had a talent for making rash decisions. My father was one of the rashest she ever made."

Rhys watched as she folded her arms across her chest, the simple act of relaying the story encouraging a physical response to protect herself. "I sense there was not a happy ending?"

"Oh no, Your Grace," she replied, returning her gaze to his, her tone somber. "I mentioned Shakespeare, did I not? They loved, quarreled, and made up with equal ferocity. They died together in a carriage accident following one such epic argument shortly after I turned twelve. They left me with a distaste for love matches in general and one for myself in particular."

It was madness, but Rhys wanted nothing more than to take her in his arms and ease the ache that so clearly held her heart. He'd only made her acquaintance less than four days past, and yet . . .

That was the problem; Rhys could not answer what came after *and yet* . . . Or he could not *bring* himself to.

Anne attempted to smirk but barely managed to hide the desperation visible on her countenance. "I told you: Shakespearean proportions."

"Well, your marriage will not end in tragedy," Rhys firmly stated.

Anne faltered and Rhys reached out to steady her, enjoying the feel of her in his arms far too much.

"I do not understand, Your Grace," she replied. Rhys felt her shiver beneath his touch, watched her breath catch as she fixed her eyes on his.

He fought the urge to quiet her question with a kiss. "I will help you find the right match." If another more deserving man was to own her future, couldn't he claim just a little of her present for himself? It was selfish of him, but he needed more time with Miss Brabourne. Craved it as a man would water when lost in the desert. Yes, it was pure selfishness, and he'd pay the price when she married and all but disappeared from his life. But it was all he had.

"There is no one more capable of finding you a husband than me," he explained, ensuring she had found her footing once more before releasing her and continuing on toward the roses. "You may have studied *Debrett's* until your eyes crossed, but I know these men—see them for who they truly are, not what they would have you believe. You cannot argue how useful I will be. And I will not watch you waste any more time only to be banished to the country. Will you have me?"

Rhys mentally cursed his last words, adding, "Will you have my help, that is?"

They'd reached the roses. Anne fingered the soft petals of a red bud, her brows knit together as she considered his words.

"It is quite a generous offer," she answered flatly. "And I cannot see any reason to refuse you, Your Grace."

"Excellent," Rhys replied, breathing a sigh of relief. He had her, at least for a little while longer.

Dearest Bea,

Though I know you'll find it hard to believe, I do have to wonder if the sixpence isn't bringing some bit of luck. The Duke of Dorset has offered to aid in my search for a husband.

Anne paused to dip her quill in the ink pot and found she could not write the next sentence. Should she reveal to Beatrice that, in the moment, she'd thought he was going to propose? And that the very idea had quickened her heartbeat until she felt sure the drumming could be heard throughout the whole of the city. And that she did not even have to think on what her answer would be.

She laid the quill down and peered out the window to where the city settled in for the evening, robed in a black night sky. Hours had passed and Anne continued to feel ridiculous. Of course he would not offer her his hand in marriage. They hardly knew each other—even if theirs was a friendship that had deepened far more quickly than Anne had ever experienced before. He was being practical—something she normally claimed of herself.

She picked up the quill again and teased her lip with the soft feathery end. It was her fast-approaching birthday at work, she was sure. Every man was becoming much more attractive a prospect, even those who were not a prospect *at all* by their own admission. No man considering a woman for a wife would offer to find her a husband.

Anne fought the swell of sadness that her last thought produced. This was no time to abandon who she was and what she wanted. She would leave love and happily-ever-afters to her friends.

She set her quill to foolscap once more.

Admittedly, I had not considered such a strategy before. But in light of my failure to find a suitable match up to this point, I don't know that I have a choice. Besides, who better to find the man I should marry than the man I could never marry?

Chapter 4

Three nights later
Lady Abingdon's Gala
Berkeley Square, London

"And I'm telling you, Anne, he's a bad choice." Rhys lounged in a leather armchair, a squat tumbler of brandy dangling from one hand.

"But you've given me no reason!" Anne paced between the brocade settee and the fireplace where he sat, pausing to confront him. "Declaring that Henry Effingham 'simply won't do' is not a sufficiently good reason to strike him from my list. I'm running out of time. My twenty-first birthday is only five weeks away. She glared at him, frustration literally vibrating through her body.

"He drinks too much," Rhys said flatly. He privately thought the man was a bloody idiot and couldn't fathom why Anne had set her sights on him.

Anne threw her hands in the air. "Every man I've met drinks too much." She pointed at the glass in his hand. "Including, apparently, you."

"I do not," he said evenly through his teeth, "drink to excess."

"Oh, very well," she grudgingly agreed. "Overimbibing is one sin the *ton* gossips have not attributed to you. More to the point, I've not heard that particular sin laid at Lord Effingham's door, either."

Rhys snorted. "Only because he doesn't drink to excess at *ton* gatherings. If the gossips could see him at gambling hells, they'd tell a different story."

"Is indulging in spirits his only excess?" Anne inquired, eyeing him dubiously.

"That, and an unhealthy tendency to obey his mother's commands." Rhys couldn't help himself. He knew how much that last claim would irritate Anne.

Anne dropped into the armchair opposite him. "Very well, I suppose I'll have to eliminate Lord Effingham from my list."

"I don't know why you need that bloody list," he growled at her. Pleased though he was at her abandonment of Effingham, her continued pursuit of a nameless, spineless husband was beyond frustrating.

Actually, in the dead of night, buried under his heavy coverlet, Rhys would have admitted it was the search for a husband at all that enraged him. But it was not the dead of night. And he was not abed. Therefore, he pushed the thought from his mind.

"You're a well-dowered woman with an impeccable pedigree. Why won't your uncle let you wait until the right man appears? Why can't he relent and let you stop hunting a husband?"

"Every woman my age is hunting a husband," she said dryly. "It's why you spend so much time avoiding their mamas."

"That's completely different," he argued. "They want the title and the money. You want independence."

Anne drew in a breath, her green silk gown tightening over the curve of her breasts.

Rhys didn't even attempt to look away. He'd been trying to fight the pull of attraction all night and failing repeatedly. Everything about her resonated within him, drew him, demanded he claim her. But this was Anne. She wanted a suitable husband. He didn't want a wife. When he'd offered to help her, he'd known how hard it would be to give her up, but he'd failed to factor in the difficulty of restraining himself while they were together.

Anne was speaking. He wrenched his thoughts back to their conversation and listened.

"Exactly. Which is why I must find a man willing to marry me who will also agree to my remaining independent. You do remember why you're here, don't you? You're meant to be helping, not hindering."

"Of course I remember," he replied, taking a long sip of brandy. How could he forget?

"My uncle will not force me into a marriage I do not want, but neither will he allow me unlimited time to choose an acceptable husband."

"I hear he's coming to town," Rhys commented idly, studying her. He didn't like the downward curve of her lips. The unhappy set of her shoulders echoed her discouragement, and he felt a twinge of conscience that his description of Effingham's unsavory character had most likely been the cause.

She glanced up at him through thick lashes and his breath caught. *Every damn time she does that, I get hard. Bloody hell.*

"Yes, on business, I presume. Marguerite was rather vague."

Behind her, the tall case clock's chimes struck the half hour in deep tones. Anne groaned, her smile rueful.

"I must return." She rose and shook out her skirt, smoothing a hand over a faint wrinkle in the green silk. "I'm certain Marguerite will be searching for me by now."

"You go ahead. I'll follow in a few moments."

She nodded and turned away.

"Anne."

Pausing, she glanced back.

"We'll find you a husband. Don't give up hope."

"I won't cease hoping, but I confess, I'm beginning to lose faith in my plan. I will write to my friends. That always lifts my spirits."

He chuckled with amusement, the brooding darkness of his

mood lifting. "I told you it was a ridiculous plan. You should have agreed with me. I'm sure your friends would."

She rolled her eyes. "Of course. Because, being male and a duke, you're always right."

"Exactly." He laughed when she shot him a mock glare. "So fierce," he teased.

"Good night, Your Grace," she said, then turned and disappeared out the doorway.

Rhys stared after her. The room was too quiet, too empty without her. He'd only recently faced the fact that this was how it would be in a few short weeks. Anne would either be married or removed to the country. Either way, there would be no more conversations in quiet libraries at balls, no more walks in the garden while her chaperone and his aunt drank tea.

He'd miss her insightful, wry comments on the vagaries of human nature the *ton* displayed in their petty rivalries and noble actions. He would miss the way she could always make him laugh when he was in a bad mood.

He'd miss her, damn it.

The situation was unacceptable. He'd have to do something to keep her in London and in his life.

Chapter 5

$\mathcal{A}$nne's maternal uncle Lord William Armbruster had been summoned to his London home via a vague and rather mysterious missive from Lady Marguerite. Uneasy with her lack of information, he'd grown increasingly concerned over the course of the trip from his country estate to his Belgrave Square mansion. The city was never enjoyable. Too many people. And far too much interaction. Lord Armbruster had earned his quiet life in the country. Lady Marguerite had been his only sister's best friend and had known him since childhood; she was well aware of his dislike for the city. Yet she'd insisted he join her in London as soon as may be. The news could not be good.

He stepped across the threshold of 812 Belgrave Square and handed his hat, caped overcoat, and cane to the butler, Timms.

"Where is Lady Marguerite?" he asked abruptly, nodding in greeting to the man.

"She and Lady Lipscombe are having tea in the yellow salon, my lord."

"Thank you, Timms."

"Will you be staying long, sir?"

"That depends," the general said grimly.

"Very well, my lord."

William strode down the hallway of his London home to enter the cozy room overlooking Brook Street.

"Ladies." He bowed perfunctorily, eyeing them with barely restrained concern. "I am here, as requested. Now, will you please tell me why I've been called halfway across England at a moment's notice? Why the urgency? Has something happened to Anne? Is she well?"

"Goodness, William, you always assume the worst," Marguerite hastened to reassure him, reaching up to pat him on the arm. "Please, do sit down. We can't converse with you hovering over us."

He glanced at Lady Lipscombe, his frown deepening.

"Marguerite is correct," she interjected before he could speak. "Looming over us and frowning won't intimidate us in the slightest. You should know that by now. Besides"—she smiled, a dimple flashing at the corner of her mouth—"I'm certain you must be famished from your journey and we have your favorite cakes, with tea."

He stared at her, intent on standing his ground, realizing not for the first time that he'd never managed to do so against the two during the entirety of their friendship. The French were nothing more than irritating toddlers compared to Marguerite and Sylvia.

"Very well. You know I've never been able to resist you two, especially when you're together. When you were young girls and joined with Bella, I was hopeless."

"We know." Both ladies' faces reflected the sadness that always accompanied the mere mention of Anne's mother. Bella had been an integral member of their circle of three when they were schoolgirls and later, as young married women. Her death had reduced them to a duo. Marguerite's current widowed state and close connection to Bella were factors that had prompted William's plea that she sponsor Anne's debut into society.

Besides, he fancied the idea of the two helping to bring Anne into the society that would become her world. He'd never admit it to the two women, but they meant as much to him as his own sister.

Marguerite poured tea, and conversation was light until William had taken the edge from his hunger. At last, he set aside his cup and plate.

"Very well, I have eaten and consumed two cups of tea. Now, tell me, why did you summon me from the country?"

Marguerite exchanged a loaded glance with Sylvia before turning to William. "We believe Anne and Rhys are becoming close."

"Anne and Rhys?" William thought for a moment before repeating his question. "Anne and Rhys?"

"The Duke of Dorset," Marguerite offered helpfully.

Which it was not. At all. "Dorset?" William asked, picturing his niece and . . .

He lifted one eyebrow and shifted his attention to Sylvia. "Your nephew Rhys?"

He shoved his chair back and stood abruptly, though he couldn't say what he planned to do next.

"William," both women said as if calming a wild animal.

The general realized he still held his serviette. Tossing the slip of fabric to the table, he pinned Marguerite with an angry gaze. "How could you let this happen?"

"I understand your skepticism, William," Marguerite started, slowly standing. "But I assure you, this is happy news."

"I cannot imagine a scenario where this development could be seen as welcome in any way," he bit out.

Marguerite eyed him warily. "William, take a moment."

"I trusted you, Marguerite—and you, Sylvia!" he said accusingly, spinning to confront the woman.

"Yes, William, you trusted me. To find a suitable match for Anne. And I have," Marguerite interjected.

His anger flared anew. "I haven't seen Anne since before the season began. Although she agreed to my request, I was by no means convinced she intended to apply herself to finding a suitable husband."

"I believe she has been perfectly honest about searching for a husband that is acceptable to her," Marguerite told him. "I am less convinced she agrees that your definition of an acceptable husband matches her own list of requirements."

"What do you mean?" William's gaze sharpened and his eyebrows lowered.

"Only that you have made it abundantly clear you want her to marry a man who will manage her affairs—and her person—with discretion and ease."

"And isn't that what every guardian wishes for their ward?" he demanded, affronted.

"Of course, William," Sylvia soothed. She exchanged a telling glance with Marguerite before leaning forward to capture him with an intent gaze. "But that is clearly not what Anne wants."

He huffed and shook his head in disgust. "I suppose she's looking for true love," he growled. "Well, I'll not have it." He glared at Sylvia, his hands tightening into fists. "I'll not have her leg-shackled to some wild young rake. I'll not lose her like I did my sister."

"Anne is nothing like her mother," Sylvia said, exasperated. "Truth be told, she's much more like you."

He gaped at her, taken aback.

"It's true," Marguerite agreed. "Anne is very pragmatic. In fact, I fear her opinion of a love match echoes your own. She's searching for a husband who is malleable, a man who will allow her to keep and manage her own funds, a man who is staid, stolid, and unremarkable in every way."

"Then what makes you think she's interested in your nephew?" he asked Sylvia. "His father and I were at Eton together and I knew him well. 'Staid' and 'unremarkable' are not words I would use to describe him. And friends tell me Rhys is very much his father's son."

"It's true," Sylvia said with pride. "Rhys is very like my late brother-in-law. But you must agree, William, this is a good thing. Like his father, Rhys is a gentleman; he manages his estates and investments with responsibility and a flare of brilliant intelligence. Additionally, his position in society is above reproach. Any young woman would be overjoyed to gain the interest of a duke."

"All of which only proves my point, Sylvia," William replied. "If Anne is searching for a manageable husband, she won't choose a gentleman with intelligence and a sense of responsibility. Such attributes would surely mean he would demand to have influence in her life." He frowned. "Also, if memory serves me, Rhys is infamous for his avoidance of marriage-minded females."

"Precisely." Marguerite clapped her hands with gleeful satisfaction. "Yet he seeks out Anne at every opportunity. She and I join Sylvia for tea and a long visit several times a week. Rhys often chooses that moment to drop in and visit his favorite aunt."

"If his attentions are that marked, why haven't I read anything about it in the gossip rags?"

"He's very circumspect," Sylvia hastened to reassure him. "Rhys would not do anything to cause a scandal or gossip," she said firmly. "But nonetheless, to those of us who know Rhys well, and Anne"— she nodded at Marguerite—"it's clear that they're drawn to each other. Sylvia and I feel it wise to encourage the friendship. But we cannot push or Anne will bolt. They must come to understand their feelings for one another on their own."

"I see." William pondered their comments. Marguerite and Sylvia would not lead Anne down the same path that Bella trod, of that he was sure. Could they be wrong about the duke? The women knew William better than he knew himself, so it was unlikely. But still, a possibility. And if they were not? Anne would be a duchess, her life settled and serene, just as she deserved.

He had no choice but to trust them. Blast, but it felt as if he were back on the battlefield with no practical options left. "So, what is your plan then? I assume you have one."

"We will keep a watchful eye on the two and send you regular updates," Marguerite said. "You must reject any offers from other suitors."

"And what about him? Is he likely to wait for her to come around to your way of thinking?"

The two women burst into peals of laughter. "Oh, William," Sylvia finally managed to say. "Rhys has no idea that Anne is the one woman for him. And if the thought should happen to fleetingly occur to him, I'd wager he'd immediately deny it."

"He needs as much time as Anne to realize what Sylvia and I recognized in the space of a week." Marguerite smiled warmly.

William shook his head. "Women. I'll never understand them."

Chapter 6

The Maldens' Annual Musicale
Mayfair, London

"*I* do hate a musicale," Uncle William muttered as he led Marguerite and Anne into the Maldens' grand music room.

Anne stifled a laugh as Marguerite chided the man gently, pointing to where rows of chairs were arranged before a number of instruments. "Come now, William. Behave. There are enough seats available in the front row for us all. And next to Lady Lipscombe. What luck!"

"That is not luck, Marguerite," Uncle William answered, slowing his pace. "Quite the opposite. No escape route should the evening prove unbearable."

Anne patted her uncle on the back and gestured toward the chairs. "It is lucky, Uncle. Both you and Lady Lipscombe share the same opinion when it comes to musicales. You shall be able to commiserate to your heart's content," she assured him, looking about the room for the duke. "Go. I'll be with you in a moment."

Uncle William huffed with displeasure but did as he was told, allowing Marguerite to lead the way.

"I abhor musicales." The low tone sounded very near Anne's ear and she attempted to restrain a shiver of anticipation.

"You and my uncle, both," she replied, turning to face the duke. "Fortunately, you're not here for the music." The only hope Anne had of subduing the worrisome reaction both her mind and body produced in the duke's presence was to stay the course. She needed to find a husband. And the duke needed to be more helpful. And soon.

Anne peered over the duke's right shoulder and nodded. "Lord Abrams is in attendance, I see."

The duke turned to take the man in, returning his gaze to Anne's almost immediately, disapproval in his eyes. "Habitual gambler. He'd have your dowry reduced to rubble within a year."

Anne stifled a groan. She could not abide a man who would so frivolously waste money—and most likely his life and hers. "All right. And what of Lord Finch?"

"Believes a woman should bear no less than six children if she's to hold her head high in public," the duke replied dryly, eyeing the rather portly earl with severity. "And, some say, he has a rather passionate interest in women's toes."

"I never said I would refuse children," Anne countered, weighing whether his proclivity for feet crossed him off the list.

Deciding it most definitely did, Anne searched the room. "Ah, there now, Lord John Thorpe. Surely you cannot find fault with him."

Anne felt a swell of satisfaction. The duke couldn't possibly have anything to say against Lord John. No one ever did.

"He plans to move to America once his overbearing mother passes on."

"Oh," Anne replied, attempting to buoy her mood. "Well, I'll admit, I've never thought to go so far afield. It would be an adventure, I suppose."

The duke eyed her doubtingly, then stepped closer, lowering his voice. "And leave your three dear friends?"

Anne willed her body to ignore the duke's closeness and concentrated on the newfound information. It was enough to break her heart, the thought of Ellie, Bea, and Cordelia so very, very far away.

And the duke, her internal voice whispered.

"Why are you doing this?" she whispered, feeling overly warm.

He tipped her chin up, concern pooling in his eyes. "Are you feeling well, Anne? You look flushed."

Almost every last piece of her heart wanted him to answer. But the last sliver? It knew she could not bear to hear the truth.

"I am tired, that is all," she offered, looking to where her uncle and Marguerite waited. "Tired of waiting for you to find a suitable match. I don't mean to sound ungrateful, but you've yet to produce even one possible candidate. I'm running out of time, Your Grace."

"I know," he ground out.

His stern tone urged Anne to look at him. The brilliant blue hue of his eyes had darkened as a sky threatening to storm would. "I said I would help, Anne, but I never said I would compromise. You deserve better."

"It doesn't matter what I deserve," she answered, surprised by the passion underlying her words. The room was growing too hot. Anne could feel perspiration gathering at the nape of her neck.

Her very idea of what she deserved was changing. What had he done to her?

"Don't ever say such a thing, Anne," he growled. "You deserve the best. And I will see that you have it."

No more. Not tonight.

The Malden girls walked toward their instruments and those still milling about took their seats.

"Come, we must join the others," Anne said, refusing to meet the duke's gaze.

"Anne," the duke said, reaching out for her arm.

Anne avoided his fingers just barely, moving toward the safety of her uncle and Marguerite. And away from the danger of the duke.

Chapter 7

The following morning, Anne sat at her writing desk in her bedroom. Sunlight shafted through the tall windows, casting bars of bright, warm yellow over the blue, gold, and red of the carpet. Quill in hand, she bent over a sheet of foolscap. A creased, well-read letter lay open atop the desk's polished cherrywood surface.

She read the letter once again, smiling at her friend's chatty news, and dipped her pen in the inkwell to reply.

Dear Bea,

I was so pleased to receive your note. How I miss you, Ellie, and Cordelia and long to have you all here in town with me. Society events are sadly dull without your company but have been enlivened by the Duke of Dorset's assistance in my search. While it's true I've yet to find a husband, I feel sure the duke's help will lead to a marriage.

My uncle has joined us in Belgrave Square so we are a threesome now. I know some find him off-putting, but I adore the man, even if he's misguided when it comes to my future.

I must close, my dear Bea, as I am promised to join Marguerite and Lady Lipscombe for a museum visit. Please write soon and tell me

*everything. I so love to hear about your days in the village although I wish
you were near me in London.*

   With love,
   Anne

Anne had not exactly lied. She'd simply omitted some of the
truth. The duke most assuredly did enliven events, in a manner of
speaking. The Maldens' musicale the evening before would have
lacked in frustration, vexation, and a few other choice words that
ended in "ion" if not for the duke. He claimed to be on Anne's
side, even her champion in the search for a husband. And yet, no
less than three potential candidates were wiped from the list, all
thanks to him.

What was he playing at? Anne honestly didn't know. But one
thing was for sure: He needed to stop. She was running out of
time—and men. And she suspected her heart could not take much
more of his brand of help.

"WHY ARE WE in a museum and not at Tattersall's inspecting the
newest arrivals?"

Rhys glanced sideways at his friend and noted the black scowl.
"You didn't have to come with me, Lucien," he said mildly. "I told
you I would meet you later."

The frown on the Earl of Penbrooke's face only darkened. "Didn't
want to chance you being delayed by your aunt."

"I promised to join her party this afternoon and view the exhibit.
I didn't pledge to spend the day here. We'll be off to Tattersall's
within the hour."

Lucien grunted. "Don't know why you agreed to ramble around
a bloody museum with a pack of females."

Distracted, Rhys only half heard his friend's grumbling as they
left the anteroom and stepped into the expansive space that hosted
a new exhibit of Egyptian artifacts. Fashionably dressed groups

of ladies and gentlemen strolled across the marble floor, pausing to view selections or gather in clusters to chat. Impatient, Rhys scanned faces but didn't see his aunt Sylvia.

"There she is." Lucien nodded to his left.

Rhys turned and found his aunt, standing with a group of women, halfway down the long room. At that moment, she saw him and lifted a hand in a gracious gesture, beckoning him. He acknowledged her with a slight nod, but before he could move, Anne's attention was caught by his aunt's wave. Her features lit with pleasure when she turned and saw him. Green eyes sparkled with delight, her hair gleaming gold against the frame of a sky blue bonnet, trimmed in cream, that matched her pelisse.

The world instantly brightened. Damn, he thought, bemused by her smile and unaware he smiled back. Somehow, she made even Egyptian relics seem irresistible.

"Well, well." Lucien's deep voice held amusement and a distinct male interest. "Now I know why you insisted on joining your aunt. Who's the chit?"

"None of your damn business." Rhys strode forward, ignoring Lucien's chuckle as he followed.

"Good morning, ladies." Rhys sketched a bow, his gaze moving over the five females standing with his aunt. "I trust you're enjoying the exhibit?"

"We are," his aunt replied. "It's kind of you to join us, Rhys. And you as well, Lord Penbrooke."

Rhys automatically murmured appropriate greetings as his aunt introduced him and Lucien to the three young women he hadn't previously met. When she made Lucien known to Anne, however, his attention sharpened. He barely restrained the instinct to step in front of Anne and block Lucien.

"A pleasure, Miss Brabourne," Lucien drawled, interest sparking in his eyes as he bent to brush his lips against her gloved fingers. He stepped back and met Rhys's gaze. "And why have you not introduced me before, Rhys?"

Rhys narrowed his eyes at his friend. "Perhaps because you refuse to attend any suitable social occasions where such introductions are made."

"Alas." Lucien pressed his palm to his chest and gave a theatrical sigh. "If you had told me how beautiful and charming your friends were, I would have attended without fail."

Rhys stifled an expletive. "Of course." The wry disbelief in his voice was obvious and Anne's eyes sparkled as her gaze met his.

"Let us move on," his aunt interrupted. "There is much to view, and I for one wish to see each of the exhibits."

"Of course." Rhys held out his arm to Anne. "Miss Brabourne? Shall we?"

"Yes, Your Grace, let's do proceed." Anne took his arm and they strolled off, joining a slowly moving throng idling down the long room. "I didn't know you would be here today," she commented.

"I promised Aunt Sylvia I would." Rhys looked down at her. The blue ruching of her bonnet framed her hair and face as she tilted her head back, her expression open and warm. No artifice, no holding back, she always looked at him as if she were seeing him, Rhys the man, and not Rhys the duke. No other woman of his acquaintance ever looked at him quite the way Anne did, he realized. He liked it. Liked the way it warmed his heart and erased the distance he normally felt from friends. He'd never thought of himself as solitary, or lonely. Now he thought he might feel exactly that were Anne to disappear from his life.

"And do you enjoy Egyptian artifacts?" she asked.

"Of course."

"You said that so smoothly, I suspect you are not being entirely truthful," she teased, eyes twinkling up at him. "But I'll let it go."

"I am curious about Egyptian history," he amended, "but I hate uncomfortable furniture with arms and legs shaped like crocodile feet."

"Ah, yet another thing we can agree on." She tugged on his arm, steering him toward a sarcophagus displayed against the wall. "Come, let us investigate this intriguing piece."

Rhys and Anne strolled across the marble floor, viewing objects both large and small. While he registered comments and voices of the rest of the group following behind, he paid little attention. They found themselves in an alcove, bent over a glass-topped cabinet to view the jeweled daggers within.

He braced his hands on the case, bracketing her much smaller form, and leaned forward. Her bonnet brim kept him from her skin, but her slender shoulders met his chest and the swell of her hips was a bare inch from his.

"Are you fascinated by the daggers, or is it the jewels that have caught your rapt attention," he murmured, pleased when she turned her head to look up at him.

"It's the artistry," she replied, her voice a musical whisper. "They're really quite beautiful."

He didn't look away from her at the case. "Yes, they are."

She blushed, color staining her cheeks, and her small hands fisted on the case next to his.

"Your Grace," she murmured, his name on her lips a soft almost-plea. "Is Lord Penbrooke here for my consideration? I'll admit he was never on my list, but I trust that you have my best interest at heart. And, as you are well aware, I am running out of time. I do not want to lose faith in your abilities, but after last night, I am beginning to wonder whether your standards are not higher than my uncle's."

A high-pitched giggle broke the alcove's quiet privacy.

"We must find the jeweled daggers, Abigail, I'm certain Lord Endsley specifically said they were along this wall."

Rhys dragged in a deep breath and stepped back. With controlled restraint, he tucked Anne's hand through the bend of his arm and led her out of the alcove. "No, Lord Penbrooke is most certainly not here for you. And do not doubt me. I will find you a husband if it's the last thing I do."

She tilted her head back and looked up at him, her eyes bright with emotional turmoil, before focusing on a guide's lecture. Rhys drew another deep breath and forced himself to focus on the droning commentary, but didn't register a single word.

It was more than an hour later before he and Lucien took leave of the women and reached the street.

"Well, that was an enlightening hour," Lucien commented as he settled into the ducal coach.

Across from him, Rhys also leaned back against the squabs. "Why enlightening? Did you actually find the company of my aunt Sylvia enjoyable?"

"Of course, the marchioness is always entertaining," Lucien replied. "But even more interesting was watching you with the lovely Miss Brabourne." He leveled a finger at Rhys, a grin curling his hard mouth. "You, my friend, are trapped."

"What?" Rhys glared at him.

"You heard me. Trapped. Ensnared by the charms of a beautiful woman. Never thought I'd see the day." He shook his head in mock dismay. "Next thing we know, you'll be getting leg-shackled and spending your nights at home. I don't relish the prospect as that means I'll be visiting the gambling hells alone. Of course"—he paused thoughtfully—"this also probably means I won't be losing as much of my blunt to you at cards. You've been annoyingly lucky lately."

"Perhaps we should give Tattersall's a miss and go to Jackson's club. I feel the need to knock you about in the ring."

"I must decline." Lucien waved a negligent hand. "You promised to look at the bays and I want your opinion. Later, if you still feel the need to punch me, we can visit the club."

"I seriously doubt I'll lose the urge to injure you in some way," Rhys said dryly, failing to be amused. "Nonetheless, I can't have it said that I broke a promise. Tattersall's it is."

Chapter 8

Dear Anne,

Bless you for writing so promptly for I, too, cherish the newsy letters from my friends. I confess I am intrigued by your observations of the Duke of Dorset as I was unaware you were acquainted. My neighbor tells me he has a reputation as a bit of a rake, but if Marguerite has approved your friendship, all must be well. Her wisdom on such matters has always proved reliable. You are so fortunate your uncle chose her to be your companion. I quite adore her. I'm so pleased you have the duke's company and happy that he's been enlisted to help in the husband search. I must admit that it never would have occurred to me to employ such tactics, but it does rather make sense.

All is well here and we have enjoyed lovely weather with fair skies, which, as you know, I so adore studying. I must close, for the vicar's wife requires my company for a visit to the Wallingford shops. Please write soon—I vow I am breathless with anticipation, awaiting further news of your progress.

With love,

Bea

"I shall be glad to dine at home this evening," Marguerite commented.

Anne looked up, searching the older woman's face from across the table where they shared luncheon. "Are you feeling unwell, Marguerite? We needn't go out every evening if you need to rest. Declining invitations will likely only make us more desired by hostesses."

"Nonsense." Marguerite waved a dismissive hand. "I'm perfectly fine. However, I confess I'm looking forward to enjoying the comfort of our own dining room."

"Will Uncle be joining us?" Anne asked. The oxtail soup was delicious.

"Yes," Marguerite replied. "He set off on some sort of business not long ago but said to expect him back in time."

"So we shall be three, then," Anne said.

They sipped their tea in silence before Marguerite continued. "Sylvia had a letter from her sister—Rhys's mother, that is. She's sprained her ankle and will be delayed in coming to London."

"Oh, I hope she is all right," Anne exclaimed, noting her marked interest too late to recover. "And there are his sisters to consider, of course. They must be disappointed by the delay."

"Yes," Marguerite concurred. "If Rhys were married, of course, his sisters could be chaperoned by his wife."

"So, his mother and sisters are anxious for him to marry then?" Anne sought to keep her query casual but feared she failed when Marguerite smiled at her with warm affection.

"What mother does not want her son to marry and produce grandchildren? And then there's the necessity of continuing the family line. Having said that, Sylvia and the rest of his family appear to be genuinely concerned that Rhys marry a woman who will appreciate his many excellent qualities. There's no question that he would make a fine husband for having been raised with six sisters, he may well understand a wife's needs far better than other, lesser men."

"In what way?"

Marguerite smiled fondly. "He seems to equally indulge and support them, while expecting them to meet standards normally held for males. When he was eight, his sister Mary, a year younger, wanted to study mathematics. Rhys demanded that she be allowed to join him in lessons. The tutor was a bit taken aback but Sylvia said their father simply shrugged and agreed. After that, all the girls joined Rhys's lessons. They're all astonishingly intelligent women. Which"—Marguerite sighed—"only means it is becoming increasingly apparent that finding husbands for them will be equally difficult."

"What a marvelous story." Fascinated, Anne wondered what life would have been like in a home filled with siblings, books, and all the lessons a duke could afford for his children. "It must have been a wonderful house to grow up in," she said genuinely.

"Indeed." Marguerite's expression softened as she met Anne's gaze. "I dearly loved your mother, but coping with her dramatics could not have been easy. Especially as your father was cut from the same cloth."

"That is true," Anne agreed pragmatically, grateful for the reminder. "I often felt as if I was the sensible adult and mother the temperamental child. Most often, Mama and Papa seemed either passionately happy or desperately upset. There was never any balance—for any of us."

"I suspect your experience with them may have colored your view of what would be an acceptable marriage," Marguerite said gently.

"How could it not?" Anne asked, both Marguerite and, admittedly, herself. Anyone would be a fool to ignore such a lesson, wouldn't she?

"They were two very passionate people. Unfortunately, it was their nature to react to common circumstances with an outburst of dramatic flair," Marguerite agreed. "But that is not how every marriage plays out, my dear. Surely you know this?"

"Of course," Anne said. "I've met many couples who are perfectly complacent in each other's company. They appear to live comfortable lives and I can't imagine they endure daily tantrums. Passion and outbursts are unlikely to have a place in their world. That's what I want in my marriage," she added firmly. "Peace. Predictable days. A husband willing to let me determine my own activities as I leave him to his. That would be the perfect situation for a woman such as me."

"But, Anne, you make no allowance for affection, for love, not to mention passion," Marguerite protested.

"I suppose I would welcome affection. But love? Passion? No." Anne shook her head, hopeful she appeared as resolute as she once felt on the topic.

"Surely you do not truly feel this way." Marguerite's shock was reflected in her voice and expression.

"I do." Anne didn't realize how tightly she gripped her teacup until she returned it to the saucer, the china rattling as she did so. She clasped her hands together in an attempt to still their trembling. "They had a terrible row at luncheon that day. I begged Mama not to go, but she wouldn't listen. She insisted she must keep her fitting appointment for the gown she was to wear to the Standish fete. At the last moment, Papa insisted upon driving her. I'll never forget how I felt when they drove away. Helpless. And angry. Even then, I could see all the destruction such powerful feelings could cause."

"It was an accident, Anne. A lorry veered in front of them. There was nothing your father could have done to avoid it. It wasn't his fault."

"That is what my uncle told me after they died," Anne confirmed.

"But you don't accept his word?"

Anne sighed. "I understand his view of the situation. I certainly don't believe my uncle, or you, would lie to me. But that doesn't change what I saw that day—indeed, what I saw and heard nearly every day for the first twelve years of my life. My parents loved and quarreled with equal passion. They died after a very loud argument. Even if that argument had nothing to do with their deaths, their marriage is not one I wish to emulate. I found the constant shouting, tears, and slamming doors made the days and weeks unbearable. I don't want a marriage with passion." Her chin firmed. "I will not have a marriage like that."

She was not lying. But Anne had begun to wonder if love always came with arguments and disagreements, blind anger and senseless actions.

"Oh, Anne." Marguerite's eyes were limpid with unshed tears. "If your mother were here, I vow I would shake her. She taught you nothing of the joys of marriage, and having lost her at such a tender age, you cannot remember anything but the tribulations." She drew in a deep breath, her own round chin firming with determination. "I shall have to change that."

Dear Miss Brabourne

Rhys sat at his desk and stared at the words he'd just written. "This is what it's come to?" he asked the silence that surrounded him in the study. When no one answered, he picked up his crystal glass and sipped at the brandy within. Anne had said writing to her friends always lifted her spirits. He'd never been one for writing letters and could not remember the last time he'd done so. Still, it was worth trying. After the visit to the museum, something had to be done to ease the tension coursing through his veins. He took up the quill again.

Dear Anne,
    Let me begin by saying this is all your fault. Up until the moment I met you, I'd successfully avoided emotional entanglements of any kind. And then you appeared. Attractive? Yes, but so were all the other women of my acquaintance. No, you were, rather are, something altogether different. I should not have offered to help you find a husband. It was entirely selfish on my part, meant only to secure more time in your presence. But now I pay by the second, wanting nothing more than to claim you for my very own, all the while knowing I cannot ever do so. You said yourself I am an unsuitable match, and while many would disagree with you, your uncle would not. I am in an impossible situation—all of which I blame on you. Because this is my letter and I shall do as I please.

Rhys threw down the quill and crumpled the foolscap in his fist. And then he heaved a heavy, long sigh. The text was childish. Selfish. And somewhat untrue. But Anne had been right. Letters could lift your spirits—just not in the way Rhys had expected. This letter would never be sent, not one single word within read, but it had, for a few moments, allowed him to indulge what he'd been attempting so hard to deny. He loved Anne Brabourne.

Chapter 9

*A*nne swept down the stairs the following morning to find Rhys waiting for her in the marble-floored entry.

"Good morning," she called, tugging on her riding gloves and ignoring the shiver of awareness as his gaze swept over her. The blue velvet of her riding habit seemed suddenly insubstantial and too snug across her breasts.

"You're very alert this morning," Rhys replied, his normal deep voice rougher, darker. "I suspected you would be awake far too late last night reading the novel you found at Hachette's last week."

"How did you know about that?" Anne said. "I don't remember mentioning it."

"You didn't," he replied, his gaze drifting over her from head to toe. She felt the brush of his look as if he'd touched her. "Marguerite told Sylvia. For some reason, my aunt felt I should know about it."

"Hmm, that's odd." She shrugged. "As to the novel, I must confess, I found it most entertaining."

"Really?" He lifted a brow, eyeing her with bemusement. "It seemed very much like fairy tales to me—Sylvia mentioned a kidnapped heiress and an earl disguised as a masked highwayman."

He looked truly confused and Anne couldn't restrain a laugh. "Perhaps it's not the sort of novel you would choose to read?"

"No." He shook his head and grimaced. "Most assuredly not. That's not the odd part, though. What puzzles me is that it does not sound like the sort of book you would read. Far too fanciful for your tastes, wouldn't you agree?"

Anne would agree, actually, just not out loud. Doing so would mean she'd have to explain why such a tale suddenly appealed to her. And she wouldn't do so with the duke. She couldn't.

"Would you allow your sisters to read such an adventurous novel if they wanted?" Anne asked, redirecting the conversation away from her.

"Of course. Why would I not?" His gaze narrowed over her. "Are you suggesting you believe I should monitor them?"

"No," she said firmly. "I do not. I merely wondered if you believed a male, who is also a duke," she teased with a roll of her eyes and a smile, "should have the right to tell his sisters what they must read."

Rhys shook his head at her in disbelief. "Clearly, you have not met my sisters or you would never think they would agree. It's also clear," he added, "you must believe me to be the worst kind of tyrant to deny them such pleasures."

"Many men would not consider themselves autocratic, but rather believe duty required they oversee their sisters' choices."

"Many men were not raised with six sisters," he scoffed. "My father gave me sage advice when I was very young. He said a wise man understands that his comfort is dependent on living in accord with the women in his life and not attempting to command them." His eyes lit with mischief. "He told me this after I loudly complained my sisters had refused to obey my orders while they were crew on my pirate ship. Since they had just mutinied and pummeled me with pillows and pirate hats, I took my father's words to heart. I believe there were some wooden swords involved as well. I had bruises, if I recall."

Anne burst out laughing. "I should have loved to have known you as a child, and your sisters as well. You must have had a great deal of fun."

"We did."

Timms held the door as they left the quiet house. Anne's uncle and Marguerite were still above stairs, and the peaceful silence was broken only by an occasional sound of a servant's footsteps.

Stubborn wisps of fog shrouded the trees in the square's central park as they descended the steps. A groomsman held the cheek strap of a pretty chestnut mare and a black gelding.

"Good morning, George," Anne said.

"Morning, miss." The amiable groom dipped his head.

Anne paused to stroke her palm down the blaze on the mare's forehead, murmuring with pleasure when the horse nickered and affectionately nudged her muzzle against Anne's hand. With one last pat, Anne stepped away, but before she could use the mounting block, Rhys caught her waist and lifted her.

Startled, she clutched his forearms and felt the heat and flex of powerful muscles as he tossed her up into the saddle. His hands lingered, steadying her until she had her balance. For a moment, his gaze held hers, heat flickering to life in the depths of his eyes. His hands tightened before he abruptly released her and stepped back to swing aboard his horse.

The groomsman rode a discreet distance behind as Rhys and Anne left the square and headed toward Hyde Park. Workmen hurried about their business, and the streets were busy with drays and hacks; still, traffic was much lighter than it would be later in the day. They reached the gates to the park and left the busy street, trotting down the quiet, deserted gravel byway of the Serpentine.

Anne glanced sideways and caught the gleam in Rhys's eyes.

"Shall we let them stretch their legs?" he asked.

She nodded and, without waiting for his reply, lifted her mount into a run.

RHYS FOLLOWED HER, arrested by the sight as muted sunlight found its way through the fog and highlighted Anne's graceful figure atop the equally beautiful thoroughbred. Distracted as he was, he was slow to realize his grip had tightened on the reins and his mount was objecting. Anne looked over her shoulder at him, her cheeks flushed with color, her green eyes sparkling with challenge as she leaned forward, urging her mare faster.

Rhys abruptly eased the reins and the galloping horses left the groom far behind as they raced on, hoofbeats thundering, until they reached a tree-shadowed section. Rhys was on Anne's heels and had nearly overtaken her when the mare faltered and slowed.

His mount responded instantly to Rhys's hand on the reins but still, he was several yards beyond Anne before he could turn the gelding. As he drew near, Anne slipped from the saddle to lead the mare onto the grass and beneath a tree. The mare was obviously favoring her left front leg.

"What happened?" Rhys asked, swinging down from the saddle.

"I think she may have picked up a stone," Anne replied, looking up as he reached her. She stroked a hand down the horse's cheek, her tone worried. "She's limping."

"Let's take a look." Rhys handed Anne the gelding's reins and bent to lift the mare's hoof. A rock was wedged against the shoe. Rhys pried it loose with a quick, careful tug before he lowered the mare's leg. She shifted, restless, and instantly limped. "I think the frog may be bruised," he commented. "Nothing some rest won't put right."

"Are you sure?" Anne queried, anxiously looking at him.

"Yes, but I'm afraid you can't ride her." Rhys looked back down the gravel they'd just traversed but the lane was empty; they were alone here in the shadow of the large old oak. "We'll wait for your groom to arrive. I'll put you up on his horse and he can walk your mare home."

Anne groaned deeply. "It is my fault. If I hadn't been intent on winning . . ."

"Don't. It's not your fault. Accidents happen."

Her gaze searched his before she gave a brief nod, the worry easing from her features.

She tugged off a glove, slipped her hand in a hidden pocket of her skirts, and pulled out a lump of sugar. "My poor Guinevere," she murmured as the mare lipped the treat from her palm. Strong teeth crunched the sweet and her ears pricked as she waited expectantly. Anne laughed softly. "She likes treats." Three more lumps of sugar were quickly devoured before Anne stroked the mare's nose. "I'm sorry, but that's all I have."

The chestnut nudged her palm and Anne laughed, giving her a final pet before turning her back to step toward Rhys. "It appears sugar can cure all ills," she said. "Perhaps I should—"

The mare bumped her muzzle between Anne's shoulder blades in a demand for attention. Unprepared and already in mid-step, Anne went flying, knocked off stride.

She landed against Rhys's chest and he caught her, instinctively wrapping her protectively in his embrace, one arm at her waist, the other tight around her upper back.

He froze, paralyzed by the swell of breasts pressed against his chest and the inward curve of her slim waist beneath his hand. He sucked in a harsh breath, and the scent of lavender assaulted his senses. She was sweet, warm female in his arms, her body lying trustingly against his, her skirts tangled around his legs, and just that quickly, he was seduced and ensnared.

She tilted her head back, and bare inches separated their faces as she looked up at him. Her thick-lashed eyes were wide with surprise and her lips parted as she caught her breath, the inhale pressing her velvet-covered breasts more firmly against him. The tip of her tongue slicked over her upper lip in a quick, unconsciously seductive movement.

Lured by the plump pink curve of her mouth, he closed the scant distance between them and traced the damp path her tongue had left across the sweet bow of her lush lip.

Anne gasped, her fingers gripping the lapels of his coat.

She tasted like everything he'd ever wanted and never had. He craved more and slowly fitted his mouth fully over hers, his hand leaving her waist to cradle her cheek and hold her closer, exactly where he wanted her, needed her. She didn't protest, murmuring her acquiescence as he tested the angle and fit of her mouth beneath his. He was lost, submerged in heat and a driving need to possess, stunned by the depth of pleasure that swamped him.

A rhythmic thump interrupted him, tapping insistently on the edge of his senses. He tried to ignore it, push it away, but it grew louder, drawing him back to an awareness of his surroundings.

Damn it. Hoofbeats. The steady trot of a slow-moving horse was growing closer. He knew he had to release Anne, now, or risk discovery.

Reluctantly, he lifted his head, sucked in a breath, and nearly lost himself when she opened her dazed eyes to look up at him.

"What?"

"I'm sorry," he murmured, forcing himself to take a step back. She swayed and he caught her, hands closing over her upper arms as he shifted to place himself between her and the drive, blocking her from view. "Someone's coming."

She stared at him, uncomprehending, and then stiffened, stepping back and away from him. Her gaze flew over his shoulder and down the graveled drive, the swift panic on her features giving way to recognition and relief.

"It's George," she said, naming her groom.

"Good," Rhys said. "He likely didn't see us, but even if he did, I'll have a word with him." He searched her features but she wouldn't look at him. "Anne," he murmured, "I'm sorry. This shouldn't have happened."

She jerked, stiffening, her gaze flicking to his. Hurt and rejection, devastation, blazed in the emerald depths before she lowered her lashes. "I know," she said with relative calm. "And we shall pretend it did not."

"No, that's not what I meant." Rhys cursed his clumsy wording. He reached for her, intent on telling her he regretted their first kiss happening on the side of a public byway. He didn't regret the kiss itself. In fact, quite the opposite. Though he knew it could lead nowhere, Rhys would not regret it. No, he would cherish it for the rest of his life.

She stepped away, avoiding him, and moved quickly across the grassy verge from the tree to the gravel, lifting a hand to wave. "George," she called. "Over here."

The groom kicked his mount and hurried toward them, his presence preventing any private conversation as the three focused on the mare and returning her safely home.

Anne effectively blocked Rhys from any discourse beyond the occasional polite comment as she insisted upon accompanying the groom and her mare. George provided a more than adequate chaperone as the trio slowly traversed the city blocks from Hyde Park back to Belgrave Square. As luck would have it, her uncle was just descending the steps as they arrived and he lifted Anne down, then kept Rhys engaged in explaining the mare's injury. When the groom took the horses to the mews in back, Anne slipped into the house, leaving William and Rhys in conversation before they parted ways.

Frustrated, Rhys swung aboard his gelding and left the square.

Anne couldn't avoid him forever. He would have opportunity to clear up the misunderstanding this evening, for they were both due at the Hanscomb fete.

But Rhys searched for Anne in vain at the gala. He finally located Marguerite late in the evening and was told Anne had stayed home with a headache.

Rhys was very sure Anne suffered from a distinct aversion to seeing him.

Bloody hell. She can't avoid me forever, can she?

By the fourth day, he was beginning to wonder if she could.

Determined to speak with her, he set off for Belgrave Square just after lunch.

Chapter 10

Timms welcomed Rhys and showed him into the anteroom, promising to inquire whether Miss Anne was at home to visitors. A few moments later, the butler returned and led Rhys to a sitting room, ushering him inside before closing the door on his back.

Although the butler hadn't promised Anne was waiting, Rhys hoped to see her in the blue and gold room. Disappointment flooded him when he didn't find her seated on the divan, or in any of the matching chairs.

"She's not here."

Rhys turned quickly, his gaze searching the room. Anne's uncle stepped out of the shadow where he'd been half concealed by a gold-tasseled, blue brocade drapery and crossed the carpet, halting several feet away.

"Good afternoon, General."

"That remains to be seen," the older man replied.

His voice was cool, underlaid with incipient anger. Rhys braced himself.

"What are your intentions toward my niece, young man?"

And there it was. Rhys was surprised Anne's uncle hadn't approached him long before. He hated deception of any kind and felt a wash of relief that the moment had finally arrived.

Still, he wasn't certain he wanted to be completely candid. Not yet.

"What do you mean?"

"Don't be daft, son." The general waved a hand, indicating their quiet, intimate surroundings. "You two have been spending time together in rooms like this for weeks. You know you endanger her reputation. So I'll ask again: What are your intentions toward my niece?"

Rhys sighed. "Only the most honorable, I assure you, General."

"Then I'll expect you to call on me tomorrow morning with an offer for Anne's hand in marriage."

"I'm sorry, sir. I can't do that."

The older man stiffened, seeming to loom larger and more intimidating. "Explain yourself."

"Your niece . . ." Rhys paused, searching for words that wouldn't bare his soul. He found none. Blunt truth appeared to be the only option. "Anne wants a biddable husband, without the annoying encumbrance of love. I find myself unable to meet her requirements."

William's eyes narrowed, probing as he studied Rhys. "I know what she wants from marriage and I don't agree with it. I wouldn't expect you to allow her to manage her own funds."

Rhys thrust a hand through his hair, scraping it back off his brow in frustration. "I don't give a damn what she does with her money. She can throw it on the grate and burn it for all I care. I have far more than her fortune, many times over. I don't need her funds." He glared at the general.

"So," William replied almost genially, his body relaxing into a less threatening mode, "if it's not the matter of her fortune and how she spends it that's holding you back, what is it?"

Rhys ground his teeth, unwilling to answer. The general, however, merely waited, his expression calm. He looked as if he was prepared to stay in this room, forever if necessary, until he had an answer.

"First, I'm not biddable. Just because I don't care about her damn fortune doesn't mean I'd allow her free rein in all things. I want a partner in life, sir. Someone who is as interested in offering her opinion on my affairs as I would be in hers."

"Rather progressive of you, Dorset, but not entirely insane." The general nodded his head in agreement. "And the second thing?"

"I find myself unwilling to contemplate spending the rest of my life with a woman who doesn't"—Rhys couldn't force the word "love"—"care for me and is only marrying me to gain control of a fortune."

"Hmmmm." William eyed him consideringly. "Yet that's the basis for most *ton* marriages," he said mildly. "The man is sufficiently well funded while the woman is of good family and ready to be the mother of his children. Why is yours and Anne's situation any different?"

"Because she isn't any other woman and our situation isn't comparable to most *ton* marriages," Rhys ground out.

"Cut line," William barked. "Out with it. Why isn't the usual arrangement good enough for you two?"

"Because I love her," Rhys shouted. "I love her," he repeated in a whisper, savoring the feel of the words on his lips.

William stared at him, his expression unreadable. Then he harrumphed, the sound a second cousin to Anne's adorable groan. He slapped a meaty paw on Rhys's shoulder. "Marguerite and Sylvia assured me you'd come around. In all honesty, I wondered if you had the bollocks to say it." He turned and crossed the room to the collection of crystal decanters on a silver tray atop a credenza. "Let's drink to women, son. They're never easy, and that's the truth of it." He eyed Rhys. "I'll give you a bit more time to convince Anne but know I expect you to settle this between you. And soon. I'll tell my solicitor to begin preparation of the marriage contracts."

"Yes, sir." Rhys took the glass, saluted William with it, and tossed the brandy down, unbelieving of what had just transpired. "You are aware of my reputation?"

The general nodded before finishing his brandy with one large swallow.

"And yet you'll allow Anne to marry me?" Rhys pressed, aware he was in fact looking a gift horse in the mouth, but needing to be reassured he was not, in fact, asleep and dreaming this conversation.

The general poured them a second round. "I am a military man, through and through. Great displays of affection are not in me. But let me make myself clear: I could not love that girl any more if she were my own daughter. When Marguerite and Sylvia told me of their scheme, I was inclined to kill you myself. But they assured me you are the man for Anne. So don't muck this up, young man. Or I *will* kill you."

He had the general's approval to court Anne. Now all he needed was Anne's consent. He downed the second glass of brandy and wondered if a decorated general could be harder to convince than the woman he loved.

He held out his glass for a third.

ANNE PACED ACROSS her bedroom carpet, sat at her writing desk, stared at the blank sheet of foolscap for several moments, then stood and paced once more.

She simply could not settle. She had never been this indecisive and emotionally fraught in her entire life. It was pathetic.

She groaned. Even her groaning was pathetic.

I cannot avoid Rhys forever but how can I face him?

Not knowing if she would be able to control her emotions if she had to say more than hello to him was terrifying. He regretted kissing her. After he'd shattered her belief that she was immune to any interest in passion and made her rethink her convictions as to romantic connections—he was sorry he'd kissed her. The knowledge she had been alone in having the foundation of her world well and truly shaken was devastating.

And this was Rhys. No doubt he'd kissed many women, perhaps dozens, or hundreds. How could she face him, knowing that she was one of many and she alone had been affected?

Oh dear God. It didn't bear thinking about. She dropped her face into her hands, awash with the heat of mortification, regret, and pain. The wall she'd erected between herself and any passionate feelings had crumbled and disappeared at the press of his mouth on hers, and he wanted her to forget it had happened. How could she?

She'd tried to wrest back control of her feelings over the days since he'd held her in Hyde Park. She'd failed miserably. Those moments kept replaying in her head. The heat of his body against hers, the strength of his arms, the warmth of his bare hand cradling her face, the aching need for something more when he'd set her away from him . . .

She couldn't stop thinking about him and how he'd made her feel, made her want, made her body ache in ways she had never before.

Was this what her mother had felt for her father? If so, Anne no longer wondered why she had acted with such abandon.

I will not become my mother. I will not.

Perhaps what she needed was distance from Rhys to recover her balance. A trip to her uncle's country estate might be in order. Surely a break from the rush of the season would refresh and settle her into her accustomed equanimity.

The dainty French clock on her mantel chimed the hour. With firm steps, Anne left her room for the dining room and breakfast with Marguerite.

Chapter 11

"There you are." Marguerite looked up from her seat at the table as Anne entered the room. "I'm delighted you feel well enough to join me, although you do seem a bit pale. How is your headache, dear?"

"Much better, thank you." Anne slipped into a chair across from Marguerite. She did not like lying to the woman, but Anne had no choice. The truth was simply too much to share.

"I'm so happy to hear that." The older woman's smile held affection. "I was becoming quite concerned."

The two chatted casually about Marguerite's visit to the dressmaker yesterday and the progress being made on a new day dress. They lingered over tea, and Anne prepared to broach her desire to spend a few weeks in the country. Before she could begin, however, Marguerite leaned forward and fixed her with a serious gaze.

"Anne, I really feel you should accompany me today. Our friends are asking for you and I know they'll be much relieved to see you out and about. We can make calls on only a select, small group of friends and stay only the shortest of acceptable visits."

"Must I, Marguerite?" Anne nibbled on a remaining bit of toast spread with marmalade, putting off replying before she looked up at last. "I have no desire to go out. I fear I'm still not feeling myself.

In fact, I've been considering the benefits of a sojourn at Uncle William's country estate for a few weeks. I'm hoping you would like to accompany me."

"No." Marguerite returned her cup to her saucer with a decided clink. "I'm afraid that won't do, not at all." She studied Anne before her worried gaze softened and she sighed. "Anne, won't you tell me what's wrong? Rhys asked about you at the Hanscomb fete the other night and seemed concerned. I know you're good friends. Has something happened between you to change that?"

Anne sipped her tea, mulling how she should proceed. She didn't feel as though she could share the entire story. But perhaps there was a way to answer without answering. "I believe we are not as good friends now as we were," she finally said.

"I'm very sorry to hear that," the older woman murmured. "Can you tell me what happened to change things?"

Oh now, really. The woman wasn't playing fair. The polite thing to do would be to change the subject. And if Marguerite refused to do so, Anne would have to. "Wouldn't a stay in the country be lovely this time of year?"

"You are avoiding my question," Marguerite answered flatly, not taking the bait. "Anne, what happened with Rhys?"

Well, the woman had some nerve, Anne had to give her that. But Anne had more. "We . . ." Anne halted, dreadful, ridiculous emotion clogging her throat. "I fear I . . ." She lowered her cup to its saucer, staring at the Wedgwood china pattern, willing herself not to cry.

The silence stretched. Marguerite leaned forward, her slim, cool fingers closing over Anne's where they fisted on the linen tablecloth.

"My dear Anne, I've thought for some time that you may be developing a . . ." She paused delicately. ". . . a tendre for Rhys. And he for you. Did something of a romantic nature occur between you?"

Anne turned her hand over, gripping Marguerite's fingers. This was exhausting. And clearly pointless. The woman had far more years of wisdom and wiles to draw from. "Yes."

"I see." Marguerite squeezed Anne's hand encouragingly. "When you were riding a few days ago?"

Anne nodded. "We were exercising the horses. Guinevere picked up a rock and we stopped to care for her. While we were waiting for the groom to reach us, Guinevere pushed me. Rhys caught me. And"—she looked up, meeting Marguerite's kind eyes directly—"he kissed me."

"Is that all?"

"Yes. But then he told me it should not have happened. I told him he was right, of course, and we should pretend it did not."

"And then what?"

"George arrived almost immediately and we came home. Uncle was here when we arrived, and I left them discussing Guinevere's injury and entered the house. I haven't seen Rhys since."

"I see." Marguerite studied her. "Am I right in assuming you are avoiding Rhys?"

"Well, yes. What else am I to do?"

"Were you upset by the kiss? Do you wish he hadn't kissed you?"

Anne set her cup and saucer down. "Yes, I was upset—am upset. He said it himself: We should not have done such a thing. Obviously he was upset. And I am upset. Seems the natural order of things in such a situation."

Marguerite winced. "Can you tell me what about it upset you? Did you not find it to your liking?"

Anne sighed. "It was lovely. While it was happening," she hastened to add. "But after . . . Rhys regretted it. Clearly, it was not to his liking. And, if I'm being absolutely honest, I truly dislike the emotional chaos that has resulted from that kiss. All of this," she said, waving a hand in the air, "from one silly kiss."

Marguerite blinked, confusion crossing her fine-boned features. "My dear, I doubt very much that Rhys did not enjoy kissing you. However, I am concerned that you appear distraught over the event."

The word "distraught" caught Anne's ears, sending a jolt of sudden panic through her. "Don't worry about me, Marguerite.

You know I am not one prone to such dramatics. All I need is a bit of time away." Anne gripped Marguerite's fingers tighter, leaning that slight bit forward to underline her words. "Which is why I want to retire to the country. Just to find my balance. Will you go with me?"

"Anne, I'm afraid going away will not be helpful."

"But I . . ."

Marguerite shook her head, her voice gentle but firm. "I'm afraid it doesn't matter how far you go, Anne. Wherever you go, you take yourself with you. You need to see Rhys and clear up what I am certain is a misunderstanding."

Anne adored Marguerite, but she was beginning to annoy her. "I don't need to see him over a silly misunderstanding."

"But you do."

"No, I don't!" Anne ground out, shoving her chair back and standing. "That is the last thing I need to do."

"Because your feelings for Rhys have changed, from friendship to love, I daresay?" Marguerite asked gently.

Anne caught her breath, tears welling to spill over and roll slowly down her cheeks. She began to walk the length of the room, willing it to go on forever. "I don't want to love him," she said brokenly. "I don't want to love anyone."

"Oh, my dear Anne." Marguerite left her seat and rushed to join Anne in her pacing. "You've nothing to fear," she soothed. "It will all come right, I promise you."

Anne could not respond. And so the two walked the length of the room, down one end and up the other, for how long she couldn't say. But it was long enough for Anne to carefully consider her dear friend's words—and her own heart's yearning. She tugged at the gold chain about her neck and took up the locket, wanting to know just what the sixpence was up to.

ANNE WOKE REFRESHED and feeling much more herself the following morning, finally able to contemplate her situation with some equanimity. While her emotions as concerned Rhys left her feeling vulnerable and unsure, still, she would face him, and herself, and discover precisely what he meant when he said he shouldn't have kissed her. Marguerite continued to insist she had mistaken his intent. He would surely be at Lady Lipscombe's that afternoon and she would make certain to find a private moment to speak with him.

She joined Marguerite as they made social calls, stopping to sip tea and chat in amiable comfort at several homes. When their carriage pulled up in front of the Marchioness of Lipscombe's elegant home, Anne attempted to tamp down her nerves. She grew more tense as they entered the house and were announced. A quick scan of the room revealed Lady Lipscombe's salon was occupied by a group of females and two younger gentlemen.

Rhys was not present. Anne sighed with disappointment, unaware she'd been holding her breath in apprehension.

"Are you all right, my dear?" Marguerite murmured quietly as they took seats next to Sylvia.

Anne managed a smile. "Yes, of course."

Marguerite gave her a quick, shrewd glance before nodding and turning to Sylvia. "Will Penelope Gainesbury be joining us? I've copied down my cook's recipe for the lemon tarts she's so fond of."

"I'm afraid not," Sylvia replied. "She sent a note this morning to say she's gone to Bath with the Athertons for a short visit. I expect her back in a few weeks, however, and if you would like to leave it with me, I'll be happy to give it to her."

"That would be perfect." Marguerite retrieved the folded note from her reticule and passed it to Sylvia.

"And how are you feeling, Anne?" Sylvia inquired. "Headaches can be so debilitating. I've been quite concerned for you."

"Much better, thank you," Anne assured her.

"I'm so glad to hear you are well. I vow there has been a rash of ladies afflicted with pains recently. I am convinced it's the London air that's causing so many problems," Sylvia said firmly. "The fog was particularly dense when I returned home early this morning."

Marguerite nodded solemnly. "I remarked on that very thing not three nights past, did I not, Anne?"

Before Anne could agree, the door to the salon opened and three young ladies swept into the room, their excited voices drowning out the butler as he announced them. The elderly lady accompanying them was clearly attempting to quiet them and failing on all counts.

Anne had a difficult time sorting out what they were saying for they talked over each other, each seeming to attempt to be the first, and loudest, to impart her news.

"Ladies, ladies!" Sylvia clapped her hands smartly. The three stopped in mid-sentences, eyes wide at her commanding tone. "Please, have a seat. We cannot understand a word any of you are saying."

The three immediately perched on silk-covered chairs. They bore a family resemblance in their fair skin, brown hair, and blue eyes, and Anne deduced they must be sisters.

"Now." Sylvia fixed them with a reproving glance. "I perceive something of note has happened." She turned to one of the young women, whose fresh face declared her barely old enough to be out in society. "Miss Sheridan, as you are the eldest, perhaps you will inform us as to the reason for your outburst."

Abashed, the young woman flushed under the subtle chastisement. "I beg your pardon, Lady Lipscombe. Please forgive us if we were too forward. It's just that the news is so very startling. And the duke is your nephew. And we did not expect to be the first to share . . ."

Anne caught her breath.

"What gossip have you to regale us with, pray tell?" Sylvia's voice turned frosty, her eyes narrowing over the three.

"It seems the duke and Lord Penbrooke were involved in a race," one of the other young women put in, breathless with the importance of her news, "and the duke's phaeton turned over when it failed to make a sharp turn."

Shock held Anne immobile, her fingers clenching together in

her lap. Marguerite leaned toward her, one hand closing over hers, grounding her as the world spun.

"Where did you hear this?" Sylvia's voice was sharp. A quick glance told Anne the older woman's face was leached of color.

"Some of the *ton*'s gentlemen were there, to watch and place bets, and they informed their wives. The ladies told us."

"But no one knows who was hurt," the third young woman objected. "Apparently, it wasn't the duke who was driving, but rather his friend, Lord Penbrooke. There's some confusion as to who was injured, whether it was Lord Penbrooke or the duke."

"I must go." Anne bent to whisper fiercely in Marguerite's ear. "Now."

"But Anne . . ."

"I must."

"Sylvia will send a footman to Rhys's home to inquire, Anne," Marguerite murmured. "There is no need for you to go in person. If you're seen, the gossip would ruin your reputation."

"I must see for myself that he is unharmed. If he's been hurt—" Anne broke off, afraid she might cry. "If he's injured, I need to be there." She was no longer confused, torn between wanting to avoid Rhys and longing to see him. The prospect of his being injured had erased murky indecision and snapped her view of their connection into sharp clarity. Faced with possible injury or death, there was no question as to how she felt about him. Nor where she must be.

"I see." Marguerite's wide eyes flared with understanding. She patted Anne's hands and bent to whisper to Sylvia. The other woman's gaze flashed to meet Anne's and she nodded once, a subtle tip of her head. She murmured a reply and Marguerite stood, drawing Anne up with her.

They said their good-byes amid the confusion and excited speculation. When finally they left the room, their departure was barely noted by the chattering women. It was all Anne could do to obey Marguerite's iron grip on her arm and move with seemingly casual intent. The moment the salon door closed behind them, however, they hurried down the hall and descended the stairs to the entryway.

"Sylvia ordered her own coach to wait outside and take you to Rhys's home. It would not do for you to be seen arriving alone at a gentleman's home, and our carriage is clearly marked with our crest. No one, however, would remark on his aunt's conveyance at Rhys's residence. I'll have our coachman drive me home and await word from you as to the situation." They moved quickly down the marble steps where two carriages waited, doors held ajar by footmen and steps lowered.

Marguerite stopped Anne just as she was about to enter Sylvia's carriage. "Send word to me as soon as you can. If Rhys has been injured, I will hurry back to bear Sylvia company."

"I will." Anne gave her a quick, fierce hug. "I promise."

Chapter 12

*A*nne gathered her skirts and entered the carriage. The moment the door closed, the coachman set off, keeping a brisk pace despite the London street traffic.

Nevertheless, the short journey seemed interminable to Anne. At last, the coach rocked to a stop in front of the imposing house and she gathered her skirts. A servant dressed in the duke's livery pulled open the door and she stepped out.

Anne wanted to run up the marble steps to the portico but managed to rein in the impulse, moving as quick as was acceptable, her steps brisk. She waited impatiently for the butler to open the door.

"Good day, madam." The liveried butler bowed, ushering her into the entryway. "May I help you?"

"Rhys—His Grace," she amended. "I have come to inquire as to his injuries."

"I'm not injured."

Anne spun, hand at her throat. Rhys strode down the hall toward her. All propriety forgotten, she ran to meet him, clasping his hands as she searched his face, unmarked but for a smudge of dust along one cheekbone. A quick frantic inspection revealed a torn jacket sleeve and streaks of dirt on his breeches, his normally impeccably polished black boots dull with dust and scrapes.

"You are unharmed? Truly?" Her voice trembled. She didn't care that she was overcome with emotion. All she cared was that he was well and in one piece.

He cradled her cheek in his palm, his blue gaze intent. "Truly, I wasn't hurt. Lucien, however, was. He's upstairs; the doctor has just departed." He looked up and over her head, toward the entry. "Andrews, I'm not at home to other callers."

"Yes, Your Grace."

"Come." He tucked Anne against his side, his arm holding her safe against his warmth, and led her toward the salon.

THE MOMENT THE door closed, Anne burst into tears. Rhys wrapped her in an embrace and she burrowed against him. She slipped her arms beneath his coat and hugged him tight, the hard, tensile strength of male muscle and bone warm and blessedly alive beneath her hands.

"Anne." His deep voice rumbled, threaded with concern. "You're shaking." He pressed her closer, one hand moving soothingly over her back from waist to nape, then back again. "Sweetheart, I'm okay."

"But you could have been killed." Her voice shook, echoing the trembling that shivered her body.

"But I wasn't," he reassured her. "Lucien broke his leg and is scratched up a bit, but he'll recover."

"Racing carriages is dangerous," she said, catching her breath as she struggled to stop shaking. She tilted her head back to look up at him. "You must promise me you won't race again. What would we do if anything happened to you? I would be heartbroken and the children—" She broke off, tears blurring her vision.

"The children?" He brushed his thumbs beneath her eyes, stroking away dampness. "What children?" He frowned in confusion, and then his eyes widened and a small, bemused smile curved his mouth. "Our children?"

"Of course," she said impatiently. "Really, Rhys, you can be so . . ." Suddenly realizing what she'd just said, she stopped speaking and stared up at him, eyes wide.

The heat in his blue eyes blazed at her, tempered with wry amusement.

"I promise I won't kill myself before we have children." His voice was deeper, rougher, his words a vow. "Does this mean you're no longer angry with me, Anne?"

The pad of his thumb stroked over her cheekbone, his palm cradling her face. His lashes lowered and he stared at her mouth. Mesmerized, Anne was hardly aware she instinctively lifted toward him.

His lips brushed against hers, an all too brief taste before he pulled back to look at her.

"You must promise me something as well."

She blinked, frowning up at him. "What?"

"Promise you will never again refuse to speak to me for days." He narrowed his eyes at her. "I don't like it."

She groaned, nodding. "I don't like it, either."

"Good. Then we're agreed." His mouth curved. Anne wanted to lick it. "Are we also agreed we'll be married as soon as possible?"

"What?" Anne blinked. "I don't . . ." She frowned before groaning again, contemplating his handsome features. "You've tricked me, haven't you?"

"Have I?"

"Yes," she tried to say firmly, failing when the faintly rough pad of his thumb pressed gently on her sensitive lip. "We were supposed to be friends. You won't make a manageable husband."

He laughed, eyes lighting with affection. "I suspect you'll manage me well enough. And I hope we will always be friends. You should also know," he continued when she groaned a third time. "I don't want your fortune. You can do with it as you wish, and yes, the barrister will stipulate your right to do so in the marriage contracts. I hope you'll allow me to recommend a worthy adviser, however, as the gentleman who counsels me has proven most wise."

"Well, then," she managed to get out, awash in emotions that weakened her knees. "I suppose that only leaves my uncle."

"Already taken care of. The man all but ordered me to marry you." He brushed his lips against hers once again, trailing kisses over her cheeks, temples, and the sensitive spot just below her ear.

Anne tilted her head, silently willing him to repeat the kisses that had her craving more. "I don't know what to say," she admitted, unsure that she could believe how perfectly everything was falling into place. Perhaps the sixpence had some magic to it after all.

"Then don't say anything at all." One big, warm hand cupped her nape before stroking slowly down her throat until his hand lay against the upper swell of her breast. His lips followed his hands, the feel of warm, damp kisses sending her heart pounding, her hands fisting in the linen shirt beneath his waistcoat. He pushed the sleeve of her gown off her shoulder and his lips traced her bare skin with heated kisses. Then he cupped her breast and his lips closed over the tip, the wet heat of his mouth driving all awareness of anything beyond Rhys from her mind.

She murmured, pressing closer, desperate as she shifted impatiently against him. His mouth took hers and he bent his knees, lifting her off her feet. She felt the wall at her back and then he brushed her skirt higher, tugging it upward as he stroked his hand over her knee and thigh.

He cupped her mound, fingertips brushing teasingly over silken curls.

"Sweetheart," he muttered against her mouth, his voice rough. "You're wet for me."

Heat and tension gripped Anne, ratcheting higher as he stroked her, petted her, the leisurely attention at complete odds with the hot press of his mouth against hers and the taut muscles of his body.

She murmured in protest when his fingers left her to unbutton his breeches. He hushed her, kissing her deeply, before lifting her higher.

"Wrap your legs around my waist, Anne," he coaxed. When she complied, he groaned, going still.

Anne was beyond rational thinking, assaulted on all levels by the sensual claim of his lips on hers and the hot slide of skin against skin.

She shifted, shuddering at the pressure of him against her sensitized center, and then he reached between them, nudging against her.

The need to have him inside her was a driving compulsion. Anne fisted her hands in his shirt, frustrated when he insisted on taking his time even though she felt the shudder in his muscles each time he moved deeper. At last, he surged against her, fully seated.

"Are you all right, love?" he ground out, his lips at her ear, his breath choppy.

"Yes." She realized her arms were around his neck, fingers tangled in his hair, and she tugged on the silky locks. "More," she demanded.

He growled with desire. And then began to move.

Anne lost all tether to earth and her former self. There was only Rhys surrounding her, surging inside her, and the heat and incredible soaring pleasure that teased, tormented, and consumed her. When the world exploded and Rhys shuddered, dropping his head to rest against the wall beside hers, she hugged him fiercely, refusing to let him go. He didn't try. Instead, he brushed kisses over her cheeks, temples, nearly touching each side of her mouth until she murmured a wordless protest and he took her mouth in a long, lazy kiss. When he finally let her breathe again, she could only smile.

Rhys lifted his head and looked at her.

"I need another promise from you," she said softly.

His eyes turned wary. "And what would that be?"

She cupped his face in her hands. "We must do this at least once a day."

Surprise, then delight, spread over his features. "Now that is a promise I can keep." He eased away from her, slowly letting her slide down his length until her feet touched the floor; he paused to refasten buttons before swinging her up in his arms. Carrying her tucked against him, he walked to the sofa and sat with her on his lap, one arm around her shoulders, one hand on her bare knee beneath her gown. "I'm very glad you came to call today, Miss Brabourne," he said gravely, blue eyes twinkling with amusement.

"As am I, Your Grace," she replied politely, one hand smoothing over his chest where his loosened cravat and shirt gave easy access to warm, bare skin.

"I think we should marry soon." He tucked a loose strand of hair behind her ear, and Anne shivered at the brush of his fingers.

"I'm happy to set a date as early as may be but I'm certain Marguerite will want to organize a wedding party. That will surely not happen quickly. And I must have my best friends with me before I can walk down the aisle." She gazed up at him, struck afresh at how very handsome her Rhys was. Her Rhys. She suddenly realized that she had been thinking of him as hers for some time now.

"Your friends, will they approve of me?"

Anne looked up at Rhys, needing nothing more than him, letting the sweet, clear admission wash over her. "How could they not?"

Rhys tightened his hold on her. "Do you know what your uncle told me? He warned me not to muck this up. Or he would kill me."

Anne studied his face, the determined, fierce look in his blue eyes, the hard set of his jaw. He would never be a biddable husband, but perhaps he could be managed. She smiled. "You will have to get used to his rather direct ways." She kissed him gently, then added, "And he was not joking about the not mucking it up bit. He would kill you. In a heartbeat."

The fierceness in his blue eyes dissipated, replaced with electric heat.

Ah, yes, she thought as he kissed her back. *This is the husband I need. My Something New.*

Something Borrowed

ELIZABETH BOYLE

Chapter 1

North Audley Street, London
Less than a week before the wedding of
   the Duke of Dorset and Miss Anne Brabourne

Dear Cordelia,

   Here is the sixpence we found all those years ago. I am passing it along to you as promised. There can be no doubts that your faith in its powers was well-placed as it has worked for me, and now, dear friend, it is your turn, even if it is, as your Aunt Aldora writes, that you've already found an eligible parti. Still, I do hope and pray that this coin will ensure that he is the one and I insist you have this paragon accompany you to my wedding. How else can your aunts and I can pass judgment on him if you do not bring him to Hamilton Hall?

   Your friend always,
   Anne

*M*iss Cordelia Padley set the letter down and turned the old sixpence that had come with it over in her hand. For all her faith that this coin would bring the four of them happiness, Cordelia now found herself filled with doubts.

For here was Anne expecting her to arrive with the man she intended to marry.

Save for one small problem. She didn't have a betrothed.

"Is that the fabled coin?" Kate Harrington asked. Her hired companion set down the morning paper and looked with nothing less than a raft of skepticism at the battered bit of silver.

Cordelia went to agree, but then she realized one thing. She'd never told Kate about the coin. "What do you know about this?"

Kate huffed a little bit and picked her paper back up, showing a renewed interest in the gossip columns. "Nothing more than what is written in your journal."

"My journal?" Cordelia set the coin down beside Anne's letter. "You read my journal?"

Nose in the air, Kate turned the page. "You needn't sound so incredulous."

"That is private."

"Not when it is so dull. And now that I see that coin, it seems rather dull as well. Hardly capable of leading one to true love."

"Apparently it worked for Anne," Cordelia replied, holding up her school friend's letter. "She's betrothed to the Duke of Dorset."

The mention of such a lofty prospect brightened Kate's interest, but not in the way Cordelia might have supposed. "Is this Anne pretty?"

Cordelia nodded. "I haven't seen her since I left school, but most likely she's very pretty. She was as a child."

That seemed to answer Kate's curiosity. "Then I'd say her good fortune had more to do with her face and not some old coin." She returned to her paper, then paused. "What did the note from your father's solicitor say?" She glanced at the unopened missive from the singular Mr. Abernathy Pickworth, Esq., the one Cordelia had pushed to one side earlier.

"I have no idea. I suppose I will have to meet with him soon enough." If it was anything like when she'd left India, having had to use nearly all her money to pay her father's remaining debts, it was a meeting she was going to avoid for as long as she could.

She might have had the comfort of her family's fortune while she'd been at Madame Rochambeaux's, but in the ensuing years, her father had lost nearly all of it in imprudent investments and reckless speculations.

At least there was still this house, well situated as it was in Mayfair. It had been let out for years, and would have to be again. Not that she was overly sentimental about the place. Cordelia hadn't lived in it since she was nine, before . . .

Well, before her mother had died in Paris and everything had changed. With the loss of his beloved wife, Sir Horace had abandoned England, fleeing to India on a pretense of scientific explorations and leaving Cordelia at school. And then when he'd died the previous year, Cordelia had discovered that his true legacy hadn't been one of intellectual discoveries, but one of debt and expenditures.

She wagered Pickworth's note was going to be more bad news. So with one finger, she nudged it under a napkin and changed the subject.

Or rather, returned to the previous subject.

"Kate, don't you believe in the magic of love at first sight?"

"No." The answer was direct and firm. "Not unless the gentleman in question is standing before his vast and prosperous estate with a battalion of servants behind him ready to do my bidding. I'm quite certain I'd be vastly smitten at that point. As should you be instead of writing about lowly sailors."

Cordelia blushed. "Whatever were you doing, going through my belongings?" After all, she'd kept her journal tucked in the very bottom of her trunk, beneath her undergarments, if only to ensure her privacy.

Kate sighed. "It was a long five months on that ship from Bombay. What else was I to read when you insisted on going up every night to look at the stars? And to answer your other great question, no, I don't think you were in any danger of being kissed by that particular first mate—he rather fancied one of the lads."

Cordelia shook her head. She knew hiring Kate, against the

advice of every lofty matron in Bombay, hadn't been the most proper decision of her life, but she liked the forthright widow for all the reasons that were now coming back to haunt her—mostly that Kate Harrington wasn't opposed to a bit of unorthodoxy or impropriety. And her knowledge of the larger world, the world beyond drawing rooms and good society, had seemed more insurance than risk at the time.

Of course, that was before the woman had unearthed Cordelia's journal and read it.

Meanwhile, Kate continued to stare at her as if expecting something. Knowing her companion, it was probably an apology. Or to be thanked for her insight as to the first mate.

So Cordelia returned to the original subject. "Yes, well, this is the fabled coin, though I hardly see how it will get me out of my current predicament."

"You could always change your mind about that coal clerk," Kate replied, glancing back down at the ads on the front page.

"Tallow," Cordelia corrected.

From the wrinkle of Kate's nose it was clear that she saw no difference.

Truly there wasn't.

And there was the rub. The difference was lost on her aunts as well—all they saw was an eligible bachelor in need of a wife.

"I probably shouldn't have written Aunt Aldora that letter," Cordelia admitted.

Kate sniffed. There was no need for words, for her intent was clear. *You think?*

But she had. Written her aunts that she was betrothed to a perfectly eligible and amiable gentleman. She'd only done it so they would stop sending her lengthy letters extolling the virtues of their new vicar, or offering up Sir Randolph's second cousin's son—who, despite an unfortunate wen, had, as Aunt Aldora had written, "high hopes of a promising career in tallow."

Tallow. Cordelia shuddered.

No, no, if she arrived at Hamilton Hall alone her lie would most certainly be laid bare, and her aunts would immediately set about scrambling to find another vicar (for fortunately theirs had found a bride), or another second cousin twice removed (for even Sir Randolph's unlikely tallow-loving cousin had found a matrimonial candidate), or whatever fellow—breathing or otherwise—they could prop up beside her in front of the local vicar all to see her *properly* and *promptly* wed.

Picking up the coin, Cordelia turned it over a few times, remembering when she and the others had found it in that dreadful old mattress.

From across the table, Kate sniffed. "I hardly see how that coin can conjure up a likely fellow—you are far more apt to find a promising candidate in the gossip columns. Take this fellow Captain Talcott. You know him, don't you?"

"Yes, but that was a long time ago," Cordelia replied, not bothering to ask how Kate knew about Kipp.

Not when he was often featured in her journal. As in every time she spied a mention of him in the paper.

Which, given the captain's splendid career in the navy, had been quite often.

"He's a veritable rogue—if any of what I've read is to be believed. How unfortunate it's his brother who's the earl—a dull, stodgy one, from all reports." Kate sniffed at the waste of a good title. "But your Captain Talcott, oh my stars! He's a devil. Opera dancers. Some mention of the brokenhearted daughter of Lord W—" Kate paused for a moment as she tried to puzzle out who that might be, but then dismissed it as unimportant. "He'd do well."

Cordelia shook her head. "Do well for what?"

"For a betrothed, you peagoose. You could borrow him for a sennight. He'd be the perfect fellow to toss you aside and break your heart."

"Borrow him? It isn't like he's an extra hair ribbon or a spare stocking one can make use of in an emergency."

Kate got straight to the point. "I'd say your current straits qualify as an 'emergency,' or do you like the idea of smelling tallow for the rest of your life?"

Well, Kate had the right of it there. But this wasn't so much an emergency, more of a reckoning of sorts. Like seeing Kipp again.

A flicker caught her eye and she glanced down at the coin, which seemed to be winking at her, but when she blinked again, she realized it was just a bit of light streaming in from the window. And out the window, there lay the garden, where she had played as a child. The familiar curved path to the house next door with all its memories . . .

And of promises once made.

Cordelia stilled. No. She couldn't. She didn't dare. And yet, she couldn't shake the recollection of something old and most opportune.

Rising from the table, she went to the window as if pulled by a thread, by that long-ago vow, and took a searching look at the house next door.

Perhaps Kate had come up with the perfect plan.

"I wonder . . ." she murmured, and knew very well that behind her, Kate was grinning like a well-pleased cat.

"YOU'RE UP EARLY."

Winston Christopher Talcott, the fourteenth Earl of Thornton, shrugged off his brother's surprise, and took his place at the head of the table. "Couldn't sleep."

"Getting married will do that to a man," Captain Andrew Talcott commented, glancing up from the note he'd been reading.

"I'm not even engaged yet, Drew."

"Ah, but you will be before the day is out," his brother remarked—no, make that teased—and tossing aside the note he'd been reading, he got up and refilled his plate. "Wish you'd told me you were in the running for Miss Holt's hand. I could have made a fortune in wagers. I don't think your name has even been mentioned."

"I can hardly believe it. But Holt himself assured me the other night that his daughter was inclined to my suit, and now there is only one thing left to do." Kipp stole a glance over at the well-laden sideboard and shuddered a bit, finding that he didn't have the stomach for any of it.

Not even the bacon.

Not so his younger brother, who returned to the table and heartily dug in. Newly returned from sea, the much decorated and celebrated Captain Talcott ate each meal as if he hadn't had a decent one in years.

Then again, he hadn't the prospect of marriage weighing him down like an anchor.

But suddenly Drew seemed to sense his brother's reluctance and put down his fork—a feat of sorts. "Demmit, don't marry the chit if you don't want to."

"It isn't what I want that matters. The estates are . . . well, you know damn well how Father . . ." Kipp didn't need to finish the sentence.

They both damn well knew how their errant sire had left things.

A complete and utter ruin. As had his father and his father before that. For nearly a century, the once prosperous Thornton estates had been slipping into disarray, and none of their forebears had taken the time (or blunt) to right their falling fortunes.

Which left it up to this Earl of Thornton to remedy. And despite all of Kipp's hard work and attempts to raise the sinking ship, he'd come to the bleak realization that no matter what he did, it would all be for naught without one thing—gold.

And lots of it. Which Josiah Holt had in spades and was willing to share with the man who would elevate his only child and beloved daughter, Miss Pamela Holt, to a lofty position in society.

Say, that of a countess.

"You know I have money—" Drew began.

"No!" Kipp couldn't say the word with any more emphasis. He wouldn't think of it.

This was an argument they'd had a number of times—Drew

would offer his prize money and Kipp would refuse it. But before Drew could continue—which he always did—the door to the dining room opened and both brothers glanced up.

"Yes, Tydsley?" Kipp asked the butler.

But the man had his gaze fixed on Drew. "Captain Talcott, your guest is becoming most insistent. She claims the matter is of some urgency."

At this Drew groaned.

"We have a guest?" Kipp glanced from his brother, then back to his butler, having given the man's words a second recall. "Tydsley, did you say 'she'?"

"I did indeed, my lord," The older man's bushy gray brows rose in a disapproving arch. "She's a most presumptuous young lady. And impertinent. Barged right in," Tydsley added, most likely in his own defense.

"Demmit, Drew," Kipp said, pushing away from the table. "How many times do I have to tell you, you cannot make this house your personal harem."

"Oh, it was only that once," his errant brother shot back, retrieving the note he'd discarded earlier. "Why, this is all madness," he said, shaking the bit of paper. "The dollymop can't even sign her name without leaving a blot of ink." Once again, he tossed the note aside.

"Nonsense or not, I want her out."

Drew groaned and slowly rose to his feet. "Just some gel trying to entrap me."

"Truly?" Kipp replied. Granted, Drew was wealthy in his own right, but this was too much. "If that is the case, then we'd best both go in there and discover what scheme she's managed, so she can't claim you ruined her under my roof—that is, if you haven't already."

"I most certainly have not." Drew blew out a breath as if he hadn't the time for such nonsense, when, in fact, he had nothing but time for mischief. "Like I said, she's just some mad bit and I'll have her dispatched posthaste."

"I don't need a scandal blowing up in my face right now. Would ruin everything," Kipp told him, getting to his feet. He was about to follow his brother to the door, but the missive caught his eye, and he picked it up, following Drew to the foyer.

"Oh yes, how could I forget," his brother prosed on. "Proper Miss Holt, and all. Dreadful shame if *she* was to withdraw her affections."

Kipp looked up from the mysterious note. "She has very exacting standards of conduct and I won't have you going and ruining everything with one of your flirts."

Drew stopped before the salon door. "My flirts? You would do well to spend some time with one of my flirts. Give you something to be passionate about."

"I have no time for passion," he replied. "I have an estate to save."

There was a huff of impatience from his brother. "Still, a little bit of passion might loosen up some of that boring starch of yours. I do say, Kipp, this Miss Holt has made you dreadfully dull. I don't even want to think of what she'll do to you once you are—"

But Kipp had all but stopped listening, having started to scan the note again.

Drew poked it. "I told you, it makes no sense." He shook his head. "Look at what she writes. 'I have need of your services,'" he intoned. "What do they teach these misses these days?"

"Who is this RSE?" Kipp asked. Yet even as he said it, the squared initials, arranged one atop the other, prodded at some old memory, pushed him to look again at the small "blot" Drew had described, which as it turned out was hardly a case of sloppy penmanship, but rather a perfectly drawn miniature of a compass rose.

A voice from the past whispered in his ear. *It must be a compass. For the RSE will go in every direction. We'll go, Kipp. You and I.*

A jolt of something ran through him and his gaze jerked up to the door before them.

No . . . It couldn't be.

Tydsley announced them, and over Drew's shoulder, Kipp could see a slight figure turn from the garden window.

The pixie curve of her face, the soft brown hair, the eyes like cornflowers, they were all the same. And yet now those very features that had intrigued him as a child were all grown up.

Cordelia.

And for the very first time in what seemed like a lifetime, his heart did something most odd.

It thudded to life in a wild cadence.

One might even say passionately.

Chapter 2

Cordelia turned from the window when she heard the door open and the butler making his announcement, not quite sure what to expect. For a moment, all she could do was stand there and hope, the sixpence clutched in her hand.

Yet everything was wrong. The man standing in the doorway before her was hardly what she expected. Oh, he had the same dark hair, the same blue eyes, but somehow the pieces did not add up the way she'd expected. "Captain Talcott?"

"Yes." There was a note of question in his reply as he hesitantly stepped into the room, his head tipped as he studied her. "Have we met?"

She let out the breath she'd been holding. Absently dropping the sixpence into her pocket, she moved forward, her hands outstretched. "Kipp, is it truly you? 'Tis me, Cordelia."

But Captain Talcott hardly appeared happy to see her, for he stepped back and then turned slightly. "Kipp, indeed! Now whose services are in question?" he asked, not of her, but of the man behind him, the one she hadn't noticed.

But the moment he shouldered his way past Captain Talcott and came to stand before her, her world righted. Well, no, actually it rather tipped in a most haphazard fashion.

For here, all the pieces fell into place. The wide chest, the solid jaw, the firm set of his lips. And his eyes, so blue and clear, as if they could see far beyond the horizon.

This was exactly how she'd imagined Christopher Talcott all grown up. But she'd never expected how the sight of him would make her feel—her mouth went dry, and her knees and resolve wavered.

For there was none of the spark to his expression that she remembered. That adventurous light to his eyes. Something, someone, had extinguished his grand curiosity, his *bon vivant*.

And worse, he stopped short of taking her outstretched hands, his hands moving toward hers and then, as if remembering himself, he let them drop back to their proper place at his side. "Miss Padley? Is it truly you?"

Such a stiffly formal greeting did not bode well. "Indeed, Kipp, it is me." She pulled her own hands back, feeling horribly foolish. "How glad I am you remember."

"Remember? How could I not?"

"Upon pain of death," they both said at once.

And there it was, a spark of the Kipp she remembered from her childhood. A bit of mischief in his eyes, that is until the other man spoke up.

"Oh, this is going to be good," he muttered, as he moved into the room.

"Leave us, Drew," Kipp told him.

"Oh, I hardly think so. This is far more interesting than the morning paper." He settled himself down on the settee and folded his hands behind his head, making himself comfortable. "Besides, I want to hear more about these services."

"Drew—"

Cordelia turned toward the captain. "*You're* Andrew?"

"One and the same. I still don't know who you are though."

Kipp intervened. "Drew, don't you recall Cordelia from next door, or as you liked to call her, Commander Whey-Face."

Drew's expression widened and then he laughed. "Good heavens, Sir Horace's scamp of a daughter, all grown up. Nicely done, though." And then the rogue had the audacity to wink at her.

Why, he was as bad as Kate had said, perhaps worse.

Cordelia blushed, but she couldn't let the record go uncorrected. "You were the one who christened me Commander Whey-Face, Kipp." Then she turned to Drew. "You used to pull my hair and once dared me to eat a worm," she replied. "Which was hardly the proper beginning for a future vicar."

The rapscallion barked a laugh. "Oh good God! I'd nearly forgotten that was where I was intended. Yes, well, fate intervened and I was shipped off to sea," he told her.

"Oh my, I am confused," she confessed. She turned to Kipp. "All this time, I thought you were Captain Talcott."

"Him?" From behind her, Drew laughed again, and she glanced over her shoulder at him. "Hardly. Nothing so pedestrian for my brother, Miss Padley, or as I recall you liked to call him, Major Pudding-Legs." Now it was Kipp's turn to flinch. With a flourish of his hand and a slight bow, he said, "You have the honor of addressing the most honorable and industrious Earl of Thornton."

"Lord Thornton? Oh, but you can't be," she managed as she sank into a nearby chair. "Kipp, good heavens, that ruins everything! How could you?"

KIPP TOOK A step back. How could he what? Not inherit? As if it had been his choice.

More to the point, what the devil was Cordelia Padley doing here? And today of all days.

"Truly, you inherited?" she asked.

She needn't sound so horrified. Most people thought inheriting an earldom was a brilliant stroke of luck. Though if he was being honest, he rather shared her sentiment.

The abrupt change in the line of succession had overturned his entire future.

"I did. My older brother—perhaps you remember him—" She

nodded at this. "Well, yes, he died in an accident not long after you left."

"Oh, how dreadful," she said, glancing between him and Drew.

"Turned everything upside down," Drew added. "Instead of Kipp being shipped off to sea, I was hauled off to Portsmouth, and he got sent to Eton."

None of that seemed relevant to the more essential question. Kipp straightened, an odd feeling of foreboding pressing at him.

Like his life was about to cast into the briars yet again.

"Miss Padley, whatever are you doing here? When did you return from Egypt?"

"Egypt, no, I wasn't—" She shook her head. "I never went to Egypt. I've been in India."

"India?" All these years he'd envisioned her sailing on the Nile and exploring ancient tombs with her scholar father.

"Yes, India. I fear it's a long story and hardly matters right now, for I find myself in a terrible predicament, and didn't know who to turn to—" She glanced from one brother to the other. "Oh, I know I am going to make a tangle of all this, but I suppose I should just say it." She paused and took a deep breath. "I need someone willing to marry me."

Behind them, Drew bolted to his feet. "Marriage?" His brows arched up in panic. "O-o-oh! That sort of predicament. Too rich for my blood. I'm out of here." He strode past them, but not before he slapped Kipp on the back. "Best of luck to you and the little *predicament.*"

Cordelia's cheeks flushed a rosy pink as she realized exactly what sort of trouble Drew was suggesting. "It is hardly that—"

"Yes, well, I only know of one sort," Drew told her as he fled.

Of course he left. Drew might be able to face England's enemies without batting an eye, but mention anything that hinted at "marriage" and the need for a hasty one at that, and he was the first one to drop sails and make a mad dash for open waters.

"Oh dear, that did come out rather badly," she muttered, more to herself.

Kipp wasn't too sure if there was a way it could have come out otherwise, but then again, he hadn't the least notion of what she was suggesting, or rather asking him. And as she continued, he only grew more confused.

"It wouldn't be a real engagement," she explained, "just a temporary one. Until my affairs are in order. Or rather my aunts are in order."

Aunts. He vaguely recalled them. A trio of crones worthy of *Macbeth.* Her father's aunts actually, if he wasn't mistaken. Why, they must be ancient by now.

And apparently just as meddling.

Meanwhile, Cordelia continued on. "Yes, well, I fear I am guilty of a bit of dissembling. I've been deceiving them for a number of years on a certain difficult subject."

He only knew of one difficult subject. One he himself was mired in at the moment. "Marriage?"

She heaved a sigh as if relieved that he understood.

He certainly did not. But this was Cordelia. She'd always been high-spirited and rather nonsensical.

He took a deep breath and knew eventually all this would make sense.

At least he hoped so.

"My aunts kept putting forth the most dreadful list of prospects—men they were convinced would be a good and proper husband for me—and had become most insistent that I choose one. Especially after Papa . . ." She paused there and looked away. "After he . . ."

She didn't have to finish; he could guess, having seeing the flash of grief in her eyes. Sir Horace was gone.

But the solution, it seemed to Kipp, was rather easy. "Why not refuse them?"

She made a rather inelegant snort. He doubted there was a miss in London who would dare such an unladylike sound, but here was Cordelia—the girl who had never quite fit in. "You don't know my aunts. Now that I'm back—in England—they will insist upon me making a match, especially when they discover—" Then she bit her lower lip, holding back the rest of her admission.

Considering what she had confessed so far, he wasn't too sure he wanted to wade in any further. He glanced at the door and wondered if perhaps Drew's instincts had the better of it.

"Discover what?"

Sighing again, she looked up and directly at him. "Well, you see, I'd written them—only to stop their interference—that I had already engaged in an understanding with a certain gentleman."

Kipp sat back as he saw where this was going. At least so he thought. "And this certain gentleman has refused?"

She shook her head. "I don't know. I'm rather in the middle of asking him."

As her words set in, Kipp blinked. He couldn't have heard her correctly, but as the seconds ticked by and Cordelia sat looking at him, rather expectantly, he realized he had. "Me? You told them we were engaged?"

Biting her lip again, she shrugged a little, made a tip of her head. "Well, it is terribly hard to find a willing man—at the very least, a tolerable one—and simply put, you are the only one I know. At least I thought I knew." Her words ran together in a rush as if she hoped they might lessen the truth of the matter.

"You told them *we* were engaged?" He had to ask it again, because it seemed rather important to make sure he had the answer correct.

"If you insist on being precise about the matter, then yes."

Yes, he did want to insist. And then he wanted to sit down. No, he needed to, he realized as he slumped into his favorite chair.

If this were nosed about town . . .

"You don't have to marry me," she added quickly. "Our engagement need only be for a few days."

"A few days?" He shook his head. He had another matter that was about to take place in the next few days. Hours, to be exact.

At precisely three this afternoon, Miss Pamela Holt was expecting him to call.

And pose a certain deciding question.

Meanwhile, Cordelia did her rambling best to quell his obvious panic. "Then you can cry off and break my heart."

She said it so matter-of-factly.

Cry off, indeed.

He'd never be so dishonorable.

Then he looked at her, her cheeks aglow, her lips slightly parted, and a look of desperate need in her eyes.

In that one glance, the strangest notion uncoiled in his gut. *The last thing I would ever do is break your heart.*

"I would never—" he began, and stopped in the blink of an eye, suddenly wary of whatever magic she seemed to be unspooling around him.

"Why ever not? It is most essential that you toss me aside. Leave me in a state of emotional ruin. Then my aunts won't dare push some wretched country rector in my direction. At least not for a year. Mayhap even two, if I'm lucky. You see, I am determined that I will not marry for anything less than to follow my heart."

Kipp straightened, as if tugged by her words. Oh, how they held a tempting lure to them.

But not one he could afford to latch on to.

"So write them that I have done so," he told her. "Thrown you over and broken your heart." That seemed the sensible choice. Why, then she wouldn't have had any need to come see him.

Following one's heart, indeed!

He stole another glance at her, that pointed chin, those blue eyes. Yet, for some unspeakable, maddening reason, he was ever so glad she had.

Need of him.

For the sight of her was like a distant candle on a dark, stormy night.

Though whether Cordelia was the candle or the storm was yet to be seen.

Storm, he would reason, for here she was, as madcap as ever, and still drawing him into her disastrous schemes.

Which, he reminded himself, had always led him into a raft of trouble.

Cordelia, on the other hand, was shaking her head at his suggestion. "No, no, a letter will simply not suffice. They need to see you. Meet you. Or else they will suspect that I've . . ."

She paused, biting her lower lip.

But he knew what she'd been about to confess, for apparently her aunts knew Cordelia for the romp that she was. "Fabricated the entire situation?" he offered.

She nodded quickly. "Yes, I fear so. If they have seen me with you, seen me terribly in love and then destitute over the loss of your companionship, they will believe the entire farce."

Kipp groaned. She wanted him to pretend an engagement and then cry off. Why, it was utter madness.

Meanwhile, Cordelia continued on and he was only half listening until she got to one very essential piece of information. ". . . I must be there when Anne marries the duke. That, and Anne is ever so fond of my aunts—and they, her—of course she's asked them to come to the wedding."

That single word tolled though his own musings. "Wedding?"

"Yes, I explained all that. My dear friend Miss Brabourne—we went to Madame Rochambeaux's school together—is getting married and I must be there. And you, of course."

The web she was weaving began to tangle around him. "When is this wedding?" he dared to venture.

"Saturday."

"When do your aunts arrive in London?"

"London?" She shook her head. "No, no, you misunderstand. The wedding isn't in London." Taking a deep breath, she continued on. "I fear this is where the favor becomes a bit complicated—"

At this, Kipp couldn't help himself. He grinned. "More so than it already is?"

She laughed a little. "Yes, well, I suppose this sounds like a great coil to you. But truly it is rather uncomplicated. The wedding is at Hamilton Hall."

"Isn't that the Duke of Dorset's—"

"—Yes. The duke is marrying Anne."

"But isn't Hamilton Hall near Bath?"

Again she nodded.

"That's two and a half days from London," he pointed out.

"Oh yes, I suppose it is." She pressed her lips together and sighed. "Oh bother! I suppose my request does entail more than just a few days. But no more than a sennight . . . at the most." She smiled, her lips quavering just slightly, and there was a wary cast to her glance. Then she came over to him and took his hand without any hesitation, much as she had when they were children.

He glanced down at her fingers twined around his own and had the sense that as improper as this was, as much as he should get up and leave before she managed to talk him into this madness, he couldn't.

"Oh, Kipp, I know it's been ages, and I know this is such an unexpected and most impractical and quite impossible thing of me to ask, but I need your help. Desperately. And if you haven't anything of import in the next week, I would be forever in your debt if you could—"

Already he was shaking his head, pulling his hands free of her grasp, for the warmth of her touch was . . . was . . .

Beguiling. Tempting.

And Drew had been very right about one thing—his life had been entirely too dull for far too long. And predictable. And boring.

Up until he'd entered this room. "Cordelia, I don't see how—"

"You'd be lending me grave assistance," she rushed to add. "Which, you might remember, is the first rule of the RSE pledge."

Those words, that pledge, sparked all the rest of his memories of her, of their charter for the Royal Society of Explorers. RSE. She'd been adamant that they would always come to each other's aid. The very heart of a good society, she'd insisted.

And he recalled one of the other rules she'd insisted upon adding. And once again, some odd, impish spark ignited inside him.

"What of Rule 18?" he asked, if only to tease her. "Does that still stand?"

He hadn't any idea why he'd just said that or why he'd even thought of it, but the result was seeing Cordelia blush quite prettily.

"I—I—I—I . . . I don't see . . . That is, I don't believe that rule is relevant to this particular situation." She straightened a bit, as if gathering her wits and fortitude about her. "I only need your assistance. Not *that*."

"How unfortunate," he replied. "From my vantage point, they seem to go hand in hand."

"Now you sound like your brother," she shot back.

"That's hardly fair, nor will it gain you my help."

"So you will—"

"Will I what?" He leaned a bit closer.

To his chagrin, her brows rose and she sat back. "Come with me to Anne's wedding." This time she smiled, a fragile little turn of her lips, and he could see that while most of Cordelia was brave and intrepid, she truly did see him as her only hope.

Which cut him right through the heart.

"If you refuse—" she was saying.

"Yes, yes, I know. Upon pain of death."

But really, what choice did he have?

Chapter 3

*L*ater that day, the Earl of Thornton found himself being shown into an elaborately decorated room—a showy display of Mr. Josiah Holt's legendary wealth.

Now, Josiah might be shunned for still having a bit of dirt under his nails, but not even the snootiest matrons could deny that his finest treasure, his beloved daughter and only child, Miss Pamela Holt, was nothing short of the rarest of Diamonds. For even now, seated as she was beside the window, the sunlight streamed down on her fair head like a halo.

She'd created a tremendous stir when she'd made her debut— both for her beauty and for the depth of her dowry. But Pamela was also Josiah's daughter, canny and smart, and had kept her affections close to her heart, so that suitors far and wide came to court her to see if they could claim this most coveted prize.

"My dear Lord Thornton, what a pleasant surprise to see you," she said, smiling and nodding slightly, regally deigning to allow him into her presence. That her affections had fallen on him, an impoverished earl, would be a bit of shock to most of the *ton*, when it had been wagered at the beginning of the season that she would most likely start the summer with a duchess's coronet on her fair brow.

Yet for some reason, Pamela had quietly and discreetly turned her discerning eye toward him, and Kipp, having passed all the trials to gain this prized lady, now stood at the last hurdle: asking that fateful question.

Just be done with this, he tried telling himself.

He coughed slightly, trying to push the lump in his throat out of the way. Truly, he had no idea why this suddenly had become such a struggle. He'd woken up this morning resolved to do what needed to be done.

Ask the heiress to marry him and thus save his lands and title from ruin.

Then *she'd* arrived.

Cordelia Padley. With her ridiculous request to lend her assistance as any RSE member in good standing would do.

Save that he'd made that promise when he'd been all of eight. And there was no Royal Society of Explorers—with all its lofty edicts of honor. Of course he'd had to refuse her.

He had obligations he must satisfy. To his tenants. For the future of his family name.

Even Drew, madcap and reckless as he was, had reluctantly agreed it was the only course.

"Aunt Charity," Miss Holt said, directing her attention to the crone seated like a gargoyle on the other side of the room. "Would you please ask Ruskin to bring in the tea tray?"

Her aunt, who acted as her chaperone, hesitated for a moment, mouth pursed with consternation at the very idea of abandoning her charge. Another pointed glance from her niece sent the woman on her errand, but not before the old crone sent one more chastising grimace at Kipp.

And then they were alone. He and Miss Holt. Which should be the impetus to making a lofty declaration.

Yet, instead of getting on with it, he found himself looking around the splendid room, a showplace of wealth and fashion, and instead of being awed by all the elegant touches of gilt, and the expensive furnishings, he suffered an uncomfortable flash of foreboding, that all too soon he'd see his beloved old relic, Mallow Hills, being dressed up in the same manner, like a Covent Garden whore trying to be a lady.

No, no, he couldn't think like that. He had to recall all the other improvements that could be made. Fields drained. Cottages repaired. Barns full of prized horses. Fat sheep dotting the meadows.

"My lord, is there something amiss?" Miss Holt asked as she carefully settled her hands down atop the frills on her gown . . . the sort a lady wore to go for a carriage ride—which he assumed she would insist upon after he got done with the business at hand, if only so she could be paraded through the park and thus spread the news of their betrothal that much more quickly.

Beautiful and shrewd. And very much her father's daughter.

"No, no," he said, running a hand through his hair. "Nothing's amiss."

Yet everything was, as if he was being prodded down a ship's plank by the point of a sword.

He did his best to remember this was nothing more than a business matter to be bartered and sealed. For her, a countess's coronet, and for him, the security of a fortune.

A fair and equitable exchange.

But one thought raced through his head.

I will not marry for anything less than to follow my heart.

Oh, damn Cordelia for reminding him of yet another impossible thing.

Love.

Only she would disavow security and position for such mercurial and mysterious flutters.

He nearly groaned. Love, of all things!

When he looked at Miss Holt, he knew there would never be the flicker of such an unprofitable emotion in her eyes. No, when she looked at him, Pamela saw nothing more than the certainty of her future . . . as Lady Thornton, and with that her ascendance in society as the premier London hostess.

A future so set in stone, so immobile, so entrenched that before he could even stop himself, a panicked rush of words came tumbling out.

"I fear I've some bad news."

The words startled even him. Good God, what had he just said? He tried to force out a retraction, but those words refused to budge. For he'd gone and let the cat out of the bag, and with that done, there was no stuffing it back in.

And to his shock, he didn't want to. Kipp straightened, his resolve bringing with it a sense of something long lost now suddenly found.

Meanwhile, Pamela smiled as if she hadn't heard him correctly. "I hardly think that possible," she replied, so certain in her value, her position. Her glance rose to meet his, a silent prod. *We both know why you are here. Get on with it.*

Yes, that was what he needed to do. *Get on with it.*

But instead, Kipp had the creeping sense of standing in wet concrete—if he didn't move quickly, he'd be trapped.

For the rest of his life.

Just as his inheritance had extinguished the life of adventure he'd once boasted about to Cordelia. He was going to be a famous cartographer. Tramp hills and mountains and islands that had never been surveyed. Tame them all.

The entire globe his to discover.

All of which had been snuffed out the moment he'd been elevated from spare to heir.

But seeing Cordelia again had rekindled that spark for adventure, the one he'd thought long lost. Oh, this had all the marks of that perfidious mistress, Fate. How else could he explain why Cordie had arrived back in his life this very day? Offering him one last adventure before this mire he stood in hardened.

But you must come with me. Upon pain of death, she'd teased him, a sly smile on her lips, and more telling, lighting her blue eyes.

He looked over at Pamela, who was also smiling, a beguiling turn of her lips that left the poets among her swains racing to put pen to paper.

Yet now, of all times, he noticed that her smile never reached her eyes.

Not like Cordie's did.

"I must leave London," he said, no longer drowning in panic, having found his footing. "First thing tomorrow."

"Tomorrow? I don't see how—" Annoyance pinched at her nose.

"'Tis a matter of honor, Miss Holt. I must go."

"You *must*?" Now that wrinkle tugged at her brow and her smile slowly straightened into a hard line. Because she had been raised with her every need being met, with her every expectation being fulfilled, he might as well have come in speaking Sanskrit, for it was obvious she couldn't imagine anything that might take precedence over his proposal of marriage.

To her.

But now that he'd launched this ship, he found himself being pulled by both the tide and a favorable wind. "Yes. I made a promise. To a friend. Long ago. The news—rather their request—came this morning."

In the form of the most madcap, impossible female one could ever have met. But he wisely chose to leave that part out.

"I can hardly fail them at such a desperate time," Kipp added. "It is, after all, a matter of *honor*."

Faced with this most aristocratic of demands, Pamela could hardly protest and not look exactly like what she was—the jumped-up daughter of a rag merchant. Composing herself and straightening as well, she nodded her acquiescence. "I would expect nothing less of you, my lord." Then she got right back to the business at hand. "When will you return?"

Here was the rub. "A sennight at the very least, a fortnight at the most."

"*A fortnight!* But—" She stopped herself right there, her hand coming to her mouth to stopper back the demanding words that threatened to follow. That, and most likely because she'd heard—much as he had—that shrill note of a fishwife rising in her protest.

"I'm sorry, but as I said, this is a matter of honor. I do appreciate your understanding and patience, Miss Holt." He bowed, then turned and left.

Well, more like fled.

If he was being honest.

THE NEXT MORNING Cordelia stood on the curb, overseeing the menagerie of trunks and valises and boxes being packed into and atop the carriage. While that might be her butler's duty, she had done it so many times over the years for her father that she still preferred to do the task herself.

If only life could be ordered so easily.

Her gaze lifted to the house beside hers, her hand going instinctively to the sixpence in her pocket.

"Looking for him and wishing he'd arrive won't make it happen," Kate remarked, having guessed, in her annoyingly canny way, Cordelia's line of thought.

"I'm not wishing any such thing," she lied.

"You've been woolgathering since yesterday."

"Hardly," she shot back. It wasn't truly woolgathering when one couldn't put something out of her mind no matter how hard she tried to dismiss it. Say like the rugged turn of Kipp's jaw. Or the hard line of his lips.

Not to mention Rule 18.

And with her usual startling clarity, Kate asked, "Whatever did that man say to you to put you in such a stew?"

"I am not in a stew," she replied tartly. "And I told you what he said. He had other obligations and couldn't assist me."

Which was for the best. Especially in light of her sudden preoccupation with how Kipp had turned out. So taciturn. So chiseled. So very handsome. So very kissable . . .

Oh bother, there she went again.

Meanwhile, Kate, never one to keep her opinions to herself, continued on. "I told you not to wear that dreadful gown."

"As if any other gown would have changed his obligations," Cordelia replied.

"You'd be amazed at the obligations a man is willing to forget when a lady wears the right sort of gown."

Cordelia chose to ignore her worldly companion, for now it would only be wishful thinking.

And wishes wouldn't bring back the Kipp she remembered. That Kipp was long lost.

The Kipp she'd whiled away hours with as a child, lying side by side on the floor of the library, paging through atlases and planning their own expeditions. Kipp charting the course and Cordelia endlessly making lists of what they would need.

That Kipp who hadn't cared what she wore, only that she loved adventures as much as he did.

"How is it you, of all people, didn't know he'd inherited?" Kate was still askance that Cordelia—mindful of every detail—had missed this very significant one.

"After my mother died, we never returned to this house. I went to school for all those years and then I followed Papa to India. I had no idea he was . . . that he wasn't . . ."

Her Kipp.

After all, she'd spent years imagining him bravely facing a hurricane or charting faraway waters, standing on the deck of his ship looking for all accounts like a member in good standing of the RSE.

And just the notion that he'd gained his heart's desire, when she had not, had been enough to warm her a bit.

Her lips pressed together as she considered the man he'd become—a reserved and guarded nobleman with the weight of the world on his shoulders. Hardly the carefree, intrepid explorer she'd fancied.

What surprised her more was the realization that had woken her up in the middle of the night: Perhaps Kipp needed rescuing as much as she did.

But how, she hadn't the least notion. Or the time to spare.

She had her own reckoning to face.

Just then the coachman tied off the last of the ropes at the back of the carriage. "There, miss, I got them just the way you like them. All ready to go."

So there it was, time for her to face the consequences of her impetuously penned betrothal.

If only . . . she wished.

Then, like a lifeline that comes out of nowhere, someone asked, "Is there room for me?"

Cordelia paused for only a second, for that voice, those words, were like the string on a top, spinning her around.

"Kipp?" She shook her head. "I mean, my lord—" For it might be Kipp's voice, but before her stood the perfect English gentleman through and through—a majestic and forbidding creature in a grand traveling coat with its bright silver buttons glinting in the sunlight.

All imposing and proper. And so very handsome. Cordelia knew she was gaping, but how could she not? For here he was, like a knight errant, all ready to rescue her.

He was here to rescue her, wasn't he?

"And me as well," added another, prodding her out of her trance.

It wasn't until then that she realized it wasn't just Kipp, but his rapscallion brother as well. Drew. The pair of them stood side by side, leading their horses and carrying well-worn valises in hand.

She tried to say something, but she was still a bit mesmerized by the sight of Kipp.

"Yes, well, I was able to rearrange my schedule," he told her. His words came out a bit stiffly, but if she wasn't mistaken, there was a hint of the old sparkle to his eyes. "It would hardly do to have a fellow member of the RSE traveling alone," he replied, a slight tip of his lips that suggested an attempt at smiling. "That is, if you haven't found another member of the Royal Society . . ." He glanced around as if he half expected some other fellow in traveling togs to be standing about.

She shook her head. "No, I suppose you will have to do," she managed, immediately feeling foolish for not having said something more enticing.

But then again, it was probably better than the confession that nearly tripped from her lips.

Why would I want anyone else?

Kate, on the other hand, having measured up the situation in the blink of an eye, stepped forward. "Lord Thornton, I believe?" She held out her hand, which the earl took and bent over. "I'm Mrs. Harrington, Miss Padley's companion." But Kate's gaze had already risen to the man behind the earl, a sly smile turning her lips. "And you must be Captain Talcott." She looked Drew up and down. "I would have expected someone taller, given the tales of your exploits." And without waiting for his reply, she strode over to the carriage and let the footman help her in, leaving Drew gaping after her.

Oh yes, Kate knew exactly how to drop a hook into the water.

Cordelia hurried to follow, partly for fear Kipp might change his mind, though from the look on Drew's face, she realized the captain would follow them to the ends of the earth.

Well, follow Kate.

"Yes, well, we'll add our bags to the collection and be off," Kipp said, nudging his befuddled brother to hurry along.

Inside the carriage, Kate was tugging at her gloves. "You didn't tell me Lord Thornton was so handsome. If I were you, I'd do my best to turn this false engagement into a real one." Her brows waggled slightly.

Good heavens, her companion was getting as bad as her aunts.

"I don't want to get married. And Kipp, I mean, the earl, is only helping me because of a promise we made to each other years ago."

Her companion made a slight snort and looked out the window, admiring the view. Which happened to be of Captain Talcott mounting his horse. "Is that the only reason?"

Cordelia ignored her.

Not that Kate was done. "Still, he's here. Which says something. Especially since you were so certain—"

"He said no," Cordelia told her. "There was no ambiguity."

"And yet, here he is. And with his brother as well." Kate smiled again and settled deeply into her seat as the carriage began to move forward. "How very curious. I wonder what changed his mind?"

Chapter 4

*L*ater that day, Cordelia stepped out of the inn and looked around, sketching case in hand. They'd stopped here in this quaint village for the night, and Cordelia—restless from being cooped up in the carriage all day—hoped a bit of a walk and the chance to draw would settle the tangled thoughts rattling about inside her head.

Much to her chagrin, Kipp had spent the day riding in silence, while Drew had taken every opportunity to move his mount alongside the ladies, pointing out the sights and regaling them with tales of his daring.

Yes, yes, Cordelia had wanted to explode about halfway through the day, *you are quite the adventurous hero, Captain Talcott, but whatever is your brother doing here? What changed his mind?*

But did she really want to know? It wasn't like she wanted a real betrothed. She was only borrowing the earl. And then she would quite happily return him to London. Which was all well and good.

Still, it was rather annoying the way he seemed to invade her every thought and yet wouldn't even look at her.

Which was for the best, she told herself, that is, until she turned slightly and realized the man himself was standing right at her side.

She jumped a little and made a bit of a squeak.

"Where do you think you're going?" He'd changed into a plain dark jacket and buff breeches, which made him less imposing, but he still managed to sound utterly stuffy.

"Out to sketch," she said, holding up her case. "And in the future, please do not come sneaking up beside me. It is ever so unsettling."

Because now her heart was pattering about most unevenly.

"I do not sneak. And how is it you are going without Mrs. Harrington?"

Yes, decidedly stuffy. This was exactly why she didn't want a betrothed, or any man, directing her life.

"She doesn't draw," she replied, ignoring the note of dismay and disapproval in his question. She was rather used to such consternation over her "unbridled independence," as the matrons of Bombay called it. She hoisted up the edge of her hem and set out across the stable yard.

"Hold on there," Kipp called after her, and he quickly fell in step alongside her, his boots squishing in the muck. "You can't wander about unescorted."

"Oh good heavens!" Cordelia came to a stop and turned to face him. "I've traveled across India, around the Horn of Africa, and all the way to England." She waved her free hand at the bucolic scene before them—the sturdy little inn and the neat row of shops beyond, green trees and even greener gardens leaving the vista soft and inviting. "I hardly think this village harbors a den of thieves waiting to pillage my pen and papers."

She continued on, but to her chagrin, Kipp followed in her wake, his wagging admonishments chasing after her.

"It just isn't done, Miss Padley," he told her.

Not Cordie. Not even Cordelia. Or even that wretched Commander Whey-Face. She'd take any of those over this formal and stiff designation. Miss Padley, indeed!

"What if you were to get lost," he pointed out.

Oh, that was the final straw. She whirled around. "However could that happen, my lord?" She notched her chin up a bit. "We're standing on an island. Eventually I would come to an edge."

This took him aback only for a moment. Then a slight smile traced its way across his lips and to her surprise he laughed. "Then I'd best accompany you . . . to see that you don't fall off."

Then he reached down and caught up her case. Took it right out of her hand. If she hadn't been so startled by the rich tones of his laughter, and the way it shivered down her spine, she would have had the wherewithal to stop him.

Why, of all the imperious . . .

"I can carry that." She went to retrieve it but he held it out of her reach.

"I'm quite certain you can." And then he shifted it to his far side and sent her one of those withering glances that only an English lord could manage. The sort that brooked no opposition.

The sort that said, *Go where you please, but you are going with me.*

Then he set off in the direction of the ruin, leaving Cordelia with no choice but to follow him.

After all, he had her sketch box.

Still, she wasn't one to give up easily. "Members of the RSE always carry their own burdens."

"This is hardly what I'd call a burden," he replied, his mouth set in a mulish line.

Well, at least one thing hadn't changed. Christopher Talcott was still the most stubborn male alive.

What else hadn't changed? That question prodded at her insatiable curiosity.

"How is it that you—" she began. *Never went to sea? Or followed your dreams? Turned into such a stuffy wreck?*

"That I what?"

"Didn't go to sea like you planned. I know you inherited and all, but that hardly seems a good enough reason—"

He flinched, only slightly, and she knew that she'd waded in too far.

But now that she was up to her neck in it . . .

"You could have still gone," she offered, seeing the wrinkle of his brow, the sudden pinch of his lips. The turmoil behind them.

Frustration. Anger. Regret.

Feelings she understood only too well.

He shook his head. "You obviously don't remember my father."

She thought for a moment and realized she didn't recall the previous earl, not in the least. But then again she'd been a child and hardly worthy of being presented to the neighboring lord.

"He had a general horror of Drew inheriting," he supplied.

Cordelia couldn't help herself; she laughed a little. "Not without good reason. He was such a dreadful scamp."

"Still is," Kipp told her. "I'd warn your Mrs. Harrington."

Cordelia nodded politely. It might do well to warn Captain Talcott about Mrs. Harrington, but she wasn't about to tell Kipp that, given his current obsession with propriety.

Instead she went back to the subject at hand. "So you stayed behind."

"Yes, and Drew was sent in my place."

Cordelia paused, as did Kipp. "I'm so sorry," she said, reaching out and placing her hand on his sleeve.

She didn't know why she'd done it, but the moment her fingers curled around his forearm, she regretted it utterly. For suddenly it made this entire farce of a betrothal seem very real.

He looked down at her hand first and then into her eyes, and Cordelia realized that their easy familiarity as children was nothing like being intimate as adults—for this close, all she could think of was Rule 18, and all that it implied.

Offered. Promised.

And from the wary light in his glance, she couldn't help but wonder if he was having the same thoughts. And if he was . . .

She panicked and snatched her hand back. *Oh, that would never do.*

So instead, she continued walking, Kipp in her wake, and both of them ignoring that uncomfortable moment.

Still, she thought as she slanted a glance at him, it was slightly unfortunate he wasn't more of a scapegrace like his brother.

"You've changed, if you don't mind me saying," she told him.

"You have not."

That hardly sounded like a compliment.

Not that she was angling for one, but still, it pricked at her feminine heart. "Not at all?"

He glanced over at her. "Oh, you've grown up."

"Well, thank you for noticing."

"It's rather difficult not to."

She supposed that might be a compliment, but since she'd never been offered one by a man she hadn't any idea what to expect.

But she had thought one might be more effusive with his praise, if one was to offer a compliment.

They turned the corner in the road, and the entire reason Cordelia had set out in this direction came into view. Just off the road stood an old ruined castle, which was more a pile of rubble than fortress, the once lofty walls having been pilfered for centuries by the nearby villagers.

In the far western horizon the sun was beginning to settle in for the night, throwing off the day's labors by bathing the sky in brilliant shades of pink and red, while the humble yellow stones of the castle glowed back with an ancient fire—that flicker of twilight where day and night entwined and embraced.

They both stopped, and Cordelia couldn't help herself, she reached over and caught hold of his hand.

"Have you ever seen—"

"No, I haven't. At least not in a very long time." Then he surprised her utterly. "Thank you, Cordelia, for asking me—to come along and all. I had forgotten—"

She nodded, for she knew exactly what he meant. It had been a long time since she'd stood with someone who understood. Understood her.

"If you are going to sketch, you'd best hurry," he told her.

"Oh dear, I nearly forgot," she said, reluctantly letting go of his hand and reaching for her case. With it in hand, she plopped down in a grassy spot, quickly sorting out what she needed and opening her sketchbook.

And then she closed her eyes and breathed deeply.

After a few moments, Kipp coughed a little. "Whatever are you doing?"

Slowly she opened her eyes. "Summoning all my senses. If I am to draw this scene, I want to be part of it—all of it. The wind, the grass, the birds—" She tipped her head toward a nearby hedge where trilling notes rose from a hidden bit of feathers. "Is that a robin?"

He listened as well. "No, a lark."

She smiled and nodded, cataloguing that away. "A friend of my father's—a Hindu priest—he also liked to draw, and always said that if one wanted to capture a moment, one needed to be in the moment. Have a sense of the place." She looked up and found him studying her. "Try it. Close your eyes."

"Hardly. Knowing you, this is one of your tricks to escape my detection."

"If I wanted to escape you, I would have already done so," she told him tartly.

"Then I will take your presence as a compliment."

"So you do know what one is," she muttered without thinking.

"Pardon?"

"Oh, nothing," she hurried to say. And then changed the subject as she studied the castle and horizon for the best vantage. "It is rather magnificent," she said, studying the sky, her head tipped slightly.

He nodded in agreement. "In London one doesn't get the chance to . . . that is, I don't get to . . . well, with my obligations and such."

"I'm so sorry." Though whether it was for the loss of his dreams or her impetuous touch earlier, she wasn't sure. So she made certain she was clear on the subject. "That you inherited."

"Not the usual sentiment one hears. Most people would suggest that I have the devil's own luck." He moved over to one of the toppled stones and sat down on it.

When she looked over, she had a vision of him that she couldn't explain, sitting there on that ancient stone, like a king of lore. So she flipped the page and started anew.

"Anyone who doesn't understand is obviously not a founding member of the RSE," she told him, nose tucked in the air.

Kipp laughed again. *"If life is not an adventure it is hardly worth living."*

Those words caught her unaware, pulling her concentration up from the sketch beginning to unfold before her. "Oh, you do remember!"

"Of course I remember. It is a fine motto for a society."

"Secret society," she corrected.

"Oh yes, very secret. And a good thing it is. I do believe there is a codicil about cannibalism in our list of rules. As a member of the House of Lords, it would hardly do if it were nosed about that I had once endorsed the eating of my fellow noblemen."

"Yes, but only in the case of extreme starvation," she pointed out. "And as I recall it was only gentlemen ranking below an earl who could be consumed."

They both glanced at each other and then laughed. Heartily.

Heavens, she couldn't remember the last time she'd laughed like this.

"Yes, I suppose it is a good thing the RSE canon has been lost to the ages," she said.

His brows twitched slightly and he glanced away.

"Kipp, it is lost, isn't it?"

He made a slip of his shoulder. "Until a few weeks ago I would have said as much, but as luck would have it, I was going through the library and found it tucked behind that giant atlas we used to drag about."

"How providential," she remarked. No wonder he'd remembered Rule 18. "Would have made my case much easier to prove yesterday if I'd had it to quote from."

"I daresay I'd forgotten most of the nonsense we'd written there." He glanced over at her, and if she wasn't mistaken, his eyes sparkled a bit, just like the mischievous boy she remembered.

Though as a lad, he'd protested quite heatedly to the addition of Rule 18 to the Royal Society charter.

He pushed off the stone and came to sit down beside her. "Whatever are you drawing?"

When he reached for her sketchbook, she bounded to her feet. "Oh, nothing. Besides, the light has shifted; I'll need to start over."

He rose as well, looking over at the horizon and back at her. "I don't think the sun has moved all that much. Whatever are you hiding, Cordie?"

Cordie . . .

Oh, he did still know her. She glanced up at him and found he'd moved closer than she'd first realized. A whiff of bay rum and horses and something very masculine teased her. So close she could see the darkening stubble at his chin. That if she were to rise up on her toes and catch his coat lapels in her grasp, tip her lips up toward his . . .

"I'm not hiding . . . that is . . . it isn't much," she told him, holding the book behind her back.

For actually, it was everything.

And he reached for it, and then just as quickly they were all entangled.

KIPP REACHED OUT to steady Cordelia and found himself holding her, surrounded by the exotic air of her perfume and the soft curves of her body pressed to his.

In an instance, he knew he shouldn't have come along on this madcap adventure—for here was all the ruin he'd been chastising Drew about since his brother had come home from sea.

Yet with Cordie in his arms, all he could think about was Rule 18.

That one line that had made him smile when he'd read it.

Upon the unlikely event that an RSE member never marries and reaches the matronly age of five and twenty . . .

Cordelia had insisted that specific codicil be added to their charter, much to his vehement protests. Now, looking down at the starry light in her eyes and the soft, inviting turn of her lips, parted just so in invitation, he couldn't think of a single objection to her rule.

And it had been *her* rule. Now all he had to do was endorse it.

He leaned down slightly, wondering in shock at his own reaction to having this improper miss in his arms.

He should be setting her aside, apologizing, anything that put him back in his proper place. That made them both remember that this was all a fiction.

Yet how could he when here was Cordelia Padley, all grown up?

Her hair all a tumble, stray strands falling in an enticing array of *dishabille*. He reached out and tucked one of the curls back behind her ear, marveling at the shiver that ran through her.

Tempting him to come closer.

However had she known, all those years ago, that one day they would meet again and . . . find themselves like this . . .

That is until the high piping notes of the lark in a nearby hedge drummed him back to the present, along with the warning clop of horse hooves and the crunch of cartwheels that said they wouldn't be alone for long.

He glanced up at the farmer coming around the corner, the tired-looking man eyeing the pair with an arched and disapproving brow—the sort of look Josiah Holt had sent toward the wastrels and rakes who'd dallied too close to his daughter.

A look that thrust Kipp back into the present. Where he was the Earl of Thornton. And nearly betrothed.

To someone else.

So no matter what he'd vowed all those years ago, it was a promise he could no longer keep.

"Yes, well, if you don't want to share your drawing," he managed, setting her back on her feet and taking a step away, until the teasing air of her perfume no longer curled around him like a lure.

For her part, Cordelia righted herself with all the affronted air of a cat that had been stroked the wrong way, the mischievous spell that had entwined them both shattering.

"It's nothing much," she told him as she brushed her hands over her hair, tucking the stray strands back into place. But each time she managed to quell one unruly curl, another seemed to find a way to tumble loose.

Just like the lady herself. Utterly untamable.

But oh, what would it be like to try?

"What is nothing?" he asked absently, still utterly distracted by her tangled hair.

"The sketch you wanted to see."

Ah, yes, the sketch. He'd entirely forgotten.

She opened her book and then held it up for him. There was the castle quickly outlined, with the lines of the horizon faintly added.

"Good heavens, that's excellent," he said, coming to stand beside her. "You've got quite the talent."

"No, my mother was the talented one. I'm but a poor imitator." She looked down at the page. "But this will be much improved when I have a chance to touch it up with some watercolors."

She smiled warily and then moved away from him, taking up a spot a few yards away, and continued to sketch.

Kipp returned to his spot on the stone, and thankfully they sat in silence for some time, until the scratching from her pencil stopped.

"Do you still draw maps?" she asked, looking up from her work.

He shook his head. "No. Hardly any point."

She set down her pencil and turned to him. "Why ever not? It was all you ever wanted to do."

"Do you still want what you desired at eight?" He couldn't help himself; he waggled his brows a bit, if only to tease her.

She blushed, like the way a dab of watercolor spread over a damp page—but that moment of discomfiture didn't last long. She straightened. "You mean go explore Africa?"

He laughed a little. "Yes, if that is what you want to call it."

She pointedly ignored his teasing. "Considering I cannot even walk across a village alone, I would assume the notion of a lady venturing into the furthest reaches of Africa would also be frowned upon."

"I daresay," he said, with a bit more chastisement in his voice than she obviously cared to hear.

She snapped her sketchbook closed. "Oh, not you as well."

"Miss Padley, that just isn't done."

She began to gather up her belongings. "You can do whatever you like, Lord Thornton. Travel. Make maps. Explore the world—though for some inexplicable reason you've decided to cast aside all your dreams."

She stood facing him, her haphazardly gathered belongings jutting out from every angle, her mouth set, her eyes ablaze.

Something about her ire poked at him. "I grew up and left such childish notions behind," he told her.

"Bah!" she huffed. Suddenly she was eight again, all indignant over his assertions that she couldn't form a royal society, couldn't explore the world, all for the simple and ridiculous bit of happenstance that she was female.

He doggedly ignored the fact that she'd changed his mind back then. "I don't know how things are managed in India, but here in England there is a very set way of how things were done. What is considered appropriate."

He couldn't imagine Pamela making such a suggestion. The closest Pamela would ever get to the Nile was the carved crocodile legs on her sofa.

"Appropriate?" A flash of sparks illuminated Cordelia's eyes. Like a warning. She set aside her belongings and marched toward him, stopping when she could poke her finger into his chest. "You, Lord Thornton, can follow any of those adventures we came up with simply because you are a man."

"How can you think it is that simple?"

"Because it is," she shot back. "A man can set his own course, where a woman is . . ."

"A woman is what?" He thought of Pamela and how she had nearly every unmarried man in London lapping at the hem of her skirts. "Being a woman hasn't stopped you. My God! As you pointed out, you've been to India and back."

"And yet here I am, trying to foil society's demand that I shackle myself to some tallow clerk or I will be deemed something less than a woman. Yes, I must marry, or, horrors upon horrors, I might end up a spinster."

A spinster. He nearly laughed. The last thing he could ever see Cordelia Padley becoming was some colorless spinster, especially when her perfume curled at his senses, enticing and sharp, full of an exotic world he'd never know, never see.

"If, my lord, you were so overly concerned about what is appropriate, if you have—as you claim—left behind your dreams, whatever are you doing here? Why did you come along with me?"

Her question took him aback.

Why, indeed?

He looked around at their very English setting, of the ruins before him, and he was reminded of his own pressing duties.

Obligations. The ones that had landed on his shoulders the day he'd inherited his father's earldom.

Duty kept him here. Far from the sights and far-flung corners Cordelia had trod. And a flicker of anger ignited inside him.

He was Thornton. It hadn't been his choice, any more than it had been her choice to be born female. But that was their lot and he was determined to do his duty.

"Why ever did you abandon your dreams?" she repeated in a whisper of a voice that soothed his ruffled spirit. "Don't you still dream of Egypt?"

"Of course, but—" he said without thinking. Kipp looked away. How was it that she knew? Could find that one small chink in his armor. That one crack in his carefully ordered life.

He'd resigned himself long ago that his desires, his dreams were insignificant, yet he'd been unwilling to cut that one last remaining golden thread.

And here was Cordelia pulling at it, leaving a ripple in his reserve.

"I think of it as well," she confessed. "Of sailing up the Nile in a felucca. Do you remember?"

"Yes." But now he saw that dream in an entirely new light. Of the two of them, standing in the prow, brushed by a warm, sensual breeze that teased at Cordelia's untamed and rebellious hair, leaving long tendrils to flutter in the air like butterflies.

And those eyes, her glorious blue eyes, alight with excitement as the exotic landscape slid by.

"Cordelia," he said, leaning down and inhaling deeply, an air of sandalwood surrounding him. "Those were just dreams."

He suspected he was saying this more for his benefit than hers, but not even that warning was enough to keep his hands from sliding around her waist and pulling her close.

She fit to him, her mouth opening in surprise as their bodies pressed together.

Cordelia had tumbled back into his life like a lost bird, some faraway bit of brilliant feathers, blown off course by intemperate storms. Out of place, but no less in need of shelter.

And his arms became that protective haven.

"Kipp?"

Her words came out of her in a whisper. A question or a request?

He made his own distinction and leaned down and captured her lips with his and found that Cordelia Padley brought with her a tempest unlike any other.

Her dewy mouth opened to him and the adventure began.

He explored her slowly, letting his tongue tease over her lips, caress her gently, while he pulled her closer, his hand at the curve of her hip, sliding over that rounded bluff, eager to find the other side, even as she stumbled into him, crashing against him like a floundering ship caught between the tide and the rocks.

Holding her tight, he steadied her, running his hands over her until he found the rising swell of her breast, his kiss deepening as his fingers cupped her, teasing her nipple into a tight point.

"*Oh*," she gasped in surprise, the pleasure nearly purring out of her as her fingers splayed over his chest, climbing to his shoulders and pulling him closer, her hips rocking against him. "Kipp, please—"

But before he could say anything, a wry set of notes piped up behind them, though this time it was no lark.

"She said she was just going around this corner to sketch—"

He and Cordelia wrenched apart immediately, but it was too

late, for as they turned in unison, there was a gaping Mrs. Harrington in the middle of the road. And to Kipp's horror, beside Miss Padley's companion stood Drew, rocking on his heels, hands folded behind his back, grinned widely as if he had just discovered a delicious secret.

Which, of course, he had.

"My, my, this hardly looks like sketching to me," he remarked. "Don't you agree, Mrs. H?"

CORDELIA TOOK ANOTHER step back from Kipp, opening up a gulf between them.

His horrified expression only served to make the entire situation worse.

Good heavens, had kissing her been that horrible?

She pressed her lips together and tried to still the last bit of a shiver running down her spine.

He'd kissed her.

And here she'd thought rounding the Cape in a hurricane couldn't be matched.

For her insides were just as tossed about, and she was just as dizzy—but in a decidedly different manner.

How could it not be?

It was exactly like watching a storm approach from the deck of a ship. Those anxious moments when she didn't know if he was going to or not . . . And then . . .

Oh, the joy of his lips crashing hard against hers, the way he'd teased her to open up to him.

And she had let him explore her lips. However could she not?

After all she'd been the one to insist on the inclusion of Rule 18. But at eight she'd been dreaming of some chaste peck on the cheek, not how his tongue teased her, his breath whispered over her, not how she'd want to inhale every bit of pleasure he offered.

His lips . . . His hands . . .

He'd pulled her close, the palm of his hand curved around her hip, while the other pressed at the small of her back—and then it slowly, languidly explored her, cupping her breast, leaving her gasping breathlessly as his touch left her a tangled, trembling mess of desires.

He'd surrounded her and she'd surrendered without a fight.

Why wouldn't she when it had all been so perfectly, well, *perfect*. That is, until . . .

She glanced over at Kate, who was doing her best to look furious, but the wavering tip of her mouth, the flutter of red fringe on her shawl, and the bit of sparkle to her eyes suggested that she rather approved of her charge's ruinous behavior.

Nor was there any doubt what Drew thought. He grinned his approval from ear to ear. Of course he would approve.

But his opinion hardly mattered.

In fact the only one that did was Kipp's, and to her horror, the look on his face, one of shock and dismay, said all too clearly that he regretted his rash behavior.

Completely.

A hot rush of mortification ran through her, and she had to imagine her cheeks were as bright as Kate's shawl.

"Yes, well, I assume supper is ready," Cordelia said, doing her best to look anywhere but at Kipp.

Especially not at *him*.

She quickly gathered her things and swept past the earl and the others without a glance back. One horrible, wrenching question chased her all the way back to the inn: What was worse?

The mortification of coming clean to her aunts and friends that her "betrothal" was a lie . . . or seeing that look of regret in Kipp's stony expression after he'd kissed her?

Chapter 5

*S*ir Brandon Warrick glanced out the window of the inn wondering at the sight before him—of a young lady rushing across the yard, but more to the point was the gentleman following hot on her heels.

He blinked, not trusting his eyes. "What the devil?"

Then the door swung open with a loud bang and a rather extraordinary miss came bustling through the common room in a state of some dishabille and looking as if she was in a rare mood.

She didn't pause, didn't glance around, but went straight through the room toward the back where he knew the innkeeper had private rooms for dining.

The door banged open again, and this time the gentleman came bolting inside. "Cordelia! Cordelia, come back here." He paused for a second, muttering a curse under his breath.

Brandon gaped for he'd never seen Thornton—proper, dull Thornton—in such a state.

"Did you see which way Miss Padley went?" the earl asked the innkeeper's wife as she came out of the kitchen.

Nay, demanded.

The ruddy-faced woman, used to the high-handed ways of the

nobility, just tipped her head. "In back, milord. In the room where I've set your supper."

The earl nodded. "Could you see we're not disturbed?"

"As you wish, milord."

And then Thornton was gone in a flash, much like the young lady had been before him.

Brandon shook his head. "How bloody curious," he said to himself, only to find he wasn't as alone as he'd thought.

"What is curious?"

He turned to find a tall, stately woman in an elegant traveling gown of dark blue silk and a long red shawl tossed haphazardly over her shoulders—as if it was an afterthought—looking him over with a practiced, beguiling air.

Brandon, who considered himself quite the man about town, tripped over his tongue at the sight of this unexpected and truly magnificent creature. "That is . . . I mean to say . . ."

The mature beauty glanced up from fixing her gloves and swept a measured gaze over him, the sort that left a man wondering if he met her discerning and experienced standards. "Yes, well," she managed, looking—to his horror—a bit bored. "Did you see a young lady go bolting through here?"

Brandon blinked. "Pardon?"

"A young lady," she prompted. Her full lips turned slightly in a smile as if she was used to leaving men in this state of intoxication.

A young lady? Oh yes, then he remembered. The odd creature Thornton had been chasing after.

"I did," he replied, leaving his answer as teasing as her snubbing glances.

And his spare words did the trick, for now she smiled in acknowledgment.

Ah, yes, two could play this game.

"I fear I've lost my charge. Headstrong young lady, to be certain. Did you happen to see which way she went?"

"You mean Miss Padley?"

This widened her dark eyes. "Why yes. Do you know her, Lord . . ." She paused to let him make a proper introduction.

Well, as proper as one could, given the circumstances. But Brandon didn't think this particular lady took much stock in rules.

He bowed. "Sir Brandon Warrick, at your service."

"Sir Brandon," she replied, weighing the name much as she had him when she'd first glanced at him. "How is it that you know Miss Padley, if I may ask?"

"I don't."

Her brows quirked slightly. "Then—"

"Lord Thornton asked the landlady if she'd seen where Miss Padley went. Then again, the more germane question would be, whatever put that poor chit in such a hurry, don't you agree?"

"No, I don't," she replied. "But Lord Thornton followed her, did he?"

Brandon nodded.

"And he's with her now?"

"He is." Brandon moved from the window. "I must admit, I'm surprised to see the earl so far from London. I was under the impression that he'd meant to stay until the end of the season."

"Obviously he changed his mind."

Obviously. So what the devil was going on?

Brandon had to know.

The lady moved toward the stairs, then glanced over her shoulder at him. "Do you know the earl?"

"I do."

After a bit of a pause, she nodded for him to continue.

"You could say we have a mutual interest."

As in Miss Pamela Holt. The heiress had strung Brandon along all season, and only until recently had she made it clear that a baronet was not high enough for her aspirations and that someone else had gained her affections . . . or rather, her large dowry.

The lucky bastard being the Earl of Thornton.

Brandon had left town if only to lick his wounds, but it seemed his concession might have been a bit premature.

"How is it that the earl knows Miss Padley—I only ask because they seem to be quite . . . *close.*"

The lady shrugged off his intimation. "Only because they are old and dear friends."

"I'm just a bit confused—for I've never met Miss Padley and I thought I knew all the young ladies—"

"She's just returned from India."

"India, you say?" Brandon took another glance down the hall. That explained a lot. The outlandish clothes, and Thornton's pursuit.

He'd bet his last shilling this Miss Padley was an heiress. She had to be.

"The devil take him," he muttered unwittingly.

"Pardon?" The lady had removed her shawl and tossed it over her arm, the fringe catching the last bit of daylight coming in through the window.

Brandon shook his head and lined up his wits. If Thornton was here . . . and Pamela was still in London . . . "Am I to assume you and Miss Padley are with the earl?"

Oh, the lady didn't misunderstand. "Indeed. Lord Thornton is being so kind as to escort us to the Duke of Dorset's wedding. Miss Padley and Miss Brabourne are old school friends."

Brandon did the math quickly. Thornton would most likely be gone for a sennight, quite possibly a fortnight.

"How fortuitous," he remarked.

"I don't see how," the woman replied, appearing to have grown quite bored with the conversation. "I say, are you staying the night, Sir Brandon?"

There was a bit of an invitation to her question, which he regrettably had to ignore.

"No, I fear not, my dear lady. It appears I must return to London more quickly than I had planned." But then again, being one who always hedged his bets, he added, "If only I had more time to make your acquaintance," he told her, gathering up her hand and bringing it to his lips. "Lady—?"

"*Mrs.* Harrington," she told him, slowly sliding her hand free of his grasp.

"My compliments to Mr. Harrington," he replied, bowing again.

"If he ever turns up, I shall inform him," she replied before she gathered her shawl back around her shoulders and made her way toward the back of the inn.

OH YES, A simple false betrothal. What harm could come of that?

Kipp groaned. None, if one didn't falter along the way and start kissing one's *faux* bride-to-be.

As he turned the corner into the private parlor, his gaze claimed only one sight: Cordelia, her back to the door.

To him, actually.

He raked a hand through his hair and wondered how he'd gotten himself into this mess. That is, until he realized how nicely her figure was silhouetted by the light from the fire.

Curved and rounded. Soft and yielding. So perfectly fitted to him that he suddenly saw himself kissing her yet again, but this time in his bed with his body covering hers.

He drew in a long breath to steady his once again hammering heart.

Well, he had the answer to his original question.

And, yes, he'd rather overstepped the boundaries of their arrangement.

She glanced over her shoulder at him, and the furrow between her brows said much. *You should never have kissed me.*

Rule 18, or otherwise.

Especially when now it was all he could think of.

"Cordelia." Her name came out in a whisper, for fear he'd startle her. And he'd have to watch her bolt away from him yet again.

Taking his heart with her.

No, it isn't that dire, he tried telling himself. *It was . . .*

Well, he didn't know what it was, but he was certain of one thing. "I apologize for being so . . .," he began. "So . . ."

Happy to have kissed you?

Willing to do it again?

"Highly improper," he settled on instead.

"It was?"

"Yes," he asserted. For her. And himself.

She turned and huffed a sigh. "Oh bother. I suppose it was."

She supposed?

"Yes, quite improper," he repeated. Again, he suspected, more for himself.

"You needn't worry, my lord," she told him. "I am not offended."

"You aren't?"

She smiled slightly. "I know you were just doing your duty as a member of the Royal Society."

Duty? That was rather the last thing he would call kissing Cordelia.

"Yes, well, you might've rushed things a bit," she was saying. "I am hardly a spinster . . . Yet."

He looked up and saw her there in the firelight, looking perfectly kissable yet again. "No, you are certainly no spinster." His boot wavered, as if trying to prod him into closing the distance between them and kissing her yet again.

Nor was that the only part of him wavering with need.

"I'm so sorry," he said, straightening and reminding himself who he was.

Not that she helped. "I wish you wouldn't be."

He had to suppose that was the most honest thing either of them had said in the last five minutes.

Still . . .

"As a gentleman, and you being a young lady in my care and protection, I fear I overstepped . . . I might have led you . . ."

"Led me?" Cordelia huffed, this time with no small measure of indignation. "Stop right there, my lord. My feet are my own—as are my choices. I'm not some flibbertigibbet to be ruined by some passing fancy. So I beg of you to give your conscience a rest. For my part, I've all but forgotten what passed between us."

She had? "You have?"

"Of course," she replied, crossing the room and stopping before the table where the platters for dinner were waiting. She plucked up one of the covers and inspected the fare. Then glanced over her shoulder. "I thank you for doing your duty, but we must remember our arrangement is a fiction."

"Yes, quite," he agreed.

She nodded. "We need only deceive my aunts and not allow some passing fancy to steer us off course. Why, what if we were caught—"

Which they had been, but she seemed determined to ignore that simple fact.

"Oh yes," he agreed. "Caught. Quite right."

"I assume that's why you looked so horrified," she added. "Because you thought we might have to get—"

Married.

To his shock, it was Cordelia who shuddered. "Oh heavens, that would be dreadful."

His gaze wrenched up. "It would be?"

"Of course," she told him. "I don't want to get married. That is the entire point of this ruse."

After a season of being chased by marriage-minded misses, Kipp wasn't too sure he'd heard her correctly. "It is?"

"Yes," she insisted. "Why else would I do all this?"

Why else, indeed.

"You are such a dear to help me out of this predicament." And then she crossed the room and took his hand in hers. "Oh, Kipp, I couldn't do this without you."

And there it was. The two of them connected yet again, and they were so close, it made it impossible to think straight. To remember this was a ruse. He glanced down at her, her gaze meeting his, lashes fluttering and her mouth opening slightly.

She looked to be about to say something more, but stopped herself, smiling at a spot just beyond his shoulder. "Oh, Kate, there you are. I suppose you are devilishly peckish, and here is supper all laid out." She'd let go of his hand, and that unnerving sense of being connected to her began to evaporate.

That didn't stop his fingers from curling into a fist, as if he could hold on to something so ethereal, yet all he grasped was a sense of emptiness.

And then Cordelia turned back to him and asked, "My lord, are you hungry?"

Hungry? He would hardly call the gnawing feeling inside him that. In truth, all her kiss had left him was starving for more.

As KATE AND Drew came into the drawing room, Cordelia put her back to all of them.

Especially Kipp.

She only hoped he didn't see the lie behind her bravado.

What had she been thinking? A false betrothal. And with Kipp, no less.

She'd have been better off hiring some fellow off the street or from the nearest public house.

Because for all his proper maneuverings and speeches, he was, at his heart, still her Kipp.

His kiss had proved that much.

And yet.

Her fingers curled into a fist, trying to hold on to the last bit of warmth from his hands.

What foolish thing had she said?

I've all but forgotten what passed between us.

How easy it had been to say those words.

But that wasn't the truth. For what had passed between them had started years ago when she'd climbed the wall between their yards and they'd forged a fast friendship.

And she'd never forgotten a day of it. Hours spent curled up in one of the big chairs in his father's library taking turns reading from travelogues of China. Writing the charter for the Royal Society of Explorers. Planning their navigation of the Nile. How warm and safe she'd felt there with him, how they fit together in that grand chair had seemed to foretell how they would fit together always.

That is until she'd left London with her parents destined for Egypt and he had been slated for the navy.

Even then she'd vowed to never forget. And now? Well, she had to add one more memory to that treasure trove.

For it would be impossible to ever forget how it had felt to be entwined in Kipp's arms.

"WHATEVER IS THE matter with you?" Drew asked about an hour into their travels the very next morning. "You've been brooding like Aunt Nabby since last night."

"This entire venture is a bad idea." Kipp glanced over his shoulder at the carriage behind them.

"You've just realized that?" Drew shook his head. "Rather late for recriminations, don't you think? Or would you rather be back in town being paraded about by Miss Holt like a winner's cup?"

Kipp flinched a bit at the suggestion. Especially because that was exactly what would have happened had he ignored Cordelia's request and gotten down on bended knee before Miss Holt.

Unwittingly, he shuddered.

"Yes, yes, I can see why you're so dismal," Drew laughed, nudging his horse a bit and smiling up at the sunshine that bathed the road ahead. "Such a dreadful fix we've found ourselves in."

"Speak for yourself," he replied. "I might very well have thrown aside a union that could restore Mallow Hills. Save our family from ruin."

To his dismay, Drew looked more bored than alarmed. But then again Drew always looked like that when Kipp tried to impress upon him the seriousness of the situation.

"Hardly. She'll be there when we return," Drew replied. "I'm just glad I get to see Mallow Hills this one last time."

"Whatever do you mean? The house is hardly going anywhere."

"It won't be the same once that chit gets her claws into it."

"It isn't like the house couldn't use some work," Kipp pointed out.

"Yes, but will she see the importance of your new roof or ditches or fences, or improvements to the cottages for the tenants, or will she take one look at the long hall, banish every bit of family history to the attics or worse—the dustbin. I wager she'll have half the house gutted before the ink is dry on your marriage license."

"She'll hardly do all that," Kipp shot back, though a harrowing vision of the Holts' gilded parlor flitted before him once again like an unholy specter of his future.

"We'll see." His nonchalant shrug suggested such a future was far more set in stone than Kipp wanted to believe. Nor was his brother done. "Speaking of Miss Holt, whatever were you doing dallying with Miss Padley?"

"I was hardly—"

"Hardly, nothing," Drew shot back. "Either kissing her wasn't to your liking—"

"Drew," the earl warned.

"O-r-r-r—" his brother said drawing his speculations out. "Unfortunately, it was very much to your liking."

They rode in silence for a bit and eventually Kipp couldn't help himself, he took another glance back at the carriage. "It was a momentary lapse in judgment."

Drew nodded. "If it were merely that, you wouldn't be in such a mood."

"I'm not in a mood," he snapped. Taking a deep breath, he did his best to compose himself. "It is just that she's—"

"Miss Padley?"

"Yes, of course, Miss Padley—"

Drew grinned. "Miss Holt would never put you in such a passion."

"Miss Holt would never profess a desire to go jaunting off to Africa."

Drew shook his head, as if he hadn't quite heard his brother correctly. "Africa?"

"Yes," Kipp replied. "Miss Padley thinks she should be able to gallivant off and explore the Nile. Unchaperoned."

Drew laughed. "No, never! Our Miss Padley? How shocking!" His eyes twinkled merrily.

Kipp groaned. Oh, this was going nowhere. "Miss Holt would never consider such an improper notion."

Drew barked a laugh. "Good God, no! I doubt Miss Holt could even find Africa on a map . . . of Africa."

Kipp's lips twitched, despite his best efforts to remain stern and proper. "Drew—"

Unrepentant as ever, his brother replied, "Well, she couldn't."

Yes, well, be that as it may . . .

"It is just that Miss Padley and Miss Holt couldn't be more different."

Drew snorted. "And it took you two days to notice?"

"Of course I noticed," Kipp admitted. "But I never realized how different until yesterday when she started prosing on about going to Africa. Like we were children again. As if I can just jaunt about the world."

But then Drew proved why it was he'd been promoted to captain at such an early age. He could see through the thickest fog, the biggest sham. "You probably gave her your argument about *duty*. And *obligations*."

"Of course. She hasn't the least notion of—" He stopped as Drew's brows rose and he realized his brother had been making a point.

One he pressed home in a level, steady voice that spoke not of a madcap tease, but a world of experience. "I would guess that what you really wanted to say to Cordelia was *When do we leave?*"

"Don't be ridiculous," Kipp replied. "Run off with Miss Padley? Why, that is utter madness."

Drew shrugged. "I suppose it might be if you hadn't already taken the first step. For what the devil are we doing on the Bath road with the lady, if not running away? Or for that matter, what were you doing kissing her last night? That, my dear brother, is the surest road to madness if ever there was one."

WHEN KIPP RODE up alongside the carriage, it was Kate who spoke up first. "My lord, how much farther?"

"Mallow Hills is just ahead, Mrs. Harrington." He looked at Cordelia. "That is, if you don't mind stopping early. We could make Hamilton Hall before nightfall, if we were to press on."

Cordelia shook her head. "No, I wouldn't want to arrive early, it would set everyone in a fuss."

Kate snorted, for she knew what Cordelia really meant.

I don't want to give my aunts any additional time to winkle out the truth.

For her part, Cordelia ignored her companion. "I'm thrilled to finally see the infamous Talcott home. Besides, I am most desirous of seeing the dungeon."

"The wha-a-at?" Kipp managed.

"The dungeon," she repeated, slanting a glance at him. "You once swore it was the deepest, darkest hole in all of England, and, if I recall correctly, half filled with the bones of traitors."

Kipp straightened and looked up at the road. "Yes, well, I might have exaggerated a bit."

"Might have?" she teased. She couldn't help herself. As much as she wanted to forget his kiss, every time she looked at him, she found herself filled with a dangerous, restless need.

"I was eight," he said.

She shrugged at his defense.

"What about you?" he ventured. "Did you ever tame a crocodile?"

"No," she told him, as if she would ever utter such foolishness.

"Ah, but you said—"

"Yes, well, I was eight as well."

They both laughed, and then Kipp rode ahead of the carriage.

Kate slanted a long glance at her.

"What?" Cordelia asked, feeling as if she was being pinned to the carriage seat for some unspoken crime.

Apparently she was.

"You are flirting with that man."

She scrambled to sit up straight. "I am not."

Her denial hardly seemed to change Kate's opinion. "Have a care, my dear, or you will find yourself caught and then—"

Caught . . . Oh, that conjured up such wonderful images. Caught in his arms. Caught with his kiss. *Caught.*

But instead, she decided to set the record straight. "I will have you know, Lord Thornton and I discussed that very matter last night before supper and we have agreed that any such . . . perception of wrongdoing would be disastrous." When she glanced over to see if her words had any effect on Kate—which it appeared they hadn't—she hastily added, "For both of us."

"You discussed this . . . with Lord Thornton?" Her companion shook her head as if she'd never heard such folly. "Oh good heavens, how utterly civilized of you."

"You make that sound like a bad thing."

"And was it?" Kate asked.

"Was what?"

"Kissing the earl? Was it a bad thing?"

"It was only a kiss," Cordelia said. She had rather hoped that Kate and Captain Talcott hadn't seen that.

"Was it?" Kate pressed.

"It was simply a kiss." A perfectly wonderful one.

"Hmm." Kate sat and watched the countryside pass by for a few moments before she spoke again. "And he means nothing to you?"

"No. Well, yes. In the sense that we are old friends, but certainly not in the way that you are implying."

"If I were you, I'd do my best to turn this false engagement into a real one."

Oh, not this again. "Don't be ridiculous." Cordelia shook her head. And again, her objection was met with silence. "He's too stuffy and hardly the man I once knew."

Except when he's kissing me . . .

Not that she was going to confess to *that*.

Just then, the carriage turned off the road and lurched as it hit the rutted drive.

"Goodness," Kate exclaimed, catching hold of the strap. Once she'd gotten herself settled back in her seat, she looked out the window. "Well, this is rather disappointing."

"What is?"

"His house. I do hope there is more to it than just a dungeon."

"Whatever do you mean?" Cordelia scooted over and looked out the window as well, but the sight that she saw was hardly as dreadful as Kate was making it out to be—rather a grand old relic exactly as he'd described it. "Oh, Kate, it is perfect. Most picturesque."

Kate deigned to look again as they pulled up toward the front. "It needs a new roof."

The carriage came to a stop and the front doors of the house swung open. A stout, older lady came down the steps, hurrying forward, a broad smile on her face.

"Oh my gracious heavens! Lord Thornton! And Master Andrew. Oh, you dreadful scamps. Arriving like this and not warning me. I haven't anything ready."

Drew opened the door to the carriage and warned them. "Mrs. Abbott, our housekeeper. Prepare to be smothered."

Behind him, there was a loud snort. "Whatever are you going on about, Master Andrew?" Mrs. Abbott demanded. And then she spotted that the carriage held guests. "And I daresay Cook is going to be in a fret. She'll not like this in the least." Then the woman's eyes lit on Cordelia. Her mouth fell open and she clapped her hands together. "Truly, is it so? Lord Thornton, you've finally gone and proposed to Miss Holt and here she is!"

Chapter 6

Once they were alone in their rooms, Cordelia turned to Kate. "Who is Miss Holt?"

Kate paused as she was untying the ribbon on her bonnet. "The young lady the earl intends to marry."

Her companion said this as if it was common knowledge.

"Yes, yes, I gathered all that, but—" Obviously if Cordelia had known that Kipp was . . . well, was about to . . .

"But what?" Kate asked, having removed her bonnet and looking about for somewhere to set it.

"If he is betrothed—" Cordelia didn't want to finish that sentence. Because if anyone at Anne's wedding knew that the Earl of Thornton intended to marry someone else . . . why, it put her entire plan in ruins. Not to mention . . . "It's just that—"

She couldn't put the rest of that into words. *It's just that I rather like him. Could very well fall in love with him.*

Might have done so already.

Kate, having settled her monstrous hat atop the dressing table, paused as she surveyed the room yet again. "The plain fact is that he is not engaged to this Miss Holt."

"Are you certain?" Those words rushed out a little too quickly. Too hopeful, for they sent Kate's brows arching up.

She brushed out her gown and smiled slowly. "Most certain."

"How do you know? His housekeeper seemed quite convinced."

"Yes, well, housekeepers do like to gossip. However, poor Mrs. Abbott hasn't had a chance to hear Captain Talcott's version of the events." Kate sat down in the overupholstered chair in the corner, kicking her feet up on the footstool and making herself comfortable. "Or lack thereof. What a dear man, your Andrew. A veritable font of knowledge."

Cordelia ignored the purring notes in the woman's voice and sat on the corner of the bed. Kate had a terrible affinity for gossip and innuendo . . . and men. At least she hoped the woman's interest in Drew was just more of the former and not the latter.

"So why would Mrs. Abbott think Kipp, er, His Lordship, was about to be married?"

Now who was fishing about for gossip?

"Because apparently Lord Thornton was about to propose to Miss Holt."

This got her attention. "What changed his mind?"

"You," Kate told her, once again all matter-of-fact. "He was planning on proposing to her the very day you came calling. And instead gave the lady some excuse about a long-held promise of assistance and fled London." Satisfied with the expression of shock on Cordelia's face, her companion got back up and strolled over to her trunk and began to sort the gowns inside.

Cordelia chewed at her lower lip, trying to make sense of all this. "Why ever would he do that?"

"Maybe he's not in love with the chit," Kate replied as she shook out a day dress. "Though from all accounts this Miss Holt is a beauty, what one used to call a Diamond. That, and she comes with a *fortune*."

But Cordelia had stopped listening, stuck on the notion of this so-called Diamond back in London.

A Diamond, indeed. She huffed a bit. That was something no one would ever call her.

Meanwhile, Kate continued on. "If I were to speculate, I'd say your earl panicked. In my experience, the very idea of marriage sends most men tumbling down a rabbit hole."

Cordelia tugged at the tangled ribbons of her bonnet and only succeeded in putting them in a dreadful coil.

Rather like her life.

"I can understand if he doesn't want to get married," she said, trying to sound nonchalant.

"Well, from the looks of things around here, it seems he must." Kate sniffed.

Cordelia stilled. "What does that mean?"

"Haven't you looked around? The threadbare carpets. The ancient furnishings. Those old curtains." She sniffed at the faded hangings beside the long mullioned windows. "Your earl is in search of a fortune, and unless you have one tucked away, he will need to marry for money."

"No, I fear I haven't any such boon." Just enough for her to live independently, albeit frugally.

"How unfortunate," Kate said, with a slip of her shoulder. "Especially when it seems you and the earl suit. That, and I'd rather hoped you'd given up these ridiculous notions of independence and adventures and decided to marry the man."

Marry Kipp? Cordelia balked. Her bonnet strings were now thoroughly snarled—much as she was trapped in a scheme of her own design.

And worst of all—Kipp was on the verge of marrying someone else.

Someone rich *and* pretty. And most likely, well-mannered and content to live the life of an English lady. In England. Without any thought of going to Africa. Or the far-flung shores of China.

She groaned—mostly from the realization that she'd never be able to untangle her bonnet strings; well, mostly that—or it might be because she had no idea where her scissors were packed. Instead, Cordelia resorted to yanking the bloody thing off.

She sighed when it came free, shaking her head with relief at not having that confounded piece of trumpery smothering her.

Free of her bonnet, yes. Free of Kate? One glance at the other woman said all too clearly her companion was not going to let this subject rest.

"I'm going to find a cup of tea," Cordelia announced, in haste and no small measure of panic.

"They have servants for that," Kate told her as she bolted for the door.

"I've made do most of my life, I daresay I can continue to do so now," Cordelia told her.

Without a husband, she wanted to add.

Since it seemed the only man she'd ever wanted was destined for another.

KIPP SHUDDERED AS he recalled the look of shock on Cordelia's face as Mrs. Abbott's inadvertent words had laid his secret wide open.

"Got to face her eventually," Drew said, nudging him up the stairs, though as it turned out, his brother's prodding was unnecessary, for here she was hurrying down the steps.

When Kipp glanced back, he discovered his brother had slipped away, leaving him all alone.

He didn't know who was the worse coward—him or Drew.

But then again, he wasn't the one who'd agreed to this imbroglio.

"I was just coming up to see—" he began, looking at her shoes rather than meeting her eyes.

"Everything is . . . the room is . . . most satisfactory."

He flinched. She sounded so stiff and so formal. So not Cordelia. He wrenched his gaze up and found her looking away. "I'm so sorry, Cordelia. For all of it."

For kissing you. For enjoying it far too much.

But he could hardly say that. Instead, he continued lamely on. At least it sounded so to his ears. "I meant to tell you—" He faltered and then steeled his last bit of courage. "About Miss Holt, that is."

"It matters not. I wish you well." Her words were a crisp knot that tied up everything.

Yet that wasn't quite the case and he suddenly had to tell her the rest. "It isn't settled. Or even certain she'll accept me—"

Cordelia turned toward him. "She'd be a fool not to—" The words came blurting out. Not so much words, but a confession of sorts.

He warmed inside. "I'm not that great of a catch—"

She huffed at this, and got straight to the heart of the matter. "Do you love her?"

Now it was his turn to confess. "No."

"Then why—"

"I must." He raked a hand through his hair. "I don't think you'd understand."

But this was Cordelia and she wasn't one to let a problem lay unresolved. "Then show me. Help me to understand."

Show her? Show her just how his forebears had brought low this once prosperous and respected estate? But then again . . . "Actually it's rather obvious."

Cordelia's brows knit together. "What is?"

"The estate. It's in ruins."

She glanced around. "Oh, hardly that. You have a roof—"

"A roof in need of repairs."

She laughed at that. "Kate said the same thing when we arrived. I fear I don't know much about estates. But I assume all roofs need repairs eventually."

He laughed as well. For there was one thing you could count on—Cordelia being practical to a fault. "Yes, I suppose so."

"Show me what makes you feel so compelled to sacrifice your heart and then I'll see if you deserve forgiveness." She held out her hand and he couldn't help himself, he took it, her fingers twining intimately with his, warm and strong, just like the lady.

He led her toward the doors to the garden and she stopped, digging in her heels. "Kipp?"

"Yes?"

She glanced shyly at him. "Can we start with the secret passageway to the dungeon?"

"Hardly," he told her, pulling her toward the French doors that led out to the gardens near the overgrown roses. "That is like having cake before supper."

"I've never seen anything wrong with that arrangement," she muttered under her breath.

SOME HOURS LATER, Cordelia stepped out of the secret passageway into a large, sunny room.

A vast library, to be exact.

She glanced back over her shoulder as the door closed, and it looked just like the rest of the paneling, impossible to discern.

"So there it is," Kipp was saying. "The dungeon and secret passage, as described. Does it meet with your approval?"

"Oh yes," she enthused. "That is the finest secret passage I have ever seen. Or explored."

"How many have you seen?"

"That is the first," she confessed. "So it wins easily."

Kipp laughed as Cordelia set off for the middle of the room, turning this way and that as she took in the collection of volumes.

"Oh, how glorious," she said, awestruck. Then she fisted her hands to her hips and faced him. "You never told me about *this*!"

"I like to keep *this* all to myself."

"Midas hoarding his treasure," she accused before turning to scan one of the shelves. "Oh goodness, is this Halladay's account of China? Does he add anything to the speculation of what happened to Captain Wood?"

Kipp shook his head. "You are the only woman alive who would ask such a question."

She tucked her nose up. "I would think an expedition that disappeared without a trace would be of interest to everyone." Her fingers traced over the volumes shelved there. "*Canton, A Traveler's History*. Oh, doesn't the very name, Canton, fill you with the desire to see the emperor's pavilions? Sir George went when he was only twelve."

"He was also a linguistic savant."

"Some people have all the luck," she replied. "Oh, and here are McTavish's accounts of the wilds of Canada."

"From the Nile to China to Canada," Kipp said, coming to stand beside her. "Is there no end to your curiosity?"

Cordelia glanced up at him in a bit of surprise. "No, of course not. The world is meant to be explored. To be seen. And I am determined to see as much as I can. Don't you still share that desire?"

He shook his head. "No, I suppose I don't."

"No? But—"

"Didn't you see the lands, the fields?"

"Yes, they're quite lovely, but I don't see—"

"And quite empty. And far too neglected. Something should have been done ages ago."

"But a steward could—"

"No!" His answer was so emphatic she paused. "That is exactly why the fields are undrained. The fences falling down. The cottages in such dire straits. They've been neglected for far too long."

"But . . ." She glanced out the window. "If you had the money—"

"If. Wishes do not repair fences." He heaved a sigh. "Perhaps in time. Once I've seen things brought to rights, or as Drew says, steered true. But until then . . ."

"Oh, Kipp—"

"None of that," he told her. "I won't have it. If I don't pity my position, then no one else should."

"Is it also your duty to give up your dreams?"

"Have you ever considered, Cordelia, that my dreams have changed?"

She took a step back, for it was the last thing she expected to hear.

He wanted to be here.

"And this Miss Holt can do all that—fix your fences and patch the roofs."

"Yes."

Cordelia thought that sounded dreadfully dull. "I so hate to think of you trapped by all this. The thought of you giving up."

"I don't think of it that way. Not any longer." He took her hand and pulled her away from the stories that held other people's adventures. "Come, let me show you something."

They crossed the room to a large table covered in rolls and stacks of papers.

Kipp sorted through them until he found a large sheet. He spread it out for her to see, trapping the corners with an inkwell and paperweights.

Cordelia's gaze danced over the drawing before her. "I thought you didn't make maps any longer."

"Yes, well, I was just dabbling a bit," he told her.

"This is hardly dabbling," she said, turning so the light streaming in from the long windows illuminated his work. "This is here— Mallow Hills, isn't it? Oh yes, it must be, for there is that beautiful little meadow we crossed." She turned to him and grinned.

"It is," he told her. "There is an old map of the lands—" He began picking through the sheets. "Ah, here it is. It isn't much, so last summer I thought to try my hand."

She beamed at the drawing. "You've done an amazing job. But it needs color."

He shook his head. "I haven't the talent for that, but you are correct, the right touches would bring it to life."

Cordelia went back to studying his map, with the focused gaze of an artist. "Did you survey the property yourself?"

He nodded. "I thought I knew it from memory, but it is so different to go out and walk the land, to see every detail, every problem from all the angles. A steward can't do that for me."

His words held a note of urgency and deep longing. She bit her lip for a moment and then glanced up at him, a sense of guilt tugging at her. "I do hope my request doesn't put you out with Miss Holt."

"No, I hardly think a week or two will matter. As it is, nothing is settled, so she has no real claim on my time."

On my heart.

But he didn't say that. That was just her own wishful thinking. "If it does become a problem, you can tell her I simply borrowed you," Cordelia teased.

"Borrowed?" He barked out a laugh. "Is that all I am—a volume from the lending library?"

She smiled slyly at him. "Eventually I will have to give you back."

"Yes, of course," he said, trying to sound nonchalant about their arrangement. *Temporary arrangement,* he reminded himself.

"Is she in love with you? Miss Holt?"

"I doubt she's in love—well, let me preface that—she's in love with the idea of being a titled lady. She has her heart set on it. If I were to guess, she's a bit disappointed that she's having to make due with a mere earl—it was much talked of earlier this season that despite her origins, she'd land a duke or a marquess."

"Because she has a fortune?"

"Yes, that and she's quite the renowned beauty."

"Have you drawn her?" She reached for a sketchbook, but he stopped her.

"Oh good heavens, no. She'd find that the height of impertinence. That, and I don't think she'd like the notion of her future husband doing anything so bohemian as sketching. She prefers to imagine me making grand speeches in the House of Lords, or sitting at the head of a large dinner party where she is the crown jewel of hostesses."

"And you do those sorts of things?"

"I must," he replied.

"Yes, I suppose so." Cordelia glanced around, for this was unfamiliar territory to her—her own parents had only been interested in the arts and sciences. "Miss Holt's father, is he in politics?"

"No. He's a *cit.* A very rich one. And he wants a son-in-law who can help along his business interests."

Cordelia glanced back at the map, retracing the paths they'd just explored. "And her money, rather her father's money, will do all this?"

"Yes, all that and more."

However, Kipp's gaze was set on the very real gardens and meadows beyond the windows. "My family has been here at Mallow Hills since the reign of King Edward. Kings and queens have visited this house. It was always a source of great pride for the Talcotts. And I want it to be that again. Not just some sad relic. An empty pile of stones." He paused and turned to her. "You could say I have my own sort of adventure ahead of me. Restoring Mallow Hills will be as much an adventure as exploring the Nile."

Cordelia didn't know what to say.

But Kipp did.

"Besides, this is my *home*."

My home . . .

Those words haunted Cordelia as she went upstairs to change for supper.

My home.

She'd never had one of those.

Oh yes, one might argue she did. The town house in London. Though she'd only lived in it off and on until she was nine—for her parents had always been traveling, off on one or another adventure. Never staying anywhere too long.

For a time, when she'd been at Madame Rochambeaux's, Cordelia had started to understand what that elusive word meant.

Home.

Not just the roof over one's head, a shelter for the night, but a true home. Surrounded by those dearest to you. A sense of shared history.

Anne, Elinor, and Bea. They were like sisters to her. And even Madame Rochambeaux, for all her failings, was the closest thing to a mother Cordelia had ever known.

Not even her aunts' house—where she and her friends had spent several summers—had come close, for it had been very much their domain.

So when Kipp had said with such certainty, such depth, that this, Mallow Hills, was *his home*, she'd had a glimpse into what he meant, for evidence of it was everywhere. The portraits of the previous earls that lined the halls—where she could clearly see hints and echoes of Kipp's handsome features staring back at her.

And as she curled up into a lonely ball in the large grand bed, she chewed at her lower lip and considered her own history.

Her family hadn't such deep roots, her father being only the second baronet, the title now lost in time since there was no male heir to carry it forward, no roots that held it in the past or for future generations to cultivate.

Even if she had all the money in the world, it would never purchase what Kipp held in those two simple words.

My home.

And while she might never be able to claim a place in his realm, she slipped out of bed and tiptoed her way downstairs, determined to leave her mark somewhere, in the only way she knew how.

Chapter 7

Mayfair, London

"She let him get away from town without closing the deal," Mr. Josiah Holt complained in a voice loud enough to carry to the other side of London.

As it was, even if he'd whispered his opinion, Pamela would have wanted to sink beneath her chair. It was bad enough Lord Thornton had fled town right at a time when there should be a very specific announcement being made, but here was her own father lamenting her failure at supper, and in front of their guest.

Yes, yes, it was only Sir Brandon, or as her father liked to call him, "her back-pocket swain," meaning that if Thornton didn't come up to snuff, she still had one eligible *parti* in the running, but still . . . it was rather mortifying.

Almost as much as her other major source of embarrassment. Her father.

Rich though he might be, there hadn't been a duke or marquess willing to align himself to such a gruff and ill-mannered *cit* as Josiah Holt.

No matter her dowry.

Pamela dared a glance at their guest and found him smiling at her. The rogue even had the audacity to wink.

Steady on, minx, she could almost hear him saying in his overly familiar manner. But then again, she suspected the baronet rather liked Josiah.

"I must own up, I was surprised to see Thornton on the Bath road," Sir Brandon replied. "For I was quite certain he'd stolen a march on me."

"Bah! I don't understand you fancy fellows," Josiah scolded. "If I want something I stand my ground. Bully my way into the matter. If you want something, you make your wants known and take the advantage."

Sir Brandon tipped his glass in agreement. "I shall remember that, sir."

"You say you saw Lord Thornton on the Bath road?" Pamela asked. "Isn't that the way to his estate?"

"Yes, I believe he was going to stop at Mallow Hills," Sir Brandon told her. "He and his guests."

That last tidbit brought Josiah's attention up from his well-filled plate. "His guests? What's this?"

"I told you, Papa," Pamela said, "Lord Thornton had a matter of honor to take care of. His journey must have taken him toward his estates."

This time it was Sir Brandon who sputtered his surprise. "A matter of wha-a-at?"

"Honor, my lord," Pamela replied. "Lord Thornton was called out of town on a matter of *honor*."

Sir Brandon sat back in his seat, looking all too bemused by the quaint notion. "Are you so certain?"

Up until this moment, Pamela would have staked her rather substantial pin money on the inalienable fact that the earl would ask her to marry him once he returned to London.

But there was something so superior in Sir Brandon's question, in the wry tilt of his brows, that an odd and unfamiliar quake ran through her.

Doubt, one might call it, but it was an uncertain feeling for her, a young lady who'd always been so secure in her wealthy advantages.

"I had it from Lord Thornton himself," she told him in her most lofty of tones. The ones bought and paid for at a respectable Bath school, courtesy of Josiah's ample coins.

"Yes, yes, I got all that flimflam, but if you think Thornton is off on some noble cause, I do hate to be the one to break it to you, my dear Miss Holt, but he's gulled you sorely."

Her fingers wound into the napkin in her lap, but still she straightened slightly, if only to perfect her posture. "You must be wrong, Sir Brandon. The earl is merely assisting an old friend."

"Is that what Miss Padley is? An 'old friend'?"

Miss Padley?

The shock must have shown on her face, because their rakish guest was smiling once again. "So you didn't know about *her*, did you?"

Mr. Holt coughed a bit. "I won't have it, sir. Discussing petticoat matters in front of my daughter."

"I'll assure you, Mr. Holt, Miss Cordelia Padley is no Drury Lane vestal, fetching though she is. Rather, she's the daughter of Sir Horace Padley, quite the respectable scholar and scientist. I wouldn't expect you've heard of him."

The insult passed right over Josiah's head, but Pamela felt the sting of it right down to her imported silk slippers.

Sir Brandon raised his glass, studying the wine as it swirled about. "Lord Thornton is escorting Miss Padley to the Duke of Dorset's wedding. Quite the event. Only the loftiest of guests were invited." He glanced around the table, and again, the slight slid right off Josiah like water off a duck. So he finished with an implication he knew Pamela would understand. "Weddings inspire all sorts of impetuous decisions, don't they, my dear?"

"Kipp! Wake up." His brother's voice wrenched him out of a deep sleep.

"What the devil, Drew. It's barely dawn."

Yet here was his brother already dressed. Most likely had been down to the stables. "Yes, I know, but you must come see this."

"If this is some sort of jest—"

"No, no," he insisted. "But you *must* see this."

There it was. Drew giving orders like he probably had about his packet ship. There would be no rolling back over and returning to that blissful dream of—well, never mind that or even whom it had been about.

Cordelia. All undone and lying on a divan. While he painted her. Teased her. Covered her.

"Kipp!" Drew was already at the door and hand on the latch, as if he had expected his brother to be right at his heels.

As ordered.

"Inside or out?" Kipp asked as he threw off the covers.

"In."

Thank God for small favors. He hardly wanted to be yanking on his boots and finding his pants while there might still be a hope of coming back up and catching an hour or more of sleep.

As it was, he threw on his wrapper and padded after his brother.

When they got to the bottom of the stairs, Drew turned and pressed a finger to his lips, signaling for stealth.

Oh, what the devil was this? He hadn't lurked about the house after his brother since they'd been children.

Whatever could Drew have managed to contrive? And then he saw his answer.

On the divan.

Stretched out much like she had been in his dream. Cordelia. Her hair falling free from its pins and tumbling off the edge of the sofa in a cascade of dark curls. She was fast asleep, as if she hadn't slept in ages.

But that wasn't the end of the mystery. Drew continued deeper into the large room, silent as a cat, charting a straight course to the map table.

Kipp followed, barely able to take his eyes off the sleeping figure. That is, until he spied what had Drew grinning from ear to ear.

He glanced at the table and like the artist he was, realized that it was all out of order, not to mention the collection of small pots of water, brushes, and blocks of color that were not his.

And then he saw it.

Cordelia's work.

Hers and his.

The estate map of Mallow Hills was now brought to life in vivid colors. The green meadows, the darker hues of the forested hills to the north, small bits of yellows and blues and pinks tucked in beside the hedges and fences, just like the wildflowers that grew there. Lines of blue where the streams meandered beside the fields.

Her light touch had brought every corner of the estate to life. She'd even added a hint of a sunrise on the eastern horizon, as if a new day, a new beginning was about to dawn over the ancient estate.

"Remarkable, isn't it?" Drew grinned.

It was. Truly remarkable.

But Kipp saw something else—how the woman who had tramped across the fields with him, gleefully climbed over stiles, and without a hint of trepidation gone through the dank old passageway, had captured all the joy and color of Mallow Hills—preserving it for always.

Whatever would she do in a lifetime?

He glanced over at her, asleep on the divan, and realized she was right at home there. Surrounded by his books, and the old and ancient relics from the various generations of Talcotts.

As if she was meant to be here. Even if she had insisted she was only borrowing him and his world.

Kipp drew in a deep breath. *I don't want to be returned like a book from the lending library. What I want is—*

"Should I fetch Mrs. Harrington or Mrs. Abbott to see to her?" Drew whispered. His brother seemed to sense, as he did, that it would be a crime to wake her up.

"No." For what Kipp wanted to do was to stop the clocks, fix the sun before it crested the horizon.

He never wanted this moment to end.

He wanted Cordelia.

But that was impossible. As impossible as holding back the dawn.

Or was it? As he gazed at her, asleep like a nymph, he found himself reaching for his sketchbook and a pencil, even as he began to catalogue all the things he wanted to capture. Her hair spilling down over her shoulders. The pink hue of her lips pursed together as if awaiting a kiss.

There was something so innocent, so magical about her, the entire world around him faded away as he settled into the chair across from her and began to sketch, barely taking note of Drew murmuring something about seeing to the horses.

That she wasn't his, nor he hers, hardly mattered.

For right now, with all his heart, he'd do anything to hold on to this moment, and he knew exactly how to capture it.

CORDELIA STIRRED SLOWLY awake. After a lifetime of travels with her father, she was used to waking up in strange places, so finding herself tucked into a settee in an unfamiliar room was hardly as unsettling as it might be to someone else.

But what she hadn't expected was to find Kipp sitting across from her, smiling.

"Good morning," he said.

She sat up quickly, swiping the sleep from her eyes and looking around to gain her bearings. Whatever was Kipp doing here in her . . .

Then she remembered, she wasn't in her bedchamber.

She'd come downstairs last night and been . . .

Oh goodness!

"You were up late, I gather," he said, casting a glance toward the map table.

Rubbing at her eyes again, she nodded. "I hope you don't mind—"

It didn't appear that he did, for he was still smiling. "I thought to leave it for you to discover the next time you were here—given we were to make an early start of it today."

"I'm glad I did see it. That I found you." He closed the book he was holding, and it was then she realized he had his sketchbook in hand. Telltale signs of pencil on his fingers and, of course, that guilty furrow to his brow.

Some things never changed. Kipp was just as guilty as she was.

For he'd been drawing her. While she'd slept.

She glanced down at herself, suddenly very conscious of how she must look, what he must have been drawing—including her bare foot sticking out the end of her gown. "Are you going to show me what you've done?"

"No."

"No?"

"Decidedly not," he told her.

Now she was fully awake. "You took advantage of me."

"Hardly," he told her, sitting back and grinning.

Why, of all the cheek! He was as much a rakish devil as his brother under all that proper veneer.

"You were right there in the open," he continued. "The perfect still life. Aphrodite caught unaware."

Aphrodite, indeed! Cordelia snorted at this, and did her best to ignore the slight thrill it gave her to hear him call her "perfect."

A perfect wreck, she had to imagine.

But the light in his eyes smoldered. Actually burned. With a passion that asked to be answered. *Come to me, Cordelia. Let me show you what perfection can be . . .*

Oh, whatever was she thinking? *He's not yours*, she reminded herself. *He's merely borrowed.*

Then again, she considered anew what he'd said. *Aphrodite caught unaware.* That usually meant the lady was . . .

Cordelia glanced again at her bare foot and had to wonder how much more of her leg had been exposed. She thrust out her hand. "I would see what you've drawn."

"As I said, I was drawing Aphrodite." He nodded to a spot just behind her.

And indeed, when she turned, there stood a small statue of the goddess on the table behind her. She blushed, feeling foolish.

Of course he hadn't been talking about her. Hadn't he and Kate both said Miss Holt was a renowned beauty? Why ever would he want to sketch her, plain old Cordelia Padley?

But then Kipp laughed, and stretched as he climbed out of his deep chair, and came to kneel before her. He winked at her, then opened his sketchbook, thumbing through the pages and then turning it toward her.

And to her shock, there she was. Reclined on the sofa, her hair all a mess, falling down every which way. Absently, she reached up to right the errant strands, trying to tuck them into some semblance of order, for the creature in his drawing looked . . . so disheveled . . . so undone.

Dear heavens, was that how he saw her? Wanted to see her?

"Now I have you always," he said, in a sultry whisper that left her shivering—and not because she hadn't any stockings on.

For whatever did one say to such a thing? Well, certainly not the first thing that popped into her thoughts.

I would be yours always if you would have me . . . Take me . . . Love me.

Not that she had to say anything, for Kipp reached out and tucked back a stray strand, his warm fingers curving around the edge of her ear sending tendrils of desire racing through her.

"Cordelia, I want—"

Yet before he could finish, Kate came bustling into the room. "Oh, there you are!" She came to a stop behind Kipp and glanced down at the sketchbook. "Lord Thornton, you've got quite a knack. You've gone and captured her exactly." Kate winked at Cordelia, ever the imperfect chaperone. "Though I do hope she wasn't snoring while you were sketching."

Kipp sat back on his heels as Cordelia bolted to her feet. The heat of a blush rose on her cheeks. Oh heavens, what was worse—

being caught with Kipp in such a way or Kate's indelicate disclosures?

She chose the latter. "I do not snore."

"So you say," the lady replied matter-of-factly.

"Only a little," Kipp teased, though neither lady was truly paying him any heed at the moment.

"Well, no more dawdling about," Kate announced, crooking her finger for Cordelia to follow. "Mrs. Abbott has brought up a lovely tray and is in a state that you aren't there to enjoy it. It truly wasn't to my credit that I couldn't account for you, and you know how I hate to be a subject of gossip."

And with that, Cordelia found herself pulled away from Kipp and led upstairs.

She glanced back at the library. Heavens! What had he been about to say?

Cordelia, I want—

For all she knew, he wanted kippers for breakfast.

"If you don't mean to marry the earl—" Kate began just as they reached the second landing.

Cordelia came to a stop, catching hold of the railing. "Of course I don't—"

She only wished she sounded more convincing. Because she didn't want to get married.

She didn't. Her gaze strayed down the stairs.

Kate made a grand *harrumph*, caught hold of her, and continued pulling her upstairs, lecturing as they went. "Then might I remind you that Lord Thornton isn't your betrothed."

"I know that," Cordelia did her best to look outraged. "I haven't the least idea what you are implying."

She failed miserably, for Kate gave a regal shake of her head. "Cordelia, that man isn't yours to dally with. And very soon he will need to be returned."

"I am well aware of the situation," Cordelia shot back. "I'm the one who came up with it."

"Then I suggest you have a care before any more complications develop," Kate replied, and continued up the stairs in a grand huff.

As if Cordelia needed to be told as much.

Something borrowed must always be returned.

Mustn't it?

CORDELIA HADN'T REALIZED how smitten she'd become with Mallow Hills until they went to leave an hour later.

As she glanced over her shoulder at the timeworn stones, she knew she'd never see these walls again.

Not after Kipp married Miss Holt.

That wrenching twinge in her chest left her wary of Kipp the rest of the day. Well, that and Kate's warning.

He isn't yours. And very soon he will need to be returned.

So when he rode alongside the carriage to point out sights he knew she would find interesting or bring her a stray wildflower or two for her pressing book, she was polite, but aloof.

However had this happened? A few days ago, yes, she'd been curious to see her old friend, but she had merely hoped he'd help her deceive her aunts so she could be on her merry way yet again.

At least, so she'd told herself.

But all of that had changed. Somewhere along the way, between watching Mrs. Abbott fuss lovingly like a mother hen over the Talcott brothers, and walking through the verdant meadows of Mallow Hills, and climbing the grand staircase with all the Talcott forebears watching over her, she'd fallen in love.

Of course, waking up to find Kipp there, his smoky gaze caressing her, oh, it had kindled a longing inside her that she'd never known.

To have that moment always, every day . . .

Cordelia closed her eyes as she realized how deeply entangled in this knot of hers she'd become. But oh, how devilishly hard it was not to smile back when he winked at her, or when she caught him looking at her—with that same smoky passion as he had this morning.

Right before Kate had arrived and ruined everything.

No, make that saved her from making a complete cake of herself. *He's not yours*, she reminded herself.

Just then the carriage swayed hard to the right as it turned off the road. She opened her eyes to find they'd turned onto a long, curved drive. After a few moments, the Duke of Dorset's grand house, Hamilton Hall, came into view.

Beside her, Kate let out a low whistle. "Your friend is to be the mistress of all that?" There was no mistaking the air of approval. "She's landed on her feet, now hasn't she?"

The implication being that Anne had her priorities in order. For while Kate smiled patiently at Cordelia's plans to leave England and jaunt about the world, she made no bones about her preference for a well-ordered house and a bevy of servants to do the heavy lifting.

Kate leaned out the window. "Makes Lord Thornton's pile of stones look quite shabby."

At this, Cordelia bristled. "Mallow Hills is nothing of the sort. It is a home. It is . . ." She paused, for she'd nearly said, *a perfect place to spend one's life.* But those words could hardly be hers. But she was sure of one thing. "That"—she waved her hand at the grand edifice and wings of rooms jutting out from every angle—"is a monstrosity. Poor Anne."

"Yes," Kate said in mock horror. "Poor Anne, indeed."

Cordelia didn't reply and they rode along in silence until the vast house loomed before them, much like her deception was rising before her, reaching its tipping point. Would anyone believe she and Kipp were . . . ? Her fingers knotted together in her lap and she was quite sure she was going to worry a hole into her gloves.

That, or toss up her accounts.

Kate reached over and laid her hand firmly atop Cordelia's. "Are you certain this is how you want to proceed?"

With your mad plan.

Though thankfully, Kate didn't say that. She didn't need to. Cordelia already knew it was foolhardy at best. To play at being madly in love with Kipp, and then to feign a broken heart.

Save now she knew the "feigning" part wouldn't be all that difficult.

Nor the "madly in love" part.

Yet that was also the moment that the unholy specter of the tallow salesman returned and she untangled her hands and sat up straight. "Yes. This is the only way."

"You could be honest," Kate offered.

"No. Not now." For as much as she didn't want to have to own up to her deception, she didn't want this fairy tale to end.

She wanted to have these last few days of being Kipp's beloved betrothed.

Blast Kipp and all his notions of home. And duty. And obligations. They'd taught her much in the last few days about what was truly honorable and brave and adventurous.

If only . . . she could be the one at his side to help him save Mallow Hills.

The carriage jolted to a stop and Cordelia drew in a deep breath. "Yes, well, here we are."

Up the grand stairs, the double doors opened and a gaggle of servants hurried out the opening, followed by a clutch of ladies.

Behind her, Cordelia heard Kate's huff of breath and a muttered "Good heavens, tighten up your corset."

Yes, quite.

But Cordelia hadn't crossed the plains of India and the wide expanses of ocean without possessing a sense of bravado in the face of certain danger, so she tipped up her chin and smiled, despite the way her heart hammered wildly.

Of course, that might also have been because Kipp opened the carriage door for her.

And he was grinning, his blue eyes alight with mischief.

"You can't be enjoying this," she whispered as he helped her out.

"Enjoying this?" He took a quick glance over his shoulder at the approaching flock and grimaced, as if he had surveyed the field and weighed their odds—and come to the same conclusion she had.

They were decidedly outnumbered.

"No. Actually, I'm terrified."

"So am I."

At this, he grinned anew. "Come now, Commander Whey-Face, gone feather-hearted on me, have you? We'll conquer this bloody horde together."

She couldn't help herself, she laughed. "Yes, indeed, Major Pudding-Legs. I suppose we must, now that we are up to our necks in it."

Then he took her hand, bringing it up to rest on his sleeve. The warm, muscled strength of his arm beneath her hand and his large frame beside her felt like a vast, unyielding shield protecting her. While she wasn't too sure if he'd done so to lend her strength or to gain it from her, what did it matter?

They'd conquer this together.

"Do you think you can convince your aunts that you are madly in love with me?" Kipp asked as they paused before the grand steps.

Cordelia nodded before she glanced up and into his eyes. "Yes, Kipp, I do."

Chapter 8

*A*nd after that confidence—*or rather, confession*—Cordelia found herself whisked away from her rear guard.

Not that any of them had much of a choice. Kipp and Drew were commandeered by the duke for a bit of "fortification." And when Drew mentioned something about seeing the duke's renowned stables, an immediate tour was organized.

Minus the ladies.

Nor was Kate any help. Seeing that the opposition had far superior numbers, she immediately fled the field with some feeble excuse about "supervising the luggage."

Leaving Cordelia to fend for herself in an intimate little salon surrounded by her dearest friends.

Yes, it was ever so wonderful to see them all—Anne, Ellie, Bea—her beloved school chums.

But that was only magnified by the addition of her father's indomitable aunts, Aldora, Bunty, and Landon. If that wasn't enough of a force to be reckoned with, they'd also brought reinforcements, a bevy of companions and other guests whom Cordelia had never met but were now seated all around the edges of the room.

Their excited chatter swirled in a cacophony of questions, and Cordelia grew dizzy trying to keep up.

"This is what comes of not having proper guidance."

"Yes, indeed. The Earl of Thornton? How is this?"

Aunt Bunty rushed in. "I vow, niece, you wrote it was Mr. Thornton, rather Captain Thornton . . ."

Aunt Landon sniffed and slanted a withering glance at her younger sister. "You must have mistaken the matter. Yet again."

Aunt Bunty bristled. "Hardly. I read the lines twice and you were present."

Anne, always the diplomat, smiled politely over the sisters' bickering and added firmly and politely, "It is absolutely perfect that you are here, Cordelia."

She smiled in return, grasping Anne's dear words like a lifeline. "I couldn't miss your wedding."

"And we will very soon see you married as well," Bea added. And as persistent as ever, she continued on, "How did you accomplish such a feat? The Earl of Thornton, of all people." She pursed her lips together—an unmistakable indication that she was gathering the facts around her.

And that wasn't a good sign, for if anyone was perceptive enough to see through her deception, she'd wager the sixpence in her pocket that Miss Beatrice Heywood would be the first.

And evidently she had. "I had heard that the earl was spending an inordinate amount of time at Russell Square in Miss Holt's company."

At the mention of the heiress's name there was a sudden silence about the room.

Apparently Miss Holt was quite well-known.

But that hardly lasted long, as several of the older ladies sniffed with disapproval.

"Vulgar creature."

"Thinks herself quite above the salt," one of the companions commented.

"My heavens, it seems every upstart family in England has a beauty of a daughter these days. Why ever can't these people have plain gels as befitting their station?" Aunt Aldora asked in all earnest.

Aunt Bunty nodded in agreement. "'Tis a decided disadvantage when a young lady is richer than all of us put together."

"Yes, Miss Holt has a bounty that gives her a decided advantage, but you have nothing to fear, Cordelia," Bea was saying.

Cordelia shifted slightly and glanced over at her friend. "I don't?"

"Of course not. The way Lord Thornton looks at you is proof enough."

"Proof?"

"That he loves you, you silly goose," Anne added.

"Yes, indeed," Ellie agreed.

"Quite worships you," Bea informed her.

"Surprised he hasn't had the banns read already," Aunt Landon added to no one in particular.

Cordelia forced a smile onto her lips. Clearly, step one of her plan had been managed—convincing one and all that her betrothal was no fiction.

Now all she had to do was survive the next few days of being madly in love with Kipp.

And then let him break her heart.

YET CORDELIA'S RESOLVE to carry on with her deception served only to leave her a frayed mess of nerves.

And for someone who had sailed around the Horn—*twice*—that was saying something.

The duke's industrious mother—despite being laid up with a twisted ankle—and His Grace's six sisters had every minute of the house party planned out right up until the wedding, so Cordelia found herself constantly surrounded by curious well-wishers, as well as her family and dear friends.

Aunt Aldora was the worst. She'd lost her betrothed a week before they'd planned to be wed, some fifty years earlier. Her beloved Wigstam had departed this world via, as Aunt Bunty called it in a loud aside, "naught more than a trifling cold."

Nor was Aunt Aldora about to see the same fate befall her dearest great-niece, so she fussed over Kipp like he was a newborn lamb—had he had enough beef for supper and not too much of the fish? Did he know the bones could cause desperate problems in his bowels?

All the while, there was Kipp, smiling at her. Doing his utmost to appear the doting betrothed.

Why he didn't saddle his horse and flee for London, she didn't know.

Worse, every time he came near her, every time he spoke to her, she was carried back to that morning, when he'd knelt before her in the library and been about to tell her something . . . do something.

Oh, if only Kate hadn't chosen that exact instant to suddenly decide to actually be a chaperone.

So as a new day dawned, Cordelia had high hopes the next twenty-four hours would be easier, that is, until she came to a stop in the doorway of the dining room just as Aunt Aldora inquired— most indelicately and in painful detail—as to the state of Kipp's digestion.

Listening to him falter for a polite reply, something inside Cordelia snapped and she discovered she was hardly the intrepid explorer she thought herself to be—for suddenly she was beating a hasty retreat, racing up to her room, catching up her sketch box, and fleeing the grand house as if the devil himself was chasing her.

And so it seemed he was.

"Where do you think you are going?"

The question stopped her in mid-flight. She'd nearly cleared the corner of the maze and had hoped to get to the distant hill before anyone noticed.

Yet someone had.

The last person she wanted to see. The only person she wanted to see.

"And without your breakfast," Kipp added, holding up a large bundle in a napkin. "I wouldn't want your digestion to become disquieted." This was added with the high-pitched notes of Aunt Aldora's constant fret and a waggle of his brows.

For good measure.

Cordelia hitched up her skirt and hurried over to where he stood, catching him by the arm and pulling him around the corner of the hedge and then not stopping until she'd dragged him behind a nearby oak.

Well out of sight.

"You're a dreadful tease," she told him even as he handed over his bounty in exchange for her sketch box. She glanced inside the napkin and sighed. "But you are also a dear."

"And where exactly did you think you were going?" he asked as he bemusedly watched her eat.

"I think that would be obvious by now," Cordelia told him between bites. She'd barely managed to eat a morsel during dinner, and she'd be the first to admit, she did love a good breakfast. And this roll was heavenly. "I am going sketching."

"By yourself?" He shook his head. "I thought we already settled that issue back at the inn."

"You settled it," she told him, finishing up the roll and taking a bite from the slice of bacon he'd purloined. Who knew he could be such a talented and discerning breakfast thief?

"And I will settle it now: Either you let me come along or I go in and inform the duchess and your aunts that you've wandered off. Alone."

That tore her gaze away from her breakfast. "You wouldn't dare!" Then after a few moments of poignant silence, she realized he would. "Oh bother. Come along if you must."

"I thought you would never ask," he said, taking a surveying glance at the landscape around them. "Which way?"

"As far from the house as we can manage." Cordelia nodded toward a small rise in the distance.

And so they set out. Somewhere along the way, Kipp took her hand in his and she didn't protest, for the heat of his bare fingers twining with hers was enough to send shivers of delight through her.

This is only for a few days, she reminded herself. *Whatever harm can come of it?*

Plenty, she soon realized as they walked and talked about every-thing—or so it felt like. It was the same companionable familiarity that had made them fast friends as children.

She regaled him with stories of India and he listened with a far-away light to his eyes, as if he were walking with her there. Smell-ing the sandalwood, the hot sun on his back, the clatter of a dozen languages alive around them, instead of the familiar tweets and twitters of robins and larks.

As they reached the top of the rise, a bucolic scene unfolded before them—a long green valley marked by the smudges of smoke rising from low-slung cottages nestled alongside the well-ordered fields. In the distance, an old steeple jutted up toward the sky.

"How perfect," Cordelia said, feeling that familiar desire to put her pencil to paper, and without a thought settled down atop the grass. Kipp joined her, proving his skills in larceny once again as he purloined a bit of paper and a nub of a pencil, the cartographer in him taking over as he began outlining the landscape.

"Don't forget, close your eyes first," she told him, settling in and letting the landscape surround her.

Kipp laughed and then did as she bid, but she suspected he was only doing it to humor her. "Yes, yes, I'm quite part of the land now."

She sniffed, but suspected one day he'd come to realize she had the right of it.

They drew in happy silence, only pausing to make note of the other's progress. Yet as the sun climbed toward midday, Cordelia knew the longer they were gone, the greater the reckoning. Silently, she packed up her belongings, Kipp returning the bits of pencil and charcoal he'd borrowed.

As she stood, he glanced down at her feet. "You've dropped something." Retrieving it for her, he started to hand it over, but then stopped and turned the bit of silver over in his hand. "This is old."

"My sixpence!" Cordelia swept it out of his grasp, even as a hot blush rose on her cheeks. "Oh dear, I'd be in a barrel of trouble if I lost that. Ellie would have me drawn and quartered."

"It's just an old coin," he remarked as he picked up her sketching case.

"Oh, hardly that," Cordelia said without thinking as she tucked the bit of silver back into her pocket. She'd taken to carrying it about like a talisman, but now regretted her foolishness, for here was Kipp looking for an explanation to her careless words. "It is just that we found it so long ago—Bea and Anne and Ellie and I. In a mattress. At Madame Rochambeaux's. That was where we met. And we thought, that is at the time, we decided the sixpence was"—oh dear heavens, she had to stop rambling along—"that it might be good luck. Anne has had it ever since, then recently she sent it to me."

"She did? Did her good luck have anything to do with Dorset?"

Cordelia flinched. "However did you know?"

"You forget, I just spent the last season surrounded by girls fresh out of their 'Bath schools.' By the way, whatever do they teach in those places?" The way he said it sounded like the ladies had spent their formative years learning an array of chicanery and fraud.

Cordelia tucked up her nose. "How would I know? Madame Rochambeaux's was not in Bath."

"Obviously." He had shifted the case in his hand and set off toward the path.

She hurried after him. "What does that mean?"

Kipp glanced over his shoulder. "That you—and your friends—are rather unique."

Coming to a blinding halt, her hands fisted to her hips. "And what does *that* mean?"

Turning slowly, he grinned and then stalked back to where she stood, until he was towering over her, and now she was shivering with something quite different than indignation.

Slowly, he leaned down, his breath warm against the curve of her ear. "My dearest Commander Whey-Face, how could I not find you different?"

Unable to stop herself, she reached out and laid her hand on his forearm, if only to give herself something solid to hold on to as her entire world began to waver beneath her.

"And that is a good thing?" she managed to ask, daring herself to look up at him. Into those clear blue eyes of his. The ones that made her think of the warm waters off Madagascar.

"The very best," he told her, and for a moment, she thought he was going to kiss her. Again.

And how she wanted him to. Longed to feel his arms around her, his lips crashing down on hers.

Wanted to believe that such a kiss could last a lifetime.

But in that instant, images of Mallow Hills flashed through her thoughts. Of all the money needed to save his home.

Money he didn't have, and she certainly didn't.

She stumbled back, out of reach, looking anywhere but at him. "Yes, well, we should be getting back. We wouldn't want to be late to the duchess's luncheon."

"Yes, if you insist," he agreed. "Your Aunt Aldora will want a full accounting of our morning."

Cordelia giggled. "Are you trying to frighten me?"

"I might. I know I'm terrified. Then again, does it help that there will be cakes with the luncheon? The iced ones you always liked when we were young."

"A little," she replied.

They both laughed, and once again, Cordelia found herself saying exactly what was in her heart. "I wish this never had to end."

"Indeed," Kipp agreed, with a long sigh. "But we have until Sunday. Let's make the most of it until then."

She wished she could be so carefree. "I can't help worrying that someone will discover the truth."

Kipp shrugged. "I can't think of what else we might do to prove our betrothal is anything other than legitimate, save—"

Right then they turned a corner in the path and there, just down the way, near the next bend, stood Anne and Dorset.

Not so much standing as entwined.

A sight that rather encapsulated Kipp's line of thought. For what else could they do to make their betrothal appear to be a love match . . .

Save get caught in a compromising position . . .

"Not this way," he told her, steering Cordelia in another direction.

"Yes, I suppose not," she agreed. Still, she couldn't help but take a glance back at the pair—Anne pinned against the wide trunk of the tree by the duke, who was doing a very thorough job of kissing his bride-to-be, so lost in their embrace, they hadn't heard Cordelia and Kipp's approach.

There was something so intimate, so passionate about the moment, Cordelia's fingers slipped into her pocket and wound around the sixpence there.

Had this bit of silver truly helped Anne? It was rather hard to believe.

And yet, there it was. The most unlikely of matches.

She followed Kipp away from the couple and had to wonder if all betrothed couples behaved so. And then she couldn't help herself— she had to know. "Is that how it is with you and Miss Holt?"

IS THAT HOW it is with you and Miss Holt?

Kipp stumbled a bit and then whirled around. "Good God! Certainly not!"

Cordelia's expression widened, for obviously she hadn't expected such a vehement response.

Then again, he hadn't realized his own horror until the words came erupting out of him.

"Truly? I would think—" she began, glancing back. "It is just that if you are about to be—"

"No!" Now he wasn't sure what he meant. But he was quite certain of one thing. "That is, we've never . . . that is, Miss Holt and I haven't—"

"Never?" She sounded entirely too pleased with his revelation.

That he'd never kissed Miss Holt.

And in a sense, it was a revelation to him. For come to think of it, he'd never really wanted to—certainly not with the same fervor that seemed to have overtaken Dorset and his intended, the pair thoroughly lost in their mutual passion.

"I don't think Miss Holt would approve—" he rushed to explain, as if that made it all more palatable.

"Of a kiss? From you?" Cordelia shook her head. "She sounds perfectly foolish."

"She's hardly all that," he said, rising to the heiress's defense, though not as passionately as one might think a nearly betrothed ought. "It's just that she isn't . . . well, I think she'd find that . . . not to her liking. And I certainly wouldn't want to impose myself upon her."

Cordelia hardly looked appeased. "If this lady is the one you want to marry with all your heart, and she you, kissing you . . . well, that should be her every waking thought. Her every desire."

And there it was.

For they both knew that Cordelia wasn't talking about Miss Holt.

Seeing Dorset and Miss Brabourne tangled together in such a way . . . He had to imagine Pamela would have had vapors over such an unseemly display.

Nor would Pamela ever allow such liberties. Not before she was married. And even then, he suspected it wouldn't be welcomed all that much after the parson had given his blessing.

Oh, she'd do her duty to produce the requisite heir and spare, but after that?

Hardly.

Then he looked at Cordelia. She would never settle for such a loveless, passionless match.

Not his Cordelia. And something old and long forgotten wrenched at his very soul. The same deep pang that had nearly torn him in two all those years ago when Sir Horace's carriage had pulled away, wrenching Cordie, his Cordie, out of his life.

Somehow, over the years, he'd forgotten that sense of belonging to another.

How two people could fit so perfectly. How they'd always held hands—dragging each other from one misadventure to another. How they'd finished each other's sentences, each other's drawings. How he couldn't go to sleep at night until he spied the candle in her room go out.

And now that they had been reunited, he'd rediscovered the hundred and one ways Cordelia Padley would always be the spark that ignited his heart. His very flame.

"Cordelia?"

"Yes?"

"Would it be terribly forward of me . . . no, make that highly improper of me to ask you something . . . to do something . . ."

Cordelia glanced at him. "Ask me to do what?"

"Kiss me, Cordelia," he whispered. "Like that. Like we are betrothed. Like we are meant to be—"

Together.

But he never got those last words out. Because then they were.

Tangled. Entwined.

He caught hold of her and pulled her into his arms. She'd balked before, but he wasn't going to let this chance pass.

For it might well be his last.

CORDELIA BARELY HAD a moment to blink, for one moment she was standing on the path and the next she was in Kipp's arms, and he was kissing her.

No, make that devouring her.

And she was drowning. She'd been longing for this moment since the night at the inn and now . . .

She tried to pull back. "Kipp, we mustn't. What if we are caught?" She shook her head. "You have obligations elsewhere. I won't be the cause—"

He shook his head and pulled her close. "Cordelia, close your eyes and listen."

To his breath as it brushed over her ear, sending tendrils of desire racing through her.

To the sigh that slipped from her lips as he kissed the side of her neck. To the rustle of shivers that tangled up in her very core, leaving her anxious and delirious with pleasure, longing for his touch, to soothe them into order, or to unravel her completely.

And then he found her mouth once more, kissing her slowly, teasingly.

She couldn't help herself, she was lost. And she opened up to him, his tongue teasing her to find the way, his hands exploring her, luring her. When his fingers curled around her breast, she arched, and he backed her up, until she was pressed into the curve of an oak.

And then he covered her with his body, as hard as the trunk behind her, and she sighed—for as innocent as she was, she knew now what it would mean to have him—for he was hard and long and she couldn't help herself, she reached out and touched him, felt him, let herself explore him, stroke him.

He caught hold of her hand and pulled it away. "You'll drive me mad."

"No more than you are doing to me," she offered.

"Not even close." And then he proved his point by slipping one of her breasts free of her gown and taking the nipple in his mouth and sucking it.

Cordelia gasped for air as he sent a thousand dangerous temptations through her, awakening every nerve in her body.

Every need.

Then his other hand pulled at her gown and his fingers slid along her thigh, and then higher, until he touched her—right where every bit of fire he was kindling seemed to be banked, and with his touch, he sparked pure passion.

"Oh," she gasped as he explored her, touched her. Ran his thumb over the hard nub there, and suddenly she was standing on her tiptoes—lifted by his touch, by something that drew her higher.

He stroked her, slowly at first and then as her hips began to rise and fall, he cupped her, sliding a finger inside her, drawing out the wetness and letting his fingers indulge her, pushing her higher.

Cordelia tried to breathe, tried to make sense of it, but then everything erupted and waves of pleasure sent her into a crescendo of desires found and released.

Her eyes fluttered open and she looked at him, only to find him grinning. Overly proud that he'd untangled all those knots.

He leaned down and nuzzled her neck, his lips warm against her damp skin. "Are you in the landscape yet?"

"Utterly," she managed.

He dipped his head down to kiss her again but the snap of a twig yanked them apart. For a second they just stood there, gaping at each other, both trying to catch their breath.

Kipp reached out and tucked a stray strand of her hair back behind her ear. It hardly served the purpose of giving her state of *dishabille* some semblance of order, but it brought a shy smile to her lips.

He took her hand and drew her out from behind the tree, where Dorset and Miss Brabourne—looking equally tousled and content—greeted them.

"Cordelia! There you are," Anne said, casting her a knowing wink. "If the duchess asks, we all went for a walk."

"We went sketching," Cordelia corrected as she nudged Kipp toward her forgotten case.

"Ah, yes, 'sketching,'" the Duke of Dorset agreed. "One of my most favorite activities."

And the four of them laughed and continued back to the house.

Chapter 9

*L*ater that evening, Kipp paused midway down the stairs, as he caught sight of his host and his brother in the foyer below. He couldn't help himself; he laughed.

For his part, Drew was dressed as a pirate—which wasn't much of a costume given his reputation on land and at sea. But it was Dorset who had him shaking his head.

"Ready, Thornton, for a night of madness?" Dressed as Bacchus, the duke raised the cup he held.

Now they both laughed good-heartedly.

"Wherever did you get that?" Drew asked, pushing off the opposite wall and looking his brother over from head to toe.

"Quite the mystery."

"Probably not," Drew replied.

Given that Kipp was dressed as an Indian prince, it actually wasn't much of a puzzle—a fact Drew acknowledged with a weary shake of his head before he returned to Mrs. Harrington's side.

How Cordelia had managed it, Kipp didn't know, but he knew one thing: He was willing to be whoever she wanted.

For as long as she wanted.

Until he had to return to London. For he must do that first. He must clear his conscience with Miss Holt.

For what if he was mistaken and Pamela's heart was engaged? Oh God, what would he do then?

He went to rake his hand through his hair and nearly sent the turban there tumbling over.

Like his life . . .

He looked across the foyer toward the crush inside the ballroom, searching for Cordelia even as a flicker of an idea, inspiration really, danced before him.

She might have joked earlier with Miss Brabourne and Dorset about going sketching, but the duke, an old school friend, had later asked him if he did indeed still draw maps. And one thing had led to another, the duke looking over the outline of the map Kipp had begun and on the spot offering an outstanding sum to do his entire estate.

But it isn't enough, his practical side argued. *For when that stipend is gone, then what?*

More commissions would take time. Time he didn't have.

If only . . .

He thought of that wretched sixpence of Cordelia's and wished it could actually work some sort of miracle.

Not that he thought such a thing likely.

If Miss Holt loved him, then honorably he would have to marry her, make his marriage of convenience.

Which, in truth, was no more honorable than asking Cordelia to stay in England. To work beside him, to restore Mallow Hills together. Hardly the life of exploration she longed for, but it was all he could offer.

"If I might be presumptuous—" Dorset began, breaking into his dark musings.

"Isn't that your prerogative?" Kipp tore his gaze away from the crowded room.

Dorset laughed. "Yes, I suppose. But I must ask—and only because Anne holds Cordelia in such high esteem—what are you doing? I mean to say, who do you hope to fool with this betrothal nonsense?"

Nonsense? Oh, the man had his full attention now.

"I don't know what you mean—" Kipp managed, doing his best to sound affronted.

"Yes, you do." Dorset glanced around and lowered his voice. "You forget I was in London this season as well." He paused and let his point sink in. Then he nodded toward the front door. "It would also explain why *she's* here."

"Who's here?" Kipp asked, turning in that direction.

To his shock, there in the doorway stood none other than Miss Pamela Holt, and in the shadow of her wake, the bulldog figure of her father, Josiah.

Kipp's heart sank. *What the devil?*

Pamela glanced around at the brightly clad guests, her eyes narrowing as she surveyed the merry scene before her. Heaving a sigh, she picked up her skirts and waded into the entryway as if she were being asked to walk through Seven Dials.

"Lord Thornton?" Her greeting held an edge of suspicion. As if she wasn't certain she'd actually found him.

"Miss Holt?" Kipp still couldn't quite believe it. "Whatever are you doing here?"

"I would ask the same of you," she replied. Josiah ambled up to her side and took his stodgy place beside her. "I heard the most unbefitting rumor regarding your departure . . . Well, I couldn't rest until I discovered the truth. And now I find—"

She pulled out her handkerchief and with it tightly clasped, held it to her lips as if the last thing she wanted to do was utter the words about to tumble free. "Well, to put this plainly, I trusted that yours was an errand of honor, my lord, and yet I find you in the middle of a bacchanal."

Behind him, Dorset barked a bit of a laugh, then being caught out, turned back to his other guests.

"Hardly that," Kipp replied. Then if things couldn't get much worse, Cordelia came down the stairs, stopping at his side. In a sari, no less. With one shoulder bare, a jewel pasted to her forehead, and her eyes lined with kohl, she made a beguiling and exotic picture.

Even now he could detect a whiff of sandalwood, the scent pulling him toward her.

Cheeky chit that she was, she winked at him.

Miss Holt made an aggrieved *harrumph*. "Am I to suppose *you* are Miss Padley?"

"I am," Cordelia said, coming forward and making a polite curtsy, one which Miss Holt did not return.

Instead, the heiress looked her over from head to toe, as if examining questionable goods. "Perhaps, Miss Padley, you don't understand the difficult position you have placed Lord Thornton in—how unseemly this all appears."

Undaunted, Cordelia continued to smile. "Miss Holt, there is nothing unseemly whatsoever. I merely borrowed Lord Thornton."

"Seems as if you've done more than that," the heiress shot back.

Across the foyer, Drew coughed and turned his back to the entire scene.

Whether he was laughing or choking, Kipp hoped it was more of the latter than the former.

Worse, Cordelia looked ready to rise to his defense and speak the only way she knew how—frankly.

"I think it is best if we spoke privately, Miss Holt," Kipp told her, catching her by the arm and turning her from Cordelia.

"Indeed!" Miss Holt sniffed, shooting a scathing glance at her apparent rival.

"There's a small salon—" Dorset offered in an aside.

"Thank you, Your Grace," Kipp replied as he steered Miss Holt away, not looking back—for if he did, he knew he'd never be able to do what he must do.

"Now see here—" Josiah protested as he came to the realization that Kipp was stealing away his daughter.

"Not now, Holt," Kipp replied as he quickly closed the door on the room, shutting it in the man's face.

This was a matter that needed to be settled. *Privately.*

"I have long heard rumors of His Grace's inclinations"—she began, settling herself in the middle of the room, well away from him and with her eye on the door—"but I would never have guessed that you, Lord Thornton, would be inclined to such depravities!"

Once again, she pressed her handkerchief to her quivering lips.

Kipp crossed the room. "Then don't think, Pamela. Tell me that you love me and kiss me."

She bristled. "I don't recall giving you leave to be so familiar, my lord." She stood her ground, all perfect posture and bourgeois indignation.

So he reached out for her. "Kiss me, Pamela."

She made a sort of yelp when he touched her and quickly scurried aside, putting a sofa between them. "Are you mad?" She looked to the door, as if wondering why her father wasn't breaking it down. When no rescue seemed imminent, she resorted to her Bath training. Shoulders back, nose in the air. "This orgy I've come to find you embroiled in has clouded your good sense, sir."

"It is a masked ball, Pamela," he told her. "Hardly an orgy."

"I disagree, when I arrive to find you addressing me so intimately and proposing such unthinkable . . . demanding such . . ."

"Kiss me."

"I. Will. Not."

"Why not?" He had to know. "If you love me—"

She ruffled like a wet hen. "We are not even engaged. Not formally."

"And if we were?"

Pamela set her jaw. Defiantly so. And for a moment she favored her father. Which wasn't an advantageous look for her. But it was a telling one, a glance that said only one thing.

Certainly not.

Kipp paced in front of the sofa, slanting a glance at her. "A friend told me that if you loved me . . . with all your heart, and I you, that our only thoughts should be of the desire between us."

She blinked, as if he had once again taken to speaking Sanskrit. With another deep breath, she addressed him slowly, choosing her words carefully, so—in his apparent madness—he wouldn't mistake the matter. "All I want between us is a proper and respectable distance, my lord."

"Pamela, the question is very simple." Kipp moved slowly around the sofa. "Do you love me?"

Her gaze flitted to the door. "Lord Thornton, I was under the assumption we shared a proper understanding. I am still of the opinion—even in light of recent events—that such an arrangement is to our mutual benefit."

She drew another breath and smiled at him, that winsome bit of encouragement that had engaged his interest to begin with. "I am willing to overlook this indiscretion, this so-called matter of honor, in order for both of us to achieve our future happiness and *security*."

Security, not love. It plucked at his sensibilities with all the familiar notes of a song played over and over.

Yet it offered him none of the comfort that up until a week ago it had provided.

But it was also a potent reminder that without her, his estate, his future would fall to ruin. It pricked at his pride, at his own sense of purpose.

Worst of all, it threatened to extinguish the spark Cordelia had relit within him.

Which, he realized, was far more precious than all of Josiah Holt's gold.

Meanwhile, Pamela had smoothly moved to the door and opened it. "My father and I have taken rooms at the inn in the village," she announced in a voice loud enough for him—and everyone in the foyer—to hear. "We will be returning to London in the morning. I expect you to join us."

By the time Kipp got to the door, all that could be seen of Pamela was the back of her skirt as she stalked in a regal huff down the front steps, while Josiah awkwardly and hastily took his leave. "My apologies, Your Graciousness, if we've come at a bad time. Interrupted your . . ." The man nervously glanced at the party and shook his head. "Whatever this might be."

He bent more than bowed, and hurried toward the door, pausing long enough to address Kipp. "Bad business this, Thornton. No other way to describe it. But I trust you'll come 'round. We both have too much to gain." Josiah nodded again and jostled his way out the door and down the steps to his waiting carriage.

Yet instead of seeing all his dreams for Mallow Hills flit away like a feather in the wind, he suddenly saw his future in the same bright colors and bits of whimsy that Cordelia had painted on his map.

She had brought the hues of life back into his very soul, and he wouldn't let anything, anyone, douse the passion and fire she sparked in his heart.

He couldn't help himself, he grinned at the realization.

It might take him a lifetime of commissions to save Mallow Hills, but it would be a lifetime spent with Cordelia.

If she'd have him.

Kipp turned and found the gathered company gaping at him.

In shock. In fury. In curious delight.

All of them. The aunts. Mrs. Harrington. Miss Brabourne. Lady Elinor. Miss Heywood. And several of the guests who'd come at the first whiff of a brewing scandal.

He couldn't care less what any of them thought. For there was only one person he longed to see, and she was missing.

He looked to Drew who stood by the window, as if watching to make sure Miss Holt was well and gone. "Where is she?"

His brother knew exactly whom he meant and nodded toward the garden doors at the far side of the ballroom.

By the time Kipp had pushed his way through the crush to the open doors, he saw only the flash of silk as Cordelia fled into the opening in the maze. Dashing across the lawn, he entered the hedges and then came to a stop.

The path went in three different directions and he hadn't a notion which way to go.

Demmit! How would he ever find her?

Then he thought of what she'd said the other night at the inn.

Close your eyes. Listen. Let your senses direct your hand. Become part of the landscape.

So he did just that. Paused and closed his eyes. To his right, he heard the faint rustle of silk. As he turned in that direction, a hint of sandalwood, so at odds with the laurels around him, teased him to follow.

Then he came to a turn, and he couldn't figure out which way she'd gone. "Cordelia," he called softly. "Where are you?"

"Leave me be," she replied in a grand huff, a windy bit of bombast that also gave him his direction.

A bit of movement on the other side of the hedge caught his eye—but how to get there, he had no idea. "If you're going to hide in a maze, you're supposed to remain quiet."

Then again, silence and Cordelia had never been easy companions.

A loud sniffle arose from the other side of the hedge. "I am so sorry. *Sniff . . . sniff.* I never meant to . . . that is, I wouldn't have asked you to help me, if I had known it would ruin . . . *sniff . . . sniff . . .* your dreams. Your plans."

As she sniffed and apologized, Kipp followed her voice, and again caught yet another whiff of her perfume and followed it like bread crumbs until he turned a corner, then the next, and finally had her in his sights.

"What are you doing here? You should be with Miss Holt," she protested as he trapped her in the middle of the maze.

"Promise me something," he told her as he came closer.

"Anything," she said quickly.

"Never mention that name again," he said, before he caught her in his arms and crushed his lips to hers.

A THOUSAND QUESTIONS crashed through Cordelia's thoughts in the moments before she found herself in Kipp's arms and his lips captured hers.

And then none of them mattered.

For here was Kipp and he was kissing *her*.

"I want you," he all but growled. So fiercely, she shivered.

Because it was everything she wanted. Except . . .

"But Kipp . . ." She gasped when he moved to kiss the nape of her neck, as he pulled her hair free of the simple tie that held it back.

Her protest died in the air as his warm hand slid over her bare shoulder, lifted the end of her sari, and began to unwrap her.

"Did you hear me?" His voice was rich and hypnotic.

Or perhaps it was the way he was caressing her, kissing her, but Cordelia was lost in a whirling hurricane of desire.

"I want you," he repeated. "I won't have it any other way. Tell me you want the same."

Whatever did she want?

She looked up into his eyes and saw the clear blue waters of the Indian Ocean, or was it the sky over Mallow Hills? She saw his face tanned from the Saharan sun, or was it from working in the fields beside his tenants?

But mostly she saw herself beside him. And wherever their lives took them, she knew it would always be an adventure. That she needn't walk the streets of Canton when she could walk the meadows of Wiltshire with Kipp holding her hand, explore the Roman streets of Bath with Kipp pointing out the sights, and find her heart's content.

"Yes, Kipp," she said, grinning at him. "I do."

And then he kissed her, tenderly, thoroughly, caressing her as he continued unwinding the long length of silk she wore.

As he freed her breasts, he kissed her there, taking each of her nipples in turn, sucking them deep into his mouth, until they were tight tips, and her body ached with the pleasure of it.

She slid her hands under his own robe—the one she'd bought on a lark, with some of the money she'd saved. As her maidservant in India had said, it would serve as the perfect gift for her groom one day.

"All for naught?" Cordelia asked, sitting up and looking at their stern expressions. "No, no, you misunderstand. I am to be married."

Aunt Aldora began to wail, and Aunt Bunty did her best to console her sister.

Aunt Landon huffed a sigh. "I hardly see how when Lord Talcott has deserted you for that horrible Miss Holt."

Chapter 10

"What do you mean, he's gone?" Cordelia pushed her way up to a seated position, drawing Kipp's cloak around her as she went.

"He's left. Departed. Gone into the village." Aunt Landon was not one to suffer foolish questions. "He's deserted you."

"If only he'd known," Aunt Bunty lamented.

"And if he had? Well, we know now he isn't worthy of her. Dreadful wretch," Aunt Aldora interjected, having found her way through her characteristic bout of tears. "I have said all along, we must find her a gentleman who wasn't intent on marrying her for her fortune."

Cordelia was still rather lost in the notion that Kipp had left. Gone to *her*.

The woman she wasn't supposed to name. The heiress with the vast . . .

Wait just a moment. Her gaze swiveled toward Aunt Aldora. "My what?"

It took a moment as the three sisters exchanged glances. Rather guilty ones.

"Oh dear. I had rather hoped Mr. Pickworth had told you," Aunt Bunty said, managing a wane smile.

As in Mr. Pickworth, Esq. Her father's solicitor. The one she'd been studiously avoiding. With a twinge of guilt, she remembered the still unopened pile of letters from the man sitting on her desk back in London.

"I have a fortune?"

"Yes, in a manner of speaking," Aunt Aldora said. "When you marry."

"It's all very complicated," Aunt Bunty hastened to add. "And all Landon's doing." She smiled as she shifted the blame to her sister.

Aunt Landon huffed, but didn't appear to mind overly much. "You must understand it was all done so that your future wasn't squandered."

"It all began with dear Wigstam," Aunt Aldora added, and then, as she always did at the mention of her long-departed betrothed, she began to weep.

"Wigstam?" Cordelia shook her head and looked to Aunt Landon for an explanation since one would not be forthcoming from Aldora.

Which Landon began, "You see, Mr. Wigstam—"

"Bless his heart," Aunt Aldora interjected.

Landon sniffed and continued, scowling at her sisters in a way that suggested no further interruptions would be tolerated. "Yes, well, Wigstam—while hardly the model of good health—was, in fact, quite wealthy. He had managed to make a fortune in the trade and when he decided to marry Aldora, he rewrote his will, leaving it all to her."

Cordelia figured out the rest. "So Aunt Aldora is wealthy—"

Her aunt pursed her lips as if the subject was so distasteful. "Yes, I've always found such mercantile matters so very unsavory. Besides, we have our own funds from Papa that Landon has managed ever so brilliantly."

Cordelia had never thought about it, but her aunts had always lived very well, and she'd never questioned where the money had come from.

But at this, she turned to Aunt Landon.

"Yes, well, when you were born, we agreed that the bulk of Wigstam's money should be yours—a dowry that would ensure you a good place in society."

"I fear we did not trust your father and mother to manage their inheritances with the same care as Landon," Aunt Aldora said.

Aunt Landon put it more succinctly. "Your father had no head for figures or business."

Cordelia nodded. No, her father had been content to spend as if he had a merchant's fortune behind him and no thought of what tomorrow might bring.

With that bit over, Landon got on with her explanation. "So, with Mr. Pickworth's help, I've managed your dowry."

"You have a railroad," Aunt Bunty interjected with a happy smile.

"A railroad?" Cordelia knew she was gaping.

"It is rather ingenious," Aunt Aldora told her in an aside. "It is a carriage on rails."

"Yes, I've heard of them."

"Actually you have two railroads," Aunt Landon corrected. "And shipping interests. And a large holding in an import firm. And you've done quite well with some land I speculated on in the north. Deep with coal, as it turns out. And well connected to the canals we are invested in."

"Why didn't you tell me?" Cordelia asked.

The sisters shared another guilty glance.

"We haven't told anyone," Aunt Landon said.

"Except good Mr. Pickworth," Aunt Bunty added. Aunt Bunty did like clarity.

"You see, after Wigstam died, it was nosed about that I had inherited his fortune, and dear heavens, the horrible fellows who came calling," Aunt Aldora said, sounding as sensible as Landon. "They all wanted one thing, my money."

"So we determined that you would either marry for love, or we would find a nice, steady—" Aunt Bunty began.

"—malleable fellow," Aunt Landon continued.

"—to marry you, one who had no notion that you were an heiress." Aunt Aldora sighed. "And we thought for certain you'd found the perfect match in Lord Thornton."

"I don't know how we could have been so mistaken," Aunt Bunty said, to no one in particular.

But Cordelia heard her and looked once again out the window into the darkness that still held the approaching day in its thrall.

And wondered how she'd been so very wrong as well.

CORDELIA JOLTED AWAKE just as the day began to dawn. She must have dozed off, and it took her a moment to get her bearings. She was back in her room, her aunts having seen her upstairs after they'd outlined exactly what she was in line to inherit. At first, unable to sleep, she'd curled up in the window seat, but she must have dozed off, for now day was dawning, a bit of light piercing the thick mist that veiled the countryside.

Somewhere nearby, she could hear one of her aunts snoring.

Then she remembered everything. The ball. Miss Holt. Kipp finding her in the maze. Making love. And then awakening to find him gone.

She looked again outside at the shrouded landscape and blinked.

Through the mist, she began to make out a lone figure striding up the drive.

Kipp!

Cordelia rushed through the house, out the front door, stopping only when she got a few feet from him. It was then that she remembered she was wearing only her wrapper.

He saluted her. "Is that the official uniform of the Royal Society of Explorers?" He looked her over from head to toe. "If it is, I approve."

Cordelia ignored his jest and got straight to the point. "What are you doing here?"

He closed the distance between them. "Commencing an exploration." And then he pulled her into his arms and kissed her.

Thoroughly.

When they paused to catch their breath, she said, "This appears to be more an act of piracy."

"It is. I am stealing you away. Taking you off to Mallow Hills, marrying you, and if you refuse, I shall lock you in the dungeon."

"I know the way out."

"Yes, I suppose you do."

She glanced up at him and grinned. "What if I came willingly?"

He stepped back a bit and eyed her. "You would?"

"Yes, Kipp. I would. I said as much last night. Yet so much has changed since then."

"Yes, it has," he agreed, nuzzling her neck.

"No," she laughed, batting him away. "Now I won't be coming alone."

His brows arched and he glanced toward the house. "Not your aunts?"

She laughed and shook her head. "No. I'll be bringing my fortune with me."

He stilled and stared at her. "You have a fortune?"

"Apparently so." Then she explained what her aunts had told her. "I don't think it is anywhere near what Miss Holt could bring—"

He shuddered. "You promised never to mention that name again."

"But you went to her—"

"I did. To apologize. But she was already gone, leaving a rather crisp note about having hidden my predilections from her—"

"Predilections?" Cordelia laughed. "I rather adore your predilections."

"Then you had best prepare for a lifetime of them," he told her as he gathered her into his arms again and began nibbling at a spot behind her ear.

It made it ever so hard to argue with him, but she did her best. "Is that an order, Major?"

"It is, Commander."

Cordelia grinned. Kipp was hers for always. Oh, the adventures ahead of them left her breathless. "Who am I to argue with a member of the Royal Society?"

"Founding member," he corrected, and his hand slid inside her robe and curled around her breast as he kissed the nape of her neck.

"My apologies," she managed.

One might forgive her such a mistake, given the circumstances.

Something Blue

LAURA LEE GUHRKE

Chapter 1

The Berkshire home of the Misses Aldora,
   Bunty, and Landon Padley
A few hours after the wedding of
   the Earl of Thornton and Miss Cordelia Padley

To anyone who chanced to observe them, the trio of young ladies huddled in an isolated corner of the garden would have seemed nothing out of the common way. The wedding breakfast was over, the bride and groom were about to depart on their wedding journey, the day was fine, and the roses were in full bloom. What better time and place for the bride's best friends to engage in a bit of conversation about the festivities?

Lawrence Blackthorne, however, knew there was more to this little gathering than a tête-à-tête among friends. Thanks to his friendship with the groom, he knew a plot was afoot, a plot concocted in the clever brain of the bride's friend, Lady Elinor Daventry, and since anything that concerned the Daventry family was of great interest to him, Lawrence had deemed it necessary to do a spot of reconnaissance.

Aiding him in this mission was the fact that the aunts of the Earl of Thornton's bride were passionate gardeners. The tall yew hedge surrounding the garden made for excellent cover, as long as he remembered to keep his head down.

As he circled the perimeter to where the ladies were gathered, Elinor's voice floated to him over the hedge.

"She is coming, isn't she? After insisting upon this conversation, you would think Cordelia would at least be punctual. You don't suppose she's forgotten?"

"Cordelia?" The Duchess of Dorset made a scoffing sound. "She'd never be so inconsiderate."

"Not usually, but today is her wedding day. And Cordelia's always been a bit of a madcap."

Ellie sounded anxious, deepening Lawrence's curiosity. What was this all about? According to Thornton, his bride had insisted upon a private, uninterrupted meeting with her friends before departing with him on their wedding journey, declaring Lady Elinor's entire future was at stake. Lawrence had pressed his friend for more information, but the earl, preoccupied with the events of the day, had not felt impelled to pursue the topic with Cordelia, leaving Lawrence frustratingly short on details.

He knew anything involving Ellie's future could also involve her father, and if she was hatching some scheme to rescue that scoundrel, Lawrence needed to find out what it was and stop it. He'd spent over half a year building a case against Daventry, and he wasn't about to see all his good work undone, not now, not when the earl was so close to receiving his comeuppance.

"She'll arrive soon enough, I expect," Miss Beatrice Heywood was saying as Lawrence paused on the other side of the yew hedge. "She's probably been detained by some relation of Thornton's who wants to welcome her into the family. Or perhaps the vicar's wife has pulled her aside to remind her of her duties to the parish now that she's properly wed."

Ellie groaned. "If it's the vicar's wife, we'll be here for ages. She holds on to one's pelisse while she talks to prevent any possible escape."

"Why such concern about time, Ellie?" asked the duchess. "Are you in haste to be away?"

"I am. I have an important engagement in London this very evening, and since Lady Wolford also wishes to return to town today, she has agreed to take me in her carriage. But she made it clear that if I'm not back at Wolford Grange by one o'clock, she will depart for London without me."

"Be patient," Miss Heywood advised. "Cordelia will be here any moment, I'm sure."

"I hope so, for I should hate to leave without saying good-bye. Especially since she's promised to bring me the sixpence."

That silly old coin? Lawrence rolled his eyes. Good Lord, was that what this was all about?

In their schooldays, Ellie and her friends had fancied that an old sixpence they'd found might have the magical power to find them husbands, but that was hardly worthy of a clandestine meeting scarcely an hour after Cordelia's marriage ceremony. And why, he wondered, feeling uneasy for reasons he didn't wish to explore, should Ellie be so concerned about matrimony anyway?

Her next words gave him a bit of clarification on that question.

"Lord Bluestone is coming to Portman Square to dine with Papa this evening, and I simply must be there."

Viscount Bluestone? That pompous ass? Lawrence made a sound of disdain between his teeth and regretted it at once.

"What was that?" Ellie demanded. "I thought I heard a noise."

"My, you are anxious, aren't you?" The duchess laughed. "This Lord Bluestone must be extraordinary indeed to put our Ellie on tenterhooks."

This time, Lawrence was able to suppress any vocal expression of his opinion, but only with a good deal of effort. Bluestone was as extraordinary as cold porridge and about as intelligent. That Ellie, whose wits were as sharp as her tongue, might have developed a tendresse for the fellow was ridiculous. It was, he told himself firmly, absurd.

"I have cause to be nervous," Ellie said, interrupting his efforts to dismiss notions of Ellie and Bluestone. "The viscount indicated at the Delamere ball that I have quite caught his fancy."

"I should hope so," Miss Heywood said, laughing as Lawrence's attempts at denial collapsed. "Bluestone claimed three dances with you. Or so I heard?"

"You heard rightly, Bea. Over refreshments, he mentioned his duty as the next duke and his need to marry well, and in nearly the same breath, he said Papa's invitation to dine was fortuitous. Oh, ladies, if he were to offer for me—"

She stopped mid-sentence, but the excitement in her voice had been unmistakable, leaving Lawrence strangely off-balance, as if the world had just tilted a bit sideways.

He leaned in closer, but before Ellie could reveal anything more, hurried footsteps sounded on the flagstone path, and another voice came to Lawrence's ears.

"I'm so sorry I was delayed," Cordelia said as she joined the other three, her voice breathless from running. "It was Mrs. Cranchester. She simply would not let go of my sleeve."

"We suspected as much," Miss Heywood told her. "And Ellie's been like a cat on hot bricks in consequence."

"I'm glad you've arrived at last," Ellie told her friend. "I must be away, ere I shall miss my ride to London."

"A circumstance I could not lament," Cordelia replied. "Oh, Ellie, I should so like to steer you from this course."

"Is that why you were so adamant about seeing me before departing for Mallow Hills?"

The countess must have nodded, for Ellie went on, "It's useless, Cordelia, for I am quite determined. Bluestone would be an excellent match for me."

To Lawrence's mind, that point was worthy of spirited debate, but he couldn't very well pop up over the top of the hedge like some ruddy jack-in-the-box and take up the issue. And even if he could, he acknowledged in chagrin, he had no right to do so.

"Why such concern, Cordelia?" the duchess asked. "From what

I understand, Bluestone is a gentleman of wealth and property, and he certainly comes from an ancient, powerful family. If he has fallen in love with Ellie and she with him—"

"That's just it," the countess interrupted. "Love has nothing to do with it."

Relief swept over him at that declaration, relief so profound, he closed his eyes. But Ellie's next words opened them again and underscored the brutal fact that her heart was no longer his concern. "If I marry Bluestone," she said, "I shall save my father from ruin."

So, he'd been right then. Lawrence straightened away from the hedge, letting out his breath in a slow sigh. It wasn't surprising that Ellie intended to rescue Daventry from his well-deserved fate, for Lawrence knew, better than anyone, the blind loyalty she felt toward her parent. But to save him by chaining herself for life to a prig like Bluestone? Of all the harebrained, infuriating, idiotic ideas—

"Wait." Miss Heywood's voice, sharp and incisive, cut into this stream of exasperated thought. "Ellie, you don't love this man, but you are thinking to marry him?"

"Exactly," Cordelia answered before Ellie had the chance to do so. "And how could she? Bluestone's thick as a brick, not at all worthy of our Ellie."

Lawrence concurred wholeheartedly with that sentiment, and he applauded Cordelia for her good sense. He only wished she could impart some of that good sense to Elinor, who seemed to have lost all of hers.

"We've already discussed this, Cordelia," Ellie said impatiently. "As I have assured you again and again, my mind is made up."

"But Ellie," put in the duchess, "marriage without love, or at least affection, is such a dismal prospect."

"A fine declaration from the woman who once declared she'd never marry for love," Ellie replied. "And I don't have the luxury of waiting to fall in love, Anne. Nor do I have the desire. One episode of that disease was enough for me."

"Lawrence Blackthorne isn't every man."

"Well, thank heaven for that," Ellie countered, and Lawrence felt those words like a blow to the chest.

"But since we are talking of Mr. Blackthorne," she went on, all her loathing for him in her voice as she said his name, "he is the reason I have no time to lose. He has persuaded the Home Secretary to launch a formal investigation of my father. All those ridiculous rumors from the war will be dredged up again, and Papa's name dragged through the mud. What if by some miscarriage of justice, Lawrence manages to persuade Peel's committee to have Papa arrested and brought before the House of Lords? I am not so naïve as to think his innocence would be enough to save him."

His innocence? Lawrence stirred with impatience. The man was guilty as hell.

"Yes, but Ellie," Lady Thornton put in, "you don't know that he'll be arrested. There would have to be evidence, and from what you've said, Lawrence doesn't have any."

Oh, he had evidence, all right. Lawrence set his jaw grimly. He just didn't have enough of it in hand yet to make his case to Sir Robert Peel. But he soon would, and when he did, Daventry would not only be arrested for his crimes during the war, he'd be convicted, and Ellie would have to face the truth at last.

"Even if he has no proof," Ellie said, returning Lawrence's attention to the conversation, "the mere fact of a formal investigation would be enough to convince many in society that those old rumors must be true. No smoke without fire—that's what people will say. I can't bear to see Papa and our family endure such humiliation. No, I intend to have this stopped now, before any of it can taint his reputation."

"I'm in a fog," Miss Heywood said. "How does marrying Bluestone stop anything?"

"Bluestone's father, the Duke of Wilchelsey, is on Peel's committee."

And, Lawrence, finished for her in his mind, *the duke wouldn't want the good name of his daughter-in-law's father to be ruined by scandal.*

It was a good plan, he was forced to admit, but one he intended to nip in the bud. The question was how. Before he could consider any possibilities, however, Miss Heywood spoke again.

"But Ellie, if you don't love Bluestone, you are putting your happiness and your future at risk—"

"Future?" Ellie interrupted, a note of bitterness in her voice. "What future? My most marriageable years were wasted waiting for Lawrence Blackthorne, and I'm now twenty-five. If people become convinced Papa was a war profiteer, spinsterhood shall be my future. Papa's shame will be mine as well. It will be the same for my cousins, my aunts, my uncles—all my family will suffer humiliation and disgrace."

"You don't know that," Cordelia pointed out, a sentiment echoed with murmurs of agreement from the other two, but Ellie's next words made it clear their counsel was futile.

"You're darlings, all of you, to be concerned about me, but there is no need. I appreciate fully the course I am choosing. To protect my family, to secure their future and mine, and to preserve my father's reputation, I am quite willing to marry Bluestone, if he'll have me. Which reminds me . . . did you bring it, Cordelia?"

"I did." The countess paused, and Lawrence worked a finger between the dense yew branches with care, pushing a few of them aside to peek at the ladies on the other side, and he watched as Cordelia held out the sixpence to her friend. "Here it is, though under the circumstances, I ought to refuse to give it to you."

"I'd rather you wish me the luck of it."

"I want you to be happy, Ellie."

"I shall be content."

That wasn't the same thing, and a glance at the countess's face told him he wasn't the only one who appreciated the difference. But Ellie took the coin before her friend could say anything in that regard, and the silver gleamed in the sunlight as she held it up in her fingers.

"Something old," she said softly.

The duchess curled her gloved fingers over Ellie's. "Something new."

Cordelia lifted her hand, hesitated a moment, then placed it over that of the duchess. "Something borrowed."

"Something blue," Ellie said and pulled her hand out from under the others, the sixpence still caught in her fingers. "Let's hope it's Lord Bluestone."

It won't be, Lawrence vowed. *Not while I breathe air.*

"I have to go back," Cordelia said, interrupting his thoughts. "Kipp is sure to be pacing by now, for he wants us to arrive at Mallow Hills before dark."

"We shall accompany you," Miss Heywood said, laughing, "so you shall be safe from Mrs. Cranchester until you can be bundled into the carriage and taken off to Thornton's estate."

Ellie, to Lawrence's relief, demurred from this plan. "I shall take leave of you here, for as I said before, I must return to Wolford Grange at once. Cordelia, I wish you a lifetime of happiness in your marriage."

"Oh, I do hate it when you take the high road this way," grumbled the countess, "for it obligates me to do the same, and I don't wish to, not in this instance. Can't you save your father some other way?"

"And defy the sixpence?" Ellie countered, a lightness in her voice that Lawrence could only hope was forced. "I wouldn't dream of it. Now, my dear friends, I really must go."

Farewells and expressions of good luck were exchanged, along with a few more attempts by Cordelia to talk Ellie out of her plan. But eventually, the other three moved off toward the house, talking among themselves, and Lawrence once again peered through the opening he'd made in the hedge, thinking to determine which path Ellie was taking out of the garden. To his surprise, however, he found that in spite of her desire to be away, she hadn't moved. She was staring thoughtfully at the sixpence in her hand, giving Lawrence the opportunity to study her in his turn.

She'd left her hat behind, he saw at once, and that was a pretty fair indication of her preoccupied state of mind. A lady would never dream of venturing out of doors without a bonnet, and as far back as Lawrence could remember, Ellie had striven to be the perfect lady—polished, elegant, and always *comme il faut*.

He was one of only a few people who understood the girl beneath the carefully constructed façade—a girl who was both terribly insecure and fiercely loyal, a girl who had always sensed her father's weak and greedy character but had never been able to acknowledge it, not even to herself.

And he was the man destined to force her eyes open. He'd accepted that brutal fact six months ago. His position then had been one of lowly barrister, his only ambition to become worthy of marriage to an earl's daughter, but fate had put him in the path of a certain arsonist, the first crumb in a trail leading straight to Ellie's father, and once he'd learned the truth about Daventry, there had been no going back.

Ellie stirred, bringing his attention back to her as she held up the sixpence in her fingers to study it. Without a bonnet, her profile had no shield from his view, and he could plainly see the turned-up nose, plump cheek, and dimpled chin he'd known since childhood. Sunlight glinted on her wheat blond hair, reminding him of another sunny afternoon—a cold, bright afternoon in January—when the only girl he'd ever loved had expected him to forgo his honor and ignore the truth.

Tightness squeezed his chest as he remembered the bitter words they had exchanged that day. In the end, she'd chosen loyalty to her parent over her love for him, and he'd chosen honor and duty over his love for her. Neither of them could alter their course now.

He shut his eyes, striving to lay aside the past and put his priorities back in order. Countless men had died because of Daventry's greed, and although Ellie might be willing to marry a man she didn't love in order to save her father from the consequences of his actions, Lawrence wasn't about to let her make the sacrifice. Soon, he hoped to have the final piece of evidence to make his case and prove to Ellie and the world what sort of man Daventry really was. In the meantime, however, he had to prevent her from marrying the son of the Duke of Wilchelsey.

He looked at her again, watching as she tucked the sixpence carefully into her skirt pocket, and he was reminded of just how much sentimental attachment she and her friends had to the coin. An idea sparked to life in his mind.

For his own part, he was a rational man. He believed in facts and science, not silly things like lucky charms. He knew black cats and broken mirrors did not decide one's fate, and coins had never found anyone a spouse unless those coins arrived in the form of a dowry. But though he had teased Ellie and her friends about that sixpence many times during their childhood, he had never quite convinced them it had no power to find them husbands, and that failure might work in his favor now.

Lawrence watched Ellie for a moment longer, considering, then he straightened his cravat, raked a hand through his hair, and brushed the stray bits of yew from his coat. For what he intended to do, he needed to look his best.

Chapter 2

*E*llie wasn't a particularly superstitious person, but the six-pence was different, and with that particular coin securely in her pocket, she felt a sudden, overwhelming relief. She and her friends may have fancied that the sixpence would bring them husbands in a girlish spirit of *joie de vivre*, but it was a notion that had proven true for both Anne and Cordelia, and Ellie could only hope it proved true for her as well.

At the Delamere ball, when Bluestone had made his admiration and his intentions so plain, she had appreciated at once what it could mean for her family, and she had seen her future, clear as daylight. Lawrence was determined to ruin her father, so determined that he'd forsaken her for duty's sake and broken her heart. Now she had the power to stop him by marrying another man. She thought of Lawrence's love of chess, a game at which he had trounced her many times, and she smiled to herself.

Checkmate, Lawrence, she thought, patting her pocket. *Checkmate at last.*

A slight cough interrupted her thoughts, and Ellie looked up to find the object of them standing a dozen feet in front of her. The sight of him, leaning negligently against the gnarled trunk of a plum tree, his arms folded across his wide chest, obliterated Ellie's satisfaction and relief at once.

"What are you doing here?" she demanded.

"Well, I am Thornton's groomsman." He straightened away from the tree and started toward her. "I daresay my attendance at his wedding wasn't any great surprise. You must have seen me inside the church."

"You know quite well what I mean. What are you doing here, skulking about the garden?"

"Taking the air?" he suggested with an innocent demeanor that didn't fool her for a second. "Admiring the roses?"

"Or spying on me," she accused as he halted in front of her. "Poking and prying into my family's affairs does seem to be your favorite sport these days."

"Now, Ellie," he began, but she cut him off.

"Do not call me Ellie. I am Lady Elinor to you, Mr. Blackthorne."

If she expected this reminder that she was a peer's daughter to set him down a notch, she was disappointed. "Is that sort of formality really necessary between friends? After all," he added, moving a bit closer, "we've known each other half our lives."

"My gravest misfortune," she countered, and started around him, but he did not stand aside to allow her to pass. Blocked by him, by the hedge to her right and the rose border to her left, Ellie was forced to halt. Her only other escape was retreat, and with Lawrence Blackthorne, retreat seemed a nauseating option.

"Detaining a woman when she is unaccompanied is thoroughly improper," she pointed out. "Still, it's quite in keeping with the despicable behavior I've come to expect from you."

"We're not really traversing that particular ground again, are we? It's ages ago, and besides . . ." He paused, tilting his head to one side as he looked at her. "Propriety was never of much concern to us, was it, Ellie?"

The soft question made her catch her breath, and as she did, the scent of bay rum came to her along with the scents of the garden. Memories assaulted her at once, memories of happier days, when she'd been head over ears in love with him and willing—not only willing, but glad—to risk her virtue at any opportunity just to be alone with him. As she thought of those heady days, slipping away from Lady Wolford's watchful eye to meet him in a secluded corner of the gardens at Wolford Grange or Blackthorne Hall or ducking with him into the cupboard under the stairs at Papa's London house for a few stolen kisses, her heart twisted a little in her breast. What a besotted fool she'd been.

But no longer. She was now well aware of the ruthless determination and merciless regard for duty that lay beneath Lawrence's charm, and reminding herself of those traits of his character obliterated any lingering pangs of her girlhood infatuation. Ellie narrowed her gaze on his face, and in her mind, she worked to disparage the very things about him she'd once adored. To her, his raven black hair and cerulean eyes were no longer the stunning combination they'd once been. The tiny scar above his left brow was not the least bit dashing, and his pirate smile was anything but charming. The strong line of his jaw was born of sheer stubbornness—hardly an admirable quality—and the lean planes of his face were more hawklike than handsome.

"What you mean," she said at last, her voice as hard as she could make it, "is that propriety was never of much concern to *you*."

"Fair enough," he acknowledged, and leaned toward her, adopting a confidential air. "It won't work, you know. Marrying Bluestone won't save your father."

"You were eavesdropping?" Even as she asked the question, she chided herself for being surprised. "Of course you were. I ought to know by now you are capable of any amount of reprehensible conduct."

"Reprehensible?" He moved even closer, so close that she could see the indigo ring around each of his irises. "I don't seem to remember you thinking me reprehensible at all until half a year ago."

Despite her vow, his closeness was doing strange things to her insides, and she changed her opinion about the notion of retreat. She took several steps back, but then her leg hit the stone bench behind her, making her realize she had retreated too far, and since he'd followed her, she was now trapped in the rose arbor. Scowling, she lifted her chin. "Stand aside and let me pass."

Instead of heeding her demand, he did the opposite, closing the last scrap of distance between them. "On the face of it, your plan seems sound, I admit," he murmured, his smile widening because he knew—the snake—that she couldn't slip around him without shredding her pretty frock on the thorns. "And I applaud your ingenuity. But Wilchelsey might actually be the sort of man to put his duty to his country above his duty to his family. And even if he isn't that sort, he also isn't the only man on that committee. Even if you succeed in marrying his son, do you really think Wilchelsey has both the inclination and the influence to persuade the others to ignore my evidence?"

Galling as it was that Lawrence knew her plans, there was nothing to do at this point but brazen it out. She forced her mouth into what she hoped was a complacent smile. "What I think is that the Duke of Wilchelsey has more influence than one of Peel's insignificant little undersecretaries. And when your efforts come to naught, Peel will probably demote you back to being a barrister."

If he was worried about any of that, he didn't show it. "You might be right," he said amiably. "But only if you succeed."

"And since you don't seem to think there's any chance of that," she countered, "there is no reason for you to detain me here any further."

"No?" His thick, dark lashes lowered, then lifted, and a faint smile curved the corners of his mouth. "I can think of a reason."

Her heart slammed against her ribs, and she hated that even now, he could turn her upside down and inside out with nothing more than a suggestive glance and a few well-chosen words. "While I can think of none."

His amusement vanished, and something else flickered across his face, something that might have been regret. It was gone before she could be sure, but his next words told her he didn't regret a thing. "I'm curious, Ellie, I must admit. What is it about my investigation that you fear?" he asked, bending down closer. "I think you're afraid I'm about to topple dear Papa off the pedestal you've placed him on."

She opened her mouth to fire off a denial of that ridiculous assertion, but then closed it again. He was only trying to provoke her.

"Keeping mum, I see," he murmured, his lips so close to her face that his breath was like a caress on her cheek. "Fair enough. But really, Ellie . . . Bluestone? I thought you had better taste. After all, you once considered marrying me."

"A temporary madness, I assure you."

"Was it?" His hand curved around her hip as he spoke, and she jerked at the contact, but there was no escape, and though she could feel the heat of his palm burning her hip through the layers of her clothing, she forced herself to be still. "Was it really temporary, Ellie?"

She grasped his forearm, desperate to stop his bold caress. "Yes," she said and shoved his hand away. "Very temporary."

"Much to my regret." He stepped back, much to her relief, but before she could duck around him and escape, he spoke again. "You must realize I can't allow your plan to succeed."

"There is nothing you can do to stop it."

"You think not?" Lawrence opened his hand, and silver glinted on his palm. "I disagree."

She stared at the coin in disbelief. "You picked my pocket?"

"I did." He flipped the sixpence into the air with his thumb, but before she could even think to snatch the coin out of the air, he caught it again in his long, strong fingers. "And you didn't even notice."

She looked up into his face, and at the knowing gleam in his eyes and the pirate smile that curved his mouth, she felt a fury so strong it made her chest ache. "You cad," she breathed. "You despicable, dishonorable cad."

"I'm dishonorable?" Any amusement vanished, and a sudden spark of answering anger glinted like steel in his eyes. "No, Elinor, the dishonor here lies with a man who sold shoddy muskets to the British army."

"That is not true!" she burst out, even though she already knew any argument with Lawrence on this issue was pointless. "My father didn't know they were shoddy."

"He not only knew it, he was responsible for it."

"Only responsible in that he was deceived."

"Deceived? It was his factory. The choice of manufacturing materials was his decision. He chose to use inferior metals for the locks so that he could make a greater profit."

"Nonsense. His muskets were made to the East India Company's design and specifications, using the exact same materials."

He gave her a pitying look. "Dearest Ellie, is that what he told you?"

Anger flared in her, anger so hot it made her feel positively violent, but she worked to control it, curling her hands into fists at her sides. "Any guns my father provided would have been inspected by the British Ordnance—"

"Are you joking? By the end of the war, the Ordnance procedures for inspection and recordkeeping had completely broken down. It was chaos. Your father and his fellow manufacturing conglomerates in Birmingham made over a million muskets in the last few years of the war, Ellie, and many of those muskets were so poor in quality that they wore out within weeks of being placed with the regiments."

"And where is your proof of this?"

"Just imagine," he went on, blithely ignoring that question, "the poor soldier who found himself defenseless on a battlefield when the hammer of his musket broke, or the frizzen spring wore out, or the lock jammed, and his weapon could no longer fire. How many of those soldiers died, Ellie? Hundreds? Thousands?"

"This is ridiculous!" she burst out. "My father would never knowingly allow anyone to die."

"The hell he wouldn't. He was fully aware of the inferior quality of his materials, and he didn't give a damn about that, or about who might die as a result. And at the close of the war, when the rumors about the shoddy quality of his weapons started coming out, he got rid of the metals, and he had the factory burned down so that he wouldn't have to hand over his records to the army."

She drew a deep, steadying breath. "You don't know any of this, and you certainly can't prove it. Other enemies of my father tried to ruin him with these very same rumors over a dozen years ago, and they failed, because like you, they had no evidence for their baseless accusations. Now let me pass, for I will not tolerate this slander of him a single moment longer. And I certainly won't allow you to slander him to others through your precious committee and ruin his good name."

"By marrying Bluestone?" He slipped the coin into the pocket at the waistband of his trousers. "That's rather out the window now, isn't it?"

Ellie watched him pat his pocket and she felt a sudden pang of fear, but she covered it with a sound of derision. "Do you think I need a coin to secure Lord Bluestone's affections?"

He shrugged. "I don't know. Not to take anything from your charms, but even your dimpled smile and big brown eyes might not be enough to overcome the dictates of fate."

"I'll take my chances."

"Why should you have to?" he asked, his question halting her as she once again moved to step around him. "Wouldn't it be better to have the coin on your side?" he added, smoothing his waistcoat over his pocket, "just in case?"

"Much better," she agreed at once, and held out her hand. "So give it back."

He smiled. "Perhaps we could make a bargain for its return?"

She opened her mouth to refuse, but thoughts of Anne and Cordelia and their matrimonial successes flashed through her mind. For her, the stakes were high and time was short. Despite her bravado, she needed all the help she could get. "What sort of bargain?"

"I'll give you back the sixpence if you give me your word you won't marry Bluestone for . . . say . . . two months?"

She almost laughed at that, it was so absurd. "Why? So that you have more time to fabricate a case?"

"It's not fabrication. It's truth."

"If that is so, then show me the evidence you have against him."

"You know I can't reveal that information, especially not to you, of all people."

"Yes, so you said six months ago. I was expected to simply take your word that my father is a villain. My own father, the dearest man in the world to me."

"'Dearest man,' " he echoed softly, and the corner of his mouth twisted. "There was a time when I thought I was the one who held that place in your heart."

Pain shimmered through her, and she couldn't bear to listen to any more. She flattened her hands against his chest, shoving with all her strength, and to her relief, he gave ground. "I don't make bargains with devils," she said, and stepped around him. "Keep the sixpence. I shan't need it."

She walked away, and she could only hope she hadn't just defied the supernatural.

Chapter 3

*E*llie hurried along the lane as quickly as decorum, tight stays, and the path's potholes would allow. As she walked, she tried to keep her mind on her future, but as she approached the turn that led to Blackthorne Hall, her steps slowed and she couldn't stop her mind from tumbling back into the past.

How often had she walked this lane with Lawrence? she wondered. Two dozen? Three? More?

At least that many. After meeting Cordelia at Madame Rochambeaux's, she had begun coming here for summer holidays, vastly preferring Wolford Grange to the remote grandeur of Daventry Close. Able to stay with Lady Wolford, a distant cousin, she'd spent countless summer days here, exploring the woods, eating hard pears and fat blackberries, and punting on the stream with Cordelia, Beatrice, and Anne.

That's how they'd met Lawrence—a capsized boat, four wet and muddy schoolgirls, and a boy standing on shore having a good laugh at their expense. His amused reaction to their predicament had earned him a few choice words from Ellie, but he'd made up for his lapse of good manners by a gallant rescue of their fishing poles, picnic basket, and punt, and they'd become friends.

For nearly fifteen years, she and Lawrence had spent the summer just that way—fighting and making up and falling in love. But no fight, no matter how heated, had ever been able to part them, not until that fateful day six months ago, when they'd had a quarrel that no gallant rescue, no apologies, and no compromise could resolve. One fateful hour, she thought bitterly, and fifteen halcyon summers might never have happened.

Ellie stopped walking and turned to stare up the tree-lined road that led to Blackthorne Hall. How could Lawrence have done this? she wondered, still baffled, still not quite able to come to terms with what had happened to a love she'd thought would last forever.

Not only had he chosen to believe vicious rumors rather than her father's sworn denial, he had used those rumors for his own advancement, somehow convincing the Home Secretary to give him a position in the Home Office to investigate the supposed scandal. Even worse, he had expected her to accept his word of her father's supposed crimes as truth without offering her any proof, saying she could not be trusted with the information. He'd expected her to side with him against her own father, to turn on the man who had shown her nothing but the deepest love and affection, based on nothing but his word.

The rutted road blurred before her eyes, and she looked away, blinking hard to keep back tears. There was no point in crying over the past. The man she'd loved had chosen ambition and called it honor. He had sided against a man who had regarded him almost as a son, and with that choice, he'd turned his back on her love and all the dreams she'd built for their future.

A bark sounded nearby, forcing Ellie out of the past, and she turned her head to find a mass of gray and white fur barreling down the lane, headed straight for her.

"No, Baxter!" she cried in dismay, but her words came too late to stop Lawrence's rambunctious bobtail sheepdog. The animal sprang into the air and caught her at the shoulders.

She stumbled backward, and though she tried to right herself, her foot hit a rut, her ankle rolled, and she went down, hitting the hard-packed dirt with Baxter on top of her.

She tried to push the dog off, but he was too glad to see her to pay any heed. His hundred-pound body wriggled with happiness as he stood on top of her, licking her face and barking out enthusiastic greetings. He was so happy that despite her fall, she couldn't help but laugh, and it took a minute or two before she could catch her breath and manage a command that was sufficiently impressive.

"Baxter, no," she said, shoving at him again. "Sit."

The dog obeyed at once, planting his behind squarely on her stomach. "Woof," he said in reply, looking quite pleased with himself as his dark eyes peered down at her between the tufts of fur that covered his face.

"Are you all right?" another voice called, and Ellie turned her head to see Lawrence about fifty feet away, coming toward them on horseback.

Baxter jumped off Ellie at once, and she gave a sigh of relief as he bounded away to greet his master. "Well enough," she answered, sitting up as they approached. "But it's clear your dog needs training. He's grown quite wild since last I saw him."

"On the contrary." Lawrence reined the horse to a stop near her feet and glanced at Baxter, who promptly sat down, looking the picture of canine restraint. "He's very well behaved."

"Oh yes, very," she agreed, giving him a wry look as she began to brush the dusty paw marks from her dress.

"He is," Lawrence insisted. "Most of the time. And in your case," he added as he swung one long leg over the horse's back and dismounted, "you can't blame him, really. It's been a long time since you've paid a visit to Blackthorne Hall."

"I wasn't paying a visit," she pointed out as he dropped the reins and came to her side. "I was merely passing by on my way home."

"I know, but . . ." Lawrence paused beside her, doffing his hat. "He's missed you, Ellie."

Her heart twisted a little at those words, but she looked away before his perceptive eyes could see what she felt, and she was grateful when he spoke again.

"I'm sorry he knocked you down. Are you all right?"

"I think so."

He gave a nod and held out his hand to help her up. She tried to stand, but the moment she put weight on her right foot, sharp pain shot through her ankle, and she cried out, sinking back down to the ground.

At once, Lawrence tossed aside his hat, knelt beside her, and without so much as a by-your-leave, he jerked the hem of her skirt upward.

"What are you doing?" She gasped and tried to tug her skirt back down, a vain effort. "You have no right to take such liberties!"

She was ignored, which was not surprising. This was Lawrence, after all. Instead of answering, he eased a hand beneath her heel and lifted her foot, and his earlier words echoed through her mind.

Propriety was never of much concern to us, was it?

She thought of hot kisses in a stair cupboard, with his body pressed to hers and his hands roaming over her in places far more intimate than her foot, and a wave of sudden heat washed through her body.

Mortified, Ellie glanced up, but thankfully, Lawrence wasn't looking at her. His head was bent over her foot, his attention on her possible injuries, giving her the chance to regain her control. But even as she reminded herself that the wild, ungovernable passions he'd evoked in her were a thing of the past, the heat of his hands seemed to burn right through her silk stocking and made a liar of her.

Fortunately, he slipped off her shoe at that moment, and the stabbing pain that shot through her foot banished any erotic sensations. She inhaled sharply.

"Sorry," he said at once. "But it's important to know if you've broken anything." Cupping her heel in his palm, he continued his examination, his free hand roaming over her foot, and though his examination was gentle, it seemed an eternity before he eased her foot to the ground.

"You've not broken any bones," he said, "but you have sprained your ankle, I'm afraid."

Ellie gave a groan of frustration, but she stifled it at once. She had no time for lamenting things she could do nothing about. "Then you'll have to take me to Wolford Grange on your horse." She held out her hand, but this time, he didn't move to assist her to her feet. "Well, come on," she urged, waving her hand. "I'm supposed to be away for London with Lady Wolford this afternoon. We can't sit here dawdling."

"Can't we?" He gave a shrug and looked around. "It's a lovely day. And besides, you've had a bit of shock. Dawdling seems like a fine idea."

"But if I'm late, the marchioness won't wait. She'll journey to London without me." Even as she spoke, she realized what he was doing. "Oh, I see. If I'm not in London, I can't dine with Lord Bluestone tonight."

"Just so." He sat back on his heels. "And if you're not with him, he can't very well propose marriage to you, now, can he?"

Ellie glared at him, despising the tiny, satisfied smile that curved his mouth. "The depths to which you are willing to sink in order to achieve your ends never cease to amaze me."

"But Ellie, you are embarked on what I can only regard as a rash course. This delay might give you time to think, to reconsider. Why, I might be responsible for saving you from a disastrous marriage and a lifetime of living with a useless twit."

"You're such a hero."

Her sarcasm bounced off him like an arrow off a granite boulder. "I am, rather," he said with a false modesty that only increased her ire.

"In your own eyes, perhaps." She leaned forward to shove her skirt hem back down over her ankles. "For my part, I still think you're a cad."

"Insulting me is not very wise of you, given that I am your only means of getting home."

"That fact doesn't matter in the least," she countered at once. "Because I know you will take me home, regardless of what I say."

"You seem very sure."

"I am sure. Whatever I may think of you, you regard yourself as a gentleman, and if you wish to continue thinking so well of yourself, you certainly won't leave a young lady who has been injured lying alone and helpless in the road." She held out her hand.

His lips twisted in a wry curve. "Well, you've got me there," he murmured, and much to her relief, he stood up, pulling her with him.

Her relief, however, was short-lived. After lifting her onto his saddle, he swung up behind her, and as his body pressed against hers, Ellie couldn't help but tense at the intimate contact. When his arms slid around her waist so that he could take up the reins, she felt a flush of heat and embarrassment. This unnerving state of affairs became downright infuriating, however, when he urged the horse forward, for the pace he set was so slow that even with a sprained ankle, she could have traversed the distance more quickly by limping home on her own.

"Oh, for heaven's sake!" she cried, glaring at him over her shoulder. "You're being ridiculous. If Bluestone isn't able to propose to me this evening, he'll do so another day. This ploy to keep me from him won't work."

"Probably not," he agreed with aggravating good cheer and seemingly no inclination to move along any faster.

"You cannot prevent me from marrying him. If I am delayed today, I will still journey to London tomorrow. Papa will host another dinner party, inviting Lord Bluestone, and that will be that."

"I'm sure you're right."

These mild agreements only served to make her more inclined to hammer the point home. "He will propose, I will wed him, and your plans will be foiled."

"No doubt, no doubt, but there's many a slip between cup and lip, as the saying goes. After all, I still have your sixpence."

"As if that means anything. My friends and I may have believed in that nonsense when we were girls, but nonsense is all it is."

"We'll see."

"Yes, we will." With that, she pressed her lips together, refusing to say another word, ignoring his comments on the fine day, the beauty of the countryside, and the pleasure of such a leisurely ride. They arrived at Wolford Grange far later than she had intended, but Ellie was glad he hadn't managed to goad her into any further arguments.

Servants must have been instructed to watch for her approach, for Lawrence's horse had barely ambled into the circular drive in front of the house before the doors opened and the butler, Mr. Hymes, came hurrying out.

"Lady Elinor," he greeted as Lawrence brought his horse to a halt by the steps and dismounted. "We were growing concerned about you, my lady."

"I daresay," she agreed with a withering glance at Lawrence as he slid her from the saddle and into his arms. "I sprained my ankle walking home from Prior's Lodge, and as you see, Mr. Blackthorne was *kind* enough to bring me the remainder of the way."

Her sarcastic emphasis on his kindness wasn't lost on Lawrence. He grinned, hefting her body slightly in his arms, and she jerked her chin, looking toward the butler.

"Where is Lady Wolford?"

"I'm afraid she has departed, my lady." The butler paused as she groaned, and he gave her a look of apology. "You know how insistent she is upon punctuality. And I fear she was a bit cross about your failure to arrive in time to accompany her."

"I'm sure." Elinor glanced again at Lawrence and found that he was positively smirking. "Thank you again, Mr. Blackthorne. You may set me down, now."

"And leave you to hop up those steps? No, no, I couldn't possibly. My *kindness* won't allow it." He looked at the butler. "Lead the way, Mr. Hymes."

"It isn't necessary," she began, but the butler had already turned away and started into the house. Lawrence followed, carrying her across the foyer, up the stairs, and along the wide corridor to the drawing room, where he deposited her on a settee.

"Best not to put any weight on it for the next few days," he advised as he straightened. "How you'll manage that, if you're traveling to town, I can't think. Perhaps you should postpone the trip?"

His expression was grave, but there was laughter in his eyes.

Ellie pasted on a smile in response. "What a considerate gentleman you are, Mr. Blackthorne, but I wouldn't dream of disappointing my father in such a way. He has great plans for me this season, you know." Still smiling, she waved a hand toward the door. "We really mustn't keep you any longer, sir, for I'm sure you have many things to do."

"Indeed, I do. I must be home to pack, for I'm also away for London today."

Ellie's smile faltered. "You're going to London, too?"

"I am. I'd offer to take you with me in my carriage, but that wouldn't be proper. Your father will be worried, no doubt, but I shall call upon him when I arrive in town and tell him what's happened to delay you."

Ellie's eyes narrowed with suspicion. "You only arrived in Berkshire yesterday. Just why, pray, are you returning to town so soon?"

"Unlike the other gentlemen of your acquaintance, my time is not entirely my own. I have duties to which I must attend. And entertainments to arrange."

She made short shrift of his position in Peel's office with a derisive snort and focused on the latter part of his statement. "Do you really think Lord Bluestone would forgo dinner in my father's house this evening to play cards or carouse about town with you?"

"Given that he probably sees me as a rival for your affections, I doubt it."

As always, his particular way of agreeing with her was maddening and made her even more inclined to argue. "He does not see you as any kind of rival. Why should he?"

"No reason whatsoever."

"Still, he'd never be so rude as to cancel at the last moment, and certainly not for your company."

"As to my company, I'm sure you're right. On the other hand,

Bluestone is quite fond of gambling and drink—perhaps too fond, but that's a story for another day. He might, however, deem the tables and whiskey at White's far more amusing than dinner with your father, especially if you aren't there."

"Your effort to diminish the viscount in my eyes won't succeed. And even if you somehow manage to divert him for this one evening, you won't be able to do that every evening."

"I'm sure. Your beauty far outweighs the allure of the gaming tables. Even Bluestone isn't thick enough to think otherwise. But tell me," he went on before she could take issue with his estimation of the viscount's intelligence. "Daventry knows about Bluestone, of course? And he approves the match?"

"Of course he approves," she snapped and regretted it at once. "My father did not suggest this course of action to me!"

"Nor has he tried to deter you from it?"

Ellie felt a sudden pang—of doubt or fear, she couldn't decide—but she shoved it away, reminding herself of the ulterior motives of the man goading her. "Papa approves because this is a good match for me, not for any other reason. And," she went on before he could express doubt on that point, "it's only because of you that the possibility of a good marriage for me has ever been diminished."

If he had any regrets on that score, he didn't show it. Instead, he tilted his head to one side, studying her so long and so thoughtfully that she squirmed beneath the scrutiny. "What are you staring at?" she demanded, feeling defensive, uneasy, and oddly vulnerable. "What are you thinking?"

"I'm wondering what sort of man approves of his daughter selling herself to save his skin."

She was on her feet at once, barely noticing the pain in her injured foot and wholly unaware of what she was doing. Only the cracking snap of her hand against Lawrence's cheek made her realize she'd slapped him.

At once, she pressed her stinging hand to her lips, appalled that she had allowed him to provoke her to violence.

He looked back at her, his countenance grave. "You needn't

worry about Bluestone, Ellie," he said quietly. "I shan't make any attempt to divert him from your side."

She frowned in disbelief. "No?"

"No." Once again, his face donned its usual easygoing good humor. "I have an entirely different line of attack in mind."

She took a deep breath, forcing down another pang of worry. "Do what you must," she said. "And so will I."

"I'm glad we are in accord at last, my dear," he said, touched his fingers to the brim of his hat, and gave her a bow. "Now, I shall leave you in the capable hands of Mr. Hymes and be on my way. My great-aunt Agatha will be quite worried if I've not arrived at Cavendish Square by nightfall."

He departed, but though she was relieved he was gone at last, Ellie couldn't help but wonder just what deviltry he did have in store.

With Lawrence, alas, there was no way to know. His brain could conjure up any number of schemes to cause trouble, making it all the more incumbent upon her to reach town as soon as possible.

She reached for the bellpull on the wall behind her, and gave it a tug. A moment later, Mr. Hymes appeared, and she beckoned him to her side. "I'll need assistance up to my room, Mr. Hymes. Then send my maid to me and order another traveling carriage readied."

"Another carriage, my lady?"

"Yes. I am still going to London tonight."

Hymes stared at her, aghast. "Oh, Lady Elinor, Lady Wolford wouldn't like it if you traveled to town unaccompanied."

"I have no intention of doing so. You will send a footman to Prior's Lodge to tell Cordelia's aunts of my predicament, explain that my need to travel to London today is quite urgent, and inquire if one of those good ladies could possibly accompany me."

"But, my lady, what of your ankle?"

"Hang my ankle." She paused and looked out the window, staring daggers at the broad back of the man riding away down the lane. "Sprained ankle or no," she added under her breath, "I refuse to stand meekly by while that man works to ruin my family."

WITHIN AN HOUR, Ellie had received a reply from Prior's Lodge, and much to her satisfaction, one of Cordelia's aunts would be happy to escort her to town straightaway.

Another hour, and Ellie was at last on her way, Cordelia's Aunt Bunty beside her. In honor of the fine day, the top of the carriage had been rolled down, and with her ankle comfortably propped up on a pile of cushions and the warm breeze flowing past her face, Ellie's worries began to ease away.

They'd gone a mere five miles, however, when the carriage suddenly slowed, and Ellie straightened on the seat, suddenly alert. "What is it, Avery?" she asked the driver on the box.

"One of the horses is having a bit of trouble, my lady. May have gone lame."

She watched in dismay as Avery pulled the pair of grays to a halt and climbed down to examine the hooves of the horse in question. "He's lame, right enough," the driver said at last. "Lost a shoe."

Ellie fell back against the seat with a groan. "Of all the rotten luck," she mumbled, rubbing one gloved hand over her forehead. "Now what shall we do?"

"Chipping Clarkson's just up ahead, my lady," the driver told her. "We'll walk the carriage into the village and have the black-smith take a look."

The blacksmith of Chipping Clarkson, however, proved unable to see to the unfortunate horse, for he was in bed.

"In bed?" Ellie blinked, staring in dismay at the proprietress of the Black Swan, who also happened to be the wife of the black-smith. "At this hour of the day?"

"Down with the grippe, ma'am. Our boy, too. Half a dozen other people as well."

Ellie was conscience-stricken at once. "Oh, I'm so sorry."

"They'll be all right now, miss. Leastways, that's what the doctor said this morning. Fever's broken, you see, but most of them are weak as babes, still. We've sent to Chalmsby for their blacksmith's boy, but we got word back he won't be able to come or send anyone until the day after tomorrow."

"Is there anyone else in this village with the requisite skills to replace a shoe?"

"Oh no, ma'am," the innkeeper told her. "Leastways, not just now. We're a small village here, you see, and with so many having been sick, all the able men are tending the fields. They'll be out until it's pitch dark, and off again at dawn. It's planting time, and with so few men to help, every minute of daylight is needed."

"Of course. Might we hire another pair of horses, then, to resume our journey?"

She might just as well have asked for dinner from a French chef. "Oh, miss, we've no horses to spare for hiring out. As I said, we're a small village."

Ellie began to feel truly desperate. "Perhaps one of the local men might be willing to take us to London?"

This notion seemed even more beyond the good lady's comprehension. "Oh no, ma'am. None of our men go to London. They can't be spared from their work to go that far. You see, we're a—"

"Small village," she said in unison with the woman opposite. "Yes, I see."

"Now then." The rotund, red-haired proprietress of the Black Swan opened the book in front of her with a brisk air. "You'll be wanting a room for the next two nights, I suppose?"

Ellie sighed, and Bunty patted her shoulder. "It's a disappointment, my dear. But there's little we can do. It seems we are stranded here until Wednesday."

That assessment of their situation proved too generous. The blacksmith's boy from Chalmsby didn't arrive in Chipping Clarkson for another full day, so Ellie's six-hour journey to London ended up taking three full days. She arrived at the house in Portman Square late Thursday evening, too late to see her father, who was already out for the evening.

The following morning at breakfast, the earl expressed great relief at her arrival, but also some bewilderment. "Thank heaven you've appeared at last," he said as they walked into the morning room together. "That bounder Blackthorne informed me that you had sprained your ankle and would be delayed, but three days?" He shook his head, frowning as they took seats at the table. "Really, Elinor, what delayed you so long?"

She gave him a wry look as she sat down. "Several ridiculous mishaps, Father."

"Indeed, Lord Daventry," Bunty put in as she took the chair to the earl's right hand. "It was a series of events so unlucky that it almost seemed like destiny."

Ellie stiffened in her chair, feeling again that pang of uneasiness. As Bunty related the events of the past few days, she tried to dismiss the feeling, for it was ridiculous to think there was such a thing as preordained bad luck, and the missing sixpence had nothing to do with the events of the past few days. Nothing at all.

"My, my, you have been unfortunate," the earl remarked as Bunty came to the end of her narrative.

"We may have been delayed, that's true." Ellie lifted her teacup in a toast. "But we're here now."

"Indeed," Bunty added with a laugh. "We've defied fate, it seems."

Ellie choked on her tea, causing her father and Bunty to look at her with concern. "I'm all right," she managed, but even as she spoke, Lawrence's words echoed through her mind.

Even your dimpled smile and big brown eyes might not be enough to overcome the dictates of fate.

Angry with herself, she set down her cup and reminded herself how ridiculous it was to think a coin could have any influence over her destiny. It was high time, she decided, to change the direction of this conversation to something more pleasant and productive.

"How was your dinner with Lord Bluestone?" she asked as she picked up her knife and fork. "I trust the two of you had a pleasant evening together?"

Her father paused over his eggs and bacon for only a moment, but it was long enough for Elinor to see a glimmer of worry cross his face. "Bluestone wasn't able to come to dinner, I'm sorry to say."

Her anger with herself for speculating about superstitious non-sense gave way to anger of a different sort, and she cursed Lawrence for getting to London ahead of her and making mischief. But her father spoke again, making her appreciate that blaming Lawrence had been premature.

"The viscount has caught a cold. He's all right," the earl hastened to add. "In the note he sent me, he assured me of that. His physician has prescribed bed rest, but he is certain he'll be back on his feet within a few days."

"Well, that's a relief." She paused a moment, noting that her father did not seem to share that opinion.

"It is," she insisted when he didn't reply. "A cold is a trifling thing, he will soon be well, and we can try again. Supper and cards, along with several of our friends? For that sort of evening, it is perfectly acceptable to issue a spur-of-the-moment invitation."

The earl nodded in agreement. "Perhaps I should call upon the viscount this afternoon? Inquire after his health, you know, express our concern. He even might be up to receiving visitors, and if so, I could issue the invitation directly. And who knows?" His expression lightened a bit. "He might bring up the topic of your future, and we could settle things then and there."

Ellie felt a sudden, inexplicable wave of dismay. "No," she said without thinking, her voice sharp, and at her father's look of surprise, she added, "You're so old-fashioned, Papa. If I am to be honored with the viscount's proposal, I should very much like it to be made to me, not to my father. Besides, if the viscount isn't quite well, we wouldn't want to put him in the awkward position of feeling obligated to see you. Call on him, but do so in the morning just to leave your card. If his illness is as trifling as it seems, he will surely be well enough to attend the Atherton ball on Friday, and you can issue the supper invitation then. Any sooner, and it might seem a bit . . . well . . . desperate. And we're not that, I should hope," she added with a forced laugh.

Her father laughed with her, but in his face she saw a hint of the desperation they both denied, and Lawrence's voice whispered to her mind like a chill wind.

I'm wondering what sort of man approves of his daughter selling herself to save his skin.

Her father looked at her and frowned, as if he could see her apprehension written on her face. He picked up her hand. "I do so want to see you settled, my dear. It's important that happen soon, before . . ." He paused and swallowed hard, glancing at Bunty, then back to her. "I want to see you settled," he said again, and let go of her hand to pick up his knife and fork.

"Spoken like a good father, indeed," Bunty put in with approval. "Not all fathers would be so generous. Many would prefer their daughters never married and stayed forever at home to look after them."

Her father laughed again, and yet, watching him out of the corner of her eye, Ellie couldn't shake her uneasiness. *Damn Lawrence,* she thought as she picked up her knife and fork. He could find and exploit anyone's weaknesses or fears, however small, for he was so devilishly clever.

No, I have an entirely different line of attack in mind.

Just what had he meant by that? she wondered, her hands stilling over her plate. If he wasn't intending to divert Bluestone from her, what was his plan?

Unfortunately, there was no way to know. With Lawrence, it could be anything, so she gave up trying to anticipate his next move and resumed eating her breakfast. Whatever plan he was concocting, she intended to be safely wed before he could implement it.

Chapter 4

The crossing over the Irish Sea was rough, the rain torrential, and all the roads out of Dublin mires of mud. Three days had passed since his encounter with Ellie before Lawrence managed to reach Drummullin, a tiny hamlet in the middle of County Roscommon. Night had fallen and the rain had eased to a gentle sprinkle by the time he arrived at the shabby inn on the edge of the village.

His initial knock on the door yielded no response, nor did his second. He tried a third time, to no avail. He began to fear this entire ghastly journey had been a waste of time, when at last the door opened.

The elderly man on the threshold scowled at the sight of him, a reaction that did not surprise Lawrence in the least. "Damn it, man, I told you in my last letter that I needed more time to consider."

Lawrence set down his traveling valise and removed his dripping wet hat. "I fear we may no longer have the luxury of time, sir."

John Hammersmith looked him over, noting his soaked cloak and muddy boots, and heaved a sigh. "Best come in," he muttered, and opened the door wide. "But remove your boots first," he added as he started up the stairs, his gait awkward, his left leg stiff as a board. "My landlady's a tartar."

Lawrence did as he was bid, leaving his boots in the minuscule foyer, along with his cloak, hat, and valise. On stockinged feet, he followed the other man up the stairs and into a small parlor.

"I'd offer port," Hammersmith said as he opened a cabinet against the far wall. "But from the look of you, whiskey's a better choice."

With a murmur of thanks, Lawrence accepted the glass of whiskey and one of the chairs before the fire that the other man offered him.

"So, what's happened to bring you here?" Hammersmith asked, settling into the chair beside him. "Though I don't know why I should want to know."

"There is a possibility my investigation of Daventry will be quashed."

Much to Lawrence's irritation, Hammersmith didn't seem surprised. "Told you the worm would wiggle his way off the hook." He paused for a swallow of whiskey. "How'd it come about?"

"The earl's daughter may soon be engaged." He paused, finding it hard to get the words out. "To Viscount Bluestone."

"Little Ellie marrying a duke's son?" He looked up sharply. "Wasn't she supposed to be marrying you?"

"She was." Lawrence took a hefty swallow of whiskey. "Until I chose to do my duty."

"Ah." That single murmured word held a wealth of understanding.

"A duke, eh?" Hammersmith went on after a moment, and made a sound of contempt. "Well, so much for your man Peel's attempts at reform. The aristocracy's always been able to thwart justice when one of their own's in trouble, and that fact won't be changing any time soon, even if Peel gets his Metropolitan Police."

Lawrence's irritation deepened, mainly because he feared the other man might be right. "It's not only the fact that Wilchelsey's a duke. It's worse than that. He is also in charge of the investigation committee to which I shall be presenting the results of my inquiry. He will have the final say as to whether or not the evidence warrants bringing Daventry before the House of Lords for trial."

Hammersmith gave a short laugh. "Best get on with it, then, before Ellie marries into the duke's family."

"Just so. But I need evidence that ties the faulty guns directly to Daventry's munitions factory."

"When you came to me in December you said every other munitions supplier operating out of Birmingham at the time had been cleared of manufacturing the faulty guns, and that's what made you sure it had to be Daventry. Isn't that evidence?"

"An absence of evidence is hardly conclusive. Daventry can claim the other manufacturers falsified their records to cover their traces. Given that his own factory burned down, destroying his records, I don't have enough evidence to make a case against him."

"You've got Sharpe, don't you? Daventry ordered him to burn the place down, you said."

Lawrence leaned back with his glass, giving the other man a wry look. "The testimony of a man in prison won't hold any great sway."

"Even if he's in prison for arson?"

"All that would prove is that Daventry burned down his own building, not why he did it. And Sharpe's arson conviction wasn't for Daventry's factory. The only reason he offered me his story is because I was prosecuting his case and he hoped I would agree to lessen his sentence in exchange for his testimony about Daventry. I was able to agree to his terms, but for his testimony to be of any use, I still need corroboration. I have managed to acquire a collection of the faulty guns, but they all lack a maker's mark." He met the other man's eyes. "But then," he added softly, "you knew that already."

Hammersmith stiffened in his chair, apparently sensing they were about to have the same conversation they'd had in December when Lawrence had first discovered him here, holed up in an obscure speck of the Irish countryside. In that conversation, Hammersmith had confirmed his worst fears about Ellie's father, but he had refused to come forward. Lawrence's subsequent entreaties by letter had not changed his mind, and the other man's next words told Lawrence that he had still not done so.

"Surely, Mr. Blackthorne, army records can give you the proof you need. The British Ordnance—"

"The purchase orders for all guns from Daventry's factory are missing. I've searched every dusty crate of papers in the British Ordnance, and I can find no trace of Daventry's guns."

"That's a pity."

"You have a talent for understatement, sir." Lawrence's voice was bitter. "I have nothing that links Daventry directly to the manufacture of the faulty guns except the testimony of a convicted arsonist." He paused, gesturing to the other man with his glass. "And you."

"As I've repeatedly said, I can't help you."

"You were Daventry's accounting clerk. If anyone can testify as to what the earl did, it's you."

"I've already told you, I can't testify."

"And as I told you in my last letter, Peel has agreed to grant you immunity in exchange for your testimony. He wants Daventry, not you."

"I can't, I tell you!"

"Can't? Or won't?"

"Does it matter?" His face took on a belligerent cast. "I'm not living in Ireland because I like the weather, you know. Daventry thinks John Hammersmith died in the fire, and I intend to keep it that way."

"I realize you might have some trepidation about returning to England and facing him—"

"Trepidation?" Hammersmith gave a laugh, though Lawrence suspected there was no amusement in it. "You could say that, yes. I barely escaped that fire with my life."

"It was late. Daventry couldn't have known you were still there when Sharpe set the fire."

"Couldn't he? Somehow, I have more faith in the earl's ability to know things than you do."

Lawrence sighed, knowing the other man could be right. Who really knew the depths to which Daventry could sink? "I will arrange protection for you."

"How kind."

Lawrence ignored the ironic inflection in the other man's voice. "You are my best hope. You know what he did, the decisions that were made. You were there."

"I was a clerk! I couldn't do anything to stop him. He was determined to milk as much money out of it as he could, and I couldn't stop him!" There was anguish in his voice, and Lawrence felt a glimmer of hope. But after a moment, the other man fell back in his chair with a sigh. "What does it matter now?"

"Hundreds, perhaps thousands, of men may died because of Daventry's greed. Don't you care? For God's sake," he added as Hammersmith made no reply, "you were in the British navy before being invalided out after Trafalgar."

"Aye. And what did I get when I fought for King and country?" The other man touched a hand to his knee, scowling. "This."

"Forget King and country. What of the men you fought with? Your comrades-in-arms? Will you see the ones who died because of Daventry go unavenged? You say you couldn't do anything then. But you can do something now."

Hammersmith turned away, his jaw working, staring into the fire, rubbing his knee. He was silent so long that Lawrence feared he'd played his last card to no avail, when at last the older man stirred and reached for his cane.

"Wait here," he said as he stood up and left the room. When he returned a few minutes later, he had a large book in his hand, a volume worn with time and blackened by soot.

"The fire didn't burn everything." He thrust the book under Lawrence's nose. "I managed to grab this on my way out. Take it."

Lawrence did so, setting it on his lap and carefully pulling back the cloth-bound cover. When he saw the columns of neatly penned figures and the names and descriptions beside them, his heart gave a leap in his chest. Tin, he noted, had been purchased in significant quantities. No part of a British musket ought to be made with a soft metal like tin. Tin, however, could be made to look like steel in a cursory inspection, and tin was cheap.

He looked up. "But why didn't you give this record to me when I came to you in December?"

"Because you're one of them. You're part of Daventry's social sphere."

"I'm not, actually. My father was merely a squire. I have an estate, yes, but I am not a peer."

"No, but you are a *gentleman*." His contempt for that particular breed was clear in his voice. "Your lot usually hangs together when it comes down to it. I never thought you'd turn on him in the end."

"Giving me this book indicates you've changed your opinion of me. Why?"

He shrugged. "You gave up the girl."

Lawrence felt cold suddenly, remembering that January afternoon and the bitter words he and Ellie had exchanged, and the choice he had made. He downed the rest of his whiskey in one swallow. "The decision was mutual," he said as he set aside his empty glass.

Hammersmith gestured to the book on Lawrence's lap. "Does that give you the corroboration you need?"

Lawrence turned several more of the fragile pages, scanning the notations and numbers in Hammersmith's neat copperplate hand, then he looked up to meet the other man's gaze. "This might be enough, and it might not. It's hard to say. Daventry still has a great deal of influence. So does the Duke of Wilchelsey."

"Which is why your cause, while noble, is ultimately doomed."

"Not if you testify. Combined with this, your testimony would clinch the case against Daventry."

The other man glared at him, but did not reply, and Lawrence decided to take that as an encouraging sign. He waited, staring straight back, and at last, the older man spoke. "Read that first," he said with a sigh. "Then . . . we'll see."

Lawrence didn't know whether to be relieved or disappointed by the equivocation. Still, he thought, his grip tightening around the ledger in his hands, he had more evidence now than he'd had before. His trip had not been in vain. He would have to be content with that, at least for now.

During the season, possession of a large London house was of more importance than the Holy Grail. The Marchioness of Atherton was fortunately placed in that regard, and her beautiful home on Park Lane meant that the Atherton ball was always one of the most sought-after invitations of the London season.

Over three hundred people were crowded into the marchioness's ballroom by the time Ellie arrived with her father. Finding Lord Bluestone, she appreciated as her gaze roamed over the crowd, would prove a difficult task.

Finding certain other gentlemen, however, proved far too easy. Between the dancers gliding across the ballroom floor, Ellie's gaze caught the dark, chiseled countenance of Lawrence Blackthorne, and she felt a sudden pang of alarm. Ever since that man had reappeared in her life, nothing but trouble had come her way. God only knew what fresh aggravations lay in store.

As if to answer that question, he looked past the dancers to find her watching him. He grinned at once and drew something from the coin pocket in the waistband of his trousers. He held it up in his fingers, and Ellie's misgivings gave way to outrage at the sight of her sixpence. *Arrogant devil*, she thought as he tucked the coin back into his pocket. How dare he taunt her with his theft of her property?

"Lady Elinor," a friendly female voice broke into her thoughts, and grateful for the interruption, she turned to find the Duchess of Wilchelsey at her elbow.

"Duchess," she greeted, offering a bow. As she straightened, Ellie glanced around, but to her dismay, the duchess's son was nowhere in sight. "How delightful to see you."

"Is it?" The older woman chuckled, recapturing Ellie's full attention. "More delightful if my son were with me, I daresay."

Caught out, Ellie blushed, but the duchess only seemed to find that even more amusing, for she laughed again. "You'll look for him in vain, my dear. Bluestone isn't here this evening. He and his father have both left me all on my own this evening, can you believe it?"

"Oh." Ellie swallowed hard at that disappointing news, but rallied. "I shall be perfectly content with your company, Duchess."

"You're a sweet child," the other woman said, tapping Ellie's arm with her fan, "but you're not fooling me." She turned to Ellie's father with an acknowledging nod. "Daventry."

"Duchess." He bowed gallantly over her hand, retaining it as he straightened, giving her the dazzling smile that had made him quite the ladies' man in his day. "My daughter may be disappointed by the absence of your husband and son this evening, but I am not, for it means I shall have you to myself."

"Not so. Lord Wetherby has already asked me to dance the next with him."

"That villain," the earl pronounced at once, earning himself the duchess's amused laugh.

"You are a shameless flirt, Daventry. You always have been."

Ellie slid her foot sideways, delicately tapping her father's toe before he could continue this playful badinage. Papa, thankfully, took the hint. "Then, since you have been so cruel as to accept Wetherby's invitation to dance before even allowing me the chance to offer mine, you shall have to make it up to me by accepting a different sort of invitation. Supper and cards, let us say, on Monday next?"

"It sounds lovely, but I couldn't possibly accept. Not without the duke. Coming to a ball on my own is all very well, but supper and cards at the home of a widower? That is far too intimate an occasion to attend alone. My husband, you see, is the jealous type and quite possessive of me."

"Bring your husband along, then." He paused to smile. "If you must. And that son of yours, too," he added carelessly, "if he's available?"

"My dear man, I'm afraid it just isn't possible. Neither of them will be back for at least a fortnight."

"Back?" Ellie and her father said in unison. They exchanged another glance, but Ellie was the one who asked for further elucidation. "But where have they gone?"

"Somerset. Wilchelsey had an express letter this afternoon from his steward, recommending that he return to Crosshedges at once. He did so this afternoon, and Bluestone accompanied him."

Given the things that had been happening to her of late, Ellie wasn't the least bit surprised. At this point, another hitch in her plans seemed almost inevitable. "Not bad news, I trust?"

"Devastating. One of the tenant cottages caught fire. It spread to several more and burned two fields before a rainstorm came up and snuffed it out."

"Was anyone hurt?"

"Fortunately not."

Grateful for that at least, Ellie returned to the subject preying on her mind. "Will it truly be a full fortnight before they return to town?"

The duchess smiled. "Don't fret, my dear. Long faces won't bring them back any sooner. Now, I must be off, for I see Wetherby coming to claim me."

"Of course," Ellie murmured, dipping her knees for a farewell curtsy as the older woman turned to depart.

"You can have the next, Daventry," the duchess added over her shoulder. "If you're fit enough for a polka?"

At the earl's assurance that a polka was well within his physical abilities, the duchess took Wetherby's arm and departed, leaving Ellie and her father staring gloomily after them.

"Well, well." The earl turned to offer her a smile, but Ellie saw it falter almost at once. "We've had quite the run of bad luck lately, haven't we?"

"Indeed, we have," she agreed, and she wondered if that bad luck might actually be cause and effect.

Could the sixpence be to blame? Surely not. And yet, Bluestone had been on the brink of proposing, and everything had been going along swimmingly, until . . .

Her gaze slid to the man on the other side of the ballroom. This ridiculous string of mishaps and misfortunes had started with Lawrence and his act of blatant theft. But if the crazy notion in her head was true, if the loss of her sixpence was responsible for her inability to receive a proposal of marriage from Lord Bluestone, what could she do about it?

She studied Lawrence for several moments, considering the question, but she knew there was only thing she could do, and when she watched him leave his circle of friends and move to the refreshment table, she knew this was her chance to do it.

She turned to her father. "Will you pardon me for a few moments, Papa? I have some important business to attend to."

"Important business?" he echoed. "At a ball?"

"Believe it or not, yes." She moved to step around her parent, but his bewildered voice stopped her.

"My dear child, where you going?"

"To change our luck." With that enigmatic reply, Ellie started across the ballroom.

Chapter 5

awrence surveyed the pale yellow liquid in the punch bowl before him without enthusiasm. Why, he wondered as he took up a glass cup, did warm lemonade always seem to be the only beverage available at a ball?

"Lawrence?"

The sound of that voice, once so dear and still so achingly familiar, caught him quite off guard. Despite how he'd teased her by waving her sixpence about, he hadn't expected her to approach him or deign to speak to him. "Why, Ellie—"

"I must speak with you," she said, cutting through any attempt at small talk.

"Indeed?"

"Yes." Without looking at him, she took a cup from the round refreshment table and moved to stand across from him, pretending vast interest in the punch bowl between them. "You have something that belongs to me," she went on, ladling a measure of lemonade into her cup. "I want it back."

"I daresay you do." He grinned. "You've been having quite the run of bad luck lately."

"I don't know what you mean."

Her attempt to dissemble didn't fool him for a second. "First, a sprained ankle and a three-day delay getting to London. Then your precious Bluestone catches a cold—"

"How you know Bluestone's state of health baffles me."

He shrugged. "I have my spies. It seems that your plans to secure Bluestone keep getting waylaid by circumstance."

Fire flashed in her dark eyes. "I want my sixpence back, Lawrence."

"What if I don't want to give it back?"

"I'm willing to negotiate for its return."

At once, his mind began envisioning tantalizing possibilities, but he forced them aside and took a sip of lemonade. "I'm listening."

"Not here." She set the ladle back in the punch bowl and cast a quick glance around. "Meet me later, in the folly."

He was so stunned he almost dropped his cup, and it took him a moment to manage a reply that was sufficiently offhand.

"Why, Lady Elinor, what a scandalous proposition." He leaned a bit closer to her over the table. "Dare I hope," he murmured, "you have something delightfully naughty in mind?"

"Don't be absurd."

"I suppose that means no," he said, and sighed. "How disappointing." But as he spoke, he found, to his dismay, that his words conveyed none of the sarcasm he'd intended. She glanced at him, and he spoke again to divert her before she could discern what he felt. "What time would you like this rendezvous?"

"Midnight. And for heaven's sake, make sure no one sees you slip away."

With that, she used the tongs to place a slice of lemon in her cup, then she departed, leaving Lawrence staring after her as she moved to join a group of her friends.

What can this mean? he wondered. By meeting him, she would be putting her reputation at enormous risk, jeopardizing her future and her plans to save her father. She must truly be desperate to get that sixpence back.

How desperate? His gaze lowered speculatively to the creamy expanse of bare skin above the deep, square neckline of her pale pink ball gown, but after only a moment, he forced his gaze back up again with the reminder that he could not allow his body to do his thinking for him.

The sixpence, he supposed, might simply be an excuse to get him alone, but he could see no reason for it, unless she intended to seduce him into stopping his investigation, and that was a notion he just couldn't credit. As for the coin itself, it was just a sixpence, after all, and though it had a certain sentimental value to her and to her friends, it was hardly worth the risk she was taking.

The only other possibility was that despite her denials to him the day of Thornton's wedding, she must genuinely believe the myth from her girlhood about the coin's power. If so, she would regard all the hitches that had occurred in her plans during the past week not as a series of trifling coincidences, but as the result of the sixpence's absence from her possession, which meant he had the upper hand in these negotiations.

Lawrence grinned. He always did prefer having the upper hand, especially where Ellie was concerned.

Ellie might regard him as a thorough-paced villain nowadays, but he had no intention of proving it by playing fast and loose with her reputation. He said his good-byes to his hostess and departed the ball, then he circled around to the back of the house, scaled the garden wall, and arrived at the little stone folly tucked away in a corner of Lady Atherton's garden with a quarter hour to spare.

The minutes seemed to crawl by, and he couldn't help but remember the many times he and Ellie had snuck away for rendezvous like this one.

No, he corrected at once, feeling a tinge of bitterness, not like this one.

He leaned his back against the solid stone interior of the folly, his gaze on the open doorway that led into the circular structure, his mind going into the past.

All the other times they'd met like this, they'd been mad with passion. Heedless, too, convinced that since they were to marry, the risks of being alone together were well worth taking. Now?

Now, everything was different. Passion had given way to angry words and distrust, and they were no longer the reckless fools for love they'd been six months ago. Now they were two people standing athwart, their passion for each other torn asunder by their loyalty to others. There was no going back.

Sometimes, he wanted to. He'd often wished he had never been assigned to represent the Crown against the arsonist James Sharpe or that he'd listened to his story or taken that story to Peel, or run John Hammersmith to earth. He could have kept it all to himself and buried Daventry's secret, and though he'd have had a cur for a father-in-law, he would at least have had Ellie.

But he'd chosen to do his duty as a servant of His Majesty's Government, and he'd tried not to look back or think of what he'd lost. Most of all, he tried not to question if the sacrifice had been worth it.

A flicker of movement brought Lawrence out of the past, and he watched as Ellie paused in the arched opening of the folly, one hand on the stone casement. "Lawrence?" she called softly.

The shaft of moonlight that fell through the open doorway behind her prevented him from seeing her face, but it shimmered along the lines of her pale silk dress and outlined the slender curves of her body, calling to the desire he still felt for her and making him long more than ever for the old days.

"Lawrence?" she called again, more urgently this time, and he swallowed hard, forcing down memories and regrets. Straightening away from the wall, he emerged from the shadows. "I'm here."

At the sight of him, she came inside, but she halted midway across the round room, still half a dozen feet from where he stood. "We don't have much time," she said. "As I told you, I want my sixpence."

"And if I give it to you, what shall you give me in return?"

"Why should I give you anything for returning my property?"

"Because possession is nine-tenths of the law?"

"Law?" she scoffed. "That's rich. You picked my pocket, and now you dare to talk about the law?"

"Is that argument meant to persuade me? Because if so, I'm afraid you're failing. You'll have to do better, Ellie, if you truly want it back. And you did say you were willing to negotiate," he added when she didn't reply.

She studied him for a moment, then capitulated with an exasperated sigh. "Oh, very well. I'll give you what you want."

"What I want," he repeated, his gaze sliding down before he could stop it, igniting the arousal that he'd been keeping at bay for months.

In the moonlight, her skin glowed like alabaster, pale and luminous, but he knew from experience it was more like soft, warm silk. His gaze caught at the shadowy cleft between her small, shapely breasts, calling to the desire inside him.

"Stop it, Lawrence," she said as if reading his mind. "That's not what I meant."

He forced his gaze back up to her face. "More's the pity."

"You said you'd give back the sixpence if I held off becoming engaged to Lord Bluestone. Very well. I agree to your terms. I give you my word that I will postpone any announcement of an engagement between us for one fortnight."

"I asked for two months, if memory serves."

"I'm offering two weeks."

He laughed. "Since Bluestone's in Somerset for at least that long, I gain nothing by agreeing to your terms. Yes," he added as she scowled at him, "I've heard he's recovered quite nicely from his cold, and that he and his father departed London for Crosshedges this afternoon. Fire broke out and burned some of the tenant cottages, I understand. Hmm . . ." He paused a moment before going on, "You really are having deuced rotten luck these days. I wonder why."

She made a sound of impatience. "Don't act as if you believe my sixpence has magical powers, because we both know you don't."

"But it seems that you do, or you wouldn't be out here, risking your reputation in a midnight rendezvous to get it back."

The fact that she'd shown her hand so plainly didn't seem to sit well with her, for she folded her arms, and those gorgeous dark eyes of hers narrowed to absolute slits. But after a moment, she took a breath, relaxed her battle stance, and let her arms fall to her sides. "Even if Bluestone has gone to Somerset," she said with a pretense of indifference that didn't fool him for a second, "there is nothing to prevent him from proposing marriage to me by letter."

"True. But I know Bluestone of old. We were at school together, and I assure you he's not the sort for letters, particularly those of a romantic nature." He paused, donning a doubtful air. "I'm not sure he could even compose such an epistle."

"Don't be absurd. Of course he could."

"If you say so." Lawrence shrugged. "Nonetheless, I prefer to take my chances."

Despite her assurance of Bluestone's talent at composition, she seemed unwilling to trust to it. "I could arrange an invitation to Crosshedges for myself and my father."

"A move that smacks of desperation and would make any man wonder why. You're not engaged to him yet, you know. He might start asking questions, hear some long-forgotten gossip—"

"I'm not agreeing to wait two months," she interrupted, "so put that idea out of your mind. There must something else we can bargain for."

Irresistibly drawn, he lowered his gaze again. "There might be," he agreed, and moved closer to her. "What else do you have to offer?"

Her mouth opened to reply, but she didn't speak. Instead, her tongue darted out to lick her full lower lip, and the arousal within him deepened and spread, even as he braced himself to be damned to perdition.

But for the second time tonight, Ellie surprised him. "I think you already know the answer to that," she whispered, and took a step toward him. "Don't you, Lawrence?"

Arousal flared into outright lust. He sucked in a deep breath, working to contain it, but with that sharp, indrawn breath, he caught the fragrance of lemon soap, her favorite, and memories again invaded his mind, memories of many other nights like this one, when she'd snuck out to meet him and he'd reveled in her sweet-scented skin and soft, willing kisses, and he knew it was too late for containment. *So much*, he thought in chagrin, *for having the upper hand.*

She moved, closing the last bit of distance between them, her small breasts grazing his chest. "What about a kiss?" she whispered, a suggestion that set all his senses reeling. "Would that persuade you?"

He opened his mouth to say it would not, but then she lifted her face and rose on her toes, and his refusal died on his lips.

"Well?" she murmured in the wake of his silence. "Is it a bargain?"

Desperate, he made one last effort. "Ellie," he began, but she stirred against him, shredding any notions of resistance, and he stood motionless, caught like a fly in treacle as she leaned in and pressed her lips to his.

The contact was light, but the pleasure of it was so exquisite, it nearly sent him to his knees. He groaned against her mouth and capitulated utterly, his arms wrapping around her waist to pull her hard against him.

Her hand lifted to his face, and the satin of her glove felt smooth and cool as her palm slid across his cheek. Her fingers raked through his hair as her lips parted against his and she deepened the kiss.

Her mouth was hot and sweet, and Lawrence closed his eyes, savoring delights he'd thought he'd never experience again. *Ellie*, he thought, his heart yearning, his head spinning, his desire for her rolling in him like thunder.

Her hand tightened in his hair as she tasted him. Her free hand slid beneath his jacket to touch his chest, her fingers fanning out over his thudding heart. Then she moved farther down, caressing his ribs. But when she paused at his waist and slid her fingers inside the waistband of his trousers, it was like a splash of cold water on his inflamed senses, for he suddenly understood her true intent.

Anger rose up, smothering arousal, and he broke the kiss, grasping her wrist. "God, woman," he choked, pulling her hand away from the pocket where he'd tucked her sixpence, "you are a devil."

"Why?" she demanded, trying to pull away, failing as he tightened his grip. "Because I tried to retrieve my property? Because to do it, I dared to use the same tactics you used to steal it in the first place?"

He couldn't deny that, and it stung. "No," he shot back, "you're a devil because you're set on marrying another man when it's clear you still have feelings for me."

She tried again to pull her hand free as her other hand pressed against his shoulder to push him away. "That is ridiculous!"

"Is it?" he countered, holding her fast. "The facts suggest otherwise."

"Facts? What facts?"

"You're here, aren't you? Coming to me just as you used to do. What else can I conclude but that you still care for me?"

"Coming here was nothing more than a tactic."

"Yes, a tactic of seduction. Granted, it was the same tactic I used on you the day of Kipp and Cordelia's wedding, but I wouldn't have succeeded if you didn't still have feelings for me. Face it, Ellie," he added, smiling as she began to sputter, "you still want me."

"Of all the conceited, smug, arrogant . . ." She paused, clearly having run out of adjectives, and took a deep breath. "Any tender regard I felt for you," she said at last, "ended six months ago when I was forced to face the truth. You have no loyalty, only ambition."

"What?" He was so startled by that accusation that his grip slackened, allowing her the chance to jerk free.

"You needn't look as if it's a revelation," she went on as she stepped back, out of his reach. "You want to talk of facts? Very well. When you heard these old rumors about my father and you questioned him about it, he swore he was innocent."

"And I suppose I should have just taken his word?"

"Well, you didn't, did you? Instead, you went to Peel and regaled him with this . . . this gossip, and used it to finagle a position in the

Home Office, even arranging to put yourself in charge of investigating the matter."

"I didn't finagle anything. Peel offered me the position."

"And you took it. And you don't find that disloyal?"

Lawrence couldn't believe what he was hearing. "So, because the Home Secretary entrusted me to investigate this, I am a slave to ambition? Because I do not choose to ignore evidence or just take your father's word, I am disloyal?"

"What evidence? I still haven't seen it. But whatever so-called evidence you have, it was surely manufactured by his enemies, men who betrayed him—"

"Not enemies, Ellie," he shot back, then stopped, realizing he'd almost given Hammersmith away. Cursing himself, he took a deep breath. "You don't really believe your father is a victim of persecution by enemies, do you?"

"Yes, I do. Papa swore to you that he was innocent. He swore it on my mother's grave. He would never have made such a vow if he were guilty. Family is everything to us. Everything. I thought you would be part of that family, but you put your own ambitions first. That is what makes you disloyal."

"It wasn't ambition. It was duty."

"You betrayed my father," she went on, ignoring his reply. "And when you did that, you also betrayed me, Lawrence. Don't you understand? You betrayed me. And you didn't have enough trust in me to show me your evidence and prove your case to me."

"I can't show you my evidence. You're his daughter, for God's sake."

"If you don't trust me, how could you ever expect me to trust you?"

With that, she turned and fled the folly, leaving him and the cold comfort of his duty behind her.

Chapter 6

*E*llie spent a long, restless night, haunted by what had happened in the garden and Lawrence's voice echoing again and again through her mind.

You're a devil.

She rolled to her other side, trying to banish him from her mind so she could sleep, but despite her efforts, his voice continued to taunt her.

You're set on marrying another man when it's clear you still have feelings for me.

"That man is so damnably conceited," she muttered, pulling the counterpane higher around her shoulders. "And arrogant. And disloyal."

Unfortunately, these reminders of Lawrence's defects did not put him out of her thoughts, and Ellie appreciated that the tactic she'd employed in her attempt to regain her sixpence had rather come back to bite her.

A tactic of seduction.

She groaned in exasperation, grabbed her spare pillow, and pressed it over her ear, a futile effort.

Face it, Ellie. You still want me.

Waves of heat washed over her—the heat of embarrassment and

desire. She tossed aside the pillow and flung back the counterpane, but even those actions did not cool her blood. Even here in the privacy of her room, she couldn't hide from the events of a few hours ago.

Ellie pressed her fingers to her tingling lips, hot, dark desires thrumming through her body. She tried to suppress them, but they would not be suppressed, and as the night gave way to dawn, she was forced to face the fact that Lawrence was right.

She did still want him, in spite of everything. She thought of the day they'd met, when she'd stood soaking wet and spitting mad in the middle of a Berkshire stream, staring into the handsome, laughing face of the boy on the riverbank. She'd lost her heart to that boy, and even now, nearly fifteen years later, she still hadn't gotten it back.

What a humiliating realization.

Still, it didn't change anything. Ellie sat up, flinging back the bedsheets in defiance, and got out of bed. Last night was over, she reminded herself as she tugged the bellpull to summon her maid. No matter what stupid desire for him might still be lingering within her, Lawrence could never be hers. He could never be part of her life. He was the enemy, determined to ruin her father, and the only hope she had of stopping him was to marry Lord Bluestone, but that plan seemed to be slipping out of her grasp, a possibility that was only further emphasized a short time later when she went down to breakfast and found no letter from the viscount by her plate.

As she sorted through her other correspondence, she tried to tell herself the fact that he had left her no word before leaving didn't mean a thing. His departure had been precipitated by a tragedy, and she couldn't expect him to think of penning explanations for her benefit in such circumstances.

And yet, even as she reminded herself of these things, her sense of foreboding only deepened, and she was impelled to go through her correspondence again. But a second search proved futile, and at last, she shoved her letters aside with a sigh.

"Oh my dear, you mustn't worry," Bunty said, correctly interpreting the meaning of that sigh. "Bluestone did depart for Somerset only yesterday. He'll write before long, I'm sure."

He's not the sort for letters.

Ellie sighed again, a sigh of aggravation. This business of remembering every scrap of Lawrence's conversation had to stop or she'd go mad.

"I'm sure he will," she replied, trying to sound as cheerful as possible, but when she looked up, she found her father's concerned gaze watching her over the top of his newspaper, and she had to look away again at once. "Have all the papers arrived?" she asked, desperate to change the subject.

"They have," Bunty replied. "Your father has *Punch*. And I have the *Times*. But the other papers are just there," she added, gesturing with her own paper to the stack at the end of the table.

Ellie glanced at the other two papers, but she couldn't work up a scrap of interest in either. Her own problem seemed far graver than any news of the day. She began reading her letters, but that exercise was no more effective a distraction from her problem or the cause of it.

She'd never believed—not really—that the coin had the power to control the ability of her and her friends to marry, but recent events had given her cause to wonder. Ever since Lawrence had taken the sixpence, her matrimonial plans had gone awry. She feared that if she didn't get the coin back, rumors about Peel's committee would start flying about, and both she and her father would become social pariahs, subject to all manner of condemnation and ridicule. Papa might even be arrested.

She tried to shake off such a gloomy scenario. Everything that had happened to waylay her plans was likely nothing more than coincidence. But even so, she thought with renewed indignation, there was the principle of the thing. The sixpence was hers, damn it all, and Beatrice's, too. Lawrence had had no right to take it. And if she didn't get the coin back and she didn't marry, it would be just like Lawrence to bring it to every party or ball she attended from now until kingdom come, waving it in her face and crowing about his victory.

It wasn't to be borne.

Perhaps she could burgle his house. Ellie considered that possibility as she ate her breakfast, but after several minutes, she was forced to set the idea aside. Granted, he probably only carried the sixpence with him when he knew he'd have the chance to tease her with it, but still, burgling his house would never work. His aunt had at least a dozen servants.

Perhaps she could write to him, offering another bargain? The problem was that, try as she might, she couldn't see Lawrence agreeing to any bargain she might propose. Why should he? A trade of some sort seemed an equally remote possibility. What did she have that Lawrence might want?

The moment she asked herself that question, Ellie's lips began to tingle, and her body flooded with heat. *For heaven's sake*, she thought, and reached for a newspaper to hide behind. Reliving last night's events was an exercise in humiliation she could well do without.

Bunty's chuckle of laughter interrupted her thoughts, and Ellie seized on the distraction like a lifeline. "I didn't realize the *Times* could be so amusing, Auntie Bunty," she said, peeking over her paper to look at the woman opposite. "What are you reading?"

"The advertisements column. I always find it most entertaining. Listen to this." The older woman leaned a bit closer to Ellie across the table, holding up the paper. "'Experienced lady's maid seeks well-paid post with gentlewoman. Willing to travel in her mistress's service.' I daresay she would," Bunty added, looking up. "Who wouldn't? I wonder if these girls realize how cheeky they appear? Well-paid post with gentlewoman, and willing to travel, indeed!"

"But if she is experienced," the earl put in, looking up from *Punch*, "wouldn't she be entitled to expect a well-paid post?"

"Of course not, Daventry," Bunty countered. "Don't be absurd." With that, she returned her attention to the paper in her hand, leaving the earl looking utterly confounded.

"No experienced lady's maid would advertise in the *Times*, Papa," Ellie explained as she gestured for the footman to pour her more tea. "Not if she has letters of character."

"I don't see why not. An advertisement seems a perfectly sensible way to go about finding a post."

"But not for a lady's maid," Bunty said. "Not in the *Times*. The only paper suitable for such advertisements is *La Belle Assemblée*."

"Ah." Enlightened at last, Daventry lost interest and returned his attention to his own paper, while Bunty resumed sharing snippets from the *London Times* with Ellie.

" 'False teeth for sale. Genuine hippopotamus ivory.' Why anyone would want someone else's discarded teeth, I can't imagine. 'Portraits painted by talented young artist. Prices reasonable.' And an address in Soho—well, we know what *that* means, don't we? Portraits, indeed!"

"I'm not even going to ask," Daventry murmured from behind *Punch*, his wry voice making Ellie smile.

" 'Respectable young woman desires correspondence with worthy young man. Intention, matrimony.' You see, Daventry? It's just as I told you. Cheeky, these girls. Bold as brass nowadays. What can one do with them, I ask you?"

"I am impelled to take issue with that point," the earl put in, lowering his paper a notch. "My Ellie is a model of propriety and modesty. Nothing overly bold about her."

Once again, Ellie felt her body tingling and her face growing hot, and she ducked behind her newspaper as Bunty hastened to reassure her father about her virtuous nature.

"Of course, I wasn't referring to dear Ellie, Lord Daventry. Why, she's as modest and proper a girl as any father could hope to have."

Ellie grimaced, feeling neither modest nor proper, for last night's events—Lawrence's arms around her and the bold way she'd pressed her body against his and parted her lips beneath his—were all still vivid in her mind. Her behavior, she appreciated in hot chagrin, had been downright wanton.

" 'Experienced first housemaid wanted,' " Bunty's voice reading ad-

---

vertisements once again floated past her. "'Impeccable letters of character required. Apply in person, Seventy-eight Cavendish Square.'"

Ellie jerked upright in her chair and lowered her paper, diverted at last from last night's embarrassing events. "Seventy-eight Cavendish Square?" she asked, feeling a jolt of excitement. "Seventy-eight?"

"Yes," Bunty answered, seeming surprised by the sudden animation of her voice. "Why do you ask?"

At once, Ellie donned an expression of disinterest. "No reason," she lied, once again taking refuge behind the *Daily Mail*. "No reason at all."

TWO HOURS LATER, Ellie stood in the belowstairs sitting room of Mrs. Pope, housekeeper to Lady Agatha Standish, hoping she looked convincing as the sober, respectable, and thoroughly fictional housemaid Jane Halloway.

Mrs. Pope was a redoubtable woman of sixty-odd, whose stout proportions and iron gray dress conveyed the impression of an unsinkable battleship, and under her shrewd blue gaze, Ellie had to fight the urge to wriggle like a guilt-ridden little girl. Mrs. Pope, she appreciated, looked as if she ate deceitful housemaids for breakfast.

Still, Ellie thought, she was an earl's daughter, and there was little the housekeeper of Lawrence's great-aunt could do to her. If caught, she would simply claim it was all a prank. And it wasn't likely she'd be caught.

She glanced down as the other woman's silent scrutiny lengthened, reassuring herself that her appearance was convincing. She'd borrowed the dress of plain gray cotton, sensible black boots, and knitted white gloves from a maid in her own father's household, and her bonnet of unadorned straw was the plainest, oldest one she owned. There was nothing about her appearance that might expose her as a fraud. And she intended to accomplish her mission here and be gone before anyone could appreciate that she had little familiarity with the specific duties of housemaids.

"You were thought of quite highly in your previous post," Mrs. Pope commented, looking up from the letter of character in her hand, her voice so dry that Ellie feared she might have overdone the praise of her abilities.

"Lady Elinor Daventry is a generous lady, ma'am," she murmured.

"Humph." That sound of skepticism took Ellie back a bit, but the housekeeper spoke again before she could speculate as to its cause. "I confess, I am curious. Why did the earl's housekeeper not provide your reference? That is the usual way these things are done, you know."

Ellie, who hadn't known any such thing, nodded. "Yes, ma'am, but Mrs. Overton is . . . ahem . . ." She coughed, inventing quickly. ". . . laid up."

"She is ill?" Mrs. Pope's brows lifted a fraction. "Too ill to write a character?"

It did sound unlikely. "Broken arm, ma'am. So, of course, she can't write anything at present, and she asked Lady Elinor to compose my character. Lady Elinor didn't mind a bit," she added truthfully. "She's ever so nice, Lady Elinor."

Mrs. Pope, much to Ellie's chagrin, gave a dubious sniff. "If you say so, though there's few in this house who would agree. A more fickle little minx was never seen, if you ask anyone here. Jilting a nice, handsome young man like Mr. Blackthorne . . . disgraceful, that's what I call it."

Stung, Ellie opened her mouth to refute that inaccurate and most unfair account of her break with Lawrence, but thankfully, Mrs. Pope spoke again before she could defend either her actions or her character.

"In light of that, I'm a bit concerned how you would fit in here, Jane. Your high opinion of your former mistress does you credit, of course, but it won't go down well in this house, as you might understand."

Ellie swallowed her pride and forced herself to offer the meekest possible reply. "No, ma'am. But," she added, pressing a hand to her bosom and striving to look the picture of earnest sincerity, "if I might address your concern, I feel strongly that my first loyalty should always be to my present employer."

"I see. And you're sure you won't miss living in the country most of the year? This house is Lady Agatha's only residence."

Ellie's eyes widened in a pretense of innocence. "Oh no, ma'am. I prefer London. As I said earlier in our interview, my aunt who lives here is ill, and being so far from her for most of the year is the very reason I decided to leave the Earl of Daventry's employment and seek a position in town."

Much to her relief, Mrs. Pope gave a nod. "Very well, then," she said as she folded the letters and stood up. "The post is yours. You will share with Betsy, second housemaid. I will introduce you to her, and she will show you your room. You can meet the remaining staff at luncheon."

"Yes, ma'am." Ellie couldn't help a grin and a gleeful little skip as she followed the other woman out of the sitting room. This part of her plan, at least, had been easy as winking. Her only regret was that she wouldn't be able to see Lawrence's face when he discovered the coin was no longer in his possession.

Perhaps at the next ball, she would be able to show him where it had gone, and as she contemplated the idea of standing across the ballroom floor from him, flipping her sixpence into the air and giving him the same sort of smirk he'd given her, she found it an enormously satisfying prospect.

LAWRENCE STARED OUT the window of his carriage as it made the turn at Charing Cross, but though he was only minutes from his offices at Whitehall, his mind was not on his work.

That fateful January day when he had broken their engagement and walked away, he'd been sure he'd never hold her in his arms or taste her lips again. He'd striven to get over her, and he thought he had, but now he knew he'd only been fooling himself.

He closed his eyes and leaned back against the seat, reliving yet again those intoxicating moments in Lady Atherton's garden. Even eleven cold and sleepless hours later, he could still feel the soft press of her lips and taste the sweetness of her mouth. Just the memory of her body against his was enough to send desire flooding through him and rekindle all the yearning he'd spent the past six months keeping at bay.

And it had all been a jade's trick—her kiss hadn't been for passion, but distraction. Her hand sliding down his chest hadn't been a caress. Lust-filled idiot that he was, he hadn't seen that it was all a ploy until was almost too late.

Making matters worse, he couldn't even blame her for her actions. The coin belonged to her. He'd taken it to use as a bargaining chip, but when that had failed, he ought to have just given it back to her. Instead, he'd taunted her with it across a ballroom floor, and now he was the one being taunted—by his own memories of what he'd once had and lost. For that, he had no one but himself to blame.

He opened his eyes, staring at the black roof of the carriage overhead, but in his mind, he saw nothing but Ellie's moonlit face and parted lips.

What about a kiss? Would that persuade you?

The arousal in his body flared even higher, and he groaned, rubbing his hands over his face and cursing his folly. Why hadn't he just given her the blasted thing when she'd asked for it? If he had, he'd have been spared this torture. And yet . . .

His hands fell to his sides, and he closed his eyes again. Yes, he'd have been spared the taste of her and the scent of her and the feel of her in his arms. But if he had it to do over again, he realized in hot chagrin that he wouldn't change a thing. He still wanted her, and despite the agony of having to relive it afterward, the episode in the folly had allowed him the illusion of believing, if only for a few heavenly moments, that he'd never lost her.

The carriage jerked to a stop. Lawrence opened his eyes and

glanced out the window to find that he had arrived at his offices. Unfortunately, he was also rock-hard, burning with unrequited lust, and not fit to be seen.

He fell back in his seat, took a deep breath, and raked a hand through his hair as he worked to contain his arousal and remember his duty. He had work to do, and that work didn't stop just because memories of Ellie's kiss were making an unholy mess of his body.

By the time his driver had rolled out the steps and opened the door, Lawrence felt he was sufficiently in control that he could enter the offices of His Majesty's Government without eliciting raised eyebrows and chortles of laughter from his colleagues, but though his body might once again be under his regulation, he soon realized that his brains were a different story. When he turned to reach for the portfolio that contained the evidence Hammersmith had given him, he found that he had left it behind.

Of all the brainless things to do. Muttering an oath, he looked at his driver. "I'm afraid we have to return home, Jamison. I've forgotten something."

"Very good, sir." Jamison rolled up the steps and closed the door, and half an hour later, the carriage was pulling up in front of his great-aunt's house in Cavendish Square.

As Lawrence entered the house and ascended the stairs to his room, he vowed that when he departed for his offices this time around, he would not only bring Hammersmith's evidence and his own wits with him, he would also leave any thoughts of Ellie behind. He would not see her, he told himself, nor even think of her, until after the trial was over. He would avoid her like the plague.

The moment he opened the door of his bedroom, however, any notion he would be able to steer clear of Ellie Daventry went straight out the window because she was standing right in front of him.

Chapter 7

"What in blazes are you doing?"

Even as he asked Ellie the question, Lawrence glanced past Ellie and knew the answer, for he could plainly see one blackened corner of Hammersmith's account book on his writing desk.

He looked at her again, noting the drab gray servant's dress, white cap, and apron, and rage flared up inside him like white-hot sparks, igniting all the other emotions he'd been trying so desperately to contain since last night.

She seemed to appreciate the depth of his fury, for as their eyes met across the room, hers widened a fraction. When the door slammed behind him, the sound made her jump. And when he started across the room toward her, she retreated, but she'd barely taken one step before her bottom hit the edge of the desk behind her and she was forced to stop.

With no choice but to brave his ire, she faced him squarely. "I came for my sixpence."

"I see." He leaned a little sideways and noted that along with Hammersmith's account book, several of the other man's letters were scattered across his desk. "And yet," he said through clenched teeth, "the sixpence doesn't seem to be what you found."

"Lawrence," she began, but that placating word was too much for his fraying temper.

"Don't," he ordered fiercely. "You've been caught poking and prying amongst my things, even reading my private correspondence. By God, if you make any attempt to justify yourself, I will throttle you."

"You needn't worry." She looked away. "You interrupted me before I could find out anything useful."

"Even if that's true, which I doubt, you've nonetheless read far enough to compromise my entire investigation."

She tried to step around him, but he grabbed her arms. "Oh no. You're not going anywhere. Tell me exactly what you know."

She tried to free herself, but when he didn't let her go, she gave a sigh and went still. "I know John Hammersmith is alive, for one thing. Although why he's living in Ireland, I can't imagine."

He felt a jolt of panic. "What do you intend to do with that information?"

She didn't answer, and he gave her a little shake. "Do you intend to tell your father?"

"What if I am?" she countered, her dark eyes flashing. "What will you do to stop me? Lock me in a prison cell?"

He studied her face, noting the defiance in her eyes, the press of her lips. It was a look he knew well, the same sort of look a mule might give when being pulled in a direction it did not want to go. Having dealt with Ellie's stubborn streak many times in his life, he reminded himself that in such circumstances as these, persuasion could often be far more effective than dominance.

He took a deep breath, forcing anger down. He relaxed his grip on her arms, though he did not let go. "You know, putting you in prison is a splendid idea. A few days down there, in a dark, damp cell with the rats . . ." He paused as if contemplating it, and when he felt her shiver, he pressed his advantage. "Big, hungry rats that bite and gnaw your flesh. There's also the maggots. They squirm about in your daily bread ration and—"

"All right, all right," she cried. "I discovered that when he

worked in the factory my father owned, Mr. Hammersmith seems
to have paid for great quantities of tin."

"Quite right. And what conclusions did you draw from that?"

She didn't answer, and he went on, "Hmm . . . what could a factory that manufactures guns possibly want with tin? Oh yes," he
added brightly when she didn't answer, "the faulty guns sent to the
British army by your father's factory had some components made
of tin. That's right."

"That's not evidence. That's a theory. Even if you could somehow prove that this tin supposedly purchased by Papa's factory was
used to make the flawed muskets, all purchasing decisions would
have been made by Mr. Hammersmith."

"Ah, so that's the way your mind's working, is it? It's all Hammersmith's fault, and your father was an innocent dupe?"

She lifted her chin a notch, her favorite pretense at haughty dig-
nity. "I saw nothing in what I read that proves Papa knew anything
about what Mr. Hammersmith was doing."

If what she said was true, then she hadn't yet seen where Hammersmith had recorded the actual dates the flawed guns had been
shipped and to which regiments they had gone. Or perhaps she had,
but she hadn't yet appreciated just what a valuable trail of bread
crumbs such a record would be.

"If that's all you know," he said, watching her closely, "then you
didn't read very far. Good."

Her attempt at hauteur wavered a bit, and a hint of fear showed
in her eyes. "So you see? What I know is very little. You can let me
go now."

"Not a chance. I want to know every scrap of information you've
gleaned. Every scrap, Ellie, no matter how trivial."

She didn't answer.

"If you continue to keep mum," he murmured, "we shall have to
return to the topic of maggots."

She gave an aggravated sigh. "I read through his letters to you.
Try as you might, you haven't been able to persuade him to come
before your precious committee and tell his lies about my father.

So, all you have is an account book that Hammersmith may very well have fabricated. And though I didn't have the chance to read much of that before you came in, it's obvious to me that without Hammersmith's actual sworn testimony, the book doesn't do you much good. You still need corroboration. Isn't that what you barristers call it?"

He cursed himself for all the times he'd discussed the law with her when he was a barrister. "You have no idea what other evidence I have," he said instead, trying to take solace in the fact that she didn't know about Sharpe. "And you won't, until your father goes before the House of Lords. But tell me," he added before she could reply, "have you any theories as to why Mr. Hammersmith is unwilling to testify?"

"Because he'd have to lie under oath?"

His gaze locked with hers. "Or because he's afraid for his life."

She stared at him for a moment, then shook her head, laughing as if the suggestion was outrageous. "What are you saying? That my father would . . . would harm John Hammersmith? That's absurd!"

He didn't reply. Instead, he studied her face, noting the uncertainty in her expression, watching it grow stronger with each passing second. Uncertainty was something he'd never seen in her face before, and hope stirred within him. "You thought the idea of Daventry being a war profiteer was absurd, too. Until today."

"Be damned to you!" With sudden violence, she twisted sideways, landing a blow to his ribs with her elbow. It knocked the wind out of him enough to slacken his hold, and she pulled free and ducked around him. But she'd barely taken one step toward the door before he turned and caught her again, his arms wrapping around her as tightly as a straitjacket.

"Let me go." She struggled, legs flailing as he lifted her off the ground. She tried to kick him in the shins with her heels, but hampered by her skirts, she couldn't land a blow painful enough to loosen his hold. "Let me go, damn you!"

"The hell I will."

"I'll scream."

"Go ahead. Do you really want my aunt's entire household to come running and find you here? That story would make quite a sensation. I can see the headline in the scandal sheets now: 'Lady Elinor Daventry caught in Mr. Lawrence Blackthorne's bedroom!' My, my, what will Bluestone and his father make of that, I wonder?"

She stilled, panting. "God," she choked between clenched teeth as she turned her head to glare at him over one shoulder, "how I hate you."

He studied her face for a long moment, and though he saw resentment mingled with her new uncertainty, he did not see the loathing for him that she so vehemently declared. "I don't think you hate me," he said, crossing his fingers that he wasn't engaging in a serious bout of wishful thinking. "What you hate is that you've been blatantly lied to by your own father for most of your life, and you're now beginning to realize it."

She shook her head in vehement denial. "My father would never hurt or kill anyone."

"Even the man who can expose his crimes in full? Hammersmith knows—"

He stopped in chagrin, realizing he had almost revealed crucial information to Daventry's loving, loyal daughter, a woman he couldn't trust an inch.

But, God help him, he wanted to.

He wanted to tell her everything he knew. He wanted to confide to her every detail and show her all the evidence he had because he still loved her, and if he could somehow convince her of her father's guilt, he might regain the love she'd once had for him. But that was a fantasy, and even if it weren't, his duty remained.

Lawrence shored up his resolve and shoved foolish hopes aside. "I have all the evidence I need to prove your father's guilt, and I will prove it. When I show the committee what I have, he will be brought before the House of Lords, he will be tried for misappropriation of military funds, for war profiteering, and—if I have my way—for treason. No matter what you may know, or what you may tell your father, you cannot stop him from facing the consequences of what he did."

"He didn't do anything wrong, and nothing you say will convince me otherwise. Even if my father's factory made those flawed guns, even if my father himself and not Mr. Hammersmith was the one who made the decision to use flawed materials for their manufacture, nothing will convince me he knew such a decision would harm anyone. He didn't know."

The doubt in her voice was stronger now, strong enough to be unmistakable. Because he couldn't be sure of what she actually knew, the only card he could safely play to gain her silence was her own conscience. "Mr. Hammersmith," he said, "doesn't seem to share your faith."

"I told you, Papa would never harm John Hammersmith. Why, the man's my godfather. The two men have been friends since boyhood. Papa would never do anything to hurt him."

"No? Hammersmith allowed everyone to believe he died in the fire that burned down your father's factory. Why would he do that? Why would he remain in hiding for the past thirteen years, living in a foreign country? He's terrified that if Daventry finds out his whereabouts, the earl will have him killed. Like it or not, Ellie," he said, as she shook her head, "if you tell your father anything about what you discovered today, you will be putting a good and honorable man at risk. Would you do that? Would you put the life of your own godfather in jeopardy? A man who called you little Ellie and carried you around the factory floor on his shoulders? A man who, according to everything you've ever told me, loved you like a daughter, and still does?"

She shuddered, and a sob came from her throat. "My father is not a war profiteer or a criminal," she cried, and once again began thrashing in his hold, denying the truth for all she was worth. "He's not a murderer or a traitor. He's not. He's not. He's not!"

With each denial, her vehemence lessened, whether due to fatigue or futility, he didn't know, but at last she stilled again, sagging in his arms. "He's not," she whispered, panting, staring at the floor.

"Either way, the question remains. Are you going to tell your father what you've discovered?"

"Will you put me in prison to stop me?"

The bitter tinge of her voice was like a knife slicing through his chest. "No," he muttered. "I'm an utter fool, I daresay, but no."

"What . . ." She paused and lifted her chin, but she didn't turn her head to look at him. "What are you going to do, then?"

His options, he knew, were limited. In fact, he had only one. "I'm going to let you go." He eased back, but before she could step away, he put his hands on her shoulders and turned her around. "Last night, you accused me of not trusting you. Well, you'll have to take it back, because I'm choosing to trust you now. I'm trusting that you won't tell your father anything of what you've discovered."

"You expect me to sit back, meek and silent, while you build your case against him?"

He couldn't help a laugh at that. "Expecting you to be meek and silent would be as pointless as expecting England to have a drought." He paused, and took a deep breath, hoping like hell what he was about to do would not further compromise his investigation or put Hammersmith's life in jeopardy. "I am trusting that you have enough affection for your godfather not to take the slightest chance of endangering his life. I am trusting you'll start to think about the men who died, good men who fought for England and didn't deserve to die with faulty muskets in their hands. And I'm trusting you to find the courage to confront your father with all those rumors from years ago. Look him in the eye as if you don't know anything, and ask him about the muskets and about the fire that burned down his factory—"

"Why should I ask him about the fire?" She stared at him in shock. "That fire was an accident!"

"Was it?"

"Of course it was!"

"If you ask him, I'm sure he'll say it was. In fact, he'll deny any wrongdoing, just as he did with me. But when he does deny it, be sure you're looking into his eyes, Ellie. That way, I'm hoping you'll see the truth."

"I already know the truth."

"Or perhaps the truth is what you've always been afraid to face."

That flicked her on the raw, he could tell. Her chin went up again, all the proud hauteur of an earl's daughter in her face. "I'm not afraid of anything. I'm not a child."

"I didn't say you were a child."

His voice was mild, but it seemed to raise her ire even higher. She stirred, scowling at him. "I am quite capable of facing unpleasant truths."

"Good. Then confront your father, ask him what really happened, and see what he tells you."

He lowered his arms and stepped back, releasing her, and at once she started for the door, but he spoke again before she could open it.

"Ellie?"

She paused, one hand on the knob, and looked at him over her shoulder.

He met her inquiring gaze with a hard one of his own. "You know Hammersmith is alive, you know from the text of his letters that he is living in Ireland. I can't do anything to change that. But I want your solemn word that you won't tell your father about him, or about anything else you've discovered today. I know you don't believe you would be putting the man in danger, but you must trust me when I say that caution and complete discretion are called for here."

She seemed inclined to argue the point, but after a moment, she bit her lip and gave a reluctant nod. "Very well," she said. "I won't tell Papa or anyone else about Mr. Hammersmith, and I won't reveal to anyone what I've learned today. I give you my word."

With that, she opened the door and departed, and as he watched her go, he knew he'd just taken the biggest gamble of his life. He could only hope it hadn't also been his biggest mistake.

ELLIE STARED OUT the window of her room at the house in Portman Square. There wasn't much of a view now, for the rain was pouring down and night had fallen, but it hardly mattered, for in her mind's eye, there was only one view, and it wasn't a picture of the neatly pruned trees and manicured patch of lawn visible beneath the streetlights below. No, the only thing she could see was a column of accounting entries denoting purchases of tin and prices paid.

What could a factory that manufactures guns possibly want with tin?

She slumped against the window, resting her cheek on the cool pane of glass, Lawrence's question forming a sick knot in her stomach. It was the same sensation she'd felt upon her discovery of the book and letters in his desk. It was fear.

A carriage rolled past, neighbors departing the square for the evening amusements of the season. Ellie had an engagement this evening, too—supper and cards at Lady Wolford's with her father. But though she was already dressed in evening clothes and the darkness outside told her it must be nearly time to depart, she did not move from her seat by the window.

She felt curiously lethargic. Her wits seemed thick as tar. The only thing she seemed able to think about was what she'd discovered this morning, and Lawrence's suggestions for what she ought to do with her newfound knowledge.

Look him in the eye as if you don't know anything, and ask him about the muskets and about the fire that burned down his factory.

She'd never deemed that necessary. Throughout her life, there had been rumors surrounding her father's munitions factory, and suspicions about how it had burned down. There had been speculation about how his income from his estates could possibly support his lavish lifestyle. But to Ellie, all that had been nothing but malicious gossip. To her, his innocence had always seemed obvious, and the rumors so absurd that she'd never felt the need to ask her father for explanations. Her faith in him had always been her armor against any whispered rumors.

But what if her faith in him had been misplaced?

The moment she asked herself that question, everything within her wanted to shout that it was impossible. And yet, the questions kept coming. What if the rumors were true? What if her father really was a war profiteer? What if, when confronted by Lawrence, her father had lied?

That, she realized, was what made his guilt seem so impossible. Her father was not a liar.

Or was he?

She tried to consider the question objectively. She thought back to her childhood, but in all the memories of her life, she could remember no lies. The dislocated shoulder she'd had falling out of a tree when she was nine—Papa had told her straight out how much it was going to hurt before he'd popped it back in place. She went further back, to when she was five years old and Mama was sick. She'd asked him if Mama was going to die, and with infinite tenderness, he'd told her the truth. And when the end was near, and she'd wanted to say good-bye, he'd ignored Nanny's protests and taken her into the sickroom. And when he'd held her on his lap in the nursery afterward while she'd sobbed her heart out, he'd smoothed her hair and told her that everything would be all right, but he'd also told her that her life would never be the same without her mama. He'd been telling the truth then, too.

Never, not once, could she remember Papa ever lying to her about anything, even if a lie would have been kinder, or easier, or more convenient. That, more even than her love for him, was what made her faith in him so absolute and Lawrence's accusations so absurd. She'd been sure, sure with all her heart and soul, that her father would never lie to her.

Ah, but lying to her wasn't the issue, was it?

That pesky little question slithered through her mind like the serpent's whispers to Eve in the garden, insidious, persistent, and impossible to ignore.

Her father had never lied to her, that was true. But she had never been the one to ask him any questions.

And when Lawrence had done so, accusing him straight out of war profiteering, he had denied it unequivocally, even going so far as to swear on the grave of his dead wife that he was innocent.

Despite such solemn assurances, Lawrence had not believed him and had acted accordingly. Ellie still wasn't sure if ambition had played some part in Lawrence's actions or not, but she did know that he wouldn't have proceeded if he had believed her father's denials.

She'd always thought Lawrence's refusal to provide her with actual evidence meant he didn't have any, but now she was forced to face the fact that he did, for she'd seen at least some of it with her own eyes. He'd said there was more.

But no matter what evidence Lawrence had, there could be sensible and innocent explanations for all of it. Even as that thought passed through her mind, so did Lawrence's suggestion.

Ask him.

The door opened, and Ellie turned her head as her maid, Morrell, came in. "The carriage has been brought around, my lady."

Ellie stirred, but she didn't move, for ennui still enveloped her like a fog. "The carriage?"

"Yes, my lady. To take you and His Lordship to Lady Wolford's. Surely you haven't forgotten?"

"Oh no, of course not." She mustn't have sounded very convincing, for a little frown creased the other woman's brow, and Ellie felt compelled to invent an explanation. "It's only that talk of the carriage surprised me. It's just two blocks to Lady Wolford's, and we usually walk."

"It's pouring rain, my lady."

"Oh yes, of course." Ellie sighed, trying to work up the will to move. "Where is Papa?"

"He's downstairs, waiting for you."

With those words came all the implications of the evening that lay ahead, and the knot that had been sitting in Ellie's stomach all afternoon twisted tight and made her feel sick. Supper and cards meant she'd have to sit across from her father at the dining table and perhaps at the card table. He'd know something was wrong. He'd see it in her face. How could it be otherwise? There was no way she could hide from him the doubts that plagued her.

"I'm not going. Tell Papa to go without me." She turned away, feeling like the most craven of cowards. She'd assured Lawrence she wasn't afraid of anything, but she was. Oh God, she was.

It wasn't what her father would see in her face that she feared. It was what she might see in his.

Ask him.

"My lady?"

Ellie jumped, looking toward the door to realize that her maid was still there. "I'm sorry, Morrell," she mumbled, and rubbed her fingers over her forehead. "Was there something else?"

"Are you . . ." The maid paused, and Ellie looked at her, only to find Morrell's frown of bewilderment had deepened to one of concern. "Are you all right, my lady?"

"Of course. I just have a headache, that's all."

"Would you like some tea brought up? Or a tray of supper?"

Ellie's stomach lurched, and she pressed a hand to her mouth, shaking her head. "No. Nothing, thank you."

"Very good, my lady. I'll tell your father you won't be going, and then I'll come back up to dress you for bed. You'll have a hot water bottle, too," she added almost defiantly, as if she expected Ellie to argue about it. "You could be catching a chill. Or the ague."

The ague was not what ailed her. "I'm perfectly well, Morrell. I don't need cosseting. I'm not a child."

I'm not a child. I'm quite capable of facing unpleasant truths.

Suddenly, the fog that had been enveloping Ellie all day dissipated, and she felt as clear and cold and sharp as a sunny day in January. "Wait," she said as her maid turned to go. "Never mind, Morrell, I will go down and talk to my father myself."

She squared her shoulders and strode past her astonished maid. "I will talk to him right now."

Chapter 8

A loud clap of thunder sounded, one loud enough to divert Lawrence from the account book, reports, and letters spread across his desk. He glanced at the window as lightning lit up the sky, and in that brief flash, he saw that the rain was coming down in absolute sheets.

The lightning vanished again, returning the sky outside to pitch black and making him appreciate that the hour must be quite late. The last time he'd looked up from his work had been to light a lamp at dusk.

A glance at his pocket watch verified that it was half past eight, but he had no intention of going home, for he had a great deal of work yet to do.

After letting Ellie go this morning, he'd ventured belowstairs to inform Mrs. Pope that her new housemaid was gone and would not be returning, and while he was there, the footman had given him his letters from the morning post. One of them had been from Hammersmith, agreeing to testify if Lawrence could promise immunity from prosecution and protection from Daventry.

Lawrence had returned to his office at once, and he'd spent every moment since then sifting through the accounting ledger Hammersmith had given him, working to link together all the pieces he had in a report for Sir Robert Peel. That report would also recommend immunity for Hammersmith, and suggest in the strongest possible terms that the committee be convened at once with a view to demand the Earl of Daventry come before the House of Lords and answer for his crimes.

Lawrence was determined to finish the report tonight and present it to Peel first thing tomorrow. Once that was done, the matter would be out of Lawrence's hands, and he could return his attention to all the other duties of his position, duties he'd been neglecting in his pursuit of Daventry.

With a wry glance at the stack of files and papers collecting dust at one end of his desk, he tucked his watch back in his waistcoat, banished any thought of going home, and returned his attention to compiling his report. It took another hour for him to finish, but at last, he was able to put down his pen.

He leaned back in his chair and rubbed his hands over his tired eyes. He'd done all he could to see justice served, and by tomorrow, Daventry's fate would be in the hands of his peers. Lawrence knew he ought to be relieved, but when he thought of Ellie, relief was not what he felt.

He was sure she would keep the promise she'd made to him this morning; at least, he was as sure as one person could be about another. For though Ellie loved her father beyond reason, she had far more character, kindness, and courage than her parent would ever possess, and he was positive she would keep her word. But about other things, he was not so sure.

Would she confront her father, as he'd suggested? And would it matter? Daventry would surely lie to her, and she could very well choose to believe him, despite what she now knew. She might not believe him, and yet still carry on with her plans to marry Bluestone in an attempt to save the earl from his fate, gambling that Wilchelsey would come up to snuff despite the evidence.

But what if she made a different choice? Hope rose inside him, but he quashed it at once. If her father was arrested, tried in the

House, convicted of war crimes, it would be a humiliating experi-ence for her and her entire family, and she could very well see Law-rence as the man responsible for her family's shame. How could there be any place in her heart for him after that?

A tap on the open door had him looking up, and he was startled to find the object of his thoughts standing in the doorway.

"Ellie?" He stood up. "What in blazes are you doing here?"

She made a rueful face as she stepped inside his tiny cubbyhole of an office. "That's the second time in about twelve hours you've asked me that exact question."

"Yes, well, you've developed an unnerving tendency to pop up in the places I least expect you to be."

Before she could reply, the stalwart frame of Jim McGowan, the night watchman, moved to stand behind her in the doorway. "Beg-ging your pardon, sir," he said, doffing his cap. "I told 'er visitors aren't to be 'ere at this time o' night, and that it's against the rules. But . . ." He paused, self-consciously twisting his cap in his hands, giving Lawrence a piteous look. "But she's a *lady*, sir."

As a gentleman of low rank, Lawrence fully appreciated the pres-sure brought to bear on commoners to give way to the aristocracy in all circumstances. He didn't always agree with that particular rule of society, but he understood it. "Quite so, McGowan. You may return to your watch. I will see the lady out myself."

The watchman nodded and donned his cap, giving Lawrence a look of gratitude. Then he departed, closing the door behind him, and Lawrence returned his attention to his unexpected visitor.

"You should not be here, Ellie," he said, gathering up his report, letters, and papers, and stuffing them into Hammersmith's ledger. "Not at this time of night," he added as he opened a drawer of his desk and dropped the ledger inside. "And certainly not unchaper-oned."

"I know. I was supposed to be at a supper party, but I pleaded a headache, and Bunty and Papa went without me. After they'd gone, I ducked down the back stairs, hailed a hackney, and came here to see you."

"Ellie, if this is an attempt to persuade me not to go forward with my investigation—"

"That's not why I came."

"Good, because I have no intention of stopping. In fact," he added, driven to underscore the facts as brutally as possible, "I'm giving my recommendation to Peel first thing tomorrow that the committee be convened—"

"Lawrence, I didn't come to dissuade you from that course. I came because . . ." She paused and took a deep breath. "I wanted to see you."

"How did you know I'd be here?"

"I remember how fond you are of working in the late hours, when it's quiet and no one's around to bother you."

It was his turn to smile. "Well, I don't know if 'fond' is quite the right word—"

He stopped mid-sentence, his attempt to lighten the situation demolished as he noted the pale weariness of her face. "Ellie, are you all right?" When she didn't answer, he shut the drawer, circled his desk, and closed the short distance between them in two strides. "What's happened?"

"I needed to see you because I . . ." She paused and looked up, meeting his gaze. "I followed your suggestion."

Hope and joy and relief rose in him, shooting up like fireworks, but he tamped those emotions down and told himself not to jump to any conclusions. "What suggestion would that be?"

"I talked to my father."

"And?" He edged closer to her. "What was the result?"

Her brown eyes seemed to darken, looking suddenly haunted. "I think you can guess," she whispered.

"He admitted culpability?" Even as he put forward that notion, Lawrence just couldn't credit it, and he was not surprised when she shook her head.

"No. I never asked him to admit anything. I didn't . . ." She paused, ducking her head to stare at the floor. "I didn't have to."

Lawrence frowned. "I don't quite under—"

"All I asked him was what metal muskets are supposed to be made of." She looked up and gave a laugh, a soft, humorless sound that twisted his heart in his chest. "All these months—years—I've denied that the gossip about Papa was true. And when you came to me six months ago, I would not let myself believe you, especially since you refused to show me any proof. But when I asked him about muskets today, his answer and his face told me everything. I saw the truth as plain as day."

"What was his answer?"

"'Steel and brass, of course.' That's what he said. And he said it without hesitation, without even blinking, looking straight in my eyes, so, so glib, as if he'd been waiting for the day when I would start asking questions. And that's when I knew he knew all about those faulty guns. I knew what you said was true. Because he never asked me why I'd want to know something like that."

"Do you think he realizes you know the truth about him?"

"I don't think so, although I can't be sure. It's amazing," she added softly, "how one simple question, when you finally work up the courage to ask it, can destroy everything you thought was the truth."

He watched a tear slide down her cheek, glistening in the lamplight, and he wanted to cut his heart out. He'd started this; he'd pushed her down this road. He had wanted her to learn just what sort of man her father was. Now he'd gotten his wish, and he felt like an utter bastard in consequence.

"Ellie," he began, and moved closer, but when he put a hand on her arm, any comforting words he'd been about to utter went straight out of his head.

"God, woman," he muttered instead, grasping a fold of her dark green cloak, "you're absolutely dripping."

She laughed a little at that, a genuine-sounding laugh that lightened the weight pressing his chest. "Well, it is raining," she pointed out, brushing the tear from her cheek with her gloved fingertips. "Pouring down in sheets. And I was so anxious to come and find you that I forgot my umbrella. Your watchman wouldn't open the gate for my driver, but he let me through and brought me here. Crossing your courtyard, I suppose I got soaked."

Erotic images of Ellie with wet, transparent clothes clinging to her body flashed through his mind, making him acutely aware of the intimacy of their situation. "We need to get you home," he told her. "Before you catch a chill."

"No, no, I'm perfectly all right. Please," she added as he started to argue. "I don't want to go home. Not yet."

Letting her stay was not, he knew, a good idea. Already, he could feel desire rising up within his body. "Ellie, you can't be out like this at night. It's not proper."

For some unaccountable reason, she smiled. "This from the man who's always saying propriety isn't important."

"Yes, well, there may be times when I'm wrong about that. This is one of those times." He glanced uneasily at the darkened window, aware they could be seen from the courtyard below, and even though the only one likely to see them was McGowan, he hastily jerked the curtains closed. "The point is, you should not be here. I have to take you home."

"Can I at least dry off a bit before we go?"

He watched in dismay as she lifted her hands to her collar, and as she worked to unfasten the frog that held her evening cloak together, his imagination once again began conjuring delectable images of her soaking wet, sending his arousal rising higher.

He seized her wrists and pulled her hands down, but any thought of hauling her toward the door ended there. "Let me do it," he said instead.

But the moment he took over the task of undoing her cloak, he appreciated that he was stepping onto very thin ice. As he worked the damp knot through the tight loop, his knuckles brushed the silky skin of her throat and his mind went back to the heady days when they would duck inside a stair cupboard or behind a hedge, and where, in defiance of all proprieties either of them had ever been taught, they'd engaged in some very passionate kissing.

His body was on fire by the time the frog finally came undone.

He pulled her sodden cloak off her shoulders and hung it on the coat tree beside the door with a sigh of relief, but as he returned his attention to her, any relief he felt vanished at once.

Her evening gown of shimmering green silk, though damp, wasn't wet enough to be transparent, but that didn't matter, for the low-cut bodice drew his gaze like a magnet. He inhaled sharply, the scent of lemon soap filled his nostrils, and his desire deepened and spread.

She felt it, too, for her lips parted a little and her lashes tilted down, and then she stirred. "Lawrence," she began, but he didn't let her finish. Instead, he bent his head and kissed her.

Of all the kisses they'd ever shared, this was the sweetest, and he savored it because he knew that as long as he lived, he would never taste anything sweeter. But he also knew he was headed straight for a cliff, and when he fell off, the crash at the bottom would annihilate him. He broke the kiss while he still had the strength.

"Ellie, this has to stop." He grasped her arms, but he didn't have quite enough resolve to push her away.

"Does it?" She rose on her toes, bringing her close again. "Why?" she asked, her lips brushing his.

"You're in a very vulnerable condition right now. So am I," he added, painfully aware of that particular fact. "And you don't realize what you're playing with."

"Yes, I do," she whispered, her lips brushing his as she spoke. "Do you think I've forgotten the old days when you used to pull me into the stair cupboard?"

Lawrence decided he'd best keep his attention and hers firmly fixed on the present. "Aren't you supposed to be marrying Lord Bluestone?"

"That was my intention." She slid her arms up around his neck. "But someone stole my sixpence and jinxed all my plans."

The touch of her lips and the warmth of her so close was sending desire thrumming through every nerve of his body. His wits were slipping, too, and his sense of honor and duty. Everything in him, in fact, was giving way to the baser side of his nature. Desperate, he grasped her by the arms, shoved her back a step, and let her go. "Ellie, stop trying to seduce me. You don't know the first thing about it."

Her laugh interrupted him. "Says the man who spent every summer from the time I was sixteen showing me how it's done."

"Yes, but that was different. We were . . ." He paused, swallowing hard, finding it hard to say what needed to be said. "Back when I'd pull you into that stair cupboard, I didn't think taking liberties of that sort mattered much because I was sure we were to be married. I loved you. Damn it," he added as pain pierced his chest. "I loved you."

Some of the pain he felt shimmered across her face. "I loved you, too. I . . ." She paused and swallowed hard, but she didn't look away. "I still do."

He stiffened. "That's a convenient change of heart."

"I realize that's how it seems," she said, but even as she spoke, he could see in her eyes something he hadn't seen for six long months, something he never thought he'd see again, something that raised his hopes all the way to the sky.

He took a deep, steadying breath, reminding himself how much it had hurt when she'd chosen her loyalty to her father over her love for him. If she made that choice again, he didn't think he could endure it. "I don't see why I should believe you."

"Because I'm here." When he didn't reply, she smiled. "Oh, Lawrence, do you really think I didn't know what might happen if I came to you now?"

He suspected she didn't have a clue. Despite their stolen moments ducking into stair cupboards and hiding behind hedges, they'd never had the opportunity for the culmination of all that passionate kissing.

When he didn't reply, she rose on her toes again and pressed a kiss to his cheek. "I came alone," she reminded, touching her lips to one corner of his. "Unchaperoned," she added, kissing the other side of his mouth. "At night."

Christ, have mercy, he was coming undone. The only way out

of this was to be blunt. "Ellie, I swear, if you stay here one more minute, I'll lose my head and take your virtue. Right here, on top of my desk."

"I hope so." He must have looked doubtful about her sincerity, because she leaned even closer, rose on her toes, and kissed his ear. "That's why," she whispered, "before I came, I took off my corset."

That information pushed him over the edge and sent both his chivalry and his sense of self-preservation to oblivion. Wrapping an arm around her waist, he pulled her hard against him, bent his head, and kissed her.

She yielded at once, her lips parting beneath his in willing accord. She pressed her body closer, inflaming his arousal almost beyond bearing, and he needed to slow down. He was taking her virtue in a musty cubbyhole at Whitehall, but the moment did not have to be as unromantic as their surroundings.

He eased back, tasting her mouth in long, slow kisses, his hands cupping and shaping her breasts through the gown, working to ignite her with the same desire he felt. He must have succeeded, for she moaned low in her throat, and her knees gave way.

He caught her at the waist, and he held her tight against him, still kissing her as he turned them both around in the cramped space. But then he pulled back and his hands slid away.

"You're not stopping?" she cried in dismay.

"Hell no," he muttered, and reached for the lamp and inkstand on his desk. He deposited them on the tiny table beside the chair, safely out of the way, then once again moved to stand in front of her. "I'll only stop if you tell me to, Ellie."

He leaned to one side, and with one sweeping motion, his arm cleared everything that remained on his desk. Books hit the floor, papers scattered, and she giggled.

"Find that amusing, do you?" he asked.

"Yes, because it's not the least bit like you to be so heedless with your things."

"You might give me some credit," he said as his hands encircled her waist. "At least I remembered to move the lamp first."

"Yes, burning down Whitehall would have put quite a damper on this evening."

"To hell with Whitehall," he said, and lifted her onto the desk. "A fire would give you time to change your mind."

"I won't change my mind," she promised, still laughing as she leaned back to rest her weight on her arms, but when her gaze met his, the intensity in his blue eyes made her breath catch, and her laughter faded away.

"Lift your hips," he told her, and when she did, he shoved her skirts up, bunching them around her waist. His palm slid across her thigh, hot against the thin muslin of her drawers, and excitement rose up within her, for she remembered what this meant.

"You remember this, don't you, Ellie?" he murmured as if reading her mind, his hand easing between her legs, inside the gap of her drawers. "Do you?"

"Yes," she answered, but that one word was all she could manage, because then he touched her most intimate place, and the sheer pleasure of it made words impossible. She moaned, tilted her head back, and closed her eyes as he caressed her, and soon she was breathing in frantic little gasps and the pleasure was rising to a pitch more fevered than anything she'd ever felt before.

Her hips worked frantically against his hand, everything in her seeking something she couldn't understand or even identify. And then it came, pleasure so acute that she cried out his name. Her thighs closed around his caressing hand, her body striving to gain every exquisite shred of sensation, until, at last, she fell back, panting, against the desk.

He pulled back, and she opened her eyes, her gaze focusing on his hands unbuttoning his trousers. When he pulled them down his hips, she felt a sudden pang of alarm. He seemed to sense it, for his hands stilled. "Ellie, look at me."

She lifted her gaze to his. His blue eyes seemed dark, unreadable, and even in the soft lamplight, his face bore a harsh expression, almost as if he were in pain. Their breathing mingled in the silence, hers soft and quick, his hard and ragged.

"Tell me you're still sure about this," he said, but even as he spoke, he was easing closer, moving to stand between her legs, shoving her skirts higher, and when he touched her again, she gasped, for his touch was scorching hot.

"Tell me," he ordered, his hands sliding beneath her hips, cupping her buttocks.

"I'm sure." She nodded, urging him on when he didn't move. "I'm sure, Lawrence."

That was all the reassurance he needed. He pulled her to the edge of the desk, and instinctively, she spread her legs wider, sliding her hips against the tip of his hard arousal, reawakening her own desire. She felt deliciously wicked, and she moved with an abandonment that both shamed and excited her.

But then his hands grasped her buttocks, and the hard part of him pressed deeper, entering her. He thrust forward, shoving deep, and she cried out as pain seared her from the inside.

He lifted her from the desk, and instinctively, she sat up, wrapping her legs around his hips and her arms around his neck, as he pulled her close and held her there, impaled and shocked, against his body. "It'll be all right," he told her, pressing kisses to her face and her hair. "Ellie, Ellie, it'll be all right."

"I'm not so sure about that," she murmured against his neck, her voice shaking, her arms tight around his neck.

"I promise it will." Still holding her, he turned around and perched himself on the edge of the desk.

"What are you doing?" she asked.

"Letting you take the lead." With that enigmatic comment, he leaned back, pulling her with him, guiding her so that she was astride him, and he was once again inside her, with her hands on his shoulders and her knees on either side of his hips.

"There," he said, smiling a little, though his breathing was ragged. "You're in charge now."

"I'm not sure what to do."

He closed his eyes. "Do what you feel."

She stirred, wriggling her hips with care, but the pain, thankfully, had subsided. Reassured, she moved again, rocking, trying to accustom herself to the feel of him inside her.

He groaned, and she stopped, unsure. "Lawrence?"

"Don't stop," he told her, grasping her hips. "Ellie, for God's sake, don't stop."

She smiled, appreciating what he felt, and she began to think this part might not be so bad after all. She used her body to caress his hard length, up and down, over and over, relishing the way he groaned with pleasure beneath her. She moved faster, then faster still, until his breathing was coming hard and his hips were thrusting up to meet hers.

Then with a sudden hoarse cry, he pulled her down to him and wrapped his arms around her back as his hips thrust hard against hers. Shudders rocked him, and then he groaned, low and deep, and she knew he was feeling the same delicious pleasure he'd already given her. He thrust against her several more times, then went still, his hold on her easing.

She sat up, smiling down into his face as he opened his eyes.

"Are you all right?" he asked, reaching up to cup her cheek.

She nodded. "I think so. You?"

"God, yes." He lifted himself toward her, and she met him halfway. She kissed his mouth.

"Well, it's done now," he said, his hands caressing her cheeks as he once more sank back against the desk. "Your virtue's utterly gone."

"Yes," she agreed, and she laughed, joy rising within her and spreading outward, farther and wider, until she felt as if it could fill the world. "So it is."

He didn't laugh with her. Instead, he frowned, and her happiness dimmed a fraction. "Any regrets?" she asked softly.

"Only one." Still cupping her cheek with one hand, he reached beneath him with the other and pulled a pen from under his body. "Next time we make love," he said as he tossed the pen over her head to hit the door behind her, "we're damn well doing it in a bed."

Chapter 9

The rain had stopped by the time Ellie and Lawrence departed his offices, and despite the late hour, he easily secured a hackney to take them home. They did not talk much on the way, and Ellie was glad of it. She feared that any conversation would inevitably lead to a discussion of her father, and she did not want that to intrude on the happiness she felt at this moment.

Nonetheless, as they drew closer and closer to home, the more she felt her joy receding and the cold, hard realities of her future intruding.

She had no illusions about what had happened tonight. She believed Lawrence's assurance that he would proceed with his case, and though she no longer resented him for the choice he'd made six months ago, she also knew the devastating effect his choice would have on her family.

She also had no illusions about her father, not anymore. She now faced a future where her beloved parent was a scoundrel and a war criminal and her family was shamed and disgraced by association, but there was no going back.

"What about you, Ellie?" Lawrence's voice broke into her pensive thoughts, and she looked up to find him watching her with a somber, thoughtful expression.

"Sorry," she said, shaking her head, smiling a little. "I was wool-gathering. What did you say?"

"You asked me earlier if I had any regrets about what happened. I don't. But do you?"

She didn't even need time to consider. "No. None."

That pleased him, she could tell, for though his countenance remained grave, he reached for her hand and kissed it. Before he could reply, however, the carriage came to a halt.

Ellie peeked out between the drawn curtains, and in the dim light of dawn, she could see the plain stone façade of the back side of her home. "Good thing you told the driver to pull to the back," she said as she let the curtain fall back into place. "It's already growing light outside."

"I won't help you down," Lawrence said. "We might not be right at your front door, but nonetheless, it wouldn't do for me to be seen with you at this hour. Not that it matters, I suppose," he added, then lifted her hand in his and kissed it again. "Since you're going to marry me."

Those words sent a strange shiver of foreboding along her spine, but she forced a smile, not wanting him to see what she felt. "That's not a very romantic proposal."

He looked at her over the top of her glove. "I'll offer a better one once I've obtained the license," he said, kissed her hand again, and let her go as the driver opened the door.

She exited the vehicle and went down the stairwell to the servants' entrance as the hackney drove on. Morrell had left the back door unlatched, just as she'd promised, and Ellie slipped inside the house as quietly as possible.

Not even the kitchen maid was up yet, fortunately, and Ellie was able to duck up the servants' staircase and get to her room without encountering anyone. As Lawrence had said, it didn't really matter if her reputation was compromised at this point, but as she undressed, Ellie couldn't shake the vague sense of apprehension that had come over her in the hackney at Lawrence's words about matrimony. She had no time to determine the cause of her uneasiness, however, for as she slid into bed, exhaustion overrode all other considerations, and she fell asleep the moment her head hit the pillow.

It was nearly lunchtime when she awoke, still groggy and heavyheaded. She had her meal brought up on a tray, and after an omelet, a fillet of sole, and several cups of strong tea, she felt much better.

She inquired of Morrell where her father might be, and was relieved to learn he'd gone to his club. The last thing she wanted right now was to see him and pretend that her question hadn't opened up an abyss between them that could never be breached. Even worse, if he had realized she knew the truth, she'd have to endure his efforts to explain, or worse, justify himself.

She dressed, then went out with Bunty, paying calls and shopping to occupy her afternoon. Still, she couldn't avoid her father forever, and eventually she was forced to return to Portman Square. The earl, the butler told her, had returned, but only for an hour, and then he'd gone out again, taking with him a trunk and a valise.

Ellie stared at the butler in shock, for of all the things she'd thought her father might do, leaving wasn't one of them. "Did he say where he was going, Brandon?"

"No, my lady. But he left a note for you in the drawing room."

She was up the stairs and in the drawing room within fifteen seconds, and sure enough, there was a note on the mantel, tucked between the clock and the spill vase. She opened it, dread opening inside her as she unfolded the single sheet of paper.

My dearest Ellie,

By the time you read this, I will be well on my way to Dover. By sunset, I will be on a ship, bound for parts unknown. Given the dire circumstances I face, living out my days in some obscure corner of the world is the best course.

I hardly need explain to you the reasons for my departure. I know you all too well, my dear, and in your eyes last evening, I saw that you have somehow been persuaded to believe the wretched lies about me. It breaks

my heart that you should take the word of my enemies, but I have not the
time to offer you explanations now.

This afternoon, Wilchelsey informed me that the Home Secretary
intends to convene an investigation into the odious rumors that have
dogged me for so long. I assured the duke that though Blackthorne's
allegations seem to have taken in Sir Robert Peel, they are utterly false.
Wilchelsey, alas, was unmoved by these assurances, and offered the
opinion that there is sufficient evidence to warrant my arrest.

I cannot bear the thought of that! You know me well, dear daughter,
and I daresay you are well aware that my greatest fault is my pride. I
refuse to bow down before lies and give my enemies the satisfaction of
seeing me shamed and besmirched in the House of Lords, and I know
you cannot bear to see me thus, so I have chosen to save us both from that
humiliation.

I doubt I will ever be able to return to England, but I take comfort in
the fact that I am leaving you in the capable hands of my cousin, Lady
Wolford. Do not worry about me, my dear, and know I am safe from my
enemies on some distant shore.

Your affectionate father,
Daventry

Ellie read the letter twice, the first time in a state of numbness
and shock, and the second time in acceptance, relief, and even forgiveness.

Her father, she saw so clearly now, was a weak and selfish man,
and though his letter spoke of sparing her the humiliation of a
trial, she suspected that her well-being had never entered into his
consideration. He was not, she knew now, the heroic, persecuted
figure she'd always thought him to be. A hero did not abandon his
daughter and run away. Her illusions had been stripped from her,
but she felt no inclination to wish them back. The truth, however
hard, was better than self-deceit.

She stood up, thinking that perhaps she should inform Lawrence
of her father's departure, for unless he moved quickly, his quarry

would slip free of him forever. But then she stopped and read the first paragraph of the letter again.

By sunset, I will be on a ship, bound for parts unknown.

She looked at the clock on the mantel, took a peek through the window, and then she sat down and thought long and hard about the ramifications of what she was about to do. Her mind made up, she folded the letter, set it back on the mantel, and went to the library for a book. It was at least two hours until sunset, and in the interim, she needed something to do.

It was twilight by the time Ellie felt it was safe to proceed. She dashed off a note, informing Lawrence of what had occurred, and sent it with a footman to Cavendish Square. Half an hour later, Lawrence strode into the drawing room, looking like thunder.

"Run away, has he? Coward," he added when Ellie confirmed his question with a nod. "Where's he gone?"

"I don't know, but he left me this." She held out the note.

Lawrence took it and began to read, but after a few moments, he stopped with a sound of derision. "Enemies?" he said and rolled his eyes. "I suppose to his way of thinking, anyone who wants justice served is his enemy."

"I'm sure," she agreed.

Lawrence returned his attention to the letter and read the rest. "Unbelievable," he said at last, shaking his head. "All he talks of is himself. His humiliation, his shame—in this entire letter, there is not one speck of consideration for you, your welfare, or your future."

"He did commend me to the care of Lady Wolford."

"How good of him." Lawrence glanced at the letter again, and gave a laugh. "He thinks his pride is his greatest fault? What a joke. His pride pales in the face of his greed and his cowardice."

Ellie didn't reply, and Lawrence looked up. Something in her face made him frown. "He is a coward, Ellie. Don't tell me he's not."

"Oh, I won't," she replied at once. "He is a coward, and no mistake."

Satisfied, he returned his attention to the letter. "Sunset," he muttered. "Well, he's long gone, then, for it's dark out now." He looked up sharply. "When did you get this?"

She could have lied. A lie would have been the easiest thing in the world, but unlike her father, Ellie was not a liar. "About three hours ago."

"Three hours?" He stared at her, an angry frown furrowing his brow and etching his face into hard, implacable lines. "You've known about this letter for over three hours, and you're just now showing it to me?"

"Yes."

"Why the devil did you wait so long?" He gave her no time to explain. "You did it on purpose," he accused, his eyes narrowing. "You wanted him to have enough time to escape."

"Yes." She squared her shoulders, facing her choice and his wrath head-on. "Yes, I did."

"How could you do this? You know what he did. You already acknowledged to me that you know he's guilty as hell. He's shown not a shred of remorse for his crimes. But thanks to you, he's slipped the hook."

"Possibly." She bit her lip, her gaze scanning his scowling face. "Are you very angry with me?"

"Angry?" He shook his head with a laugh that had no amusement in it whatsoever. "Woman, angry doesn't begin to describe how I feel at this moment. Why, Ellie?" he demanded, his voice hard as granite, his brilliant blue eyes glittering like jewels. "Why would you do this?"

"Because," she said simply, "he's my father."

Lawrence sucked in his breath, then let it out slowly. "A very poor father," he muttered.

"Yes," she agreed. "He's a scoundrel of the first water, I daresay, and a coward. And I freely admit he would have deserved every bit of punishment the law would have thrown at him, and more besides. But . . ." She paused and sighed. "I still love him, Lawrence, in spite of it all."

"He has far less regard for you than you do for him."

"I know. But there it is. I fully realize the ramifications of what I've done, and I'm sure you must resent me right now—"

"Resent? That's an understatement."

She took a deep breath and persevered. "I wouldn't blame you if you cried off and decided not to marry me—"

"I can't cry off," he interrupted again. "Your virtue's been compromised. No gentleman could cry off in such circumstances."

The bitterness in his voice was unmistakable, and pain squeezed her heart. "I don't know if you can ever forgive me for ruining your case, but I hope you can, because I love you, and I want to marry you more than I've ever wanted anything in my life, and I don't think I could bear it if the only reason you went through with it was a sense of obligation about last night."

He didn't reply, and in the face of his silence, she closed her eyes, fearing that her choice had made a breach between them that could never be healed. It seemed an eternity before he spoke.

"You didn't ruin my case."

At those muttered words, she opened her eyes. "I didn't?"

"Not by a long chalk." His eyes narrowed, and he glared at her. "I'll soon determine what ship he took, and where he went, and I will employ all the investigators required to find him. I don't care how long it takes. I don't care if we've been married two decades and have a dozen children, Ellie, I will find that scoundrel you call a father."

At those words, joy and relief flooded her, banishing all her doubts and fears. She opened her mouth to reply, but he cut her off.

"And if the Crown allows it, I will have him dragged back here to face his peers in the House of Lords and account for what he's done. So," Lawrence added, tossing aside the letter and folding his arms with a belligerent scowl, "perhaps you are the one who wants to cry off?"

"No." She shook her head. "I don't. If you do find him and bring him back, then he'll have to take his punishment, and I shan't weep for him."

"Good." He relaxed a little, his arms falling to his sides. "So we are getting married?"

"I suppose we are." She sighed, giving him a look of mock aggravation. "Even though I have not yet received a proper proposal."

"Don't push your luck." He wrapped his arms around her and pulled her close. "I still have your sixpence."

"So you do," she said, smiling as she slid her arms up around his neck. "Which means I can't take anything for granted when it comes to matrimony, can I?"

He pulled back to retrieve the sixpence from his pocket. "You know," he said musingly as he held it up between them, "I shouldn't wonder if there's something to this coin's power, after all."

She studied it, considering. "There have been times in the past week that I've wondered about it, too. But I don't see how it's possible, Lawrence. I mean, the sixpence was supposed to be my key to finding a spouse, but it hasn't been in my possession for over a week, and I'm getting married anyway. Doesn't that prove it doesn't work?"

"On the contrary." He flipped the coin into the air, caught it again, and gave her a wink. "You're not the only one getting married, you know."

"That's true," she agreed, laughing. "That must mean it works for whoever has it, not just for me and my friends. But, heavens, if it does work, you mustn't lose it."

"Don't worry," he said and tucked the coin back into his pocket. "Until you are safely wedded to me, I am keeping this sixpence with me every single moment. But what am I to do with it after that? Save it for our first daughter?"

"Certainly not! You have to give it to Bea."

"Bea won't want it. She's always said she'll never marry, sixpence or no."

"If we're right, I doubt she'll have a choice. We might see her put the sixpence in her shoe before all's said and done."

"Her shoe?" Lawrence looked at her in bewilderment. "What's a shoe to do with it?"

"It completes the rhyme, of course. 'Something old, something new, something borrowed, something blue, and a sixpence in her shoe.'"

"Ah, I'd forgotten the last line. But I'm not sure the rhyme quite hangs together."

"But it does, Lawrence. The coin is obviously the 'something old.' And Anne's duke . . . he was definitely 'something new' in her life. And then there's Cordelia—"

Lawrence's chuckle interrupted her. "Well, that part fits, at least. Borrowing someone else's fiancé? Who but Cordelia would think of a harebrained idea like that? I ask you."

"It was rather madcap, wasn't it? But that's Cordelia all over." She looked up at him, smiling. "And then," she said softly, "there's us."

"And that's where we veer off course. You must have thought Bluestone would be your 'something blue,' but you're not marrying him. You're marrying me."

She shook her head, bemused. "Only a week ago, I believed marrying him was my destiny. What on earth was I thinking?"

"Well," he began, but she cut him off.

"It was a rhetorical question," she said sternly.

"Either way, your plan to marry Bluestone didn't work out, thank God." Lawrence's arms tightened around her, and a frown of puzzlement creased his brow. "So what the devil is your 'something blue'?"

She laughed, looking into the brilliant blue eyes of the only man she had ever loved. "You are, my darling," she said, rose on her toes, and kissed him. "You are."

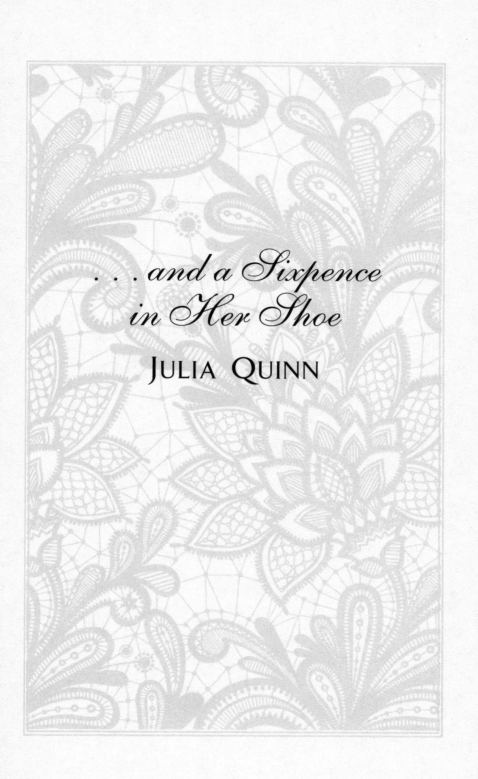

. . . and a Sixpence in Her Shoe

Julia Quinn

Chapter 1

An upstairs bedroom in Wolford Grange
Herefordshire
Immediately following the wedding of
   Lawrence Blackthorne and Lady Elinor Daventry

"*Y*ou're joking."

   But it was clear from their faces that Anne, Cordelia, and Ellie were *not* joking. Bea could only stare, first at them, and then at the coin that had been laid in the palm of her hand.

   Then back at them, because, really, *they* were the ones with the ability to form thoughts and take action and change the future. Not the coin.

   Never the coin.

   "You made a vow," Cordelia said.

   "Oh, come now—"

   "A *vow*, Bea."

   "We were children!" Bea looked over at Ellie, hoping to find some spark of sanity in her eyes.

   But Ellie was nodding right along with Cordelia. "It worked for us, Bea. You should give it a try."

   "I cannot believe the three of you think that this sixpence"—Bea thrust her hand forward, as if they didn't already know precisely what she was holding—"that this . . . this *coin* has supernatural powers."

"I'm not saying it *does*," said Anne, whose recent marriage to the Duke of Dorset made her one of the highest-ranking ladies in the land. "I'm just saying I'm not convinced that it doesn't."

"I had wretched bad luck when Lawrence had it in his possession," Ellie admitted.

"I still can't believe you gave it to him," Cordelia scolded.

"He picked my pocket!"

"*I* can't believe you married a pickpocket," Anne said, shaking her head. Her expression was admirably grim, but she managed to keep it that way for only a second before a snort of laughter burst through her lips.

"Well, he's *my* pickpocket," Ellie said, "and that's all that matters." She turned to Bea. "*You*—"

"*Don't* say that I could have my own pickpocket," Bea warned her. Good heavens, her friends had lost their minds. Was this what love *did* to a person?

"You have to take the sixpence," Ellie said.

Bea's gaze dropped to the silver disk in her hand. "I believe I've already taken it."

"You have to *use* it," Ellie clarified.

Bea rolled her eyes. "Most people would agree that the *normal* use for a sixpence is to spend it."

"Bea!"

It was a collective shout, from all three of her friends. She looked at them, still dressed in their elegant gowns. Ellie was in her wedding dress, for heaven's sake. Lawrence was probably pacing a trail through the rug in the sitting room on the ground floor, waiting for her to come down so they could leave for their honeymoon.

Instead they were holed up in a bedchamber, arguing over *this* nonsense.

Cordelia reached out and folded Bea's fingers over the sixpence. "Put it in your shoe."

"Now?"

"It's the only way we'll believe you've done it."

"You do realize I could simply remove it as soon as I've gone?"

"But you wouldn't," Ellie said, "because you don't break promises."

Bea opened her mouth to argue, then groaned. They had her there. This was the problem with friends. They knew you too well.

"The thing is," Bea said, "I don't even want to get married."

Anne looked up briefly from the gloves she was sliding onto her hands. "So you say."

"So I mean!"

"You should reconsider," Anne said with a frank shrug. "The marital state has a great deal to recommend it."

"I might agree," Ellie said pertly, "if I ever managed to leave this room to join my new husband."

"I'm not stopping you," Bea pointed out.

But Ellie was undeterred. "I'm not going anywhere until you put that bloody coin in your shoe."

Bea sighed. There was no winning this one. Not with all three of her friends staring her down like a tribe of lost gorgons. She turned the coin over in her hand a few times. "Well," she said thoughtfully, "I suppose it counts as something old."

Anne grinned and tapped herself on the chest. "And I'm something new."

"What?"

"I'm a new duchess," she explained.

"You're stretching this old wives' tale for all it's worth, aren't you?" Bea remarked.

Anne shrugged unrepentantly.

"Well, I borrowed my fiancé," Cordelia said.

Ellie waggled her hand in Bea's face, her sapphire betrothal ring glinting in the fading daylight. "And I've got something blue."

"It all fits," Anne said. "It's brilliant." She pointed to the coin, then to herself, Cordelia, and then Ellie as she said:

> "Something old,
> Something new,
> Something borrowed,
> Something blue . . ."

No one needed prompting to finish with: "And a sixpence in her shoe."

Well, except Bea. She kept her mouth shut the whole time. But in the end, she could only shake her head. "I can't win, can I?"

"Shoe," Anne ordered. "Now."

"You've become quite the duchess," Bea grumbled, plopping down on a nearby chair so she could remove her slipper.

"She was always this bossy," Ellie said. She flashed a smile at Anne, which was instantly returned. Bea couldn't help but smile a little herself, even as she sighed in defeat. This, she thought, was the very definition of friendship. The shared laughter, the smiles that didn't have to be hidden behind a hand. The knowledge that if she ever needed anything, ever found herself alone or adrift . . .

She would never be alone or adrift. That was the point.

Bea didn't believe for one moment that a sixpence could help a lady find a husband, but she did believe in friendship.

She put the coin in her shoe.

One week later
High Street, Wallingford
Oxfordshire

Bea frowned and shook her foot at the ankle, hoping no one would notice the strange hopping gait she'd adopted for the last ten or so paces. One would think that a coin—especially one so flat and worn down—would be nearly impossible to feel underfoot, but no, it felt like there was a bloody pebble in there, wedged between her stocking and shoe.

She felt rather like the Princess and the Pea.

Except she wasn't a princess. Nor was she a lady or an honorable or anything other than the very ordinary Miss Beatrice Mary Heywood, orphaned daughter of the late Robert and Elizabeth Heywood, devoted and grateful niece to the Misses Calpurnia and Henrietta Heywood.

She lived in a very ordinary home, with three floors, two servants, and one garden. She liked to read. She liked to knit. All very ordinary pursuits. In fact, the only extraordinary thing about her (besides her circle of dear friends, which—rather improbably for a young lady of her station—included a duchess, a countess, and the daughter of an earl) was her passion for the skies. It wasn't a terribly ladylike pursuit, but Bea had never been concerned by this. When she tipped her face to the heavens, she saw nothing but possibility. And it was so glorious it took her breath away.

Every single time.

At that very moment, in fact, the cumulus cloud at about one o'clock (assuming the church spire was twelve, and Bea always made the tallest structure twelve) looked rather like the Taj Mahal. Not that she had ever seen the Taj Mahal, or that she ever would, but she had seen a colored illustration of the magnificent Indian building, and surely that was enough to render judgment on a cloud.

Over at four o'clock she saw a teapot, and at six—

"Excuse me!"

Bea snapped back to attention just a moment too late to avoid barreling into a gentleman coming the other way down the pavement. Her body connected with his with a breath-sucking thud, and her reticule flew from her fingers, skittering a few inches along the cobbles when it hit the ground. Bea would have gone down, too, if a pair of large hands had not come to rest roughly on her shoulders, steadying her before she toppled over.

"I'm so sorry!" She snatched up her purse, thankful the clasp had remained fastened. "I was looking for a bench."

"In the sky?" came the derisive response.

She felt her cheeks grow warm. He had her there. Still, he didn't have to be quite so ungracious. "Of course not," she muttered.

"I was distracted, and, well . . ." She didn't finish the sentence. What was the point? She cleared her throat and finally met the rude gentleman's eyes. "Please accept my apologies. It was very careless of—"

Of . . .

My goodness. She blinked, so startled by his appearance that for a moment she could not speak. There was a patch over his right eye, but that was of little interest. Because the other one . . . his left eye . . .

It was the exact color of the sky. A little blue, a little gray.

More than a little stormy.

"I'm terribly sorry," she said again, although honestly, who got that angry over a careless step? Had he never been jostled on the pavement before?

His lips pinched, and his brows—the same rich, dark brown as his hair—drew down. When he spoke, his tone was just as rigid as his expression. "Mind where you're going next time."

Bea felt her jaw grow stiff. "I shall."

He stared at her for one last uncomfortable moment, then grunted, "Good day," and stalked past.

"Good day to you, too," Bea muttered to the empty space in front of her. Annoying man.

Then she turned. Because she couldn't quite help herself. The insufferable man was striding down the street like he owned it, although maybe he did. She knew enough of men's fashion to know that his boots and hat were exceedingly well made. And as for his coat—all fancy blue superfine and shiny gold buttons—of a certain that had been constructed by an exclusive London tailor. No one else could have cut and stitched the cloth to so elegantly cover his muscular frame.

Which brought her to another point.

"Annoying man with annoyingly broad shoulders," she muttered. How could it possibly be fair that the worst examples of humankind so often were the loveliest to look at?

With a sigh and a shake of her head, she carried on her way, eager to complete the rest of her errands. As if to mock her, the sixpence shifted in her shoe and dug in hard under her big toe.

"Really?" she said to her foot. If this was the sort of man the lucky charm was going to bring her, she was going to chuck the bloody thing in the lake.

LORD FREDERICK GREY-OSBOURNE had three older brothers, two degrees from Oxford, and one working eye.

At present it was the eye that he found the most vexing, although his brothers generally ranked a very close second.

He supposed he should have been grateful that the wretched young lady had bumped into him, rather than the other way around. One had to take one's pleasures where one could, and it was nice to be reminded that he wasn't the only clumsy clod attempting to navigate the uneven cobbles of the Wallingford high street.

Funny how one never quite realized just how essential two eyes were to depth perception until one of them was rendered useless.

But instead, all he could remember was the look on her face when she'd finally raised her eyes to his (eye, that was, singular). She'd frozen, barely able to mask her disgust.

He had never been a rogue, never been the sort to steal kisses and catalogue conquests, but he'd been handsome; all the Grey-Osbourne boys were. He was used to seeing a tiny flare of appreciation in a woman's eyes, hearing the ever so slight catch of her breath when they were introduced. He was tall, and he was strong, and he hadn't thought he'd been vain, but clearly he'd been wrong, because the revulsion . . . the pity . . .

It was more than he could take.

No, he thought as he stepped into Plinkington's Stationery Shop (Purveyors of Fine Paper since 1745), it was obviously *not* more than he could take, because he was still here, still walking and talking and, more than anything else, still thinking, but he could not make it through the day without some reminder that he was not the man he used to be. There was probably another, more Shakespearean way of saying it, with acid in the belly, or rage firing his soul, but the truth was more simple, and probably more profound.

It made him angry.

And it kept him angry.

"Lord Frederick, sir," Mr. Plinkington said, his face lighting up at the sight of his finest customer. "A pleasure to see you. What can I help you with today, my lord?"

Frederick nodded in reply. He was relatively new to Wallingford, but he'd been in the shop many times since the accident. Mr. Plinkington was well used to his face, and if he noticed the eye patch—or the scar that escaped the edge of the fabric and snaked down his cheek to his ear—he no longer let it show.

"Three notebooks," Frederick told him.

"Already?" The shopkeeper's brows rose with his smile. "You bought some just last month."

Frederick gave a friendly shrug. "I take a lot of notes."

"'Tis a good business," Mr. Plinkington said with a nod, "a stationery shop so close to a university. You academic types always seem to want to write things down."

"One would think you'd fare even better were you in Oxford proper," Frederick pointed out.

"Ah, but then the rents would be higher."

"A fair point," Frederick murmured. He wandered over to the far side of the shop while Mr. Plinkington ran his fingers along the spines of the many notebooks that filled his shelves, searching for the kind he knew Frederick preferred. Plinkington's carried a good selection of writing paper as well. He supposed he ought to replenish his supply; he seemed to have a great deal more correspondence now that he'd purchased a small estate of his own. Close work usually left his good eye exhausted by the end of the day. He knew there was no shame in dictating his letters to someone else; this was what most of his contemporaries did, as a matter of fact.

But it still felt like a mark of failure, an acknowledgment that he was no longer as fully capable as before.

"Mr. Plinkington?" he called, intending to ask about the price of different sizes of laid paper, but before he could put words to his query, he heard the shop door open, followed by the tinny chime of the bell.

"Can I help you, miss?" the shopkeeper asked.

"Yes, thank you," replied a female voice.

Frederick stilled. He recognized that voice. It had assaulted his ears not two minutes earlier.

"I'm looking for a scientific notebook," she said.

Mr. Plinkington, all helpful good cheer, said, "I can certainly help you with that."

Frederick stepped slightly to his left, the better to both see her and partially obscure himself behind a freestanding shelf. It was the lady who had bumped into him on the street, of course. She was smiling pleasantly at the shopkeeper, her expression nothing like the one she'd directed toward him just moments before. Her eyes had been green, he recalled, or more properly, hazel. She was wearing one of those atrocious frilled bonnets ladies seemed to find necessary, but enough of her hair peeked out to reveal itself a rather ordinary light brown.

He had not been able to determine if it curled.

Not that he cared if it curled. But he was trained to observe. He couldn't *not* do it. For example, he had noticed earlier that her eyelashes were a shade darker than her brows, and just now, as she joined Mr. Plinkington near the counter, he saw that the stitching in her fine kid gloves was not of uniform color.

She had repaired them. Probably more than once.

"Unlined, if you please," she said, tipping her head toward the shelf behind her. "I frequently make illustrations alongside my notes."

"We don't get many ladies looking for scientific notebooks," Mr. Plinkington said.

The lady's smile tightened.

"Not that I'm making a judgment," the shopkeeper assured her. "Just an observation." His expression grew jolly as he pulled out several notebooks. "A scientific observation, if you will."

The lady nodded graciously and reached out her hand.

"Oh, I'm sorry," Mr. Plinkington said. "These are for the gentleman." He motioned with his head toward the back of the store. "I'll get yours just as soon as I'm finished with his order."

"Of course," she replied, her head turning instinctively to follow his motion. "First come, first . . ."

Frederick acknowledged her presence with a nod.

"Sir," she said, her tone making it quite clear that the syllable was born of polite manners and nothing else.

Frederick responded in kind. "Miss."

"Ah, then you know each other!" Mr. Plinkington said jovially. "I suppose there's no getting around it in a town of this size."

"We have not been introduced," the lady said, not *quite* turning her back on him. Frederick almost chuckled. There were those pesky good manners again. She could not bring herself to be rude, no matter how much she clearly wanted to.

"Lord Frederick Grey-Osbourne," Frederick said with a bow. He could hardly do anything else, under the circumstances. And besides, there was something rather delicious about being scrupulously polite when the other person wished to have nothing to do with you.

"I am Miss Heywood," she said somewhat primly. He wondered if she was a schoolteacher. Or a governess. She had that air about her.

"His Lordship's new to Wallingford," Mr. Plinkington said helpfully. "He's a don up at the university."

"Not precisely," Frederick murmured. He didn't actually teach at Oxford, but after a decade of study and a hefty donation to the school, he did have unfettered access to the libraries and laboratories. All in all, it was an excellent arrangement.

"What is your area of study?" Miss Heywood asked.

He couldn't imagine she truly cared, but he did give her points for inquiring, *and* he knew from previous experience that the surest way to shut down a conversation was to launch into a description of his research, so he said, "Physics, mostly."

She blinked three times. "Practical or theoretical?"

He stared. "I beg your pardon?"

"Do you study practical or theoretical physics?" she repeated.

Frederick cleared his throat. It was not a question he normally heard outside of academic circles. "Theoretical," he told her. "Mostly."

"That's quite a lot of mostlys."

Cheeky thing. He felt himself smile. "It's a complicated subject."

"I'm sure it is," she said, glancing over at Mr. Plinkington. He was wrapping up Frederick's purchase. Miss Heywood was clearly eager for him to move on to her request.

Her posture seemed to indicate that she'd had enough of the conversation, and Frederick *had* introduced the topic of theoretical physics for that very same reason, but when she'd asked him about his work, he could have sworn he'd seen a spark of actual interest in her eyes.

And something in him just couldn't resist.

He stepped forward, inserting himself just far enough between her and the shopkeeper so as not to be completely obnoxious about it. "What do *you* study, Miss Heywood?"

She turned with surprise. "Nothing," she said.

Frederick quickly realized the error of his question. This close to one of the world's finest universities, "studying" was an official thing, and not something women were generally permitted to undertake.

"Are your notebooks a purchase for someone else, then?" he asked, even though he knew they were not. She'd said she liked to make illustrations alongside her notes. But she didn't know that he'd heard her.

"No, they are mine," she admitted, looking slightly discomfited by his attention. She cleared her throat. "I have an interest in astronomy."

"Very commendable," he said.

She smiled, but it was clearly not authentic, and it occurred to him that she probably thought he was humoring her.

"There is quite a bit of physics in the science of the skies," he said. "Theoretically, we might one day visit the moon."

She let out a choke of laughter. "Oh, you're serious," she said, once she'd contained her grin.

"Quite," he replied, "although it's not anything I expect to see in my lifetime."

"Nor mine," she agreed.

He raised a mischievous brow. "Do you expect your life to extend that much longer than mine?"

"What? No, I—" Her lips pressed together, then quirked at the corners when she realized she'd been teased.

"The moon," Mr. Plinkington chortled. "Gor, now there's a rich man's dream."

Frederick offered up a wry smile. "I suppose there is a reason I don't pursue practical physics."

"I don't know," Miss Heywood said thoughtfully. "The theoretical eventually becomes the practical, or so one hopes, yes?"

He found himself staring at her for quite a bit longer than was socially necessary. That spark of intelligence he'd seen in her eyes was clearly something more like a bonfire. How intriguing to find a female who was interested in this sort of thing. Scratch that, how intriguing to find a *human* who was interested. Frederick had long since given up trying to lure his brothers into scientific discussions. He'd quite given up on the topic with anyone outside his colleagues at the university.

"Here you are, my lord," Mr. Plinkington said, handing over the notebooks. They'd been wrapped in brown paper and tied with twine, a neat little bundle of future research. "Shall I put it on your account?"

"Please." Frederick took his purchase and weighed it lightly in his hands. He ought to go. He'd got what he had come in for. There was no reason to remain.

"Unlined notebooks for you," Mr. Plinkington murmured, moving on to Miss Heywood.

"Just one," she specified.

"Will this do?" he asked, plucking one off the shelf and holding it forward.

She took it, flipped through the pages, and nodded. "It's perfect."

"Shall I put this on your account, Miss Heywood?"

"No," she said firmly, reaching into her reticule, "I will pay now. Thank you."

Frederick watched as she transferred some coins to her palm, then carefully plucked out a few to pay for her purchase. The rest she returned to her purse.

"There is no need to wrap it," she said to Mr. Plinkington. "I don't think it will rain before I get home."

"I should think not," he replied with a smile.

So she lived close by, Frederick thought. Or perhaps not. Mr. Plinkington could have been referring to the patches of blue that had been steadily pushing out the clouds. The weather was indisputably fine this afternoon. She could walk all the way to Oxford and be unlikely to encounter rain.

"Do come again soon, Miss Heywood," Mr. Plinkington said, handing over her notebook.

"Thank you, and please give my and my aunts' regards to Mrs. Plinkington." She turned her head, her eyes settling on Frederick, who was still standing by the door. She looked at him with a some-what flat expression, one that clearly said, *You're still here?*

"Thank you, Mr. Plinkington," he said with a formal nod of his head. There was every possibility that he would have felt the need to wait inside until he, too, could offer his thanks. "Good day." He nodded to Miss Heywood and repeated his farewell. "Good day."

"My lord," she murmured, and then he had absolutely no more excuses to remain. He gave her one last nod, headed outside, and started walking toward his gig.

But first he glanced up. The clouds were astonishingly fluffy this afternoon. And that one—the one that was just starting to creep behind the church steeple—was particularly majestic. Almost like the Taj Mahal.

The Taj Mahal, eh? He'd like to go see that someday, one eye or not.

Chapter 2

*T*wo days later Bea found herself back in town, walking briskly up the high street on her way to the butcher and baker, who were rather inconveniently located at opposite ends of the town. This was not in her normal roster of tasks, but Mrs. Wembley, the longtime cook and occasional lady's maid to Bea's two elderly aunts, was caring for her sick sister in Nottinghamshire, and Bea had neither the energy nor the funds to find a replacement for such a short time as a fortnight.

Aunt Callie and Aunt Hennie could manage the basics of cooking, and their housemaid Martha knew a bit, too, so they would not starve. Provided, of course, that they had provisions to prepare. Enter Bea. She was a wreck in the kitchen, but shopping was nothing more than basic maths, right? She could buy ham. A leg of lamb? Not a problem. She did wonder at the extensiveness of the list she'd been given, though. Could they really need four loaves of bread? Two rashers of bacon? How much did her aunts intend to eat?

With a shake of her head, she resolved to cut the list in half (at the very least), pulled open the door to Farnsworth's Family Butchery (est. 1612, a longstanding Wallingford tradition), and smiled broadly at the proprietor.

"Miss Heywood!" Mr. Farnsworth called out. "What brings you in? Mrs. Wembley still with her sister?"

"Yes," Bea replied, "for at least a week, I think, possibly even two."

Mr. Farnsworth sucked in his breath. "Glad I'm not a fly on that wall. She *hates* her sister."

"Really?" Bea asked.

Mr. Farnsworth—ever the gossip—nodded. "Talks about her all the time when she's in here. Wretched thorn in her side, she always says. But then again, she's not exactly a stroll in the park, is she now?"

Bea gave a little shrug and a nod, about as much of a response as she was prepared to offer. Mrs. Wembley was not particularly long of temper, but she was an *excellent* cook, and Bea saw no reason to antagonize her, even in absentia.

"Don't suppose any of you can cook," the butcher said.

"Well, we can manage toast." Bea looked down at her list. "And bacon, apparently."

"Miss Martha knows her way around a kitchen," Mr. Farnsworth said, reaching into his case. "Don't let her tell you she doesn't. Now, what do you need today?"

"Aunt Hennie made up a list," Bea said with a frowning shake of her head, "but I have to say, I think she may have been somewhat ambitious." She held it forth, letting Mr. Farnsworth's sausagy fingers take hold of the slip of paper.

He chuckled aloud as he read Henrietta Heywood's spidery writing. "Why don't I just give you what Mrs. Wembley usually takes?"

"That would be marvelous." Bea fiddled with the clasp of her reticule. "How much will it be?"

He waved her off. "You can put it on your account. I'll send a bill at the end of the month."

"No, no, I would rather pay you now," Bea said. She'd wrestled the household accounts from Aunt Hennie the previous month and had been horrified by the state of their finances. No more putting anything on account until their debts were paid off. Honestly, it was a wonder the village merchants still welcomed their business.

"As you wish," Mr. Farnsworth said equably. He did not mention that they still owed him over two pounds for previous purchases. For which Bea was quite grateful.

"Anything else?" he inquired, handing her a chicken, thoughtfully cut into pieces. "I'm leaving off the leg of lamb. I don't think you need it."

"Not to mention we don't know how to cook it," Bea said with a laugh.

"Miss Martha knows," he reminded her.

"Martha's got her hands full," Bea assured him, "but I will certainly seek her advice should we need to prepare anything more complicated than eggs and toast." She held up her package. "And bacon. Perhaps we shall eat breakfast all day long until Mrs. Wembley returns."

"Should I take back the chicken?"

"Oh no, I'm only joking. Even I would grow tired of bacon after two weeks of nothing but. Now"—she set down her packages and pulled her change purse from her reticule—"how much do I owe you?"

Mr. Farnsworth told her, and she counted out her coins, carefully avoiding the sixpence that she'd stashed in the purse after the wretched thing had nearly given her a blister the day before.

"Here you are," she murmured, dropping most of the necessary coins into the butcher's hand. "Just one more pen—oh!"

Bea didn't know how it happened, and in fact she was of enough scientific mind that she knew it couldn't possibly *have* happened, but she could have sworn the sixpence vaulted itself from her purse.

And rolled right out the door just as another customer walked in.

"Just a moment!" Bea yelped, abandoning her purchases as she dashed outside. The stupid coin might be the bane of her blistery existence these days, but she couldn't *lose* it. What would her friends say?

Practically tumbling down the two steps to the pavement, she looked this way and that until her eyes caught the glint of sunshine on metal and she launched forward.

Just in time to see someone else's hand scoop it up.

"I'm sorry," she said assertively. "That's mine."

A man she did not recognize tossed the sixpence in the air and caught it neatly in an overhand grasp. "Used to be," he said with a cheeky grin. "But it's mine now."

She drew back, startled by his rudeness. "No, you don't understand. I was in the butcher shop, and—"

"And you let it go," he interrupted. "Now it's mine."

"Sir," she said, scooting forward to block his way on the pavement. "I must protest. Mr. Farnsworth will attest to my honesty in this matter. He saw the whole thing."

But a quick glance over her shoulder told her that Mr. Farnsworth was busy with his other customer. And if Bea reentered the shop to attract his attention, the scoundrel before her would surely depart.

"Look," Bea said, trying to sound reasonable, "I'll give you a different sixpence in its place." Which was highway robbery, but what else could she do? She needed that coin. She did not believe it carried luck; in fact, she was quite certain it did not. But it was important. It held memories, happy ones of laughter and friendship.

It was the one thing she and her friends still shared.

The man drew back, his dark eyes flashing with new interest. "You'd pay me for this?"

"I would."

"You'd give me a sixpence."

"Yes," she ground out.

His hand came up to stroke his chin. "Then I think you'd pay me double."

Bea gasped. "What?"

He shrugged. "It's obviously worth more to you than a sixpence."

"Oh, for—"

"Is there a problem?" came a new voice.

Bea had never thought she'd be delighted to see Lord Frederick Two-Names again (she'd quite forgotten what he was properly called), but she couldn't have been more grateful to see him staring quizzically down at her with his one spectacular eye.

"None at all," the man—Bea refused to even think of him as a gentleman—said smoothly.

"That's not true!" Bea stood at attention, her arms like fisted sticks at her side. "This man has stolen my sixpence."

"Your sixpence," Lord Frederick repeated, his tone possibly suggesting that he found this to be quite a lot of drama for a sixpence. Or maybe not. He had rather a cool countenance. Bea found him impossible to read.

"It is my lucky sixpence," she ground out, mortified to be saying such a thing to a man of science.

Lord Frederick gave a dispassionate glance to the other man and said simply, "Give it back."

The man's upper lip curled. "I picked it up off the ground."

"After it fell from my purse and rolled out of Farnsworth's!" Bea cried, half ready to throw her arms up in frustration. "Honestly, I told him I'd give him a different sixpence, and now he's demanded double."

"Is that so?" Lord Frederick murmured. But it was much more than a murmur. There was danger lurking in his voice, and when Bea caught sight of his face, she almost backed up a step.

Some would say his eye patch lent him a menacing air, but Bea knew better. That eye patch was the only thing keeping him from incinerating the thief on the spot. His good eye was practically shooting fire; Bea couldn't imagine what it would be like to face the full force of his glare.

"Bollocks," the thief spat, flicking the coin into the air toward Bea. "'Snot worth it."

The sixpence landed on the ground, and Bea stooped to retrieve it, deciding there was no point in a display of pride. But when she stood back up, she noticed that Lord Frederick had taken a step to his left, blocking the other man from departing.

Bea's eyes widened as Lord Frederick said with devastating quiet, "You will watch your language in front of a lady."

"Or what?"

"Or I'll have to hurt you."

Bea jumped forward. "Oh, this isn't nec—"

Lord Frederick silenced her with a hand, never once taking his eye off the scoundrel's face. "Will you apologize," he said, again with the menacing calm, "or will I hurt you?"

The sixpence thief moved to slug his opponent in the belly, but Lord Frederick was too quick, and before Bea could even blink, he'd blocked the blow and landed a bruising punch to the other man's face.

Bea's mouth fell open as the bounder dropped to the ground.

She looked up at Lord Frederick, then back to the man on the ground, then back to Lord Frederick. "You didn't have to . . ."

"I assure you, I did." He gazed down at his fist with a rueful expression. "I'm going to feel this tomorrow." He stretched his gloved fingers, then bent them again, wincing as he went through the motion. "Pity."

"I should get you some ice." Bea glanced over her shoulder at the butcher shop. "Perhaps Mr. Farnsworth . . ." Her words trailed off when she realized that Lord Frederick had, without seeming to look down, planted his foot on the thief's midsection, preventing him from rising.

"An apology, if you please," Lord Frederick demanded.

"For the love of—"

Lord Frederick's boot made a rather sudden shift in position.

"I'm sorry!" the man yelled.

"Very well, then," His Lordship said, removing his foot. He turned back to Bea. "May I escort you to your next engagement?"

"Oh," Bea said, feeling strangely breathless, "that's not . . ." She took one look at his face—utterly impassive and polite, and yet with that hint of ferocity in his eye—and revised her statement. "Thank you," she said. "That would be most welcome."

He nodded and held out his arm, but she motioned to Farnsworth's. "I need to retrieve my purchases. If you don't mind . . ."

"I will await you here," he confirmed.

Bea scurried back into the shop, where Mr. Farnsworth was still helping a customer, seemingly oblivious to the drama that had unfolded on his storefront pavement.

"Miss Heywood," he said in his usual jovial tones. "It's all right there on the counter."

She nodded her thanks, and then, deciding that she had no need to witness the thief's departure, took just a little bit longer than was necessary to make her way back outside.

Sure enough, Lord Frederick was now alone on the pavement, tucking his pocket watch away just as she emerged. "Miss Heywood," he said, reaching for her packages.

Bea stood dumbly for a moment before releasing them into his care. She was so used to fending for herself—and of course for her two aunts. The mere motion of handing her parcels to a gentleman felt rusty.

"I need to stop by the baker's," Bea said awkwardly. "Some bread, I think, and scones, if she's baked some today."

He dipped his head graciously and allowed her to lead the way.

"I don't normally do all the shopping," Bea heard herself explain. "Our cook has gone to Nottinghamshire to be with her sister. She's sick. The sister, that is, not our cook."

Why on earth was she saying all this?

"With a lung ailment," she blurted out.

And why couldn't she seem to stop?

"I do hope she feels better soon," Lord Frederick said. His lips curved. "The sister, that is. Not your cook."

His voice held enough warmth to indicate that he was teasing, and she smiled sheepishly. "I'm sure Mrs. Wembley would welcome your well wishes, too. She's likely half out of her mind by now." And then, because such a statement seemed to require further explanation, she confided, "She's not terribly fond of her sister."

He cracked a smile. "All the more admirable that she's gone to care for her, then."

"It's what you do," Bea said, cocking her head to the side as she looked up at him. "When you're family."

"I suppose it is. Although I must say, I can't imagine any of my brothers rushing to my side for a lung ailment."

"No? What about—" Bea cut herself off in horror. She'd almost asked about his eye. What on earth was she thinking?

There was a beat of silence, just long enough for Bea to want to dig a hole and throw herself in it.

But then Lord Frederick turned to her with a wry expression and said, "They did come for that."

"I'm so sorry," she said, the words tumbling from her lips.

"Don't be."

"But I am. It was so terribly rude of me, and—"

"Stop," he said, and while she was still desperately trying to determine just how badly she'd offended him, he added, "please."

She swallowed and nodded, wanting more than anything to render yet another apology. But that would clearly be the wrong thing to do, and it made Bea wonder how often apologies were rendered for the sake of the giver, rather than the recipient.

"It was a carriage accident," he said abruptly.

Bea looked over in surprise. She had not expected him to say anything further on the subject. And she had the strangest feeling that he hadn't expected it, either.

"I still have the eye." He looked over at her, and she realized that he had positioned himself on her right. Did he do that as a matter of course, so that he might more easily see his companion? She closed her left eye, intending to assess her own peripheral vision, then quickly opened it again. Had he seen her? She did not want him to think she was mocking him.

He gave a little smile—a very little smile, actually, but there was just enough ruefulness to it to tell her that he'd seen what she'd done and he understood why. "I'm told it's disconcerting," he continued. "It's quite clearly sightless."

She nodded. She had seen people with blind eyes. It was difficult not to look, especially at first meeting.

"I expect that I damaged the surrounding muscle," he continued, surprising her with his forthcoming manner. "It does not move properly. Nor does the pupil dilate and contract."

"Really?" she said, turning to him with interest. How fascinating. Gruesome, but fascinating.

He blinked, looking vaguely surprised by her tone.

Bea thought for a moment. "I wonder . . ."

"What?"

"It's nothing," she said quickly. Where on earth were her manners? She had just sworn to herself that she wasn't going to ask questions, and then the very first chance, *I wonder* popped out of her mouth.

She'd always been far too curious for her own good.

"What do you wonder?" he pressed.

She sucked at the inside of her cheek, debating the wisdom of further inquiry before deciding that he didn't seem too terribly angry with her. And she *was* curious . . .

"Does it give you headaches?" she asked.

His lips twisted into an endearingly dry smile. "I was clouted on the head with the better part of a chaise and four, so yes, there have been headaches."

"No," she said, laughing despite herself, "I mean now. Because of the light."

A wrinkle formed in his brow. "I'm not certain I grasp your meaning."

"If your pupil does not expand and contract properly," Bea explained, "it cannot regulate the amount of light entering into your eye."

His head tilted, indicating for her to go on.

"I am sometimes afflicted with a headache when the air is overly bright," she continued. "But is that because I am *seeing* the light or simply because it's there?"

He stared at her.

"Does one actually have to *see* the light to be caused pain by it," she explained. "Or to be more precise, to *realize* that one sees it. I wonder if . . ." She felt her cheeks begin to grow warm. Her words had wandered off among her own thoughts, something they did all too often in the face of scientific inquiry. "I'm sorry," she said, forgetting that she hadn't meant to apologize to him again. "You must think I'm terribly silly."

"No," he said slowly, "I think you're probably quite brilliant."

Her lips parted. Honestly, she forgot to breathe.

"I do get headaches," he confirmed. "But I have no idea if it's because of the light. I'm not sure that there is a way to determine the cause."

"I suppose not." Bea frowned. The sciences had not been a feature of her education at Madame Rochambeaux's, but what she had lacked in formal schooling she had made up for with a voracious appetite for books, and she was well familiar with the scientific method. To properly determine if bright light was causing his headaches, one would need to eliminate all other causes, but surely that would be impossible, given that he had, as he'd said, been whacked over the head with a good portion of a carriage.

Or perhaps it was the bad portion. She rather thought any portion of a carriage was bad if it was connecting with one's skull.

"Miss Heywood?"

She looked up into his amused expression. "Sorry. Woolgathering."

"I'd offer you a penny for your thoughts, but I rather think a sixpence would be more in order."

She gave him a rueful smile. "I suppose you think I'm very silly."

He quirked a brow.

"Lucky coin and all that." She was embarrassed even to mention it, but after his gallant behavior, she didn't think she had the right to avoid the topic. Although he would never know the full truth of it—that her friends were convinced it would lead her to true love.

But Lord Frederick only shrugged. "If it's special to you, that's all that matters."

"I've had it for years," she said, wondering what it was about this man that led her to share her secrets. "We found it at school."

"We?"

"My friends and I. There were four of us. Ellie, Anne, Cordelia, and me. We were inseparable."

"Do you miss them?"

"Very much. We don't have much opportunity to see each other now. They are all married. Quite grandly, too." She caught him looking at her curiously, and she hastily added, "I never intended to marry, you see. I have the care of my aunts."

"That is very commendable of you," he murmured.

And all at once, Bea was sick of being commendable.

But she plowed on regardless. "They cared for me," she said, almost defensively. "I must do the same."

He nodded slowly.

"I was quite young when my parents died," she said. "Barely eight."

"I'm sorry."

She accepted his condolences with a tiny smile. And then, for reasons she could not identify, she kept talking. "It was smallpox."

He winced.

"Both of them," she continued. "Half the village caught it. And half of those died. Likely the only reason I survived was that I'd just been sent to school." She stared off in the distance, and as always, the irony of it all forced a hopeless smile onto her lips. "I cried so desperately when they forced me to go, and it probably saved my life."

"It does make one consider the possibility of fate," Lord Frederick said.

"I know," she agreed. "I've never believed in such a thing, but—" She caught him giving her a dubious look, and she had to add, "I don't *really* think the coin is lucky."

"Of course not," he said, clearly humoring her.

Bea pressed her lips together, trying not to smile. "Anyway," she said, "I was most fortunate. I mean, if it had to happen, that I went to my aunts."

"The best case scenario in the worst possible situation."

"Exactly." She looked up at him, right into his perfect cloudy-sky eye, and there it was. A strange, unfamiliar sort of kinship, like she'd finally found the one person in the world who understood.

Which was madness. She had Cordelia and Ellie and Anne. They all knew her sad history, and they all had acknowledged something similar.

But it hadn't felt the same.

Maybe it was because she was an adult now. Or maybe it was the sixpence burning a hole in her reticule. It made her fanciful.

And she wasn't fanciful. She couldn't afford that luxury.

She gave herself a mental shake. "Most of the time I was away at school. My aunts thought I should be with other children. But of course I had to leave when I was twenty."

"Twenty?" He looked surprised.

"I taught for two years after I was done. I would have stayed longer, but the school was closed. The headmistress retired, and no one wanted to take over."

"Did you enjoy teaching?"

"Very much. I was given great latitude. It was the first time the school offered the sciences. Not physics, I'm afraid." She looked up with a lopsided smile. "I'm not qualified for that. But we studied the plants and the trees, and of course astronomy when the weather cooperated."

"Then you are self-taught," he observed.

She shrugged and looked down at her feet, embarrassed and proud at the same time.

"It is very impressive."

She risked a glance at his face and felt a rush of delight at the sincerity in his eyes. "Thank you."

He paused in his steps, tilting his head as he looked at her.

"Is something wrong?" she asked.

"No," he said thoughtfully. "It's just that . . ." Then he blinked, and something seemed to clear in his face. His voice was much crisper when he said, "There is an excellent observatory at the university. Have you been there?"

Bea shook her head. "No. I've seen the exterior, of course, but

I've never been inside." One couldn't just walk up and demand entrance.

"Would you like to go?"

Her entire body snapped to attention. He had not just offered to take her to the Radcliffe Observatory. He had *not*. "I beg your pardon?"

"I hope it's not too forward—"

"It's not too forward," she interrupted, excitement fizzing through her like bubbles in a stream. "Well, it is too forward, but I don't care."

"I'm at liberty to use the facilities when I wish, and I'd be happy to take you."

"That would be marvelous. Amazing. Thank you. Oh my goodness, thank you." She couldn't stop herself from rising to her tiptoes—not because she was trying to approach him in height, although that wouldn't be such a bad thing—but rather she was so unbelievably, stupendously, *incandescently* happy. She had to put that energy somewhere.

Since she couldn't very well throw her arms around him and hug him.

Hug him?

What on earth?

She stumbled. She shouldn't even be *thinking* about hugging him.

"Miss Heywood?"

"Sorry," she said quickly. She needed to get ahold of herself. He was going to think her the veriest ninny, so unsophisticated that she fell over from excitement at the thought of visiting an observatory.

And that's all it was. Excitement. This man was going to fulfill her lifelong dream—to view the stars with clarity.

To travel closer to the heavens.

If she'd had the urge to embrace him, surely that was all it was. Gratitude. Very well-deserved gratitude. Lord Frederick Two-Names could have no idea just how big a wish he was granting. He was a man, wealthy and titled. If he wanted to look through a telescope he could just walk right up and ask. It would never even occur to him that he might be refused.

But she . . . she had never thought . . . aside from the very basic handheld scope she'd borrowed once from a retired ship's captain . . .

She sighed.

"You're happy," Lord Frederick said.

She looked over at him and beamed. "More than I could ever say."

"I shall have to inquire as to the availability," he warned as they resumed their journey to the bakery. "Generally, one must schedule one's time."

"Of course," she said promptly.

"As soon as I know the possibilities—"

"I can go at any time. Any time at all."

He nodded.

"I have nothing on my schedule. Well, nothing that cannot be changed." She was going to the Radcliffe Observatory. She'd reschedule *church* if it came to that.

"Truly," she said, as if she had not already made herself clear, "I shall make myself available at whatever time you deem convenient. I am the essence of flexibility."

What she *was* was the essence of a blithering madwoman, but he didn't seem to mind. If anything, he looked like he understood.

Of *course* he understood. He was a scientist. Still, she smiled sheepishly and apologized for her excitement. "I'm sorry. I'm talking a mile a minute. I can't help myself. It's just, well . . . it's a long-held dream of mine."

"I think you will find it most interesting," Lord Frederick said. "There are quite a few telescopes there."

"Quite a few?" she echoed, barely able to believe he might catalogue one of the finest collections of astronomical instruments in the world as *quite a few*. "There is a transit telescope by John Bird!"

"Is he a particular favorite of yours?"

"Oh yes," Bea answered, her excitement gushing through her

voice. "He's brilliant. I know that some people prefer Dollond, and of course Sir William Herschel is to be admired, but I have long felt that the quality of Bird's instruments is beyond compare."

He blinked a few times. "Then you've used them elsewhere."

"No," she admitted, feeling a light flush of embarrassment color her cheeks. "But I've read about them." She swallowed. "You can infer a lot about the quality of astronomical instruments by reading about them."

"Of course," he said, and she wished she could tell if he meant it or if he was only being polite. "I've met Sir William," he remarked. "Several times. And his sister. She's his assistant, you know."

Bea nodded. "It's very enlightened of him."

"I'm glad we are making these plans," Lord Frederick said. "It is high time I went myself. I haven't been since—" His voice hitched. It was barely noticeable, just enough to add an extra flash of silence before he said, "Since the accident."

Bea's lips parted, and she held her words for a moment before asking, "Will your injury make a difference? The telescope is a single-lens apparatus. One puts only one eye to the glass."

"Indeed, but it was the other eye I preferred."

"Oh." Bea swallowed, hoping her expression conveyed her sympathy because she had a feeling he didn't want any more words to that effect. Then her natural curiosity took over, and she found herself winking back and forth, left-right-left, puzzling over how the street scene in front of her seemed to move back and forth depending on which of her eyes was open. It was just a fraction of an inch, but it was noticeable.

"It has to do with which eye is stronger," Lord Frederick said.

She stopped winking and looked over at him curiously. "Did you know all this before your injury?"

"I never had reason to be curious about it."

She sucked on the inside of her cheek, thinking. "Do you wear the patch all the time?"

"No," he confirmed. "Not when I'm alone."

Bea wanted to ask if it was uncomfortable, or scratchy or hot, but that seemed the height of rudeness, and besides, they'd reached Mrs. Bradford's Pies and Pastries (The Finest Scones South of Scotland). Lord Frederick tipped his head toward the door. "Your bread awaits," he said.

"Did you want to come in?" Bea asked. It seemed rude just to leave him out there, holding her packages.

"I don't know. Are they really the finest scones south of Scotland?"

"I cannot prove that they are *not*," Bea replied, and with a jaunty grin, she walked inside.

Chapter 3

*T*hey walked in together, immediately enveloped by the cozy scent of warm bread. "Oh, there's nothing like a bakery," Bea said, taking a deep breath. She saw the owner bending over a shelf near the back, and called out, "Good morning, Mrs. Finchley!"

"Not Bradford?" Lord Frederick inquired.

Bea shrugged. "Not for a hundred years, or so I'm told."

"Miss Heywood," Mrs. Finchley said with a smile. "So nice to see you this morning."

Bea looked over at Lord Frederick, but he'd turned away, distracted by the enormous gingerbread house on permanent display near the front window.

"Mrs. Finchley's mother is from Heidelberg," she murmured as he bent down to inspect the workmanship. She moved past him to the front counter, smiling to herself when she looked back and saw him giving the icing a surreptitious tap.

Probably assessing its tensile strength. She loved that he was checking that.

Mrs. Finchley was waiting, so Bea gave her her attention and said, "We'll take our usual order, please, but with two extra scones."

"Hungry, are you?" Mrs. Finchley said with a chuckle. She

reached under the counter for a freshly baked loaf. "And how are your dear aunts? I haven't seen them in weeks."

"The same as ever. Aunt Hennie has taken it into her head to create a new sort of number puzzle."

"She always did like her puzzles."

"It does seem to be taking some practice," Bea confirmed. "We're going through paper at an alarming rate."

"And Miss Calpurnia?"

"Still trying to domesticate the ducks. I shall have to hide your bread from her, or we'll have no toast for breakfast."

Mrs. Finchley laughed. "I have a two-day-old loaf that didn't get bought yesterday. You can have it for the ducks in return for an egg if she ever succeeds."

"I'm afraid it will be a very bad bargain for you," Bea said. "Aunt Callie's been bitten three times this week. Those ducks are vicious."

From beside her, she heard Lord Frederick's deep voice. "Can ducks bite?"

Bea startled. She hadn't heard him approach.

"I don't believe they have teeth," he murmured.

"It *feels* like a bite," Bea amended, having unfortunately experienced it herself. It probably had served her right for trying to help her aunt when she knew the cause was doomed.

She looked back over at Mrs. Finchley, who was watching her with patient expectation. Ah, right. Introductions. Always a sticky situation when one did not recall the full name of one's companion.

"Lord Frederick," Bea said, thankful that his title enabled her to introduce him in this manner, "may I present Mrs. Finchley? You have likely eaten her bread already now that you've, er . . ." She paused for a moment, blinking. "You do live near Wallingford, don't you?"

"Two miles out," he confirmed before turning to Mrs. Finchley and—thankfully—giving his full name. "Lord Frederick Grey-Osborne, ma'am."

Mrs. Finchley's eyes went very wide, then she bobbed a curtsy, mumbling, "My lord."

"I have recently purchased Fairgrove," he said, more to Bea than Mrs. Finchley.

"Oh yes, from Mr. Oldham," Bea confirmed. She looked over at Mrs. Finchley. "He's gone down to Brighton, has he not?"

But Mrs. Finchley had busied herself behind the counter and was now talking too loudly to herself about the hardened bread, and how it was perfect for ducks.

Bea looked over at Lord Frederick with a little shrug, but his expression had gone shuttered and cold. "I will await you outside," he said, and with a little bow, he was gone.

Bea watched him in openmouthed incomprehension, murmuring, "Whatever could be the matter?" as she pivoted back to Mrs. Finchley.

Who had popped back up like a jack-o'-lantern.

"Oh, that poor man," she said. "Oh, that poor, poor man."

Bea looked helplessly at the door, now firmly shut, then back at Mrs. Finchley. "What are you talking about?"

"His eye. It's so tragic. That poor, poor man."

Bea wondered if she'd be going on so if she'd seen Lord Frederick dispatch her sixpence thief earlier. The man had either a future or a past in boxing. "He seems perfectly capable to me," she said.

"A shadow of his former self," Mrs. Finchley said with a slow shake of her head.

"You knew him, then?"

"Of course not. But I heard all about the accident. We all did."

"We did?" Bea echoed. Because she was fairly certain she had not.

Mrs. Finchley shrugged, and Bea felt vaguely scolded by the gesture, as if she had neglected her civic duty by being unaware of such critical gossip. "Perhaps I was visiting friends," she murmured. There had been an awful lot of weddings lately, all of which had required her extended presence away from home.

"His father is the Marquess of Pendlethorpe, you know."

Bea's eyes widened, and once again, she caught herself glancing toward the door, not that she could see Lord Frederick through the warped and wrinkled glass. Everyone knew of the Marquess of Pendlethorpe. His grand country estate was nearly twenty miles away, but he was still the highest-ranking nobleman in the area.

As his fortunes went, so did the village's.

"It was a terrible, terrible thing," Mrs. Finchley went on. "Oh, that poor man. It breaks my heart, it does. He was so very handsome."

"He still is," Bea retorted.

Mrs. Finchley looked at her with a kindly expression. Kindly and perhaps a little bit pitying. Bea felt her teeth clench.

"They thought he would die," Mrs. Finchley said. "The coachman did, although not right away."

Bea gasped, her hand going to her mouth. What a terrible thing to endure. To live when another did not . . . She could not imagine how a person could survive such a thing and not feel crushing guilt for it.

"There was someone else in the carriage as well," Mrs. Finchley said. "A friend, I think. I don't remember the name. But his injuries weren't severe. Certainly nothing to compare to an eye. *He* will be able to go on with his life."

"He?" Bea echoed.

"The friend," Mrs. Finchley clarified. "But poor Lord Frederick . . . No one will ever look at him the same. You can pretend you don't notice it, but I think that's almost worse."

"If I lost an eye," Bea said tartly, "I should think I would be more concerned about loss of sight than my appearance."

Mrs. Finchley handed over two loaves of bread, one still warm and smelling of yeast, the other hard as a rock and ready for ducks. "Perhaps," she said, her little shrug making it clear she was only being polite. She filled a bag with scones and held that forth as well. "Half a dozen, as always. Oh, but you wanted two more." She quickly piled those in. "Is the extra for His Lordship? I shan't charge you for it. It's the least I can do."

"Thank you," Bea said, glancing worriedly toward the door.

Lord Frederick had said he'd wait for her outside, but she did not want to make him wait too long, not after Mrs. Finchley had been so rude . . .

Or had she? Bea frowned. *Had* Mrs. Finchley been rude? In all honesty, Bea wasn't sure what *had* happened. One minute Lord Frederick had been friendly and smiling, and the next he was out the door. Mrs. Finchley hadn't said anything impolite, but then again, the way she'd been going on and on about that poor, poor man . . . If her pity had shown in her face, it was no wonder Lord Frederick had felt he must leave.

Bea tried to imagine what it would be like to wear one's injury so prominently. She'd meant it when she said that she'd be more concerned with the loss of her sight than her appearance, but perhaps she had been naïve in her thinking. Single-eye blindness was at least a private thing. A patch . . . a scar . . . Those sat on one's face forever, for all to see. Bea had never liked being the center of wide attention, and when she thought about how others would stare . . .

It must be awful.

For Lord Frederick Grey-Osborne to suffer such an injury and endure . . . He must be a remarkable man indeed.

"Do you want to put it on your account?" Mrs. Finchley asked.

"N—" Bea's hand froze on its way to the reticule. "*Yes,*" she said firmly. She didn't have time to make change. "Please."

And then she hurried out the door.

"SCONE?"

Frederick blinked himself out of his sulky reverie. Miss Heywood had exited the bakery and was now standing before him, a currant-flecked scone in her outstretched hand.

"I know it's terribly uncouth to eat and walk at the same time," she said, "but I won't tell if you don't."

"Thank you," he said, taking the pastry. He didn't eat it, though. For some reason he didn't want to. He waited for her to say something about his distempered behavior, but she did not, instead look-

ing up at him with bright eyes and, if not a smile, at least something
that was not a frown.

"I'm sorry for that," she said.

He tilted his head in question.

"She means well," she said, motioning toward the bakery. "I
don't think she intended to be rude."

"She wasn't rude," Frederick said, but he had a feeling his
brusque tone undercut his words.

"No," Miss Heywood said, "I suppose she wasn't."

Frederick's eyes narrowed. He had not expected her to agree.
Perhaps more oddly, he had not wanted her to.

"But, I don't know . . . I shouldn't like to bear that sort of reaction," she went on.

He snorted. "Revulsion?"

She looked at him with surprise. "I was going to say pity."

"It's human nature," he said with a little shrug.

"I suppose it is," she agreed. She nibbled at her scone, her tongue
flicking out to catch a currant before it detached itself and fell to
the ground. Frederick was mesmerized, and a little flicker of heat
snapped in his chest.

He went still. He hadn't felt such a thing in over a year. If his
breath hadn't caught, if his heart hadn't sped up at same time, he
might not have recognized it.

Desire.

Or maybe it was more of a yearning, a reawakened sense of
wonder and fascination. What would she do if he kissed her? Not
here, of course. All of Wallingford was bustling around them, noisy
and brisk and decidedly unromantic. But what if the world slipped
away?

What if there was nothing left but two people and the air and sky?

Miss Heywood brushed away a crumb and looked back up. "But
surely not everyone reacts so," she said, her brow furrowing into a
thoughtful frown. "With pity, I mean. I didn't."

He gave her a look.

"I didn't!"

She had, as a matter of fact. He remembered it vividly. And it still bothered him.

"No, tell me," she protested, even though he had not said a word. "You think I reacted rudely when I met you?"

But he didn't have a chance to reply before she punched in with: "If I did, it was because *your* behavior was abominable."

"I beg your pardon," he said icily. That was insupportable. If *he'd* been rude, it was because she'd acted like he was some sort of hideous beast.

She sniffed, her chin rising with disdain. "If I behaved badly—"

"You stared at me as if I were a monster."

"I most certainly did not."

Again, he just looked at her.

"I didn't! If I looked at you oddly—" Her words slammed into an abrupt halt.

"What?"

"Nothing."

"*What?*"

"Eat your scone."

He threw it off to the side. "Tell me." He felt ridiculous. For the love of God, he didn't even know this girl's given name, and yet he had to know. What had she been about to say?

She let out a little puff of air, her chin rising as she said, "If you must know, I was looking at your good eye."

That halted him in his tracks. "My . . . good eye?"

Her lips pressed together, and she looked slightly embarrassed when she finally said, "It's the color of the sky."

He glanced up.

"Not *today*. Oh for goodness' sake," she muttered.

"Not today?" he echoed stupidly.

She shifted her weight from right foot to left. "It was cloudier," she mumbled.

He had a feeling he'd lost the talent for intelligible speech, because once again all he could do was repeat her. "Cloudier?"

She flicked a glance up at the uninterrupted cerulean sky currently gracing the English countryside with its benevolence. "Your eye," she said. "It's blue, but it's not completely blue."

"I have always thought they were gray," he heard himself say.

"Oh no. Certainly not. There is quite clearly a bit of blue." She leaned in, her hand motioning toward his eye as if he could possibly make out the spot she was trying to indicate. "Right there at the edge of the iris. It's a little . . ."

Her words trailed off, and her lips parted with surprise, as if she'd only just realized how odd and irregular the conversation had become. "Excuse me," she said in a halting voice.

She looked a little stunned.

He *felt* a little stunned. And he wasn't exactly sure why. One thing was clear, however:

"I must apologize," he said.

She looked up at him with gorgeous, questioning eyes.

He was not used to making such amends, but the words came forth with remarkable, heartfelt ease. "I clearly misinterpreted your expression when we first met. I do beg your pardon."

Her lips parted with surprise, and once again, her tongue flicked out, sending a spark to the very tips of his fingers.

"I'm sure it's understandable," she said. "If you're used to people behaving such . . ."

"Nevertheless, I should not have jumped to conclusions. And at the very least, after a long enough acquaintance to sketch your character, I should have revised my initial assumption."

"Thank you," she said softly.

And then, to his great surprise, he blurted out, "I don't know your name."

Now she looked vaguely aghast. Or maybe just startled. He was beginning to wonder if one needed two eyes to properly read a woman's expression.

"Your given name," he clarified, despite his embarrassment. "I do not know it."

There was no reason he *should*; they were both well aware of that. He had no intention of bucking propriety by calling her anything other than the properly proper Miss Heywood, but there was something rather irritating about not knowing if she was a Mary or an Elizabeth, or maybe a—

"Beatrice."

Beatrice. He liked that. It fit her.

"Most people call me Bea."

He nodded. There was nothing in her voice to indicate that she was inviting *him* to do so, but in his mind, in his dreams . . .

In his *dreams*?

And there went that spark of desire again, this time threatening to explode into flames.

What the bloody hell was wrong with him?

"My lord?"

He started, suddenly realizing that he'd let an awkward amount of time pass since she'd spoken. "I beg your pardon, Miss Heywood," he said. "I fear I was lost in my thoughts."

Again, she regarded him with that wide, open gaze, as if she thought he might say more. Maybe even that she *hoped* he might say more.

"Is it an occupational hazard?" she asked.

"Getting lost in one's thoughts?"

She nodded. "Theoretical physics. It's all in one's head, is it not?"

"Not really," he told her, "but one does spend a staggering amount of time staring off into space."

"I'd offer you a sixpence . . ." she said with a teasing smile.

"I would never take your lucky sixpence."

"Well, I didn't say I'd give you *that* one," she bantered, "although you probably deserve it. Thank you, again, for intervening on my behalf."

"I hate bullies," he said with a shrug. What he didn't say was that it had felt bloody *wonderful* to use his fists against that cretin.

She smiled, and once again, it was as if the sun shone a little brighter, just on them two.

"I do, too," she said, leaning forward conspiratorially, "but I lack your right hook."

"Left," he said with a grin, giving his hand a little flex for fun. "I write right, but I throw left."

"How intriguing."

Frederick thought of all the times he'd heard those words . . . standing at the edge of a ballroom, sipping a brandy at his club . . .

How intriguing . . .

How delightful . . .

How diverting . . .

No one ever *meant* it.

Except . . . He rather thought that *she* did. Miss Beatrice Heywood. The remarkable Miss Beatrice Heywood.

He wasn't ready to say good-bye.

He cleared his throat. "May I escort you home?"

"Oh, it's not far," she said in a rush.

"If you'd rather I didn't—"

"No, it's not that. Just that it isn't necessary."

"I never thought it was necessary," he told her quite seriously, and as he looked at her, at her wide hazel eyes and the freckles that danced across her upturned nose, it suddenly occurred to him that he could fall in love with her, and maybe, just maybe, she wouldn't care that he was no longer whole.

Or maybe that was *why* he thought he could fall in love with her. Because she had looked at him and seen not an injury but a fascinating scientific question. What happened when the light hit his retina? Did it make a difference if a one-eyed man used a telescope?

In that moment, it became somehow imperative that she allow him to see her home. It was as if his entire world hung in her balance, and he could see it, two lifelong paths stretching before him, his journey to be decided by her simple yes or no.

And he knew—he *knew*—that he would never be able to live with himself if he did not try to tip the scales.

He held out his hand and said, "Please."

Chapter 4

The following week
The drawing room of Rose Cottage
Home to the three Miss Heywoods

*B*ea had never considered herself prone to giddiness, but as she waited for Lord Frederick to arrive to escort her into Oxford, she was practically bouncing from foot to foot. Which would have been bad enough, but she'd put the sixpence back in her slipper, and it kept sliding around beneath her stocking, refusing to settle down into anonymity.

She felt the veriest fool. Here she was, a woman of science, preparing herself for a scientific outing with a man of science. And she was putting a sixpence in her slipper because some nursery rhyme had declared that it would find her a husband.

And while she still could not bring herself to believe that a coin might contain magic, she *had* accepted the fact that if she were by some chance to find a husband . . .

Bea wanted it to be Lord Frederick Grey-Osborne.

She was in love. She had never expected it, never even thought she desired it. But something had happened that day he walked her home. He had held out his hand, and she'd taken it, and the most astonishing thought had burst into her mind—that she wished they were not wearing gloves, that she wanted to feel his warm skin against hers.

She'd tipped her face toward his, and for one shining moment she thought he might kiss her.

But of course he didn't. They were standing in the middle of town, for heaven's sake. She could not help but wonder, though— what if they had been somewhere else? What if the world had blurred around them, and it was just they two, alone under a sky sunny and blue?

Would he have kissed her?

Would *she* have kissed him?

Lord Frederick had called upon her at Rose Cottage twice since then, once to inform her that he had made the necessary arrangements for their outing to the Radcliffe Observatory, and once— rather thrillingly—for no particular reason at all.

He was not due for another ten minutes, but he liked to be early. She knew this, not from experience, but because he had told her so during their two-hour-long conversation the time he'd come to see her without giving a reason. She also knew (also not from experience, but *please*, this much was common knowledge) that gentlemen did not ordinarily stay for two hours when they paid a lady a call.

Despite advice from females more experienced than she that a lady should not appear too eager, Bea was waiting in the drawing room with her gloves on, her hat at the ready. For heaven's sake, he *knew* how excited she was to visit the observatory; it was ludicrous to think that she might somehow make herself more desirable by pretending she wasn't ready when he arrived.

But of course they could not travel to Oxford together without a chaperone, no matter how academic and high-minded their outing. So Aunt Callie was also waiting in the drawing room, pretending to knit as she watched Bea watching the window.

Eventually she gave up the pretense altogether. "Are we waiting for a glimpse of a carriage?" she asked, coming over to stand by Bea's side.

Bea didn't even bother to pretend she didn't know what her aunt was talking about. "We are."

Aunt Callie nodded. "He likes you."

Again, Bea did not dissemble. "I like him, too."

Aunt Callie held her tongue just long enough for Bea to settle into her own thoughts, and then—

"You should marry him."

Bea's head swung around. "Aunt Callie!"

Calpurnia Heywood—always the more forthright of the Heywood sisters—gave a blunt shrug. "You should."

"I might point out that he has not asked."

"He will." Aunt Callie's eyes met Bea's in a rather knowing expression. "If you give him a little encouragement."

"Encouragement?" Bea echoed.

"Indeed."

"I cannot believe you're saying this."

Aunt Callie's brows rose.

"Very well, I can believe it," Bea said. Her aunt had never been known for circumspect speech.

"Mind that it's the *right* kind of encouragement," Aunt Callie added.

"I'm terrified to ask," Bea said.

"It's not what your *other* aunt would think is the right kind, that much I'll say."

This did not clarify the matter in the least, but Bea judged this not to be a question that desired further discussion.

"Regardless," Aunt Callie declared, "I am glad you've finally got yourself a suitor."

"I—"

"And don't say he's not your suitor because we both know that he is."

Bea had, as a matter of fact, been about to say that Lord Frederick was not her suitor. She *thought* he was interested. She thought he knew *she* was interested. But he had not declared himself in any sort of formal manner, and she did not want to jinx herself by making assumptions. It did not seem right to give him a label he had not claimed.

"Furthermore," Aunt Callie continued, oblivious to Bea's inner turmoil, "given that you *do* finally have a suitor . . ."

"You make it sound as if there is something wrong with me," Bea said, taking advantage of Aunt Callie's habit of inserting dramatic lulls in her sentences.

"Not at all. I am well aware that you have declined to pursue normal matrimonial goals so that you might remain with Hennie and me." She turned to look at her niece, and her eyes softened. "You would be married with a family of your own by now if not for us."

"Oh," Bea said, suddenly humbled. She had no idea that her aunts understood the sacrifice she had made. It seemed like it must be obvious, but they had never spoken of it.

And as for Bea . . . she herself had not realized the extent of her own sacrifice. She'd told herself she hadn't cared if she never married. She'd even believed it. But with all her friends happily paired off, and then meeting Frederick . . .

"We do appreciate you," Aunt Callie said softly.

Bea reached out and squeezed her hand. "And I you."

Her aunt allowed herself one sentimental smile before resuming her brisk lecture. "As I was saying," she announced, releasing Bea's hand so that she might assume a more authoritative pose, "given that you do finally have a suitor, I am most gratified that it is Lord Frederick. I don't give two figs that his father is a marquess . . ." She paused, frowned. "Well, maybe one fig. One cannot discount the perks of such a position, even if he is unlikely to gain the title."

Bea bit back a smile.

"He seems like such a sensibly-minded young man," Aunt Callie concluded. "I reckon that accident was the best thing that ever happened to him."

"*What?*"

"Oh, I'm sure *he* will never see it that way, but adversity is often the making of a man, especially a man who has never had to work for his supper."

Bea was so shocked she practically had to force herself to close her mouth. "Aunt Callie, he lost an eye."

Her aunt frowned. "I thought you said he still has it."

"He lost the use of it. It's much the same thing."

"I'm not sure that it is, but no matter, that's not my point."

She wasn't going to ask. Bea swore to herself she wasn't going to ask. And yet—

"What *is* your point?" she asked.

Aunt Callie shrugged. "I think you will find that his handicap forces him to view the world differently. Because the world now sees *him* differently. And I suspect this cuts to the bone."

It was at times such as these that Bea could not reconcile this wise elder with the woman who spent half her time herding ducks.

"Ah, here he comes now," the duck-herding wise elder said.

Bea looked up, and sure enough, Frederick's carriage was coming down the drive. A shiver of anticipation fizzed through her.

"You're smiling," Aunt Callie said.

Bea did not look over, but Aunt Callie was smiling, too. She could hear it in her voice.

"I declare I am brimming with excitement," Aunt Callie said, pulling on her gloves. "A telescope! And here I thought I was done with new experiences."

"What a silly thing to say," Bea told her.

"I *am* in my seventh decade, my dear." She made for the door. "Come, let's await him outside. You're far too keen to get to Oxford to waste time sitting prettily in the drawing room."

"Quite right," Bea said, hurrying out. Maybe her eagerness was unseemly, but Frederick would understand.

After all, it was why she'd fallen in love with him.

Oxford University
Later that afternoon

"Here we are," Frederick said, motioning across the lawn toward the Radcliffe Observatory. He'd always liked this building, with its distinctive octagonal tower and soothing yellow stone. It was near the city center, but not quite in it, so they had been able to bring the carriage quite close. Bea's aunt seemed of hearty constitution, but she had to be at least seventy, and there were stairs enough within the observatory without her having to fight the university crowds.

"I'm so excited," Bea said, for what had to be the fortieth time.

He wanted to reach out and squeeze her hand.

"I can't stop smiling."

He looked over at her. If ever a smile came from the very bottom of a woman's soul . . .

He wanted to spend the rest of his life making her that happy.

"I still think we're a trifle early," Miss Calpurnia said, frowning up at the sky. Frederick supposed she had a point. It wasn't even properly dusk. It would be well over an hour before the stars found their twinkle.

"I can look at the clouds," Bea said.

Her aunt rolled her eyes. "There are only three."

"All the better for when night does fall. The constellations will be magnificent."

Calpurnia nudged Frederick in the arm. "That one has always looked on the bright side of things."

"A most becoming trait," he murmured.

"I have always thought so," she said, oblivious to the blush that was now creeping across Bea's face. Or maybe she wasn't oblivious. He had a feeling Miss Calpurnia Heywood was a great deal shrewder than she liked to let on.

"I know I should be proper and sedate," Bea said, "and murmur things like 'This will be so diverting,' but I can't." She looked up at him with eyes aglow. "I couldn't sleep last night for all my excitement."

Frederick knew that the bulk of her excitement was for the collection of telescopes currently awaiting them at the top of the tower, but he thought that a sliver might be reserved for him. At least he hoped so, because he was fairly certain that he'd fallen quite desperately in love with her.

Who would have imagined it? When he'd purchased his small estate and taken up residence near Wallingford, it had been with the intention of removing himself from society. More than anything, he'd wanted to get away from the pity and the constant stares that were making it so difficult for him to move. He'd imagined a life more solitary.

Instead he'd found Beatrice Heywood.

She was not the sort of lady anyone would have anticipated for him. Of gentle birth, to be sure, but hardly likely to cross paths with the son of a marquess.

Not that he cared. Not that he cared at all. It was almost enough to make him glad for his injury.

If that stag had not jumped in front of his carriage . . . if the driver, God rest his soul, had not swerved . . .

If they hadn't rolled, and if the wood hadn't splintered . . .

If he hadn't lost his eye.

He wouldn't have met her.

He suddenly realized it wasn't *almost* enough to make him glad for the accident, it *was* enough. He would always mourn his driver, and Frederick knew that nothing, not even his happiness, could make up for the loss of his life. But as for his eye . . .

It seemed a small thing indeed compared with a lifetime with Bea.

She was endlessly fascinating. Fiercely intelligent, but unlike so many of his academic peers, she also possessed a healthy dollop of common sense. And when she smiled . . .

His heart felt light.

He knew that others might consider hers to be a relatively ordinary face, and yet when he looked at her he saw—no, he *felt*—a radiance that warmed him to his toes.

Suddenly, the promise of a happy life was no longer quite so unreasonable.

He had not declared himself to her. That seemed premature, even if she had to know at least some of the extent of his feelings. He'd called upon her twice. In one week. She had to know what that meant.

He loved her.

Very well, she probably didn't know *that*. But she had to know that he was very interested. He'd almost kissed her twice. There was that time in front of the bakery—he thought she'd looked as if she saw the desire in his face. In fact, there had been that heady moment . . . when she'd swayed just a fraction of an inch . . .

She had wanted him. She might not have realized it, but he'd seen it in her eyes.

The second time he'd almost kissed her had been just a few days earlier. He'd called upon her at Rose Cottage and stayed a staggering two hours, laughing and talking and every so often lapsing into a moonish silence.

One of those moments had occurred when they'd gone for a brief walk in the Heywoods' garden. She'd been showing him the eponymous roses, and he'd been overcome with the most incredible urge to haul her into his arms. She had not realized; he was fairly certain of that. She'd been focused on the roses, explaining some new grafting technique she'd read about in a journal, and he'd actually forced himself to step away, so tenuous was his hold on his emotions.

But dear *God* he had wanted to kiss her. He'd wanted to do a great deal more, to be completely frank, and it was hardening his resolve to declare himself soon.

It was rash, and it was crazy, but if he asked her to marry him . . . surely she would say yes.

Wouldn't she?

She didn't seem to even notice his eye.

She made him feel whole.

"Here we are," he said, motioning toward the observatory. "Your telescope awaits."

"Oh, Frederick," Bea sighed. "Thank you."

If she'd wanted the world he would have given it to her, but this was Bea, and so he'd give her skies instead.

He must have been wearing his lovesick expression because Bea's aunt said, "You look nearly as happy as she does."

He coughed. "Merely delighted to be escorting two such beautiful ladies."

"Merely?" Calpurnia said with a scoff. "There's nothing *mere* about it, my boy."

"Oh, Aunt, stop," Bea said with a shake of her head.

"No, no," Frederick said, feeling gallant and flirtatious and all sorts of things he'd thought he'd lost forever. "She is quite right."

"I generally am," the elderly lady said.

"You must stop encouraging her," Bea said.

"Don't be ridiculous," her aunt told her. "Of course he must encourage me. It's the surest way for him to encourage *you*."

"Aunt Calpurnia!"

But Calpurnia only shrugged. "She loves me dearly," she said to Frederick. "Indulging me can only endear you to her."

Frederick tried not to laugh. He truly did.

"I'll bet you treat your mother nicely, too," Calpurnia said.

"Always," he said solemnly.

"Oh look, we're here," Bea said loudly.

They weren't, not quite. But Bea took the last few steps in record time, and soon they were entering the observatory.

"I must say, this is very grand," Calpurnia said, looking about.

"Wait until you see the upstairs," he told her.

She looked over at the staircase with a frown. "That's quite a lot of steps."

Bea immediately moved to her side. "Will you be all right? The observatory is all the way up in the tower, so it will be quite a few more steps than those."

"I will be fine," Calpurnia said. "Slow and steady wins the race, I always say."

"You've never said that," Bea said.

"Well, I'm saying it now. I'm not missing my chance to see that telescope."

"Telescopes," Frederick murmured. "There are several."

"Even more reason to attack those stairs. Onward!"

Bea looked over at him as her aunt marched forward. She smiled and shrugged before she followed, and together they made their way to the library, where Calpurnia sank gratefully into a leather reading chair.

"Go on without me," she said to Bea, who was gazing at the next flight of stairs with a longing that was palpable. "I'll be along shortly. I just need a moment or two to catch my breath."

"Are you certain?" Bea asked, even as she edged toward the stairs.

"Beatrice Mary Heywood, for the love of all that's holy, go see your telescope."

"Scopes!" Bea called out, abandoning all pretense of decorum as she tore up the stairs.

Frederick grinned.

"You'd better follow," Calpurnia said tartly. "I won't be out of breath for long."

Frederick's grin fell right into openmouthed surprise, and then, no dummy he, he dashed up the stairs after Bea.

Chapter 5

"Oh my," Bea breathed. If heaven existed—and after a lifetime of Sunday church services she had no reason to believe that it didn't—surely it looked like this, with gleaming brass quadrants, a magnificent zenith sector, and a transit telescope pointed at the sky.

She walked slowly through the three rooms that made up the observatory, gazing at all of the magnificent instruments, barely able to bring herself to touch them, much less place her eye to a lens to look through.

She wasn't sure how long she'd been wandering the rooms before she remembered to look up at Frederick. He'd been following silently—or at least she thought he had. In truth, she'd been so lost in her joy that she'd quite forgotten she wasn't alone.

"I'm sorry," she said with a sheepish smile.

"For what?"

"For ignoring you. I just . . . it's all so . . ." She waved her hand toward the transit telescope at her side, as if such a meager gesture could possibly indicate the level of reverence she felt for it.

"I enjoy watching you," he said softly.

Her heart caught mid-beat.

"Most people don't find passion in their lives," he said. "That you have, without even the benefit of a worthy education, is re-markable."

"Thank you." She wasn't sure what else to say. He was looking at her with such intensity she wasn't sure if she could even find more words.

"May I show you something?" he asked. His voice was very quiet, almost grave.

"Of course."

She thought he would lead her to some hidden gem, perhaps a tiny abacus tucked away in a corner, or an important document displayed on a desk. But instead his hands went to his face.

And he began to remove his eye patch.

Bea held her breath as he slid it up and over his forehead. The magnitude of his gesture was not lost on her. He was laying himself bare, trusting her with his deepest pain.

For several seconds she did nothing but study him. In some ways his damaged eye looked perfectly normal. It sat in its socket just like its partner, and although Frederick would always bear a jagged scar across his cheek, it somehow had not changed the shape of his eye.

But it looked darker than the other, much darker, and it took her a moment to realize it was because his pupil was permanently dilated.

He'd told her that his eye was quite obviously sightless, and she supposed he was right, but there was something beautiful about it, something almost innocent.

Almost holy.

She swallowed, her hand reaching forth before she remembered to ask, "May I?"

He nodded.

With light fingertips she touched his scar at its very edge, where it melted into normality near his ear. His good eye fixed upon her face as she traced the puckered skin. Most of the scar had faded to white, but there were still traces of angry red woven through like the tight fibers of a rope.

"It must have hurt terribly," she whispered.

"It still does," he said. "Sometimes. Not often."

She moved closer to his eye, skimming across his cheekbone. "How long did it take?"

"To heal?"

She nodded.

"Months. It was . . ." He swallowed. "I don't like to talk about it."

"That's all right."

"But someday . . . I will. To you."

Her eyes flew to his, which seemed crazy, since all she'd been doing the last minute was staring at his face. But somehow, when he said that, she moved from his eyes to his soul.

"I love you," he said.

Her lips parted.

"I know it's been barely a week, and I know I will not ever deserve you, but I love you, and if you will only grant me the opportunity, I will spend the rest of my life devoted to your happiness."

"Frederick," she whispered.

"Will you be my wife?"

She nodded. There were so many words swimming within her, but she could not seem to piece them together. She could not seem to do anything but stare at his beloved, imperfect face and think how much she loved him.

"I don't have a ring," he said suddenly. "I hadn't intended to do this now."

She was so glad he had.

"I love you," he said again.

She tipped her face toward his. "I love you, too."

He touched her cheek, his gaze moving to her mouth.

Bea's eyes widened, and then, in a moment so perfect it rivaled the stars, his lips touched hers.

It was exactly how a first kiss should be—reverent and chaste, with just a hint of—

"It's not enough," he growled, and before she knew it, he had pulled her into his arms, his mouth taking hers in a fiery kiss of possession.

No, she thought, glorying in the strength of his body against hers, *this* was how a first kiss should be.

This was how all kisses should be.

Long, deep, and with the promise of wicked intention.

"This will be," Frederick said, his mouth trailing along the line of her jaw, "a very short engagement."

Oh yes, Bea thought. Anne and Cordelia had dropped tantalizing little hints of married life, but it wasn't until this moment, with Frederick's hands and lips performing a naughty dance upon her skin, that she had even an inkling of what they'd meant.

And then, all too soon, he pulled back, his hands cradling her face. "Soon," he promised. "Three weeks."

"No special license?" she teased.

He groaned. "If I thought I could get it any faster . . ."

She smiled, then reached up again to touch his temple. "To survive such an injury," she murmured. "I am so lucky."

His eyes flared with love, and for a moment she thought he might kiss her again, but then they heard the startlingly heavy footfall of Aunt Calpurnia.

"Oh my goodness!" Bea yelped, jumping back. She tried to smooth her hair, but she had a feeling there was nothing she could do about the glow of bliss on her face.

"Good as new!" Aunt Callie called out. "Well, almost new. I don't think there will ever be anything new about me again."

"Aunt Callie, don't be silly," Bea said, bustling over to her side.

Her aunt looked at her through narrowed eyes. "You look . . . different."

Bea choked on air.

"Lord Frederick!" Aunt Callie called out. She turned and walked toward him, leaving Bea to her distress. "Show me one of these telescopes."

"Your niece is far more knowledgeable about such things than I."

"I'm sure she is, but she's a bit too thunderstruck to impart her expertise."

Frederick looked over at Bea with widened eyes.

"You took off your patch!" Aunt Callie exclaimed.

Frederick jerked straight, and his hand flew up to his face. It was rather endearing, Bea thought, his surprise at having forgotten it.

"Ehrm . . . it was a bit itchy."

"Really?" Aunt Callie said. "I would have thought it might get in your way."

"Well, that, too," Frederick improvised.

Bea spent the next ninety minutes explaining the various instruments to her aunt—the magnificent twelve-foot zenith sector, used for measuring latitude, the gorgeous brass mural quadrants, and her favorite, the Bird transit telescope.

"Isn't it gorgeous?" she gushed.

"Well," Aunt Callie said. "It certainly is impressive."

Bea just smiled. She knew that her aunts had never shared her passion for astronomy. But they loved that she loved it, and that had always been more than enough.

"Is there something you wish to tell me?" Aunt Callie murmured, as they bent their heads together near the rotating mechanism.

"Soon," Bea said. She would tell her aunts when she returned home. For the next few hours she wanted to keep Frederick's proposal close to her heart.

Aunt Callie gave her an assessing look. "I see," she murmured.

Bea had a feeling that she did.

"Where do those stairs go to?" Aunt Callie asked, wandering over to the base of the twisting staircase that wound up to the dome.

"The upper gallery," Frederick answered. "From there you can exit to the roof."

"Goodness no," Aunt Callie said. "I'll just look from here." She wandered over to a telescope. "Do you think it's dark enough to see anything yet?"

"There is only one way to find out," Frederick said, and he adjusted the dials until it was ready for her to look through.

"Oh my goodness!" Aunt Callie said, moving just far enough back from the eyepiece to twist her head toward Bea. "It's beautiful. Spectacular."

Bea beamed.

Then Calpurnia Heywood did the most un–Calpurnia Heywood thing Bea had ever seen.

She swooned.

"Aunt Callie!" Bea shrieked. She rushed forward to steady her, but Frederick was faster, catching her before she hit the ground.

"Oh my," Aunt Callie said in a wavering voice. "I can't imagine what . . ."

"We have been standing for quite some time," Frederick said. "You look very pale."

No paler than normal, Bea thought, but then again, Aunt Callie had always prided herself on her milky complexion.

"Thank you, my dear boy," she said. "I would surely have toppled if you had not come to my aid."

Except she wouldn't have toppled. Aunt Callie had definitely swayed, and she'd flung a hand to her brow, but it had all happened close enough to Frederick that she would never have hit the ground. It was, Bea was coming to realize, the most carefully choreographed swoon in the history of carefully choreographed swoons.

And Bea had a feeling that carefully choreographed swoons had a long history indeed.

"It is all so overwhelming," Aunt Callie said, fanning herself in a most uncharacteristic manner.

"Are you certain you're all right?"

"I will be," Aunt Callie said. "I just need to sit down."

"Here," Bea said, "let me escort you—"

"No!"

Bea blinked.

"I mean no, you mustn't. This is your dream, Beatrice. I could not ask you to give up even a moment of your allotted time."

"But—"

"I believe I'll go back to the library," her aunt said, sounding ever so slightly more robust. "I quite liked the chair I used earlier."

"Downstairs?" Bea murmured. Because it was becoming increasingly obvious what was going on here.

"Quite right. That's where I'll be." Aunt Callie looked over at Frederick. "Don't mind me. I shall be just fine. Please, take all the time you need."

And then she turned back to Bea and winked.

Well. That cleared up the matter of what sort of encouragement Aunt Callie thought she should give to Frederick.

Before either of them could offer again to escort her out, Aunt Callie hurried down the stairs, repeating, "All the time you need!"

"Should I have seen her out?" Frederick asked with a thoughtful frown. "She seems to have made a near complete recovery."

"Oh, indeed."

He looked at her, his eyes lighting with . . . something.

Bea decided to take a chance.

"She didn't swoon," she said.

"No?"

She shook her head. "She never swoons."

Frederick's lips began to curve, and Bea's heart began to flutter.

"In fact," Bea said, "she has quite the most sturdy constitution of anyone I know."

It was, in Bea's opinion, as close to yelling, *Kiss me* as she could possibly manage.

He took a step toward her. "Did you want to look at the telescope again?"

She shook her head. "It can wait."

"Really?" His brows rose. "You'd ignore the stars?"

"Just this once."

"Why, Miss Heywood, I think you might be flirting with me."

And because love made Bea feel very bold, she touched her finger to his cheek and said, "We're engaged to be married. Surely I'm allowed."

"Encouraged, even."

Aunt Callie's face flashed in Bea's mind, reminding her to offer Frederick encouragement. An unladylike snort burst from her lips.

"What is it?" he murmured, smiling down at her.

She shook her head. Her aunt had been more than obvious this evening. Bea didn't need to compound it by admitting that she'd been plotting all along.

"I could torture it out of you," he teased.

"Or you could kiss me."

"Or I could kiss you," he agreed, and his mouth swooped down to capture hers again.

"Wait," she said, and when he pulled back, a confused expression on his face, she whispered. "Or I could kiss you." With gentle hands, she guided his face toward her lips, gently kissing him at the corner of his eye.

And she realized that whatever his eye had lost, it did not include tears.

She kissed those away, too.

Epilogue

One month later
A guest bedroom at Farringdon Hall
Home of the Marquess of Pendlethorpe

"*W*hat do you think we should do with it?"

The Countess of Thornton—Cordelia to her friends—held out her hand, the sixpence in her palm.

The Duchess of Dorset looked up from the bed, where she was trying to make herself comfortable. Anne wasn't that far along in her pregnancy, but she seemed to be tired all the time. "We should wait for Bea," she said. "It wouldn't be right to make a decision without her."

Cordelia looked over at Lady Elinor Blackthorne, who stood by the window, pensively gazing out. "Ellie?" And when she didn't answer: "Ellie!"

Ellie startled and turned. "Sorry?"

"What do you think we should do with the sixpence?"

Ellie frowned. "Where is Bea?"

"*That* seems to be the question of the hour," Anne said in an exceedingly dry tone.

"I told you," Cordelia said, "I saw her sneaking away with Lord Frederick."

"Bea would never do that," Anne said.

"I believe we've all done things we would previously have said we'd never do," Cordelia commented, tipping her head toward Ellie.

"Why are you looking at me?" Ellie protested, thrusting her arm toward Anne. "She's the one with child."

"I've been married over a year!" Anne retorted.

"And Bea's been married over an hour," Cordelia said smoothly. "Have you seen the way he looks at her?"

"It's very sweet," Ellie said.

"There's nothing sweet about it," Anne said tartly.

Ellie gave her a peevish look. "Says the pregnant woman lounging on the bed."

"The married pregnant woman," Anne reminded her.

Ellie smiled. "I tease."

Anne smiled back. "I know."

Ellie glanced to each of her friends, eyes widening with excitement. "Do you think they anticipated their vows?"

"They're already married," Cordelia reminded her.

Ellie rolled her eyes. "I meant before this."

Anne thought about this for a moment. "Not Bea."

Cordelia shook her head with perhaps more vigor than one might have expected. "Not *Bea*."

She looked at Ellie.

Anne looked at Ellie.

Ellie's lips parted in consternation. "What?"

"Did you?" Cordelia asked.

"What a question," Ellie muttered, her face going into an immediate flush.

"You did!" Cordelia gasped.

"Did *you*?" Ellie demanded.

Cordelia's cheeks took less than a second to reach the same shade of pink as Ellie's.

"Oh ho ho!" Ellie crowed. "Pot meet kettle."

And then, as if by telepathic agreement, both ladies turned to the bed, where Anne lay, watching the exchange with interest.

"You're awfully quiet," Cordelia said.

Anne pretended to look at her nails. "I haven't anything to say."

Ellie crossed her arms.

Cordelia planted her hands on her hips.

"Oh, fine," Anne capitulated. "We did, too."

"All three of us," Ellie said, shaking her head.

"But not Bea," Anne said firmly. "Bea would never."

As if on cue, the door opened, and Bea slid inside, the smile on her face matched only by the high color of her cheeks.

"Sorry I'm late," she said, clearly attempting to regulate her expression. "Have you been waiting long?"

"Not too long," Ellie said, biting her lip.

"Probably not long *enough*," Cordelia said devilishly.

"What?" Bea asked. She looked from friend to friend. "I'm sorry, I don't understand."

"We're just happy you're happy," Anne said, her words more of an announcement than anything else. "We were just talking about how much we all like Lord Frederick."

"Oh." Bea beamed, gazing at her three closest friends with love. "I'm so happy you do. I'm so happy I . . . well, I'm just so happy!"

"He's very dashing," Ellie said.

"I know. He has beautiful eyes, doesn't he?"

Her friends blinked.

"Well, the one you can see," Bea amended. "You'll have to take my word on it for the other."

"Does he always wear the patch?" Anne asked.

"Most of the—"

"We don't have time for this," Cordelia cut in. She looked at Bea apologetically. "Not that his injury isn't of the utmost importance."

Bea gave an acknowledging nod. She knew her friend meant no offense.

"We have to decide what to do about this." Cordelia held forth the sixpence.

Bea took it from her, allowing its familiar weight to settle in her palm. "I don't know. We don't really need it anymore, do we?"

"We all got our money's worth," Anne said.

Bea looked over at her. "Oh, that's terrible."

Anne shrugged. "I'm so tired these days, all I can do is make bad puns."

"Perhaps we should save it for our daughters," Ellie suggested.

Bea thought about that. "It seems rather calculated."

"And we weren't?" Cordelia countered.

"I don't think it's right for us to leave it for so many years," Anne said. "It seems unfair."

"To whom?" Bea asked.

She shrugged. "The rest of humanity, I suppose."

"So what do we do?" Ellie asked. "Hide it again?"

Cordelia's eyes widened. "Why not?"

"But where?" Bea asked.

"Back in a mattress," Cordelia said firmly.

They all looked at the bed.

Bea's eyes bugged out. "*Here?*"

"Who knows when we'll next be together," Cordelia said.

"But at my father-in-law's house . . ." Bea said. "Surely no one sleeping here will need such luck."

"*We* did," Anne said baldly. She scooted off the bed and yanked at the sheets, exposing the side of the mattress.

"I agree," Ellie said. "It would be wonderful if we could take it to a school like Madame Rochambeaux's, but we can't. So let's make do."

"Does anyone have a knife?" Anne asked.

Bea jumped forward. "You can't cut into my father-in-law's mattress!"

"No need," Anne said. "There's a tiny hole right here."

Ellie leaned down to look. "It's as if it was predestined."

"You know I don't believe in any of this," Bea said, but she handed over the coin.

"Apparently you don't have to believe," Anne said, shoving the sixpence into the mattress. "You found Lord Frederick anyway."

"I did," Bea said softly. "Or maybe he found me."

"You found each other," Ellie said.

"Help me tuck the sheets back in," Anne said.

They all knew how. No matter how high they'd risen in the world, they'd started out at Madame Rochambeaux's, where all girls had to make their own beds.

"Who knows how long it will take for someone to find it?" Ellie wondered.

"Maybe a hundred years," Anne said.

"Maybe longer," Cordelia said.

Bea's lips parted. "Do you think . . ." She looked at her friends, so incredibly dear to her. "Do you think someone hid the sixpence for us to find?"

"There's no way to know," Ellie said.

"No," Bea murmured. "But I think they did. I think there were four girls—"

"I thought you were the skeptic among us," Ellie said.

"I am." Bea shrugged helplessly. She thought of Frederick, waiting for her downstairs. "Or maybe I was."

She looked at the mattress and laughed out loud, startling all her friends. "I have to go," she announced. She blew a kiss to the sixpence, nestled in its new home, and called out, "To love!"

She had a marriage to begin.

XAFIC
12/16